T5-AWI-956

WITHDRAWN

WITHDRAWN

BEFORE

Short Stories About Pregnancy
From Our Top Writers

BEFORE

Short Stories About Pregnancy From Our Top Writers

EDITED BY

Emily Franklin and Heather Swain

THE OVERLOOK PRESS
Woodstock & New York

First published in the United States in 2006 by
The Overlook Press, Peter Mayer Publishers, Inc.
Woodstock & New York

WOODSTOCK:
One Overlook Drive
Woodstock, NY 12498
www.overlookpress.com
[for individual orders, bulk and special sales, contact our Woodstock office]

NEW YORK:
141 Wooster Street
New York, NY 10012

Copyright © 2006 by Emily Franklin and Heather Swain

All Rights Reserved. No part of this publication may be reproduced or
transmitted in any form or by any means, electronic or mechanical,
including photocopy, recording, or any information storage and
retrieval system now known or to be invented without permission in
writing from the publisher, except by a reviewer who wishes to quote
brief passages in connection with a review written for
inclusion in a magazine, newspaper, or broadcast.

∞ The paper used in this book meets the requirements for paper
permanence as described in the ANSI Z39.48-1992 standard.

Cataloging-in-Publication Data is available from theLibrary of Congress

Book design and type formatting by Bernard Schleifer
Manufactured in the United States of America
ISBN 1-58567-740-X
1 3 5 7 9 8 6 4 2

To our husbands

Contents

Acknowledgments

WE WOULD LIKE TO OFFER OUR MOST HEARTFELT APPRECIATION TO our wonderful agent, Faye Bender, who saw this project from its conception to its birth. Thank you also to Peter Mayer, our publisher, for giving this book a home; to David Mulrooney, our editor, for all his valuable input; and to the entire staff at The Overlook Press for their enthusiasm and support. Special thanks go to Thisbe Nissen and Robert Birnbaum, two talented writers, who graciously put us in touch with many of the contributors to this collection.

Editors' Introduction

WE MET BECAUSE WE WERE WRITERS; BOTH WITH OUR FIRST NOVELS coming out within a month of one another. Then we became friends for all the subtle and wonderful reasons two people find each other interesting and amusing. Soon afterwards, our friendship deepened when we both wound up pregnant at the same time. Six months later, we traveled together, promoting our books, with our swollen bellies propped out in front of us. Our daughters were born ten days apart.

This book came together after a conversation in which we both lamented the fact that we had written short stories about pregnancy that hadn't been published. "We should do an anthology of pregnancy stories," one of us said. "But let's include stories about parenting, too," the other one added. We guessed correctly that other writers would have their own stories that elucidate the joys, anxieties, humor, and sadness of the most universal project: childrearing. *Before: Short Stories About Pregnancy From Our Top Writers* is a collection created by some of today's most exciting best-selling novelists and masters of the short story who have come together for the first time to tell the untold stories of pregnancy, parenthood, and possibilities.

Between the two of us, we've experienced six pregnancies, three labors and deliveries, one c-section, and two losses. We have four children total and we aren't done yet. For the past several years, our life's work has been a continual balance of having and raising children and writing. And we couldn't think of a better way to spend our time. Except, perhaps, reading what other writers are thinking about pregnancy and parenting. Since you've picked up this book, you must have similar interests.

We know from experience that when you're expecting a child your time is limited, but like us, you probably still love a good read, especially one that speaks to the fascination, fears, and wonder of pregnancy. While medical texts about pregnancy are invaluable, sometimes you need a reference point for your experiences and sometimes you simply want to be entertained while being amused, consoled, or reassured.

We've gathered twenty-four short stories about pregnancy by some of the best American authors writing today. (In *After: Short Stories About Parenting*, you'll find stories about parenting.) We've arranged the stories in a way that we think will make an engaging read from the first page to the last and have done our best to represent a variety of experiences: to have children or not, the effects of pregnancy on relationships, the potential humor of labor, the gravity of complications during delivery, the elation of creating new life, and the struggles over fertility. There is something for nearly everyone in here, whether you are reading to reaffirm your own experience or to understand what someone close to you is experiencing.

Having been there (many times) we also know that when you're expecting a child, you don't necessarily want to read about every aspect of pregnancy. Sometimes we simply want to be happily reassured that everything will be fine. To that end, we've included a chart in the back of this book that provides a summary of each story. If you want to read selectively, please refer to that chart. If you want to be surprised, please ignore it.

However you choose to use this book, we hope that you enjoy reading the stories as much as we have enjoyed compiling them. Our deepest gratitude and respect go to all the authors who have contributed to this collection. We are honored to have worked with such an astoundingly talented group of people who have given so selflessly to a project that would literally be nothing without them.

—Heather Swain & Emily Franklin

BEFORE
Short Stories About Pregnancy From Our Top Writers

Emily Franklin

In the Herd of Elephants

SMILING CADILLAC WIDE, JULIA ROBERTS STARES OUT AT US FROM the television. She's riding on top of an elephant somewhere—Thailand, maybe—and manages to look graceful, hair piled up, and unfazed by the heat. In our ninth and eighth months, Lucy and I are considerably less cool; sweat dollops run their jagged course from temple to Lucy's jaw while perspiration seeps through my bra, oozing from the underwire until I can feel it on my stretched stomach.

Bloated like a pair of bullfrog cheeks, we are nevertheless sitting right next to each other, not bothering to leave a space in between.

"I wish I had a trunk," Lucy says putting her forearm to her nose and flinging her wrist. "I would splash myself in a waterhole."

We debate the merits of a trunk versus a marsupial pouch then drink the last of our Russian Iced tea. Lucy's mother made a jug of it—loose tea tied in cheesecloth sacs submerged into hot water—and stuck it in the fridge and we've been sipping at the ginger-orange of it until our tongue tips are slightly burning.

"What about Ella?" I say to Lucy.

We still haven't settled on names for the babies now too big to swirl inside us so they just punch and roll, and we are desperate enough these days that we look to every day objects or anyone we encounter to see if we can pick something suitable; Lottie was the bag packer at Shaw's Market, Jinelle was the vacuum brand Lucy thought sounded good for a girl. The Baby Romaine from our salads didn't seem right for a child, but we decided it would work for the rock group we'd never form.

"Ella's nice," Lucy says. "You could have Ella and I could have Louis."

We don't know if we are carrying boys or girls or one of each, but the husbands, who both work on the farm, have a feeling they'll soon be surrounded by a herd of females. Today they sift through the harvested brussel spouts and bunch the snap beans into crates to be shipped. When they come home linted with cornhusks we'll go out to the truck and see what remnants they've got in back and fashion dinner out of the bruised tomatoes or button mushrooms.

On the television, Julia heads into the jungle to be with orangutans, leaving the heft of elephant she rode on to wait in the dusty shade.

"There's only two kinds of elephants," I say, "The Asian elephant and the African—the African's the biggest, so that's me."

"Give me another couple weeks," Lucy says still facing the screen, "Then we'll see. You'll be in labor and I'll be sitting here, sweating and packing on the pounds."

Since I'm due three weeks before she is, Lucy is terrified I might have the baby and suddenly leave her behind, back in the world of the non-parenting.

"Maybe we'll go at the same time," I say to try to make her feel better, even though it's best if she is full term. The last thing I'd want is to have Lucy stuck in the NICU while I'm home breastfeeding on the couch.

Lucy perks up. "Maybe we will! Can't you see it? The guys running back and forth, checking on us, comparing how much dilation."

We joke about being crops the men need to tend, about wetting through the pick-up's seat when our waters breaks, or the way my husband's face would curl up if he were rushing me to the hospital, driving with his chest pressed to the wheel like he did when the main pipe burst and nearly flooded the cabbage crop two years ago.

I flip channels for a minute to look at the weather, which annoys Lucy.

"Can't you just leave it? You know it's still hot out, so why bother checking?" she asks. She fans herself with a paper towel and then says, "This isn't working."

"Hey—what about Windy or Cloudy or Cirrus?" I ask, going back to our name game.

"Cirrus isn't bad—for a boy."

"Those are ice clouds," I say and then, feeling the need to explain myself, "I only know this because I watch the Weather Channel too much."

I tell her about thin stratus clouds that sheet the sky, the patchy altocumulus ones that are made of water but hardly ever produce rain, and the mammtus clouds that have pouch-like shapes hanging out like bosoms.

"Hey—we're mammtus," Lucy says and makes me turn back to the animals.

Back at the documentary, one of the orangutans is old and might not make until the end of filming. Movie-star Julia is clearly upset and watches mothers bug-pick their children to feel better while the gray-haired one ails in the distance. Lucy starts to cry when Julia talks to the camera about her experience in the jungle, about how it changed her, how she liked watching the primates use sticks to fish a row of ants out from a hole in a log, about how surprised she was by the way the group communicated.

Watching Lucy cry makes me start. When we watched a documentary about seagulls, we learned that, depending on the species and where they lived, a quarter of all newly paired gulls split up. Lucy's first fiancé died in the water and when the seabirds dove in, beaking for their dinners, alone and apart from their mates, Lucy told me again about how part of her still missed Matt. Here she was, married to Justin and having a baby, but the slice of her that still loved Matt would always wonder what love and children would have been with him. Maybe those feelings will trickle away, thin out and fade as she gets further into life with Justin, when the baby is born.

I know what she means, though, the curiosity about what might have been. This pregnancy is my fourth. My first three didn't take. Actually, the first one wouldn't have worked at all—it wasn't with my husband, but with my first fiancé, Hull, who went off to teach an outdoor course in Colorado the summer after our engagement and never came back.

My real husband, Jay, saw me heaving behind my bakery before Hull had gone. He stopped his truck and offered help I didn't take until about a year later when I burned an arm making rolls and he drove me to the emergency room. At our wedding, each guest left with loaf of braided molasses, the same kind of dough I had been making when Jay came to my rescue.

I didn't meet Lucy until a year later, when I was pregnant again and she was mourning Matt, working part time on the farm. I could say she is the sister I never had, but it's different than that. All my life I felt I deserved a friend like her, that fit like I wanted with a husband, a woman I knew I wanted to spend my life with. When I saw Lucy, crouching in the bulbous pumpkins that fall, and then later, wiping tears back as she hedged the shrubs at the farm's entryway, I knew I found her. I raked the clippings up for her and listened to her talk about her engagement, about her unused law degree, about her guilty crush on Justin, who had been Matt's good friend.

"Hey, look, she's back on the elephant," Lucy says, pointing to Julia Roberts, who has to leave the jungle and head back to Los Angeles where there are people instead of orangutans.

"She looks so different without the make-up and lighting," I say.

"She looks really awake," Lucy says.

She puts her hand on my baby-belly and I touch hers. I remember the elephant footage we saw the year we first met, when I was miscarrying again and again and she still slept in Matt's ripped tee-shirts. The elephants slugged along the dry land, females remaining with females as the males went out to live independently. The bulls liked to be alone, or didn't know how not to be, and they only long-distance communicated when it was time to mate. There wasn't a set breeding season for them, and the cow stayed in heat only three to six days at a time, so the process was tricky.

I remember Lucy saying, "Can you imagine having a pregnancy last for nearly two years?" And how that made me cry since I couldn't hold onto mine for longer than five months. But now I could imagine it, living huge and round for another couple of months, walking around ill-balanced but with a whole other person inside. In the elephant documentary we watched, we saw a cow birth a too-weak calf. The herd needed to migrate towards water and the mother elephant had to leave her baby's unmoving body to dry and disintegrate in the sun. Each year that same mother, buoyed by her female friends, revisited that place and stood for a while, remembering the baby she didn't get to have.

"Borneo," I say reading the credits on screen, "They were in Borneo, not Bali."

"Let's go make something for dinner," Lucy says and pulls me up by both upper arms like you do when someone's drowning.

"Sounds like a plan," I say and exhale hard and up, blowing the hairs off my forehead. We walk—hands linked like we're walking trunk to tail—into the kitchen where there's bread rising, and stay there together, just like this.

Ann Packer

Her Firstborn

DEAN GOES TO THE WINDOW AND STARES AT THE DARK PARKING lot, half looking for Lise though she won't arrive for another ten minutes. It's after six and the lot is all but empty, just white lines glowing with new paint. He wonders what she's doing right now. Finishing a snack? Or already locking up and heading for the car? Or, no: gathering their bed pillows and *then* heading for the car. Tonight is their first childbirth class, and the flyer said to bring pillows. He imagines them piled on her backseat—flowered, lumpy, faintly scented with the deep smells of bodies asleep—and he shudders. It seems wrong somehow, a broken rule of nature: no personal bedding outside the home, please.

She pulls in right on time, her headlights sweeping the wooden fence, and he shuts down his computer and heads out to the reception area, calling goodbye to Gregor as he approaches the elevator.

"Dean, Dean, hold on." Gregor appears in the doorway of his office with a stack of CDs in hand, an amused look on his face. "I just want to give you a little encouragement." *Incurgement* is how it sounds to Dean: Gregor's from West Virginia, which shows up in about a fifth of what he says.

"Thanks," Dean says. "It's nice to know you care."

"I do—in a kindly, avuncular way."

Dean laughs: Gregor is thirty-eight to his forty-one, blond and robust to his dark and stringy. Gregor is about as avuncular as Dennis the Menace.

"Come on," Gregor says, motioning Dean closer. "You want to be prepared, don't you? It's like anatomy class. When Jan and I went the woman had big illustrations and a pointer. She said, 'This is the uterus, these are the fallopian tubes.'"

"That was in Morgantown," Dean says. "This is Eugene, remember? There's practically a *street* named Uterus here."

Gregor laughs, but he's looking Dean over all the same. "Everything OK?" he asks in a carefully blended mixture of concern and nonchalance.

Dean nods.

"Sure?"

"I'm *fine*," Dean says. "Lise's waiting, I've got to go."

He pounds the Down button, then doesn't want to wait for the elevator. The fire stairs are at the other end of the hall, and he takes off at a gentle jog.

"I want a full report tomorrow," Gregor calls. "In exchange for bearing the lion's share of our mutual burden here."

Dean flips the bird over his shoulder, but he's grateful: he and Gregor run a small company that publishes software guides, and this is their busy season, galleys to look over, a tight production schedule to stick to. Gregor'll be here until ten or eleven tonight, easy. "You can't have a baby in the *fall*," he said when Dean gave him the news. He was kidding, but only just.

Outside, Lise's Subaru is idling at the curb. Dean slides in next to her and says, "Sorry, Gregor had to ride me a little."

"Wimmin been birthin' babies a long time, Dean."

"No, it was about how Mickey Mouse the class'll be." He pulls her close for a kiss, then takes her hand from the steering wheel and kisses it, too, on the little valley between her first two knuckles.

When she returns her hand to the wheel he notices a tiny oval sticker with the word "Kegel" printed on it, right at twelve o'clock. "Where'd you get that?"

"At my appointment today," she says with a smile. "I got a whole sheet of them, I'm supposed to put them all over the house as reminders."

A Kegel is a toning exercise for pregnant women: it's like stopping your urine mid-flow, according to one of Lise's books. For a while, Dean found himself trying it nearly every time he peed, just to see how it felt.

"I put one over the kitchen sink," she says, "and one on my bedside table, but I figured that'd be enough."

"Moderation in all things."

"Right."

He reaches for her belly and strokes it. "How was the appointment?"

"Fine, except I've gained *five pounds*. I've got to pace myself."

"Like a marathoner?"

"I've got the carbo-loading part down anyway."

They exchange a smile: Dean's the runner in the family, although he's tapered way down since their marriage. Used to be he wouldn't miss a morning with his group, but these last two years have taught him to question pretty much everything he thought he knew about himself, like that *running* was the only path to well-being. Most mornings now he sleeps in, Lise breathing quietly beside him.

"Everything else OK?" he asks her.

"Yeah, the head's down, I'll have my internal next time probably."

"That it?"

She doesn't reply, and when an odd, faraway expression comes over her face he's suddenly washed with tension, certain he knows what's on her mind. But then she says, "And twenty, and that's a hundred today, and that's *all* I'm doing, damn it," and he lets out a big breath. Kegels. That's what she was doing, just Kegels, not thinking back after all.

*　*　*

The class meets in a church basement, in a room with plastic chairs set up in a circle and the air of having seen a lot of 12-step programs in its day. Dean and Lise carry their pillows in and take seats opposite the only other couple there yet, the woman tiny and auburn-haired, dwarfed by her belly. Lise's small, too, but her belly is more volleyball-sized to this woman's Great Pumpkin.

The woman leans forward eagerly. "How far along are you?"

"Thirty-three weeks," Lise says. "How about you?"

"The same. Looks like forty, though, huh?"

"No, you look fine."

"I look enormous."

Lise shrugs but doesn't disagree. She has a knack for getting along with strangers—not so much cultivating them as keeping her distance in the most amiable possible way. Dean's just the opposite, comes off as an asshole even when he's thinking there might be a friendship in the offing.

"Do you know what you're having?" the woman says.

"We decided not to find out." Lise looks at Dean and gives his leg a pat. At the beginning, thinking it would be easier that way—easier for her—he told her that he wanted to know, but she absolutely didn't and he's grateful now. He likes to think of the baby living its secret life in there, waiting to surprise them.

"How about you?" Lise says, and the woman smiles.

"A girl."

"Nice."

"I was so nervous finding out, because I *really* wanted it to be a girl." She shrugs. "I have a friend who's pregnant with her second and she's not finding out, either—do you have older kids?"

Dean feels his pulse quicken and he turns with concern to Lise, but she just shakes her head placidly.

"I guess you wouldn't be here," the woman says absently, and this time Lise doesn't react. They're here for him, of course.

Gradually the room fills, and soon every seat is taken. Dean's certain he and Lise are the oldest, which shouldn't matter but somehow does. The teacher is a tall, blousy woman with a patch of red high on each cheek. She has an easel and a stack of illustrations, but, Gregor will be sorry to hear, no pointer. When the clock over the door says seven, she picks up a piece of chalk and writes three letters on a portable blackboard: "I-N-G."

"I'm Susan," she says. "Welcome to everybody, especially the moms. This class is going to hopefully get you ready for childbirth, and since that's a pretty intimate thing, I'd like us to get to know each other a little. Let's go around the room and say our names and also something you like to do." She points at the letters on the blackboard. "I wrote 'i-n-g' because I want you to tell us something you like *doing*." She turns to the woman at her left. "Let's start with you."

The woman blushes. "I'm Patricia, and I guess I like gardening." She looks at her husband, and he nods.

"Yeah, I'm Jim, and I like skiing."

"I'm Stephanie, and I like folk dancing."

"I'm Gary, and I like playing soccer."

Two more people and it'll be Lise's turn. Dean leans close to her. "Can I say that I like be-ing alone?"

She smiles and then takes his hand and places it on her belly, just in time for him to feel the baby move. "I'm Lise," she says a moment later. "It's pronounced Lisa, but it's spelled L-i-s-e." This is something she generally tells people within minutes of meeting them; it was one of the first things Dean ever heard her say. "I like reminding myself I won't be pregnant forever."

The whole class laughs, and Dean says, "Yeah, I'm Dean, and I like the fact that that's true."

The next person starts to talk, and it's only then that Dean realizes he didn't use an i-n-g word. I like fail-ing to follow simple instructions.

Finally it's the last couple's turn. The woman says she likes making jam, and then her husband, a big guy with a florid face and a Hawaiian shirt, says, "She's like this, so you know one thing *I* like doing!"

The class titters, and Lise digs her elbow into Dean's side. Dean looks at the guy to see if he's kidding, but the guy just seems puffed up and proud. *I like fucking? This* is what Dean will tell Gregor about tomorrow.

In a moment Susan starts talking about fear and pain. Fear causes tension. Tension causes pain.

"Actually," Lise says under her breath, "*contractions* cause pain."

Susan takes up the chalk and turns to the blackboard. "OK," she says, "let's go over what happens during labor."

Halfway through the class she gives them a break. While the women line up for the bathroom, Dean climbs the stairs and goes outside to get some air. It's an early October night, still and cool, the rains a few weeks away although the air feels moist already, expectant.

After a few minutes Lise comes out to join him. For work she wears her hair pulled back, but it's down now, and the dampness has curled the shorter bits near her face. She looks pretty in the vaguely European way she looked pretty when they met, dark tendrils and dark eyes and a small, dark-red mouth. French or Italian, he thought then, and when they started talking it was all he could do not to compliment her on her excellent English.

He reaches out and fingers a lock of her hair. "Don't they give us milk and crackers?"

"Juice and crackers. Little paper cups of apple juice and three Ritz crackers each."

"Dixie cups? With pastel seashells on them?"

"Exactly."

Back inside, the basement room seems overheated. All of the women are flushed. They've got something like two extra quarts of blood in their bodies, a slightly unnerving figure to Dean. Think of the pressure on their veins. How could you be the same afterward, shrunk back to your usual volume?

"Let's wind up," Susan says a little later, "by going around the room again and this time telling about any experience you've had with childbirth—if you've ever been with a woman during labor, or if you've actually attended a birth. And tell us your name again."

Stricken, Dean turns to Lise, but she just smiles and keeps within herself, inside the chamber where she keeps all of that.

One woman tells about having been with a friend for the first part of her labor, another says she watched her sister give birth. None of the men has anything to say.

Lise and Dean have switched seats, so Dean has to go first this time. "I'm still Dean," he says. "I have no prior experience with childbirth."

Then it's Lise's turn, and Dean feels that the whole class has been waiting for this moment, expecting it somehow. "I'm Lise," she says. "I went through childbirth myself, eight years ago." She turns to Dean and gives him a look that's almost—*apologetic*, he finds himself thinking. She holds her eyes on his, but just as he's finally mustering a dumb smile she turns away.

"I had a little boy," she says to the class. "I was married to someone else then. The baby died when he was five months old."

Dean's lips are dry, and he licks them. He doesn't know how she can stand this—he can't himself stand the fact that she has to. He looks around the room: the women are staring at her, the men at their own hands. Susan clears her throat. "How did he die?" she asks in a gentle voice that makes Dean think of murder.

"He died in his sleep," Lise says, "crib death," and then there are no more questions, no more answers, just the sound of the clock ticking and the feel of a group of people waiting for something to be over. Dean stares into the center of the room and waits, too, moment giving way to moment until finally, mercifully, the woman next to Lise takes her turn.

In bed at home later, Dean tries to look at proofs while Lise arranges the pillows she needs for sleep. He's used to this, but he half watches anyway, thinking the pillows look different tonight, distorted somehow after their time in the bright lights of the church basement. Next week, Susan promised, they'll use them.

Lise puffs a little with the effort of getting comfortable. She's on her side with one pillow between her legs, another under her belly, and a third smaller one that she's tucking between her breasts. "Can I get you anything?" he says, and she gives him a rueful look.

"A surrogate? I guess it's a little late for that."

"How about a backrub?" He gets off the bed and goes around behind her, easing himself onto the mattress. He lays his hands onto the soft flannel of her nightgown and begins kneading, pressing into her muscles with the heels of his hands. There's more flesh than before, and it seems loose somehow, sliding across her back as if not quite a part of her but rather an extra layer of clothing.

"Right there," she says, and he presses harder. "It wasn't so bad, was it?"

"The class?" he says. "It was OK. Susan's a bit caring."

She laughs, but he feels tense. In her dresser, in the top drawer, there's a picture of the dead baby, and as he stares at the drawer front he can almost see it: the blond wood frame, the baby with his little topknot curl and his toothless grin, his drooly lower lip catching the reflection of the flash.

"I thought what you said . . ." he says. "I thought you were amazing."

"About Jasper?"

The name gives him a tiny shock, as always. "Yeah."

"It was fine."

They are both silent, and for a while Dean just moves his hands across her back, kneading and pushing, pushing and kneading, until from her breathing he knows that she's asleep. The light's still on, but whereas before this pregnancy she was the finickiest sleeper he ever slept with, requiring perfect darkness and silence, she now falls asleep effortlessly, at will—even against her will, over books, carefully-selected DVDs, sometimes even Dean's conversation.

He turns off the light, but rather than climb in next to her he goes to the window and looks outside. A misty night, starless, the rooflines of his neighborhood jagged against the lightish sky. What happened to her is just too horrible. It's unspeakable—*literally* unspeakable, in a way: when he first heard, it became for a while both all he could think of about her and also something they couldn't really talk about—*didn't* really talk about, because what was there to say? Horrible horrible horrible horrible horrible. In some true, essential way that was all that could be said.

By feel he finds shorts and his running shoes, then makes his way to the front door. It ca-thuds shut behind him and he locks it, then slips his running key into his Velcro pocket. He does a few quick stretches on the front lawn, and then he sets out, first an easy trot but soon he's running all out, heaving hard, racing toward the University. His first run in how long—a week? Ten days? The dark feels like a material thing he has to penetrate. He passes the development office where Lise does graphic design, the science complex, Oregon Hall. On Agate he turns and presses even harder to get past the track—track town, he's a runner in a town of runners, out here again but alone this time, legs burning, lungs burning, sweat sliding off him in streams.

That weekend, Dean and Lise are in a Thai restaurant on Willamette when Gregor and his wife, Jan, come in. Dean hunkers in his chair, but of course Gregor spots him right away. "Dean and Lise!" he booms from across the crowded restaurant, his arm moving over his head like a windshield wiper on High. "Great! What say we join forces!"

Dean groans. After five years of working with Gregor, Dean thinks of him as a family member, but the kind with whom you don't want to be seen in public.

"It's OK," Lise says.

The hostess leads them over, Gregor beaming, Jan just behind him with a shy look on her face, her brown hair in a new, shorter style that makes her look—there's no other word for it—matronly. Dean knows her pretty well, from his bachelor days, when once or twice a month she'd phone the office late in the afternoon to tell Gregor to bring him home for dinner, but she and Lise aren't well acquainted. The four of them have been out together only once before, back when Dean and Lise weren't married yet. Jan was pregnant then, now that Dean thinks about it. Pregnant with two kids at home. She kept getting up from the table to go call the babysitter.

She sits next to Dean, leaving Gregor the chair beside Lise. He sits down and pulls forward, then gives Lise a broad smile. "I haven't seen you in must be ten or fifteen pounds," he says. "Are you eating everything in sight? You're just huge."

Lise smiles good-naturedly, but Jan gasps and blushes. "*Gregor.*" She catches Dean's eye and shakes her head apologetically. "Ignore him," she says to Lise. "How are you? You look great."

"Thanks."

"Are you ready?"

Lise shakes her head. She tucks a strand of hair behind her ear and says, "All we've got is a bassinet, plus some boxes of old clothes."

Dean swallows and stares at his placemat, the tips of his ears getting hot and, no doubt, red. The old clothes are the dead baby's, and he's afraid of what will happen next. Early in his relationship with Lise, he told Gregor about what had happened to her, and though he immediately felt he'd betrayed her and swore Gregor to secrecy, he can't imagine Gregor didn't tell Jan. He's afraid to look up, afraid to see the sympathetic, probing look he's sure Jan's giving Lise.

But: "Go shopping," Jan says, and now Dean does look up, to find Jan smiling innocently. "Seriously. Borrowed stuff's nice to have, but you need to get your own stuff, too. I didn't with our first, and I felt so guilty, putting him in these ratty little stretch suits. With the others I bought new stuff, and it really made a difference, really made me feel I was welcoming them right."

"Thanks," Lise says. "I'll keep that in mind."

Gregor gives Dean a defiant look, and Dean shrugs. OK, so he doubted Gregor. OK, so he was wrong.

"Do you have a stroller?" Jan says.

Lise shakes her head.

"That's where to spend some money. The expensive ones really do last a lot longer. There's probably nothing you'll use more."

"OK," Lise says. "We'll look into that." Under the table, she presses her stockinged foot against Dean's ankle, and he brings his other leg forward and holds her foot between his calves until their food comes.

At childbirth class the following week, Susan has them all lying on the floor, heads on their bed pillows, tensing and then relaxing each muscle group in their bodies. Tense your toes. And now relax them. Tense your ankle. And now relax it. Dean's nursing a cold and lying down should feel good, but the ceiling lights bore into his eyes and he can't stop coughing.

After the break Susan shows a short movie. It features a couple straight out of the seventies—man with sideburns and a tight, striped sweater; pregnant woman with Farrah Fawcett hair and eyebrows plucked to oblivion. The film opens with them in their motel-style living room in early labor: Dean knows this because the first thing the woman does is lean back in her chair and start breathing very deliberately, as if she were following difficult instructions. Soon the couple is in their car heading for the hospital, and she's breathing harder; next they're in a hospital corridor, walking and then stopping and then walking; and finally she's on the delivery table with a doctor nearby, his gloved hands ready. Dean turns away at the moment when the crown of the baby's head first bulges out, but he forces himself to watch as it bulges again, and then the whole head appears and it's all there, born, covered with white stuff, its arms and legs curled close to its body. Near Dean one of the women in the class sobs, and through the dark he sees Lise reach into her purse for a Kleenex and pass it to her.

Leaving the class later, the woman touches Lise's arm. "Thanks for the rescue."

"Oh, any time," Lise says. "I keep one of those little boxes of tissues in my purse."

The woman smiles and waves, but she gives Lise a curious backward glance as she joins her husband at the door, and Dean knows she's wondering about Lise's emotional state. He understands: he used to assume Lise thought about her baby dying all the time. She's said it's not like that, but every morning she opens her top drawer and looks at his picture while she's fishing for underpants, and Dean has to fight the urge to tell her to stop. *Don't*, he wants to say. *That'll just make it worse.* Like pressing a bruise.

Out in the parking lot, Lise hands him her purse to hold while she pulls her sweater over her head. Actually it's his sweater, a baggy old shetland he's had since college, burgundy and a bit motheaten, and he smiles a little, remembering a line from one of her pregnancy guides.

She tilts her head to the side. "What?"

"I was thinking of that book: 'Your husband's closet is a great place to find maternity clothes, but be sure to ask first!'"

She grins. "Like they know you better than I do. It should be called *What to Expect from an Annoying Author*. That's the same book that told me to ask myself before taking a bite of a cookie whether it was the best possible thing I could be eating for my baby. When I want a cookie I want it *because* it's a cookie, not just because it's something to eat."

"Do you want a cookie? We could go to that café."

She shakes her head. "I want a quart of mocha chip ice cream, but I think I'll just have an apple at home instead."

They make their way across the rutted parking lot, skirting puddles, walking slowly. "She reminded me of me," she says once they're in the car.

Dean looks at her.

"That woman."

His throat tightens. Was Lise crying during the movie? He was next to her the whole time, wouldn't he have noticed? Shouldn't he have?

"I mean the other time," she says. "We saw a movie every week, and every single time I cried right when the baby was born." She slides her car key into the ignition, then gives him a thoughtful look. "I don't know why I didn't tonight. I kind of thought I would, although I didn't put the tissues in my purse for that very eventuality." She smiles. "She sure thought so, though—did you see how she looked at me? Like she wondered why I needed a *box*, but it's this little thing, look." She fishes in her purse and pulls out a box of tissues about the size of a wallet. "So I blow my nose a lot."

"People have an incurable interest in what's not their business," Dean says. "They want to *know*."

Lise nods and then starts the engine, pulling onto the wet street with her tires swishing. Dean looks out the window at the porches going by—the big, wide porches of communal living, fraying easy chairs in front of plate glass windows, bicycles chained to railings. The kind of place he lived when he was new in Eugene. He had a bedroom on the third floor, half a shelf in the refrigerator. Fourteen years ago. What he remembers is the dankness of the bathroom, how his towel never really dried from one shower to the next.

At a traffic light he turns and looks at Lise's profile, her high forehead and her long, narrow nose. He thinks of the woman at class tonight, her wanting to know. What he knows isn't much: that it happened during an afternoon nap, only the second time Lise went out without him; that her husband was the one at home, the one to go in after the nap had gone on much too long. Dean still remembers the night when he heard all of this, at a little Mexican restaurant out near the airport, with red-checked oilcloths covering the tables and mariachi music coming from a radio in the kitchen. She spoke evenly as she told him about the blur after the funeral, the half-year of living back to back with her husband, the two of them moving through their house like ghosts until finally she left, taking nothing but her own clothes and the baby's. Not because she hated her husband, she said, and certainly not because she blamed him: It was just that they couldn't go on. She couldn't go on.

She's lost track of him. She doesn't even know if he's still living on the West Coast. There are moments, though, like now—sitting in the dark car beside her, knowing he could ask more about it all but not wanting to press, not wanting to press on the bruise—when Dean gets a sudden intimation of the man, of a guy his own age with a permanent pain wedged in his side like a runner's stitch, and a cold fear slides through his veins.

Very early Saturday morning, Dean is woken to complete alertness by a pack of runners passing by outside, their feet slapping the road, the muted, heaving sound of their breathing checked once or twice by a low voice. Beside him Lise's deeply asleep, her dark hair a tangle, the faint, sweet scent of her hand lotion just there under the fresh-laundry smell of the sheets. He feels as wide awake as ten a.m., but he doesn't want to get up, doesn't want to go running any more than he wants to be alone in the kitchen with the grey dawn lightening outside while he makes coffee and pages through the *Register Guard*. Up against the headboard he finds a small pillow, a stray, and he rolls over and holds it against his ear. A few months ago, a friend of Lise's from the Bay Area told him it was the early mornings rather than the interrupted nights that were hardest, but he thinks that if the baby were born already, were down the hall crying right now, he wouldn't mind at all getting up. She was passing through Eugene, Lise's friend, on her way to a family reunion in Portland, her husband and three kids in tow. She was an old friend, a neighbor from Lise's old life, and her presence had an odd effect on Lise, made the color in her cheeks a bit brighter, the pitch of her voice a bit higher. Toward the end of the visit, the friend's oldest child lifted his baby brother from the floor and flew him through the air like an airplane, and Lise said, to no one in particular, "Jasper loved that."

When Dean wakes again it's midmorning, he can tell by the light, by how empty the bed feels next to him, as if Lise's been up for a while. Her nightgown is on a hook on the back of the bedroom door, and he wanders out and finds her dressed in her denim maternity overalls, standing in what will be the nursery, a small corner room with white walls and a square, jade-green rug.

"What a sleeper," she says when she sees him.

"I do my best."

"Was there anything you wanted to do today? I was thinking we could go buy a rocking chair, maybe a few other things."

An hour later, they borrow a neighbor's pick-up truck and drive downtown, where they buy a rocking chair, a changing table, four hooded towels, a three-hundred-dollar stroller, a package of cloth diapers, a footstool for nursing, five flannel blankets, a car seat, a stack of pastel washcloths, a Snugli, a mobile with multi-colored zoo animals hanging from it, a lambskin, and the tiniest fingernail clipper Dean has ever seen. Driving home with the big things in boxes in the truck bed behind them and shopping bags strewn at their feet, Dean is exhilarated.

After lunch he mows the front lawn, and then, because it's something he's been meaning to do for weeks, he gathers up and takes to the supermarket several dozen empty beer bottles, which yield him for his trouble a few wrinkled dollar bills and a handful of change. Back at home he's not surprised to find Lise in the baby's room again, standing amid the morning's loot. He fetches his toolbox and assembles the changing table while she comes and goes, carrying stacks of things to and from the garage: in the distance he hears the washing machine churn and drain, and the thrum of the dryer.

As he's tightening the last screw on the footstool, she goes into the closet and reappears with a cardboard box.

"Careful, I'll do that," he says, but she's already set it on the floor and crossed to his toolbox for a box-cutter.

She slices open the edges first, then pulls up the still-joined flaps and cuts them carefully, so the blade won't go through what's underneath. With a feeling of discomfort, he watches as she opens the box, and then there they are, the dead baby's clothes.

She removes a handful of little white caps and sets them aside. Next is a stack of tiny white undershirts, with shoulders that somehow remind him of the way the fly looks on jockey underwear. Halfway across the room, he doesn't know what to do or say. He feels grossly out of place, and beyond that boorish, and beyond that paralyzed.

"Pretty basic stuff," she says, but then her expression brightens, and she eagerly withdraws a little one-piece yellow coverall with the head of a giraffe on the front. "Look at this," she says, looking up at him. "I'd forgotten about this one. We always called this the giraffe suit."

"I can see why," he says with an idiotic smile.

She looks at him carefully. "What do you think about using some of this stuff?"

There's no reason not to, unless it would make her feel worse. "Sure," he says. "Whatever you want."

A wide bar of sunlight brightens her lap, and she brushes absently at a spot on her overalls, then sets the giraffe suit down and rubs her lower back with both hands. "I do want us to get some new stuff," she says, "but I feel like—I don't know—I'd like to use some of these things, too. I mean, I saved them as Jasper outgrew them, for when he had a little brother or sister. Would it bother you?"

"Not at all."

The doorbell rings, and he hesitates a moment, then makes his way to the front door. Outside, his neighbor's eight-year-old daughter is standing there with a small paper bag. "Dad said you left this in the truck this morning," she says, and Dean takes the bag and thanks her, then watches as she leaps off the porch and runs home.

She goes to school just a block away: when he leaves for work each morning he sees her mother watching from the sidewalk until she's reached the schoolyard.

In the bag is the nail clipper. Dean closes the front door and returns to the nursery, not entirely surprised to find it empty. He comes back out and hesitates outside his and Lise's bedroom.

She's standing at her dresser, the top drawer open. She has the picture of the baby in one hand, something small and red-and-white striped in the other. Her head is bent, her dark hair brushing her shoulders, and Dean feels sure she's crying. He crosses the room and puts a hand on her back, and she turns. She isn't crying, but she has an air of crying about her: of just having cried or of being about to. "Sweetie," he says, and she looks up at him with her bottom lip clamped between her teeth.

"Do you know why he was smiling in this picture?"

Dean shakes his head.

"Because Mark had just pulled these from his feet and started tickling his toes." She opens her hand, and the red-and-white thing unfolds into a tiny pair of socks. "He loved having his toes tickled, he'd make this little noise, like 'Arrr.' I remember it so clearly."

Dean doesn't know what to say. His throat is lumpy and he has to try a couple of times before he can swallow. At last he remembers the bag. "Look," he says. "We left this in the pick-up."

She hesitates a moment, then turns and puts the picture away, pushing the drawer closed and pausing for just a moment before turning back. She sets the socks on the dresser and looks inside the bag. "Oh, the clippers," she says. "Good. We'll definitely need those."

Gregor calls late Sunday night, after Lise's asleep. It's a habit Dean and he have gotten into, to catch up on things before the start of a new week. Tonight they talk for a while, but Dean's distracted, and after a while Gregor's voice trails off.

"What?" Dean says.

"Go on to bed, son. Get some sleep while you can."

"That's like telling someone to eat five dinners today because he's going to have to fast for the next week. There's only so much sleeping you can do. Go on, I was listening."

"Nah, you weren't. Everything OK? Got the bag packed for the hospital?"

"Yes, Gregor," Dean says wearily, although in fact Lise packed it just this afternoon. The books said to take all kinds of crazy stuff— lollipops and tennis balls, as if you were preparing to sit in the audience of "Let's Make a Deal"—but she just put in the basics.

"Don't forget your swim trunks," Gregor says.

"What?"

"For the jacuzzi. Jan always made me get in with her so she could lean against me instead of the porcelain."

"You're loving this," Dean says. "Go torment someone else, call a catalog and pick on the operator."

"Come on," Gregor says. "I just want you to be prepared."

"I am. Jesus."

Gregor doesn't respond.

"What? I can't possibly be prepared, is that it? My life is going to change completely, I'll never have a free moment again. I know that, OK?"

Gregor laughs.

"OK, I even know that I don't really know it."

Now Gregor hesitates. "How's Lise?" he says casually. "Is she—"

"She's fine."

Gregor is silent, and Dean thinks of yesterday, all the excited shopping and then the box of clothes. "She got out his stuff," he says, but then he stops himself. What is he doing? He doesn't want to tell Gregor this. His heart pounds, and he adds, almost against his will, "His clothes."

Gregor exhales. "Jeez." He hesitates and then says, "Is she— I mean, are you guys—" He's silent for a moment. "It must be scary," he says at last, "to think it could happen again. Is she really worried?"

"You'd think so," Dean says, "but she's not." He fingers the buttons on the phone, strokes their faint concavities. Back when they first talked about getting married and having children, she told him that she saw what had happened as a one-time thing, plain bad luck—it bothered her when people expected her to fear a repeat. She said that wasn't how the world was—how she wanted to think of it, anyway.

As for him, he doesn't fear crib death, he fears . . . what? Something.

He fears being afraid.

After saying goodbye to Gregor, he goes into the kitchen. It's nearly midnight but he's far too wired for sleep. He gulps a glass of orange juice, then crosses the room and opens the back door.

The backyard is small, little more than a deck and a tiny patch of grass, but it's nicely enclosed, and last spring Lise hung Italian tiles on the fence and planted lavender and rosemary in terra cotta pots. Dean sits on a wooden bench they chose together shortly after they were married, and he leans back. The night is cool, and he feels the wind stir goosebumps from his bare arms. Overhead, the half-moon looks transparent. The faint scent of lavender reminds him of a trip to Provence he and Lise took two summers ago, and he finds himself remembering an evening there, in a village near Arles. Walking after coffee in a tiny cafe, they happened upon a kind of amateur's night at the local bullfight, and they sat and watched from rickety bleachers while boys barely old enough to shave teased and provoked bulls, then leapt to safety over the low wall of the ring. Near Dean and Lise, a small family called and cajoled to one of the boys, and when his turn in the ring was over he came and sat with them, had his head rubbed by his father and then reached to take onto his lap a little girl dressed in pink ruffles. Dean watched them openly, and when the boy looked up and met his gaze he gave Dean a look of such sweet contentment that Dean felt a rush of love not just for him but for all of them, the proud father and the fat mother, the little, over-dressed girl: love and pure longing. If it did happen again, if his and Lise's baby died too, would they survive? Would their marriage? The thing is, there's no telling. From where he sits, less than a month away from fatherhood, he sees that what they've done together acknowledges the possibility of its own undoing: that what there is to gain is exactly equal to what there is to lose.

Labor starts in the kitchen three days before Lise's due date, with a gathering of color in her face, a low moan as she bends over the counter, her weight on her forearms. In a moment she looks up and smiles, and Dean sets down the pan he's been drying and says the exact thing he hoped he wouldn't say at this moment, a line out of a bad movie: "Is it time?"

It isn't, quite. But close to midnight, after hours with his watch in his hand, timing contractions, Dean helps her to the car and they head for the hospital, Dean trying to avoid potholes while she puffs in the seat next to him, her hands on her belly.

"Jesus," she says, "I better be fucking five centimeters dilated when we get there or I'm never going to make it."

He reaches for her hand, but a moment later she moans and shakes him away. She's already told him that he's not to talk to her, touch her, or in any way get in her face while she's in hard labor. Ice chips. That was all her first husband was allowed to do, feed her ice chips.

Up ahead the hospital looms into view, and he imagines plowing right through the double front doors—the car would just about fit. The walk from the parking area takes forever, Dean standing by while Lise staggers along, bent like an old woman. Inside, a clerk takes her name and phones for a wheelchair. The orderly pushing it doesn't seem surprised when Lise refuses it, nor when, several minutes and only twenty yards later, she changes her mind.

Upstairs, minutes stretch endlessly while hours collapse upon themselves. There's a period of walking in the halls, another of standing nearby while she rests her forearms on a bar and moans. Drugs are discussed, rejected, demanded. Then for a strange interlude Dean sits in a chair next to the bed and nearly dozes, only to be startled to alertness by a bright light aimed at his wife's crotch. All the blowing and panting, the ice chips, the dial on the fetal monitor springing up and down—it's all as he was told it would be and at the same time utterly shocking. Then suddenly Lise cries, "Oh my God, I can't do this, I can't do this," and the room stills to her.

"That's the wrong attitude," the midwife says. "You have to think you can do it."

"I can do this, I can do this," Lise cries; and then she does.

Lise in the rocking chair with Danny curled in her lap. Danny asleep in the very center of Dean and Lise's huge bed. Lise on her side on the couch with Danny next to her, his mouth around her nipple. Danny staring at Dean while Dean stares at Danny. Every moment feels consequential, essential to preserve somehow and yet also infinitely repeatable. Dean watches Lise watching Danny, and his eyes brim and overflow. Lise watches Dean watching her, and tears stream down her cheeks.

Dean has never been so tired in all his life. Midnight, two four-teen, three forty-five, five oh three. Walking, walking: his shoulders have never felt so sore, his upper arms. Danny wants to be held. He's five days old, seven, and Dean still hasn't set foot in the office. Gregor and Jan arrive one afternoon while Lise is asleep, and answering the door with Danny in his arms, Dean hardly hears their greetings and exclamations, his only thought that at last he can go to the bathroom. They've brought gifts for Danny—a navy blue sleep-suit, a copy of *Goodnight Moon* and three different lullaby tapes, but the thing that touches Dean is a huge dish of lasagne, good for at least four dinners. He hugs them both.

The day of Danny's two-week check-up arrives and Dean is ready with a list of questions for the doctor. The blister on Danny's upper lip, the sucking blister—could it pop and what would happen if it did? The spitting up—is it normal for there to be so much of it?

The cradle cap, the hiccuping, the way one of his toes sort of curls under the one next to it. . . .

In the living room, getting ready to go, Dean buckles a sleeping Danny into his car seat, drapes a blanket over the handle because it's misting a little outside, and turns to Lise just as she's zipping the diaper bag.

"I'll go start the car and get the heater going."

"Good idea." There are rings around her eyes, a small smear of what looks like mustard near the cuff of her white Oxford shirt, which is actually his: since Danny's birth she's been living in his shirts—for their looseness, for how easy they are to unbutton for nursing. She follows his glance to the smear. "Oops," she says.

"Tough times call for tough people."

"Still, I think I'll change. There's no one at a pediatrician's office who won't know what that is."

She heads for the bedroom, and Dean takes the blanket off the car seat to look at Danny. He's still asleep, one round cheek resting on his shoulder: his drunken-old-man look. "You nailed Mommy," Dean says. "What a thing to do."

The doctor's office is crowded, full of small children swarming all over a colorful plastic play structure or tapping insistently on the glass of a large aquarium. Dean sets Danny's car seat in a relatively quiet corner, and he and Lise sink onto the bench next to him, each of them sighing a little as they sit down.

Lise picks up a magazine, and Dean rests idly for a moment, then stretches across her to look at Danny. He touches Danny's forehead, his cheek, his impossibly tiny fist. Danny's fingers scare Dean, how fragile they are: little matchsticks in flimsy padding.

A nurse comes into the waiting room and says "Daniel?," and Lise's on her feet waiting well before Dean gets it. He lifts the car seat and follows her and the nurse back to a small examining room, where the nurse asks questions about feeding and sleep and then tells them to undress Danny. She leaves and reappears when they've got him down to his diaper, which she untapes, then she carries him to the scale, whisks the diaper out from under him, and slides the scale's weights around until she's arrived at his.

The pediatrician comes in a little later. He asks Dean, who's been holding Danny, to set him on the examining table, and then he listens to Danny's chest, rotates Danny's legs, presses his giant fingers into Danny's abdomen. Dean stands just to the side, so alert he realizes he's waiting for Danny to learn to roll over and to roll to the edge of the table: if he does this, Dean will be ready to catch him. Danny's awake now and quiet, and when the doctor finishes his examination and loops his stethoscope around his neck, he and Dean and Lise gather and stare at Danny, watch as his ocean-deep eyes move from one of them to the next.

"Can I hold him?" the doctor asks Lise, and while Dean's wondering what's odd about this, Lise nods, and the doctor lifts Danny and cradles him against his chest. "He's a nice little bundle," the doctor says, and all at once Dean understands that what he's feeling is the awe of ownership, amazement that permission is his and Lise's to give or refuse. Just two weeks and he's an expert on Danny, on his Dannyness, each day placing into an infinitely expandable container every new thing he knows to be true about his baby. He thinks of what he knows about the dead baby—about *Jasper*—and it's next to nothing: he liked to be flown through the air like an airplane, he loved to have his father tickle his toes. Dean's had it all wrong: it isn't that Lise had a baby who died, but rather that she had a baby, who died. He looks at her, creases around her eyes as she smiles at Danny, and he feels a little space open up in his mind, for all she can tell him about her firstborn.

The doctor turns to Dean now, holding Danny out like an offering. "Dad?" he says. "Do you want him back now?"

Aimee Bender

Marzipan

One week after his father died, my father woke up with a hole in his stomach. It wasn't a small hole, some kind of mild break in the skin, it was a hole the size of a soccer ball and it went all the way through. You could now see behind him like he was an enlarged peephole.

Sharon! is what I remember first. He called for my mother, sharp, he called her into the bedroom and my sister Hannah and I stood outside, worried. Was it divorce? We twisted nervously and I had one awful inner jump of glee because there was something about divorce that seemed a tiny bit exciting.

My mother came out, her face distant.

Go to school, she said.

What is it? I said. Hannah tried to peek through. What's wrong? she asked.

They told us at dinner and promised a demonstration after dessert. When all the plates were cleared away, my father raised his thin white undershirt and beneath it, where other people have a stomach, was a round hole. The skin had curved and healed around the circumference.

What's that? I asked.

He shook his head. I don't know, and he looked scared then.

Where is your stomach now? I asked.

He coughed a little.

Did you eat? Hannah said. We saw you eat.

His face paled.

Where did it go? I asked and there we were, his two daughters, me ten, she thirteen.

You have no more bellybutton, I said. You're all bellybutton, I said.

My mother stopped clearing the dishes and put her hand on her neck, cupping her jaw. Girls, she said, quiet down.

You could now thread my father on a bracelet. The giantess' charm bracelet with a new mini wiggling man, something to show the other giantesses at the giantess party. (My, my! they declare. He's so active!)

My parents went to the doctor the next day. The internist took an X-ray and proclaimed my father's inner organs intact. They went to the gastro-interologist. He said my father was digesting food in an arc, it was looping down the sides, sliding around the hole, and all his intestines were, although further crunched, still there and still functioning.

They pronounced him in great health.

My parents walked down into the cool underground parking lot and packed into the car to go home.

Halfway there, ambling through a green light, my mother told my father to pull over which he did and she shoved open the passenger side door and threw up all over the curb.

They made a U turn and drove back to the doctors.

The internist took some blood, left, returned, and winked.

Looks like you're pregnant, he said.

My mother, 43, put a hand on her stomach and stared.

My father, 46, put a hand on his stomach and it went straight through to his back.

They arrived home at six-fifteen that night; Hannah and I had been concerned—six o'clock marked the start of Worry Time. They announced the double news right away: Daddy's fine. Mommy's pregnant.

Are you going to have it? I asked. I like being the youngest, I said. I don't want another kid.

My mother rubbed the back of her neck. Sure, I'll have it, she said. It's a special opportunity and I love babies.

My father, on the couch, one hand curled up and resting inside his stomach like a birdhead, was in good spirits. We'll name it after my dad, he said.

If it's a girl? I asked.

Edwina, he said.

Hannah and I made gagging sounds and he sent us to our room for disrespecting Grandpa.

In nine months, my father's hole was exactly the same size and my mother sported the biggest belly around for miles. Even the doctor was impressed. Hugest I've ever seen, he told her.

My mother was mad. Makes me feel like shit, she said that night at dinner. She glared at my father. I mean, really. You're not even that tall.

My father growled. He was feeling very proud. Biggest belly ever. That was some good sperm.

We all went to the hospital on delivery day. Hannah wandered the hallway, chatting up the interns; I stood at my mother's shoulder, nervous. I thought about the fact that if my father lay, face down, on top of my mother, her belly would poke out his back. She could wear him like a huge fleshy toilet seat cover. He could spin on her stomach, a beige propeller.

She pushed and grimaced and pushed and grimaced. The doctor stood at her knees and his voice peaked with encouragment: Almost There, Atta Girl, Here We Go- And!

But the baby did not come out as planned.

When, finally, the head poked out between her legs, the doctor's face widened with shock. He stared. He stopped yelling Push, Push and his voice dried up. I went over to his side, to see what was going on. And what I saw was that the head appearing between my mother's thighs was not the head of a baby but rather that of an old woman.

My goodness, the doctor said.

My mother sat up.

I blinked.

What's wrong? said my father.

Hannah walked in. Did I miss anything? she asked.

The old woman kicked herself out the rest of the way, wiped a string of gook off her arm, and grabbing the doctor's surgical scissors, clipped the umbilical cord herself. She didn't cry. She said, clearly: Thank Heaven. It was so warm in there near the end, I thought I might faint.

Oh my God, said Hannah.

My mother stared at the familiar wrinkled face in front of her. Mother? she said in a tiny voice.

The woman turned at the sound. Sweetheart, she said, you did an excellent job.

Mother? My mother put a hand over her ear. What are you doing here? Mommy?

I kept blinking. The doctor was mute.

My mother turned to my father. Wait, she said. Wait. In Florida. Funeral. Wait. Didn't that happen?

The old woman didn't answer, but brushed a glob of blood off of her wrist and shook it down to the floor.

My father found his voice. It's my fault, he said softly, and, hanging his head, he lifted his shirt. The doctor stared. My mother reached over and yanked it down.

It is NOT, she said. Pay attention to *me*.

Hannah strode forward, nudged the gaping doctor aside and tried to look up inside.

Where's the baby? she asked.

My mother put her arms around herself. I don't know, she said.

It's me, said my mother's mother.

Hi Grandma, I said.

Hannah started laughing.

The doctor cleared his throat. People, he said, this here is your baby.

My grandmother stretched out her wrinkled legs to the floor, and walked, tiny body old and sagging, over to the bathroom. She selected a white crepe hospital dress from the stack by the door. It stuck to her slippery hip. Shut your eyes children, she said over her shoulder, you don't want to see an old lady naked.

The doctor exited, mumbling busy busy busy.

My mother looked at the floor.

I'm sorry, she said. Her eyes filled.

My father put his palm on her cheek. I grabbed Hannah and dragged her to the door.

We'll be outside, I said.

We heard her voice hardening as we exited. Nine months! she was saying. If I'd known it was going to be my MOTHER, I would've at least smoked a couple of cigarettes.

In the hallway I stared at Hannah and she stared back at me. Edwina? I said and we both doubled over, cracking up so hard I had to run to the bathroom before I wet my pants.

We all drove home together that afternoon. Grandma in the back seat between me and Hannah wrapped up in the baby blanket she had knitted herself, years before.

I remember this one, she remarked, fingering its soft pink weave. I did a nice job.

My father, driving, poked his hole.

I thought it might be a baby without a stomach, he said to my mother in the front seat. I never thought this.

He put an arm on her shoulder.

I love your mother, he said, stroking her arm.

My mother stiffened. I do too, she said. So?

I hadn't gone to my father's father's funeral. It had been in Texas and I'd just finished with strep throat and everyone decided Hannah and I would be better off with the neighbors for the weekend. Think of us Sunday, my mother had said. I'd worn black overalls on Sunday, Hannah had rebelled and worn purple, and together we buried strands of our hair beneath the spindly roots of our neighbor's potted plants.

When they returned, I asked my father how it was. He looked away. Sad, he said, fast, scratching his neck.

Did you cry? I asked.

I cried, he said. I cry.

I nodded. I saw you cry once, I assured him. I remember, it was the national anthem.

He patted my arm. It was very sad, he said, loudly.

I'm right here, I told him, you don't have to yell it.

He went over to the wall and plucked off the black-and-white framed photograph of young Grandpa Edwin.

He sure was handsome, I said, and my father rested his hand on top of my head— the heaviest, best hat.

After we arrived home from the hospital, Hannah and I settled Grandma in the guest bedroom and our parents collapsed in the den: our father, bewildered, on the couch, our mother flat-backed on the floor, beginning a round of sit-ups.

Fuck if my mother is going to ruin my body, she muttered. Fuck that shit.

I brought a book on sand crabs into the living room and pretended to read on the couch. Hannah promptly got on the phone. No really! I heard her saying. I swear!

My father watched my mother: head, knees. Up, down.

At least you can DO sit-ups, he said.

She sat-up, grit her teeth, and sat-down. Some good sperm, she said, nearly spitting.

It's miracle sperm, my father said.

Excuse me, I said, I'm in the room.

Miracle? my mother said. Make it your dad then. Tell your fucking chromosomes to recreate *him*.

Her breasts leaked, useless, onto her t-shirts— cloudy milk-stain eyes staring blind up at the ceiling. She did a set of a hundred and then lay flat.

Mommy, I said, are you okay?

I could hear Hannah in the other room: She died in October, she was saying. Yeah, I totally saw.

My mother turned her head to look at me. Come here, she said.

I put down my book, went over to her, and knelt down.

She put a hand on my cheek. Honey, she said, when I die?

My eyes started to fill up, that fast.

Don't die, I said.

I'm not, she said, I'm very healthy. Not for a while. But when I do, she said, I want you to let me go.

I was able to attend my mother's mother's funeral. I kept close to Hannah for most of it, but when the majority of relatives had trickled out, I found my mother huddled into a corner of the white couch— her head back, face drawn.

I sat next to her, crawled under her arm, and said, Mama you are so sad.

She didn't move her head, just petted my hair with her hand and said: True, but honey I am sad plus.

Plus what I never asked. It made me not hungry, the way she said it.

She stopped her sit-ups at ten-thirty that night. It was past my bedtime and I was all tucked in, lights out. Before she'd fallen asleep, Hannah and I had been giggling.

Maybe I'll have you, I said, stroking my stomach.

She'd sighed. Maybe I'll have myself, she'd whispered.

That concept had never even crossed my mind. Oldest, I hissed back.

After awhile, she'd stopped answering my questions. I prodded my stomach, making sure it was still there and still its usual size. It growled back.

I heard my mother let out a huge exhale in the den and the steady count: three hundred and five, three hundred and six, stopped.

Stepping quietly out of bed, I tiptoed into the hallway; my father was asleep on the couch, and my mother was neatening up the bookshelves, sticking the horizontal books into vertical slats.

Mommy, I called.

She didn't turn around, just held out her arm and I went right to it.

My baby, she said, and I felt myself blooming.

We sat down on the couch, curled together, my knees in a V on her thigh. Her side was warmer than usual from the sit-ups, even a little bit damp. She leaned her head against mine and we both stared ahead, at the closed drapes that were ivory, specked with brown.

I'm hungry, I said.

Me too.

We stood and went to the refrigerator. I found some leftover spaghetti. My mother opened the freezer doors, rummaged around, and brought out half a cake.

I never knew there was cake in there, I mumbled, stuffing a forkful of noodles into my mouth.

It was chocolate on the outside and sealed carefully in plastic. This was from Grandma's funeral, she told me.

I blinked. No way, I said. The marzipan one? I *loved* that cake. You tried it? My mother unwrapped it.

I ate at least three pieces, I said. It was the best food at the wake by far.

She cut me a thin slice and put it on my placemat.

Most ten year olds don't like marzipan, she told me. It's Grandma's favorite, marzipan is, she said. You must've gotten the taste from her.

I nibbled at its edge. It was cold and grainy from the freezer.

Delicious, I said, savoring the almond paste as it spread out in my mouth.

My mother cut herself a piece, grabbed a fork from the drying rack, and sat down across from me.

Why do we have it? I asked.

She shrugged. You know some people keep pieces of wedding cake, she said, taking a bite.

In the morning, my father was holding the photograph of his father in his lap.

Edwin, I said. Handsome Grandpa Edwin.

He pulled me close to him. Grandpa Edwin had thick brown curls.

He really was an asshole, my father said.

I started laughing: loud, full laughter.

He put a hand over my mouth and I laughed into his palm.

Sssh, Lisa, he said. Don't laugh about it.

It's funny, I mumbled.

Don't laugh at a dead man, he said.

I had a few left in me and I let them out, but they were half their big bellylaugh size by then.

How's the hole? I asked, when I was done. Does it hurt?

Nah, he said. It's no big deal.

Can I see?

He raised his thin undershirt.

Can I touch? I asked. He nodded. I gingerly put my fingertips on the inner circle; his skin felt like skin.

So where do you think it went? I asked.

What, he said, the skin?

Everything, I said: the skin, the ribs that were in the way, the stomach acid, all of it.

I guess it's all still in there, he said. I guess it's just pushed to the side.

I think it's cool, I said, imagining a new sports game kind of like basketball that revolved around my father.

He put his shirt back down, a curtain falling. I don't, he said. But it didn't kill me, he said, and I'm grateful for that.

At dinner my grandmother cooked her famous soup with tiny hot dogs floating in a thick bean broth.

I missed this soup, I said, I never thought I'd eat this soup again. This is my favorite soup in the whole world.

Hannah promptly lost a piece of bread inside and poked around the bowl with her fork.

Let's hold hands, said my mother, before we start.

I swallowed the spoonful in my mouth.

I grabbed Hannah's hand and my grandmother's hand. One was soft and mushy and the other one was soft and mushy, but different kinds of soft and different kinds of mushy.

My mother closed her eyes.

We never say prayers, I interrupted.

We are today, said my mother.

I bowed my head.

So what do we say? I asked, looking down into my soup which was bobbing along. Something about bread?

Sshh, said my father. It's a silent prayer.

No, it's not that, said my mother, I'm still thinking.

Ow, Hannah told my father, you're squeezing too hard.

I think we're supposed to be thankful, I hinted.

Hannah turned and glared at me. Shut up, she said. Give her a second.

My grandmother was quiet, smelling her soup.

Needs salt, she whispered.

My mother looked up.

I'm not sure what to say, she said. Her eyebrows furrowed, uncertain.

Let's make it up, I said. I squeezed Hannah's hand and my grandma's hand, and at the same time, they squeezed back.

I'll start it, I said, and we'll go around the circle.

My mother looked relieved. Good, she said, that sounds good.

I would like to say thanks, I began, for my parents and my sister and for the special appearance of Grandma . . . I turned to Hannah.

. . . And for Grandma's soup which is the best soup and is way better than that fish thing we were going to eat. She faced my father.

He cleared his throat. There's usually something about survival in good prayers, he said. Thanks for that.

My mother gave him a look. That's so impersonal, she said.

He shrugged. I'm on the spot, he said. Survival is important to me.

My mother looked us all over and I could see the candle flame flickering near her eye. Her gaze held on her mother.

We all waited.

It's your turn, I said, in case she'd forgotten.

She didn't look at me. She stood up, breaking the hand-links she had made, and sat close to her mother.

My father began eating his soup.

I have a cake from your funeral, she said.

I felt myself lift inside. I squeezed down on Hannah's hand. She said Ouch.

Cake? my grandmother said. What kind of cake?

Marzipan cake, my mother said.

My grandmother smiled. Marzipan? she said. That's my favorite.

I stood up; I wanted to be the one; I went to the freezer, opened it, dug around, and found the cake wedged beneath the third ice tray like a small football.

Here, I said. Here it is.

My mother grabbed it out of my hands.

Just a taste, she said.

Let's all have some! I said. We can all eat funeral cake!

Just a little, my mother said.

Oh come on! I said. Let's make it into five pieces.

My mother looked at me.

Okay, she said. Five pieces. Her face looked lined and tired as she cut up the cake. I passed a piece to each of us. My grandmother bit into hers right away.

Mmm, she said. That is good, now that is GOOD.

My mother did not eat hers. She wrapped it back in the plastic.

My grandmother kept eating and oohing. I bit into mine. Hannah gave me hers; she hates marzipan. I nearly hugged her. My father ate his quickly, like an appetizer.

I remember, said my mother, we all thought you would've

liked it. We said you would've loved it.

My grandmother licked her lips. I do love it, she said. She pointed. Are you going to eat your piece?

No, said my mother.

Can I have it? she asked. I haven't had such good marzipan in I don't know how long.

No, my mother said, closing her fingers over her piece. I want to keep mine, she said.

Oh come on, said my father, let the lady have her cake. It was her funeral cake for God's sake.

I finished my slice. I still had Hannah's.

Here Grandma, I said, Hannah didn't want hers. I slid the whitish slab onto her plate.

Thank you dear, my grandmother said.

I want to keep mine, my mother repeated.

Hannah began on her soup. Her spoon made dull clinking sounds on the bowl.

The soup is good Grandma, she said.

Mmm-hmm, said my father.

My mother sat still at her place. The plastic-wrapped cake sat next to her spoon. She didn't touch her soup. The hot dogs stopped floating and were still.

I'll eat yours if you don't want it, I said to my mother.

She pushed over her bowl. I pretended I was her while I ate it. I imagined I was doing the eating but she was getting nourished.

When I was done, I asked: may I be excused?

No one answered, so I stayed.

Julianna Baggott

Girl-Child X:
A Story of Birthing Told
Through Three Eras

ONE

ENVISION A CHILD WHO WAS A GIFT WITH FULL BUNTING—TOES, profound umbilical wound, downy head. This was during, let's call it, the Era of Avocado-Colored Kitchen Appliances.

For our purposes we will call the child X—a girl.

Unlike many who are born again and again, X was born just once—at lunchtime. The doctors were eating cafeteria Jell-O and chain smoking. It was a grand time for such things—Jell-O and chain smoking! The Jell-O and the chain smoking symbolized our blissful ignorance, joy of joys! Second-hand didn't even exist as a cultural concept. We all smiled a wobbly desserts and smelled charred for decades. This is all very hard to explain.

Because the doctors were eating cafeteria Jell-O and chain smoking, they weren't there for X's actual regatta. In lieu of a doctor, the nurse, cocky and full of bravado, told X's father he could catch the child.

X's father, the lawyer, the engineer. As a child, a stutter collected in his mouth after his own father died. On the debate team, he was the smarty-pants who got punched.

There was a time when he was too nervous to swallow. Fatherless, stuttering, punched, swallow-shy boys aren't prepared for catching.

Was X's mother aware of these thoughts?

X's mother—imagine a woman who thought the disposable Tyvek dress would catch on; a Duponter's wife—who let her husband bounce unboiled eggs on the shag to prove the super-powered effects of the carpet padding. A woman who, despite the tourniquet of etiquette of her time, often wears her convictions with passion— as she does now, screaming: *Get this baby out of me!* And then she curses violently. This is honest. No one here will blame her. This child was her fourth and in addition to it being the Era of Avocado-Colored Kitchen Appliances, it is also the Snotty Academic Zenith of Zero Population Growth, and she has been gawked at hatefully for months. Regardless, wanting a visitor to leave after staying on for nine months is a reasonable request.

Will X's father catch the baby girl? This is the question.

The answer is simple: X does not expect to be caught. (In all fairness, she doesn't expect to be extruded either.) But even in retrospect as the story is told to her countless times—how her mother said, *Glory be! Glory be!*—X anticipates a slippery reception, a cold floor, a gliding to a rubbery halt. But here it is: wide hands, a chest, a towel—unearned. And that is what surprises X each time she thinks about it . . . this birth, this life, this gibbous head teetering on a small neck—it is a gift, again: unearned.

TWO

During, let's call it the "Golden Age of Push-Button Cable Boxes" and on into the "Glory Days of Bono's Irish Mullet," that's when X came of age. All lack of pruning, all lack of tether, she was unsuited to any kind of actual work. She was diagnosed "artistic," (a long history of slides in dim art school classrooms; photography solution wafting up from the basement darkrooms; the turpentine strumming around nudes standing still and flaccid)—but she loved, most deeply, men of all sorts. She rode them dynamically with a Marylou Retton ecstaticism. She often raised her hands victoriously when finishing (not some grubby sexual basement encounter in the TV glow of General Hospital—Nurse Bobby and Patch having it out at last!). Let's stick with the Rettonesque metaphor and call it: a floor routine—not to be too euphemistically prudish.

Perhaps you are now expecting some gynecological interruption—a finger-wagging docu-drama shown in a Catholic high school health class (or ethics class, P.E., home ec., maybe even shop)—replete with stirrups, cold instruments (isn't it worse when they warm them up first?), a prescription of Pills rattling in plastic pop-out containers that are made to look like suede wallets. Perhaps you are expecting to hear that X had an unwanted pregnancy, venereal collapse, a deformed ego. Perhaps you would like her to have the abortion for your own political reasons or perhaps you would like her to keep the pregnancy for your own political reasons.

This is not that story. (Keep your dirty political reasons to yourself! Thank you kindly!)

I should mention, however, that it was at some unknown point during this era that she formed strong opinions on children—though had little access to them—and consequently looked down upon those who:

   a. didn't have natural childbirth
   b. littered the earth with non-biodegradable diapers
   c. took children to nice restaurants (She was a waitress in a nice restaurant.)

And now, I should admit, this (part deux) is simply (or not too simply) the transition from X having been birthed through a vagina to a vagina of her own which will eventually lead to a decision (informed though artistically imagined) to use her vagina as an exit for a baby of her own.

Let me say this: In a three part structure as this, sometimes the second part is only a bridge from part one to part two—but if you prefer to stick to a Freudianly exacting metaphor, we can use the term tunnel instead of bridge. Actually, I prefer Chunnel.

THREE

Now what? We have passed the Dawn of Sensitivity Training for High-Level Management, though X's father—born sensitive (fatherless, stuttering, punched and swallow-shy) is now overly so—and X's mother has weathered The Mighty Thigh Master Movement with her dignity intact. And X herself fell in love in the midst of the Tyranny of Low-Rise Retro Bell-bottoms with a man raised in New Hampshire where he was a longtime sufferer (and still is sore to the touch because) of The Tragic Bill Buckner Error of '86. And now, in the middle of The Great American Idol Worship, she finds herself rotund with child.

She is fond of referring to the pregnancy as her "condition," because she likes how it sounds antiquated, more a la British PBS movie. Even though she has yet to have the child, she has the overwhelming urge to rattle other pregnant women by their shoulders maybe even slap them—especially the ones in Pooh Bear maternity tops getting perms at the mini mall—and scream hysterically: *We could DIE. Don't you know that! There is nothing cute about this!*

She despises home-birthers—women having babies in bathtubs, placentas caught in bowls designed for potato chips.

"Historically speaking," she is fond of saying to her husband, "this is how women die. Go to any old graveyard and read the tombstones and count how many women are buried with their babies." She's never done this and has no intentions.

"Scientifically speaking," she's fond of saying to her husband, "human beings are terrible at giving birth. We only have them one at a time, usually, and with these giant heads. We've just selected too much on the trait of brain size." For the first time in her life, this seems like a huge error in the history of mankind.

Her husband's head is large. She regards it as she would an impolite gesture.

"Personally speaking," she's fond of saying to her husband, "I'm surprised that I'm an animal, after all."

After all of what? After the invention of travel coffee mugs with rubber handgrips! After the inauguration of wheels on luggage (how many centuries did we have luggage and wheels and just couldn't fathom putting them together until some stewardesses dreamed it up?)! After the obscenity of doggie T-shirts that have Bling-Bling printed on them in fake diamonds! She omits the transition above and simply says, "Animals aren't even animals any more, for shit's sake!"

Please note: During her pregnancy, she only slaps one person—and it was not a pregnant woman. (She had a long flight with a high school marching band and an understandable incident with a sophomore flutist.)

Despite X's morbidity and all of the above, she has a strong capacity for denial—and closed her eyes during the birthing film's close up of an engorged vagina—mid-head—and its corresponding anus—bulbed beyond anus recognition. Leading up to the due date, she is inwardly cocky. She was not only a sexual *gymnast*, she also was a very good field hockey player—a forward, no less, second team All-Catholic. She believes—as so many do—that women are by and large physically doughy and that this is why they whine so much about labor—that there is some vow between all post-birth women to overhype so that they can be afforded their suffering and sympathy—and what kind of emotional miser would call a mother a liar?

When labor starts, she prisses from the pain. Ouchy. And then she tries to crawl away from it. And then she tries to breathe with the pain– as was suggested in those fucking, fucking, lame-ass, shit-ass labor classes. As she suspected, the labor educators have overplayed their hand. (Why, oh, why had she ever believed them? Breathing! It seems intentionally cruel now. Labor educators are the most vicious brand of Allen Funt-ery.)

She finds a new pain. It makes her disappear. It makes her move in the bed as slowly and silently as a large cat. Later she will think of the women who give labor in trees during floods of the rainy season. She doesn't want drugs and yet when offered she gladly risks paralysis.

And then it is time to push. It isn't lunch time, like her own birth, but the doctor is out. She expects instead of Jell-O and chain-smoking, he's having sex with the nurse from the previous shift. (Nurses and shifts have come and gone ... Lives have been lived. It's snowed some. Geese have moved onto the hospital lawn ....)

She regards her husband suspiciously. She recalls his history with Bill Buckner. "Don't let him catch the baby," she says to the nurse, conspiratorially, when her husband is in the bathroom.

The nurse laughs and tells the husband as soon as he walks back into the room. (Conspirators!)

The doctor appears at the last moment. He's too jocular. He's no doctor! He's a playboy! He's a fucking rodeo clown!

X is at a disadvantage, because she has no real idea that it is an actual baby inside of her. It is her pregnancy inside of her. It is her "condition" inside of her. But once someone announces they can see the top of the head—the downy gibbous head—the baby exists not only in her mind—but in her body. It is here and it needs to be there. *Get this baby out of me!* she thinks to herself. Animal from animal.

And the baby does come out.

And when the doctor lifts the baby for her to see—a boy!—the infant lifts his arms in the air—like a gymnast. How odd! What an odd creature!

The doctor is asking X's husband if he wants to cut the umbilical cord. Her husband declines. "I don't want to be the one, metaphorically or otherwise." He is this kind of thoughtful, big-brained husband.

Her husband will tell her all of this later. Right now she cannot hear them. Her vision is a pinprick in paper—eclipse-style. There is a swarming, oh, hive-chest, oh, like someone has yanked a cord and the old lawnmower has kicked up inside of her. This is not mortar board. She, animal, has whelped—the baby is a flesh pot, porcine and pulpy—its cells all aligned miraculously.

She does not deserve this baby.

It is—what?

A gift so lavish, it's unseemly, uncalled for—more than anyone deserves. Her husband's face is shining like a globe lit with pride. She feels both humble and divine, and she whispers, "For me? Are you sure? Mine?"

Elizabeth Graver

The Mourning Door

THE FIRST THING SHE FINDS IS A HAND. IN THE BEGINNING, SHE thinks it's a tangle of sheet or a wadded sock caught between the mattress cover and the mattress, a bump the size of a walnut but softer, more yielding. She feels it as she's lying, lazing, in bed. Often, lately, her body keeps her beached, though today the sun beckons, the dogwoods blooming white, the peonies' glossy buds specked black with ants. Tom has gone to work already, backing out of the driveway in his pick-up truck. She has taken her temperature on the pink thermometer, noted it down on the graph—98.2, day eighteen, their thirteenth month of trying. She takes it again, to be sure, then settles back in, drifting, though she knows she should get up. The carpenters will be here soon; the air will ring with hammers. The men will find more expensive, unnerving problems with the house. She'll have to creep in her robe to the bathroom, so small and steady, like one of the pests they keep uncovering in this ancient, tilting farmhouse—powder post beetles, termites, carpenter ants.

She feels the bump in the bed the way she might encounter a new mole on her skin, or a scab that had somehow gone unnoticed, her hand traveling vaguely along her body until it stumbles, oh, what's this? With her shin, she feels it first, as she turns over, beginning to get up. She sends an arm under the covers, palpates the bump. A pair of bunched panties, maybe, shed during sex and caught beneath the new sheet when she remade the bed? Tom's sock? A wad of tissue? Some unknown object (needle threader, sock darner, butter maker, chaff-separator?) left here by the generations of people who came before? The carpenters keep finding things in the walls and under the floor: the sole of an old shoe, a rusted nail, a bent horseshoe. A Depression-era glass bowl, unbroken, the green of key lime pie. Each time they announce another rotted sill, cracked joist, additional repair, they hand an object over, her consolation prize. The house looked so charming from the outside, so fine and perfectly itself. The inspector said go ahead, buy it. But you never know what's lurking underneath.

She gets out of the bed, stretches, yawns. Her gaze drops to her naked body, so familiar, the thin freckled limbs and flatish stomach. She has known it forever, lived with it forever. Mostly it has served her well, but lately it seems a foreign, uncooperative thing, at once insolent and lethargic, a taunt. Sometimes, though, she still finds in herself an energy that surprises her, reminding her of when she was a child and used to run—legs churning, pulse throbbing—down the long river path that led to her cousin's house.

Now, in a motion so concentrated it's fierce, she peels off the sheet and flips back the mattress pad. What she sees doesn't surprise her; she's been waiting so hard, these days, looking so hard. A hand, it is, a small, pink dimpled fist, the skin slightly mottled, the nails the smallest slivers, cut them or they'll scratch. Five fingers. Five nails. She picks it up; it flexes slightly, then curls back into a warm fist. Five fine fingers, none missing; she counts them again to be sure. *You have to begin somewhere,* the books say. *You have to relinquish control and let nature take its course.*

She hears the door open downstairs, the clomp of workboots, words, a barking laugh. Looking around, she spots, on the bedroom floor, the burlap sack that held the dwarf liberty apple tree Tom planted over the weekend. She drops the hand into the bag, stuffs the bag under the bed. Still the air smells like burlap, thick and dusty. She pulls on some sweatpants, then thinks better of it and puts on a more flattering pair of jeans, and a T-shirt that shows off her breasts. She read somewhere that men are drawn to women with small waists and flaring hips. Evolution, the article said. A body built for birth. Her own hips are small and boyish; her waist does not cinch in. Her pubic hair grows thin and blond, grass in a drought. She doesn't want these workmen, exactly, but she would like them, for the briefest moment, to want her. As she goes barefoot down the stairs to make a cup of tea and smile at the men, she stops for a moment, struck by a memory of the perfect little hand; even the thought of it makes her gasp. The men won't find it. They're only working in the basement and the attic, structural repairs to keep the house from falling down.

In her kitchen, the three men: Rick and Tony and Joaquin. Their eyes flicker over her. She touches her hair, feels heavy with her secret and looks down. More bad news, I'm afraid, Rick tells her. We found it yesterday, after you left—a whole section of the attic. What, she asks. *Charred*, he says dramatically. There must have been a fire; some major support beams are only three-quarter their original size. She shakes her head. Really? But the inspector never— I have my doubts, Rick says, about this so-called inspector of yours. Can you fix it, she asks. He looks at her glumly through heavy-lidded eyes. We can try, he answers. I'll draw up an estimate but we'll need to finish the basement before we get to this. Yes, she says vaguely, already bored. Fine, thanks.

Had she received such news the day before, it would have made her dizzy. A charred, unstable attic, a house whittled down by flames. She would have called Tom at work—you're not going to believe this—and checked how much money they had left in their savings account, and thought about suing the inspector and installing more smoke alarms, one in every room, blinking eyes. Today, though, she can't quite concentrate; her thoughts keep returning, as if of their own accord, to what she discovered in her bed. One apricot-sized hand, after thirteen months, after peeing into cups, tracking her temperature, making Tom lie still as a statue after he comes, no saliva, no new positions, her rump tilted high into the air afterwards, an absurd position but she doesn't care.

After thirteen months of watching for the LH surge on the ovulation predictor kit—the deep indigo line of a good egg, the watery turquoise of a bad, and inside her own body, waves cresting and breaking, for she has become an ocean, or it is an oceanographer? *Study us hard enough*, the waves call out to her, *watch us closely enough and we shall do your will*. She has noted the discharge on her underpants—sticky, tacky, scant. Egg white, like she's a chef making meringues or a chicken trying to lay. *Get to know your body,* chant the books, the Web sites, her baby-bearing friends, and oh she has, she does, though it's beginning to feel like a cheap car she has leased for awhile and is getting ready to return.

She still likes making love with Tom, the tremble of it, the slow, blue wash, the way they lie cupped together in their new, old house as it sits in the greening fields, on the turning earth. It's afterwards that she hates. She can never fall asleep without picturing the spastic, thrashing tails, the egg's hard shell, the long, thin tubes stretched like IV's toward a pulsing womb. A speck, she imagines sometimes, the head of a pin, the dot of a period. The End—or maybe, if they're lucky, dot dot dot.

But the hand is so much bigger than that, substantial, real. Her own hands shake with relief as she puts on the tea water. Something is starting—a secret, a discovery, begun not in the narrow recesses of her body, but in the mysterious body of her new old house. The house has a door called the Mourning Door—the realtor pointed it out the first time they walked through. It's a door off the front parlor, and though it leads outside, it has no stoop or stairs, just a place for the cart to back up so the coffin can be carried away. Of course babies were born here, too, added the realtor, her voice too bright. Probably right in this room! After she and Tom moved in, they decided only to use the door off the kitchen. Friendlier, she said, and after all, they're concentrating, these days, on making life.

When she goes back upstairs, she takes the burlap sack and a flashlight to the warm, musty attic, where Tom almost never goes. With the flashlight's beam, she finds, in one dark corner, the section where the fire left it mark. She touches the wood and a smudge of ash comes off on her finger. She tastes it: dry powder, ancient fruit, people passing buckets, lives lost, found, lost. She leaves the sack in the other corner of the attic inside a box marked "Kitchen Stuff." Then she heads downstairs to wash her hands.

Three days later she is doing laundry when she comes across a shoulder, round and smooth. She knows it should be disconcerting to find such a thing separated from its owner, a shoulder disembodied, lying in a nest of dryer lint, tucked close to the wall. But why get upset? After all, the world is full of parts apart from wholes. A few months ago, she and Tom went to the salvage place—old radiator covers, round church windows, faucets and doorknobs, a spiral staircase leading nowhere. Then, they bought two doors and a useless unit of brass mailboxes, numbers fifteen through twenty-five. Now she wipes her hands on her jeans and picks the shoulder up. It is late afternoon, the contractors gone, Tom still at work. She brings the shoulder up to the attic and puts it in the sack with the hand. Then she goes to the bedroom, swallows a vitamin the size of a horse pill, climbs into bed and falls asleep.

Whereas before she had been agitated, unable to turn her thoughts away, now she is peaceful, assembling something, proud. But tired, too—this is not unexpected; every day by four or five o'clock she has to sink into bed for a nap, let in dreams full of floaty shapes, closed fists and open mouths. Still, most days, she gets a little something done. She lines a trunk with old wallpaper, goes for a walk in the woods with a friend, starts to plan a lesson sequence on how leaves change color in the fall. Her children are all away for the summer, shipped off to lakes and rivers and seas. Sometimes she gets a "Dear Teacher" postcard: *I found some mica. We went on a boat. I lost my ring in the lake.* The water in the postcards is always a vivid, chlorinated blue. She answers each postcard, gets her hair cut, sees a matinee movie with her friend Hannah, starts to knit again. One night Tom remarks—perhaps with relief, perhaps with the slightest tinge of fear—that she seems back to her old self.

In the basement, the men put in Lalley columns, thick and red, to keep the first floor from falling in. They construct a vapor barrier, rewire the electricity. They sister the joists and patch the foundation. In her bedroom, she stuffs cotton in her ears to block the noise. She wears sweatpants or loose shorts now, and Tom's shirts. Each time she catches a glimpse of herself in the mirror, she is struck by how pretty she looks, her eyes so bright, almost feverish, her fingernails a flushed, excited pink.

She finds a second foot with ten perfect toes, and a second shoulder. She finds a leg, an arm. No eyes, yet, no face. Everything in time, she tells herself, and at the Center for Reproductive Medicine they inject her womb with blue and she sees her tubes, thin as violin strings, curled and ghostly on the screen. They have her drink water and lie on her back. They swab gel on her belly, and she neglects to tell them that her actual belly is at home, smelling like dust and apple wood, snoozing under the eaves. They say come in on Day Three, on Day Ten. They swab her with more gel and give her a rattle, loose pills in an amber jar. Tom goes to the clinic and they shut him in a room with girlie magazines and take his fish. At home, while he is at the doctor's, she finds a tiny penis, sweet and curled. Tom comes home discouraged—rare for him. He lies down on the floor and sighs. She says don't worry babe and leans to kiss him on the arm. She would like to tell him about everything she has found, but she knows she must protect her secret. Things are so fragile, really—the earth settles, the house shifts. You put up a wall in the wrong place and so never find the hidden object in the eaves. You speak too soon and cause—with your hard, your hopeful words—a clot, a cramp. Things are so fragile, but then also not. Look at the ants, she tells herself—how they always find a place to make a nest. Look at the people of the earth, each one with a mother. At the supermarket, she stares at them—their hands, their faces, how neatly it all goes together, a completed puzzle.

She knows her own way is out of the ordinary, but then what is ordinary these days? She is living in a time of freezers and test tubes, of petri dishes and turkey basters, of trade and barter, test and track, mix and match. Women carry the eggs of other women, or have their own eggs injected back into them pumped with potential, four or six at a time. Sperm are washed and coddled, separated and sifted, like gold. Ovaries are inflated until they spill with treasures. The names sound like code words: GIFT, IUI, ZIFT. Though it upsets her to admit it, the other women at the Center disgust her a little. They seem so desperate, they look so swollen, but in all the wrong places—their eyes, their chins, their hearts. Not me, she thinks as the nurse calls her name and she rises with a friendly smile.

One day, she moves the burlap bag from the attic to the back of her bedroom closet. It's such a big house, and the attic is sweltering now, and soon the men will be working up there on the charred wood. Before, she and Tom lived in a tiny, rented bungalow and looked into each other's eyes a lot. She loves Tom; she really does, though lately he seems quite far away. Outside, here, is a swing-set made of old, splintered cedar, not safe enough for use. But that same day, she finds an ear in it, tucked like a chestnut under a climbing pole. The tomatoes are ripe now. The sunflowers she planted in May are taller than she is, balancing their heads on swaying stalks. In the herb garden, the chives bear fat purple balls. The ear, oddly, is downed with dark hair, like the ear of a young primate. She holds it to her own ear as if she might hear something inside it—the sea, perhaps, a heartbeat or a yawn. It looks so tender that she wraps it in tissue paper before placing it in the bag.

One night on the evening news, she and Tom see a story about a girl who was in a car accident and went into a coma, and now the girl performs miracles and people think she's a saint. The news shows her lying in Worcester in her parents' garage, hitched to life support while pilgrims come from near and far: people on crutches, children with cancer, barren women, men dying of AIDs. Jesus, says Tom, shuddering. People will believe anything—how sick. But she doesn't think it's so sick, the way the vinyl-sided ranch house is transformed into a wall of flowers, the way people bring gifts—Barbie dolls, barrettes, Hawaiian Punch (the girl's favorite), and a blind man sees again, and a baby blooms from a tired woman's torso, and the rest of the people, well the rest sit briefly in the full lap of hope, then get in their cars and go home. The girl is pretty, even though she's almost dead. Her braid is black and shiny, her brow peaceful. Her mother, the reporter says, sponge-bathes her each morning and again at night. Her father is petitioning the Vatican for the girl to be made an official saint.

Days, now, while the men work in the attic, she roams. She wanders the house looking for treasures, and on the days when she does not find them, she gets in her car and drives to town, or out along the country roads. Sometimes she finds barn sales and gets things for the house—a chair for Tom's desk, an old egg candler filled with holes. One day at a yard sale, she buys a sewing machine, though she's never used one. I'll give you the instruction book, the woman says. It's easy—you'll see. Also at this yard sale is a playpen, a high chair, a pile of infant clothes. The woman sees her staring at them. I thought you might be expecting, she says, smiling. But I didn't want to presume. As a bonus, she throws in a plump pincushion stabbed with silver pins and needles, and a blue and white sailor suit. It was my son's, she says, and from behind the house come—as if in proof—the shrieks of kids at play.

That night, with Tom in New York for an overnight meeting, she sets up the sewing machine and sits with the instruction manual in her lap. She slides out the trap door under the needle, examining the bobbin. Slowly, following the instructions, she winds the bobbin full of beige thread, then threads the needle. She gets the bag from the closet. She's not sure she's ready (the books say you're never sure), but at the same time her body is guiding, pushing, *urging* her.

Breathe, she commands herself, and draws a deep breath. She has never done this before, never threaded the needle or assembled the pattern or put together the parts, but it doesn't seem to matter; she has a sense of how to approach it—first this, then this, then this. She takes a hand out of the bag and tries to stitch it to an arm, but the machine jams, so she unwinds a length of thread from the bobbin, pulls a needle from the pincushion and begins again, by hand.

Slowly, awkwardly, she stitches arm to shoulder, stops to catch her breath and wipe the sweat from her brow. She remembers back stitch, cross stitch; someone (her mother?) must have taught her long ago. She finds the other hand, the other arm. Does she have everything? It's been a long summer and she's found so much; she might be losing track. If there aren't enough pieces, don't panic, she tells herself. He doesn't need to be perfect; she's not asking for that. He can be missing a part or two, he can need extra care. Her own body, after all, has its flaws, its stubborn limits. What, anyway, is perfect in this world? She'll take what she is given, what she has been able, bit by bit, to make.

She stitches feet to legs, carefully doing the seams on the inside so they won't show. She attaches leg to torso, sews on the little penis. The boy-child begins to stir, to struggle; perhaps he has to pee. Not yet, my love. Hold on. She works long and hard and late into the night, her body tight with effort, the room filled with animal noises that spring from her mouth as if she were someone else. She wishes, with a deep, aching pain, that Tom were here to guide her hands, to help her breathe and watch her work. Finally—it must be near dawn—she reaches into the bag and finds nothing. How tired she is, bone tired, skin tired. She must be finished, for she has used up all the parts.

Slowly, then, as if in sleep, she rises with the child in her arms. She has been working in the dark and so can't quite see him, though she feels his downy head, his foot and hand. He curls toward her for an instant as if to nurse, so she unbuttons her blouse and draws him near. He nuzzles toward her but does not drink, and she passes a hand over his face and realizes that he has no mouth. Carefully, in the dark, she inspects him with both her hands and mind: he has a nose but no mouth, wrists but no elbows. She spreads her palm over his torso, and her fingers tell her that he has kidneys and a liver but only six small ribs and half a heart. Oh, she tells him. Oh I'm sorry. I tried so hard; I found and saved and stitched and tried so hard and yet—

She feels it first, before he goes: a spasm in her belly, a clot in her brain, a sorrow so thick and familiar that she knows she's felt it before, but not like this, so unyielding, so tangible: six small ribs and only half a heart. While she holds him, he twitches twice and then is still.

Carrying him, she makes her way downstairs. It's lighter now, the purple-blue of dawn. She walks to the front parlor, past the TV, past the old honey extractor they found in the barn. She walks to the Mourning Door and tries to open it. It doesn't budge, wedged shut, and for a moment she panics—she has to get out now; the weight in her arms keeps getting heavier, a sack of stones. She needs to pass it through this door and set it down, or she will break. Trying to stay calm, she goes to the laundry room and finds a screwdriver, returns to the door and wedges the tool in along the lock placket, balancing the baby on one arm. Finally the door gives and she walks through it, forgetting that no steps meet it outside. Falling forward over the high ledge, she lands, stumbles, catches her balance (somehow, she hasn't dropped him) to stand stunned and breathless in the still morning air, her knees weak from landing hard.

Across the road, the sheep in the field have begun their bleating. A truck drives by, catching her briefly in its lights. She lowers her nose to the baby's head and breathes in the smell of him. He's lighter now, easier now. *Depart,* she thinks, the word an old prayer following her through the door. *Depart in peace.* With her hands, she memorizes the slope of his nose, the open architecture of his skull. She fingers the spirals of one ear. Then she turns and starts walking, out behind the house to the barn where a shovel hangs beside the hoe and rake. It's lighter now. A mosquito hovers close to her face. The day will be hot. Later, Tom will return. She buries the baby under a Hawthorn tree on the back stretch of their land and leaves his grave unmarked. My boy, she says as she turns to go. Thank you, she says—to him or to the air—when she is halfway home. She sleeps all morning and gardens through the afternoon.

That night (Day Sixteen, except she's stopped charting), she and Tom make love, and afterwards, she thinks of nothing—no wagging fish, no hovering egg, no pathway, her thoughts as flat and clean as sheets. Tom smells like himself—it is a smell she loves and had nearly forgotten—and after their sex, they talk about his trip, and he runs a hand idly down her back. She is ready for something now—a child inside her or a child outside, come from another bed, another place. Or she is ready, perhaps, for no child at all, a trip with Tom to a different altitude or hemisphere, a rocky, twisting hike. They make love again, and after she comes, she cries, and he asks what, what is it, but it's nothing she can describe, it's where she's been, so far away and without him—in the charred attic, the tipped basement, where red columns try to shore up a house that will stand for as long as it wants to and fall when it wants to fall. Nothing, she says, and inside her something joins, or tries to join, forms or does not, and her dream, when she sleeps, is of the far horizon, a smooth, receding curve.

Adam Langer

The Book of Names

WE WILL NOT NAME HER ANDI BECAUSE THAT'S THE NAME OF MY fiancée who is currently meeting with the obstetrician while I sit out in the waiting room with a book of baby names.

We will not name her Bethany because that's Andi's older sister's name and Bethany has been trying to get pregnant for five years and hasn't spoken to us since Andi announced that we would be getting married because she was going to have a child.

We will not name her Christine because, even though I am an atheist, my mother would never speak to me again if the word "Christ" appeared in our child's name.

We will not name her Diane because I lost my virginity nearly thirty years ago to Diane Kessler when she and I were both counselors at Camp Chi and, even though Andi and Diane get along okay, I still haven't told Andi about the long-term, on again/off again relationship I had with Diane; it would just be too strange. In some ways, Andi is pretty traditional and I doubt that she would understand.

We will not name her Evelyn because the English Department secretary is named Evelyn and she became awfully flirty with me at the faculty Christmas party when she learned of Andi's pregnancy, as if she thought that both the pregnancy and the youth of my fiancée were evidence of my virility.

We will not name her Frances because Andi's father is named Frank and, even though my mother (Roz) says that she would never want a child named after her because Jewish tradition opposes naming children after living human beings, still she would be upset if we named the child after Andi's dad, particularly since my mom never understood why Yael Liebowitz married Frank and not me.

We will not name her Georgette because our birthing class teacher is named Georgette and I don't think she likes me very much—she keeps recommending campus couples' counselors to Andi when she thinks I'm out of earshot.

We will not name her Hilary because, not only is Diane's daughter named Helen, I'm not entirely sure that I'm not Helen's father, even though Helen doesn't look much like either myself or Diane's husband who is named Ira. Hilary also sounds like Hilly, which reminds me of *Hills Like White Elephants*, a short story that I assign every year to my freshmen, even though I find it to be Hemingway's weakest.

We will not name her Ida because that's too close to Ira and not only is Ira Diane's husband's name, and not only is Ira my creepy father's name, but Ira is also the name of the obnoxious frat boy who tried to punch me out when he learned that Andi had dumped him and started dating me.

We will not name her Jane because one time, shortly before my mother divorced my father, I discovered my dad gazing with apparent lust at a picture of the actress Jane Russell in *Look* Magazine and, since then, I have been unable to look at my father the same way. Or anyone named Jane, for that matter.

We will not name her Kate because I have dated three Kates and all three of those relationships ended badly, one with a restraining order, which I found completely inappropriate and exaggerated, by the way.

We will not name her Lolita for obvious reasons, despite the fact that *Lolita* is Andi's favorite book, a fact that she has never satisfactorily explained to me.

We will not name her Miranda because Miranda makes me think about Miranda rights, which are what were recited to me on both occasions when I was put in the back of a squad car for driving home from campus while I was severely intoxicated. This was before I stopped drinking; it's been three months since I met Andi and I've had two-and-a-half months clean and sober.

We will not name her Nadine, even though that's the name of the Led Zeppelin song that Andi and I danced to at the Bluebird on the night that she and I first met and she got pregnant.

We will not name her Oleanna because that's the name of the movie my department advisor made me watch when he first learned that I was dating a university student, even though Andi wasn't even taking any classes in my department, not even in the humanities, I must add.

We will not name her Patricia because Patricia is Andi's best friend, and, to be honest, she was the woman I went to the Bluebird to meet on the night that Andi found me half-drunk on Wild Turkey at the bar.

We will not name her Quinn, even though that was my first choice for a name, largely because "Quinn The Eskimo" is my favorite song. But since Andi won't listen to any of my Dylan albums or, for that matter, any albums that were recorded pre-1989 (she says that old records are "depressing"), it seems ill-advised to force the issue.

We will not name her Roberta, because I have a really gorgeous work-study student named Roberta.

We will not name her Samantha, because I have a really gorgeous work-study student named Samantha.

We will not name her Traci for reasons similar to those that I have mentioned above.

We will not name her Ulla, because that's my first daughter's name and I haven't spoken to her in years.

We will not name her Victoria because Victoria is the name of Andi's best friend who will serve as maid of honor at our wedding. In fact, Victoria is one of only four people who will attend the wedding, the others being my mom, my brother, my favorite grad student Wiley, and her husband Jamal, a jackass who works for *The Herald* and says that he would like to write an article about me.

We will not name her Wiley because Wiley's my favorite graduate student and she wound up marrying some jackass named Jamal.

We will not name her Xaviera because that sounds like the name of a porn star and porn stars remind me too much of my father. I still find it hard to believe that he would actually move to Vegas and marry someone young enough to be his daughter.

We will not name her Yael because Yael Liebowitz was the first girl who ever dumped me, and you never quite get over being dumped for the first time.

We will not name her Zelda because that's the name of Andi's obstetrician who is approaching me while I am sitting here in the waiting room with the baby name book. Zelda is asking if she can speak to me outside.

Emily Rubin

Ray and Sheila Have a Day

IT'S SIX A.M. AND I WAKE UP, STILL FUMING. WE'VE BEEN FIGHTING for three days, since Saturday night, when Ray went to the Lusty Lady for his youngest brother's bachelor party. The decision to go to a strip club, he tells me, wasn't easy. He says he didn't want to go because he knew it would upset me and because it would be bad for his health. He says cigarette smoke gives him a headache and makes his eyes water. However, he wanted to bond with his younger brother on the night before his wedding. Ray is the oldest. When his father died two years ago, he became the dad in the family, calling his siblings and mother every week to make sure that everyone and everything is under control. Since I've been pregnant, Ray's kept the phone numbers of immediate family members in a silver pendant around his neck. He tells me periodically that you never know when you might need those numbers.

Accompanying his brother to the Lusty Lady, according to Ray, was an act of parental love. I point out, calmly, that there are many ways to be parental which don't involve naked women dancing in front of drunken men. Ray tells me that the evening was harmless. He says I don't have a realistic sense of what strip clubs are like. He says they're lonely places. He only stayed for an hour; he sat and drank a beer and talked to his brother's friends and then left. He says he didn't even watch the show.

As soon as I hear the words "the show," the tiny doors in my head start slamming shut and my mouth goes dry.

"What part of the evening constitutes 'the show'?" I yell. "Does it include the part when the strippers are jiggling their asses on the laps of bastard Neanderthals? What about the part when guys go into the back room for a blow job? Is that part of 'the show'?"

"For Christ's sake, Sheila, it's 6:30 in the goddamn morning," Ray says, closing his eyes. "I'm not saying that I had a good time. It was like going to some weird sex circus with a bunch of pathetic guys. It was a complete freak show."

He gets out of bed and picks up his watch from the night table.

"Let's look at the bright side," he says. "It could have been worse —it could have been a bottomless bar instead of a topless bar, right?"

I think that I hate him. I hand him a pen and a pad of paper and ask him to draw the evening. I tell him it will help me to develop a realistic sense.

"Sheila," he says, sitting down on the bed, "I married you for your sense of humor. What happened to your sense of humor?"

Ray spends a long time on the drawing, even though it's done in primitive strokes and stick figures. This is what he draws: a woman in a bikini bottom with her arms above her head and small breasts; fat and short men standing around the stage, watching; four or five tables of men, and a few women, drinking and talking to each other; Ray sitting on a bar stool, facing away from the stage, talking to a man wearing glasses.

I study the picture when he is finished.

"Relative to the size of her body, is that how big her boobs were?" I ask.

"More or less," he says.

"More or less," I repeat. "I thought you said you weren't watching 'the show', you filthy swine."

Ray sighs loudly.

"Do you even remember that I'm pregnant?" I ask.

Being pregnant has made me batty. Just when I think I'm ready to forgive and forget, I hurl something across the room. In the last month alone, I've smashed two mirrors and a crystal vase, which I never particularly liked. Now in the evening when I'm hungry, I cry, because everything I consider eating makes me feel like throwing up: cheese, fish, saltines. Sometimes I'll be walking down the street and the urge to pee strikes me with the force of a hurricane. Where we live, just below San Francisco in Daly City, the hills are steep and unforgiving for pregnant women; last week, I had to pee in my neighbor's back yard because I couldn't make it home in time. I crawled behind the farthest rhododendron bush, which rises up against the fence. I felt like a complete pervert, with my big white stomach sticking out through the branches and my backside pressed against the fence. I hope the neighbors didn't see me.

"Good morning, fuckhead," I say, when Ray walks into the kitchen.

I am making scrambled eggs, only enough for myself.

"Sheila," he says, standing right behind me, "I'm sorry."

I turn around and poise the spatula in front of his nose.

He speaks slowly, as if explaining something to a very slow learner. "I didn't mean to hurt your feelings. I didn't mean to upset you."

I stare at him. He looks at the egg dripping from the spatula onto the floor.

"You could have left," I say, "you could have turned around before going inside. You could have done a million different things. You could have called me from a pay phone and said let's play miniature golf. Let's drive to the desert and watch the cactus grow. Let's check in at the Holiday Inn and swim in the pool. You could have left a message for your brother at his apartment. You could have told me you were a loathsome beast five years ago, when it still would have been easy to leave you."

In response, Ray sits down at the table and scribbles something along the top of the business section of the *San Francisco Chronicle*. He tears off what he's written and sticks it in his pocket.

"What did you write down?" I demand.

He shrugs and smiles.

"I never give away my secrets," he says.

"What do you mean you don't give away your secrets?" I bellow, "Did you get a blow job? What is wrong with you?"

"I don't know," he says.

When I married Ray five years ago, I married a man with allergies. The typical ones: dust, pollen, dog hair. Now the allergies are getting worse instead of better. Actually, I think they're breeding. Over the past year, he's developed lactose intolerance, allergies to air condition-ing, soap, mold, wool, and a compulsion to take notes. He takes lots of pills and doesn't eat any dairy. And he writes on everything—nap-kins, telephone books, the newspaper. The other day Ray told me that he doesn't want me pumping my own gas because the fumes will harm the baby. And no more Mountain Dew for me, either. When Ray saw the empty soda bottle on the floor of the car, he ran into the house, waving the bottle over his head and shouting, "This stuff is like drink-ing antifreeze, Sheila! Don't you know what it could do to the baby?"

I'm not sure why Ray turned out this way. He comes from a family of enormous North Dakotan men. He measures six feet, eight inches tall, his baby brother six feet, nine. These are people who lift you off the ground instead of hug. I've learned to never shake hands with them or wear open-toed shoes. When his family visits, the herd of giants tramples our domestic landscape. They break door handles and shower faucets and chandeliers. They knock over plants and floor lamps. And they inhale food. Once I watched Ray's brother eat three turkey and jam sandwiches in one sitting, for a snack. But Ray is different from the rest of the giants. For one thing, no one else in his family has allergies. His mother says he's always been special.

It's 8:30. Ray is cleaning the toilet, which he does every morning.

"Sheila," he yells from the bathroom, "Give me a goddamn break, won't you?"

I can hear the clink of the Ajax can on the tile floor.

"Someday you'll forgive me," he yells. "You know that underneath it all, you still love me. You know that, don't you?"

I lie down on the couch and close my eyes. His lactose intolerance is crap. He's just as capable of drinking milk as the rest of us.

"Go fuck yourself," I say, not quite loud enough for him to hear.

"What?" he shouts, "What did you say?"

I had a number of boyfriends before I met Ray, and I know the symptoms of a failed relationship. It starts like this: at first, you see your partner's quirks as subtle and full of charm—a stammer, a slight body odor, a tendency to misplace the keys. Then you notice that these habits interfere; they limit the person's ability to talk rationally, to function on the job, to respond to crises. Naturally, you want to help. But you soon see that the person can't or won't or is too slow to change and then you grow irritated. You begin to care less and less, until you can't make yourself care at all. Then it's time to move on. Ray and I are right in the middle of this cycle. I'm afraid that a baby will push us to the outer limits.

I start getting dressed for work and the phone rings. It's Angela, the nurse from my doctor's office. She asks me how I feel. For a second, I am tempted to tell her about the Lusty Lady, because she is a kind woman and would most likely offer sympathy. But then I realize how unusual it is for Angela to call without my solicitation. She only calls me after I've left some embarrassing message about pregnancy constipation or weird skin flaps that have emerged on my neck.

Angela gets down to business. The blood test from your last visit, she says. She sneezes and excuses herself and, with a muffled tissue mouth, says that I need to consider genetic counseling and additional testing. She tells me that my Alpha-Fetoprotein test results came back abnormal. Further testing needs to be done, she repeats, but at the present time, your results indicate a 1 in 29 chance that the fetus has Down's Syndrome.

The term Down's Syndrome slams hard against my ear. I hear myself echoing the words: "Down's Syndrome."

"You mean retarded, right?"

"Yes," she says.

As I walk into the kitchen with the portable phone, she explains the chromosomal makeup of Trisomy 21. I look at last night's spaghetti dishes on the wooden counter and then I look at the clock and then I look at Ray standing in the door frame, his hands in yellow gloves, his arms bent upwards at the elbows and his hair pulled back in a ponytail. I pour myself a glass of water and stand at the sink drinking it. When the nurse finishes talking, she asks how I'm doing. "That's a low blow," I say, and then we laugh together for a second before I start to cry. I ask what I should do next. Angela tells me to take this one step at a time. She gives me the phone number of a fetal sub-specialist and tells me to call for an appointment.

When I get off the phone, Ray hugs me for a long time. He rubs my back and tells me that we can handle this. Standing in his arms, I remember the blood test from the week before. Angela had said the blood work was important but routine, most likely nothing to worry about. They were going to run a few tests from the same blood sample: check my iron level, my Rh factor, and whether the baby was at increased risk for birth defects. The chatty phlebotomist told me knock-knock jokes to distract me from the needle. Afterwards, Angela gave me a pamphlet on the Alpha Fetoprotein test, but I stuck it in a magazine I was reading. Later that night when I went to look for the pamphlet, I had forgotten where I put it and I hadn't looked since. I guess I didn't really want to think about the implications. I figured the less I had to worry about, the better.

Ray kisses the top of my head and says that chances are good that the baby will be fine. He tells me that they shouldn't use the lowest common denominator when citing probabilities. He tells me to think of the risk as 3 in 90, or 4 in 120. That doesn't sound as bad as 1 in 29.

"We're in this together," Rays says, squeezing my hand.

"You big, tall jerk," I say, pressing my face against his chest.

Ray and I didn't plan this pregnancy. When I was a week late, we went to the pharmacy and bought a home pregnancy test, along with sorbitol-free, dye-free, fluoride-free toothpaste for Ray. I told him that I wanted to take the pregnancy test alone. I sat on the floor of our bathroom and watched the thin plastic bar slowly change color, from white to pale violet to light blue. I walked out of the bathroom and numbly handed the stick to Ray, who was sitting in the living room, listening to Steppenwolf and reading an old copy of *High Times*.

"Wow!" he said, "It's like a science experiment that really works!"

"Maybe it's not the right time for a baby," I said, biting my thumbnail.

Ray took my hand and pulled me onto his lap.

"Of course it's the right time," he said, reaching out and stroking my cheek. "Just imagine having a little baby together, a little baby with a soft face and little hands and a little mouth. It would be this big." Ray cupped his hands together and stared into them.

I looked at Ray's face, his receding hairline, the spackle of freckles on his forehead. I thought about the love we had, fragile and familiar, somehow towing us along.

"Of course, we'll have to get the place checked for lead paint," he said. "And asbestos. And radon. We can't forget about the radon. But there's time for all that."

Steppenwolf sang *Born To Be Wild* and Ray smiled, bobbing his head up and down with the music.

"This seems kind of crazy, Ray."

"Well, what isn't?" he asked. "We'll be great parents. We'll have a great kid. We can do it, Sheila." He lifted my shirt and kissed my belly.

Ray sits with me as I dial the number Angela gave me. The receptionist tells me there's been a cancellation for a 12:00 appointment today with Dr. Nelson. I take it. Then I call in sick to the Jewish Vocational Center. I teach literacy classes to Russian immigrants there, which is why I carry a ceramic poodle, a deck of cards, and a tape measure in my purse; when your students are in their 70's and barely literate, these are essential tools.

Even though I was raised Presbyterian, since I've been teaching at the Center, I feel like I'm becoming Jewish. I find myself talking over people's voices, rather than waiting for them to finish before I speak, which is a strategy I learned from my students. I've also started to repeat their funny expressions: *Whoever can't smell gunpowder shouldn't go to war. From your mouth to God's ear. In the bath, all are equal.* "With one bottom, you can't dance at two weddings," I recently told my mother, when she asked if we'd be coming home for Thanksgiving. Lately, I've been walking into class a few minutes late. I like to stand outside the door and eavesdrop, listening to the foreign accents and raised voices. They're the grandparents I wish I had growing up.

It was last Friday that I told my class I was four and a half months pregnant. All nine of my students clapped for me, and, in their mix of Yiddish and Russian and English, they congratulated me, after telling me I had waited long enough, at 34 years old. Marvin Satz, my most articulate student, stood up slowly from his folding chair and made a toast with his travel mug from Dunkin' Donuts.

"Mazel Tov!" he said. "You'll make wonderful mother! When good fortune come, pull up chairs for them!"

The others agreed. They told me to make sure to use a *moy'l* for the circumcision, if it's a boy. The *moy'l* has the "golden hand," they said. Now I wish I hadn't told them anything.

Ray takes a shower before the appointment, and I walk from room to room. It's 9:30. I pet Dashiel, the cat, as he licks water from the surface of the fish tank. He never tries to scoop up the fish; instead, he just antagonizes them by drinking their water. I watch as his tongue flits in and out of his mouth and the fish drop to the bottom of the tank. I turn on the television set and watch the anchorwoman smiling like a zombie. Then I lie down on the couch and push my face deep into the cushions and begin to sob, alternately choking on the musty scent of old fabric and reaching my hand up to wipe my nose. When I sit up, I see my reflection in the mirror: my mouth is full of dark lint.

Ray hands me a box of Kleenex.

I ask him, "Which do you think is worse—bringing a kid into the world who's doomed, or having an abortion because you're too overwhelmed to take care of a retarded child? They're both selfish acts, aren't they?"

"Let's not torment ourselves," Ray says. "Let's wait to see what the doctor says."

He takes a pen out of his pocket.

"Wait a minute," he says, looking around the room, wielding the pen as though it were a flashlight. "What happened to my Del Monte notepad?"

For the past two years, Ray has worked in the complaint department at Del Monte. It started as a temp job and then he was hired permanently. He spends his days reading and responding to loyal and not-so-loyal customers. Now he tells me that last week, he got a letter from someone who found a dried lizard in his box of prunes, and another letter from newlyweds who sent photographs of themselves on their honeymoon right before they ate the raisins that gave them diarrhea for two weeks. I just look at him. His eyebrows are arched and he's smiling like a cartoon character. There is something so dented about him. Somewhere along the way, he's lost about twenty percent of his marbles. He's not all there. Down's Syndrome or not, I'm not sure that he's whole enough to raise my child.

"Ray," I say, "listen to me. This is private, just between you and me. If I have an abortion, I want to tell everyone it was a late miscarriage."

"That's fine," Ray says, "whatever you want."

Ray asks me to put his hair in two braids. He says he wants to look like Willie Nelson for the doctor's appointment.

"Look at everything Willie's gone through," Ray points out. "The government confiscated his studio when he didn't pay his taxes, he's a reformed alcoholic, he's had a couple of bad marriages and he barely has enough money to live on. He must be 65 years old and he still has to travel around in a goddamn bus to make a living. Things haven't been easy for Willie. But people go on. It wouldn't be so bad having a baby with Down's Syndrome. It would be okay."

It cheers me up to see Ray with his little brown braids, each one tucked behind an ear. Ray suggests that I put my hair in braids, too. He tells me to sit up and then he brushes my hair with wide strokes. His cool, thin fingers press against my neck and gently pull my head back. As I weave my hair into the braids, Ray opens up his guitar case and sits on the couch near my feet and plays *Hotel California*. He plays the chorus twice at the end and then it's time for us to go.

On the long drive over to the Perinatal Center, I think about the time Ray and I had gone bowling, last summer. After putting on our bowling shoes, we looked around and saw that it was a night for kids and families with special needs. I remember watching one retarded boy pick up the bowling ball like it was a 50 pound boulder. He picked it up with both hands and a thick, baffled look, and he stood very still at the head of the lane. He looked back and forth between the ball and the white pins. After a minute, he shut his eyes and hurled the ball down the lane with such force that I thought it would crack the wooden floor. When he turned around to face his parents, his mouth was open and his eyes were wet and bright. He jumped up and down and his parents clapped and shouted, *You did it, Dennis!*

Now, I turn to Ray and ask him if he remembers Dennis. He doesn't know who I'm talking about. I tell him: *the retarded kid at the bowling alley*.

"The retarded kid," I say again.

Since I've been pregnant, I've been having the strangest dreams. Maybe it's some kind of a sign. In my second month, I dreamt that all of my top teeth fell out and I buried them in the courtyard of a monastery and then they came back to life. When I woke up, I opened my mouth wide in front of the bathroom mirror. I looked at the uneven ridges of my teeth, and my gray, glinting fillings, and the thin strands of saliva stretching from top to bottom. And even though all of my teeth were intact, I still felt my chest throbbing with terror from the dream, and I noticed shallow purple wells under my eyes. Maybe my teeth know something I don't.

As we enter Dr. Nelson's office, I whisper to Ray that he should do the talking, because I feel a force field of sobs rising up from my throat. The receptionist smiles at us and makes a copy of our health insurance card. She hands me a clipboard and pen and says she likes our braids. That almost makes me cry, but I hold it together until she calls me sweetie: "Remember to use the toilet to empty your bladder, *sweetie*."

In the waiting room, Ray puts his arm around me and asks me to tell him the story of when I was expelled from day camp for flushing all two hundred feet of the cloth hand towel, which I had cut from the dispenser, down the toilet. Telling the story is a good distraction. We laugh. It's a relief to forget about Down's Syndrome, even for a few minutes. It's good to remember that Ray is my friend.

At 12:30, we meet with Ingrid, the genetic counselor. She takes our health histories and explains that the doctor will do a level II ultrasound to look for Down's Syndrome indicators, and then perform amniocentesis, in order to analyze the chromosomal structure of the fetus. This is what she says: "During the ultrasound, Dr. Nelson will look for shortened limbs, an extra fold of skin at the back of the baby's head, unusual configuration of the heart, only two vessels in the umbilical cord, asymmetrical development of the brain . . ."

Ingrid has a long list of items that the doctor will hopefully be able to eliminate. I stop listening after the first five. The blood is pounding in my ears.

Ray is asking some question about probabilities, and I notice Ingrid's sad smile. It reminds me of the strained smile of the Planned Parenthood counselor when she gave me my first pregnancy results nearly 20 years ago, when I was in high school. When she said the test was positive, I was confused. At first I thought she meant everything was fine, very positive, I had nothing to worry about. But then I realized from her serious tone that things were actually quite negative. I could tell she'd given her little talk many times to other girls, because she didn't pause during her presentation. Just like Ingrid, she recited the facts. She said I could continue the pregnancy and keep the baby. She said I could continue the pregnancy and give the baby up for adoption. She said I could have an abortion in state with my parent's consent, and out of state without their consent. I wonder now if that fetus had Down's Syndrome.

Ray is clearing his throat and telling Ingrid about his stint with hallucinogenic drugs during college. He tells her that he doesn't think it's likely, but that it's within the realm of possibility that he was exposed to traces of poisonous chemicals mixed into the LSD. "Strychnine," he says, "the government might have been producing acid laced with strychnine." This is the first I've heard about strychnine and government-manufactured LSD. I don't know if this information should surprise me or not, since Ray is an absolute and paranoid nutcase.

"Could that be a contributing factor in Sheila's test results?" he asks.

Ingrid raises her eyebrows and says he'll have to discuss it with Dr. Nelson. Ray looks at me and shrugs his shoulders.

"You never know," he says.

While Ingrid reviews the risks of amniocentesis, I notice Ray starting to freak out, just a little, on the sidelines. His nostrils widen and he tugs on one of his braids when she says there's a four percent chance of injuring the fetus or inducing miscarriage. I take his hand and tell him to relax, that it's the right thing to do.

"We need to know," I whisper to him.

We meet with Ingrid for an hour and a half and then it's time for Dr. Nelson. Dr. Nelson is cross-eyed. Ingrid didn't tell us that part. I don't know which eye to look at. It doesn't seem right. He asks me to lie on the table, lift up my gown, and push my panties below my hips. It's such an intimate request to make of a stranger, but I comply because, I tell myself, I am the patient, I am his stranger, I am at his mercy. Ray sits down in the chair next to the table.

After Dr. Nelson smears cold gel on my round, pale belly, he turns off the light in the room, and his face is illuminated by the blue glow of the ultrasound screen. I listen to his slow, rhythmic chanting as he moves the metal device across my stomach and points to different areas on the monitor: "Heart has four chambers, umbilical cord has three vessels . . ."

It's good that the room is dark. I look away from the screen, at the shining reflection of blue on the metal cabinet handle against the wall. I don't want to see that little person floating inside of me if I might end up aborting it. A Catholic friend once told me that every woman gets one abortion without moral judgment, and after that it's a sin. One abortion per woman. That's the rule, she said.

Dr. Nelson turns the light back on. "The ultrasound looked okay," he says, "now it's time for the amnio." He explains that he will extract amniotic fluid from my uterus. He says he will use a long needle. Ray asks if it will hurt. Dr. Nelson says I will feel some pain, but mostly I will experience a popping sensation. The doctor tells me I need to lie perfectly still during the procedure, so the needle doesn't puncture the umbilical cord or come in contact with the fetus. I still can't figure out which one of his eyes to look into; they're idle, unreadable. I look just above his eyebrows, at the puffy lines in his forehead.

"I don't want to see the needle," I say, shaking my head on the pillow.

I turn my face to Ray while he watches the doctor prepare the needle. Ray looks terrified. He leans over and tells me that I'm being brave.

As the doctor inserts the needle in my belly, I make an involuntary grunting sound. I shut my eyes, and to block out the stinging pinch, I make myself remember things. Anything will do. I remember how Miss Wang's wig fell off when I was in first grade. She was the shortest, fattest woman I had ever known. She had rolls of fat on her wrists and ankles, and when she slipped on the chalk and rolled on her side, her dress tore from her waist to her underarm. Her thick flesh oozed from the ripped seam. I remember how shocked I was to see black razor stubble instead of hair on her head. Later, my mother told me *that poor woman must have had cancer and lost her hair.*

Then I remember the memorial service for Ray's father. Ray stood with his siblings at the church podium. In the rigid, wooden pew, I sat next to Ray's mother and held her hand. I remember how limp and dry her fingers were against my clammy palm. I watched Ray choke through the speech he had practiced the night before, with his great shaking hands, the creases in his pants, the plaid handkerchief collapsed at his feet.

Suddenly Ray is standing up from the chair next to me and speaking loudly about the needle.

"That needle," he points to where the doctor has his hand on my abdomen, "I'm afraid it's getting too close to the baby." Wisps of hair, escaped from Ray's braids, fly around his head as he speaks.

I whisper for Ray to calm down and Dr. Nelson tells him to please take a seat.

Dr. Nelson explains that the placement of the needle is fine; he's able to monitor fetal movement through the ultrasound screen, and the needle is currently at the opposite end from where the fetus is.

"How do you know that needle isn't contaminating the amniotic fluid?" Ray continues, his voice rising. "What if the baby's allergic to metal?"

"Mr. Evans," the doctor says sharply, "perhaps you should wait in the waiting room until the procedure is over."

"No, thank you," Ray says, "I'd prefer to stay right here and keep an eye on that needle." He smiles fiercely. His eyes are darting between the ultrasound screen and my belly and he has a twitch in the corner of his mouth.

"Ray," I whisper, "you're making a scene."

"Mr. Evans," the doctor says, "the only thing in this room endangering the fetus is you. If you do not leave, I will terminate the procedure. It's up to you and your wife."

"Please, Ray, go to the waiting room," I say. "Just go."

I reach out my hand and Ray takes it.

"Please."

Ray looks down at me. After a few seconds, he says, "Fine. I'll be right outside if you need me."

"I'll be out soon," I mumble.

After the nurse escorts Ray out of the room, I shut my eyes and the doctor continues drawing the fluid. The needle gives a sharp pinch when I breathe in and out. Dr. Nelson and I are silent together, in the void created by Ray's outburst. Hot tears seep from the corners of my eyes. My toes are cold. In my head, I compose a list about Ray. Pros and cons.

On the negative side,
    he's neurotic
    he's a patron of strip clubs
    he's taken entirely too many drugs
    he'd make our child insane

On his behalf, I note that
    he's sweet and tender
    he cleans toilets
    he'd play guitar for the baby
    he loves me

The amnio is over. Dr. Nelson tells me he hasn't seen anything suggesting Down's Syndrome, but the real test, he says, is waiting ten days for the lab to conclude its definitive cell report.

"Next time don't bring your husband," he says. "Or give him a sedative."

Driving home, we're caught in rush hour traffic, and it's 7:30 in the evening by the time we walk through the door. Ray puts his arm around me and says he'll make dinner. I'm too exhausted to argue about his eruption during the procedure, or ask about strychnine, or revisit our fight regarding the Lusty Lady. Instead, I tell him I'll take a bath. Nothing hurts, but the muscles in my body feel too close to my skin. Light and twinging. In a strange way, my body feels almost exhilarated.

I dim the bathroom light and run the hot water full blast. Globes of steam rise above the tub. I wonder if we've progressed from stage two to stage three in the doom cycle. When I step into the hot water and sit down, I watch as my thighs and belly slowly turn pink. The water is so hot it is almost freezing. Hot pink flesh. I know pregnant women aren't supposed to take steaming baths, but I need this one. I tug at the little bandage near my pubic bone, at the base of my belly. It's glued tight, trapping my birth mark and a fringe of pubic hair.

"Are you ok, little baby?" I ask my belly, rubbing the smooth, taut surface. It's round and firm, like a huge hard-boiled egg. I slide further into the water until my shoulders are covered and the top of my belly rides just above the surface of the water. I listen to the crackling sound of the air bubbles. I pull my head under.

Ray knocks on the bathroom door and asks what kind of salad dressing I want. I don't answer. I have nothing to say. I could stay in the bathtub all night if I wanted to. Maybe I'll never get out of the tub. But eventually I'll have to deal with people knocking on the door, asking me questions about salad dressing and forgiveness. I look around the tub, at the bottles of shampoo, the shaving cream, the floating candle in the shape of a star. I wish I were a little bar of soap, thin, translucent, the kind of little slip of soap that's nearly at the end of its life. Or maybe I could be a bath sponge, soaking up the extra water. That wouldn't be too bad.

Ray opens up the bathroom door after knocking a few more times.

"I brought you salad," he says, "kind of like breakfast in bed."

He lowers the lid of the toilet and sits on it, tipping the salad bowl toward me. I sit up and take a few bites of lettuce with my fingers. Ray reaches into the bowl after me. As I listen to each of us chewing, I lean back in the tub and see the shadow of Ray's face against the wall, how the dark shape looks like a bird sleeping in its nest. I close my eyes and feel the water lapping against my body. The baby flutters in my belly. I look at Ray's chest rising up and down, the salad bowl in his lap, his long toes stretched against the magazine rack.

"Ray and Sheila have a day," he tells me, his mouth full of carrots, and I nod my head, yes, Ray and Sheila have a day.

Heidi Julavits

Little Little Big Man

BIG COULDN'T REMEMBER THE FIRST TIME HE'D CONJURED THE image of himself, a grown man, wearing a belt buckle as wide as his pelvis. A gold-plated buckle, to be absolutely precise, the gold rubbed off in the raised places, the belt cinched all the way down to the new holes he'd popped with a screw driver.

He ate one baked bean a day.

Of course the women in the rodeo stands loved the lean in him, because they thought he'd never beat them like an all-there man might. He'd land in their laps after being tossed by Biscuit Killer, by Thunder Girdle, by Tom. The women would heft his featherweight self over their shoulders and carry him, his forehead banging against their flowery backsides, the skirt fabric sticky with syrup (they all owned messy children), the sticky patches matted with ragweed. The ragweed made him sneeze and he'd blow their skirts upwards around their waists, because for such a bitty fellow, he was chock full of lungs.

GAZOONTITE LITTLE MAN they'd say, and squeeze his legs together tight, as though that were the place from which the soul might make a run for it.

Of course he never said PUT ME DOWN, because he liked the way the blood felt, rock-hard and banging inside his skull. He liked to feel the women's skirts rise up and over his face, obscuring his vision of the dusty nowhere in which he lived.

Big joined the rodeo in oh-two. He weighed less than a fortnight, but even so his boney lackerings were too much for Nancy. She had a spine like a wheat stalk. She had hooves like tea cups, and a wispy, invisible mane. She wore a headdress of bird feathers; before the show she'd run sweet, skippity circles around the rodeo ring, her feathers whittling. The men would grow quiet as their futile boy-hoods overtook them, while the women wiped the sticky purple ketchup off their children's forearms, losing themselves in a pursuit of cleanliness that otherwise never spoke to them much.

Hairless little runt, the women would say, wiping the ketchup and wiping it. Colt'd split her in two. If you can't better yourself, what's your purpose?

Nancy would disappear into the hole at the end of the circle, and a real horse would fire into the cage. A rider'd tipple out along the rails with his Johnson packed high between his hip bones. When he dropped, they could hear the UUUFFFF as the spine rode him up between the legs like a wire through cheese, puppeting his single body into two, floppy bodies. The rider would fall, always he'd fall, and sometimes his head would get stepped on so that Big and the others would have to dig under it with a two-by-four and ride that seesaw until the head popped out from the dirt like a bloodied plate.

Big always rode last. He rode the tiredest horse, but this didn't keep his body down. He'd spread his legs wide over that spine, blue with horse sweat and chapped up by crotch grommets. He'd uncheck his heels and then his legs, those two filigrees, would float up as his organs—that never got leaner, that never lost their tubes or bobbles—descended toward the haunches of Biscuit Killer, of Thunder Girdle, of Tom. Sometimes he'd clap himself around the ears with his boots when his pelvis struck. It sounded like hard on soft, it sounded like the kind of sex the women were used to, and they would drop hold of a ketchuppy wrist and press a palm between their udders.

He never lasted more than four hooves. Two front hooves (down up) two back hooves (down up) and Big'd be seeing sky better than the others. He'd see that the clouds were made of nothing much, not even old water. He'd put a hand over his eyes to block out the sun and let the wind find nothing to hold onto except his tiny snap-shirt. The wind would try to sail him away but his shirt always tore into dithers, and Big'd find himself fluttering toward the bleachers and the soft sticky nest of a lady's lap.

It wasn't until the third time that something became meant by it.

Big was always winded after his landing, his lungs squashing madly to find a bit of air.

My lucky day, Sal said, opening her legs and closing them, opening and closing them, giving birth to a man with a big buckle. Sal already had six kids who were invisible on rocks, who liked the sun overmuch and scattered quicker than dirt. The rodeo men called them the lizards, and gave them the old broken candy they kept in their thigh pockets.

Hey Sal, Big said. She had a face too overwhelming for eyes of her own. She was flesh, she was teeth, she was hair. She was a most touchable lady.

Nice to see you again, Big, said Sal.

At the rodeo picnic, Big ate his baked bean cut into eight pieces. Fellows stood beside him, a wool jacket wrapped around his head, which was half broken after a bad two seconds on Randy Bottom. Fellows, the whites of his eyes all bloody, glanced at Big sideways and said, looks like you're Sal's, rightly.

Meaning what? Big asked, pushing his bean around.

Meaning it's time for a man to settle down.

You find me unsettled? Big inquired.

Sal's lonely, said Fellows. Takes a lot out of her to raise those six little lizards on her own.

That afternoon, banging home to Sal's place with his head squarely in the heart of her bottom, he knew he'd done his last turn up there beside the sun, wondering where the hell he'd land.

Sal's six lizards had six different names, but Big called them One Two Three Four Five Six. Actually, he called them Six Five Four Three Two One. He renamed them every morning. The first one he saw would be Six. If he saw two at once, the shorter would be Six, the taller Five, and so forth. The lizards loved it, because it meant their bad and stupid ways didn't follow them from day to day. They became unpunishable.

Sal wasn't a bad lady, and she never cried over her former husband. Big said to his rodeo friends She's not a bad lady, and they understood this to mean he was some form of smitten.

You smited, ain't you? Fellows jockeyed.

Yessir, he be smote, said Yardarm.

Smy on you, said Lawrence Ray.

And he didn't correct his friends, because they seemed happier to perceive him as a man of appetites. He didn't know if he loved Sal; he did know that he knew her in an awkward fashion far beyond the Biblical. Big was so winnowed that he made love to Sal by crawling all the way up into the dark, plummy middle of her. He could be stealthy and unnoticed, but Sal preferred a fight; she'd taken to insulting him before he entered her (head first) because the more he bucked inside of her, the more he kicked and punched and resented her, the better she felt. He'd lie in that warm culvert afterward as Sal slept. Once he decided to explore. He slithered northward, through the stretched neckhole of her uterus, where each of the lizards had briefly lived. He found the graffiti on her womb, scraped into the pitted flesh by the pupil-sized fingernails of lizards Six Through One.

Written upon the skin, sagging and domed like an overused bathing cap, were the following promises: I'LL PUT THIS FORK THROUGH YOUR MUTHERFUKEN EYE SAL, YOU KNOW I HAYTE MUSTERD GREENS, QUITE YER CATERWHALING, GIMME A DADDY-SIZED PIECE OF THAT THER HONEYPOT.

Sneaky little fuckers, Big thought. He liked to use both hands to scruffle their moldy hair in the mornings. The lizards arched under him like alleycats, pretending they wanted to get away but always going absolutely nowhere.

Still, it was all about the lessening of himself, no matter if his wife called him Lady Man and mocked his bean eating. This was achieved through various methods, of which starvation was only the most obvious. There was the wind, which he allowed to lick him down each morning when he was weakest. He stood naked next to Sal's ex-husband's bird-shitted gas grill and let the whipping gravel past his skin take pieces of him with it. Then there was the bloodletting, done in secret next to the horse pen. In the spring, when the snow turned into river and avalanched oceanward as only squeezed water can, he tied himself off the south-most girder of the Fourth Avenue Bridge and let the river pulverize his body, snapping veins, unrooting whiskers, shaving down clavicles.

When he was feeling most reduced, when the wind barely snagged on his joints and blades, when the stray dogs passed him by without once thinking of food, he'd visit Nancy.

Going out, he'd say to Sal who was always knitting by the white noise machine that winded out the noise of the lizards. She believed the machine was an air conditioner too, and stripped down in front of it to better receive the cool. He could not look at her udders and her sag as she stubbornly purled him another cardigan, sizably meant for the man she wished he was.

Cold out, Lady Man, she'd say, indicating the coat tree mossy with acrylic cardigans, tens and tens of them.

What? he'd say.

Nothing, Sal'd say.

He'd unhook a cardigan heavier than a drunk, he'd drag it as far as the road, he'd leave it over a failing bush that looked like it needed protecting. He'd run the two miles to the horsepen and he felt the final excess pieces of himself lifting into the night.

Big originated from a wispy father who sought to see his son grow tall and wide, who sought him to beat pets and love sports, to make his own elfin irrelevance seem less his fault. His father was a sickly, twine-thin fellow, always coughing up yellow fluids into a glass decanter and speaking quietly toward the curtains. He never beat his family. The domestic tyranny he created with his diligent, long-suffering sweetness and his needy leers was more insipid than any fist or belt lashing. His wife cowered and will-o-wisped around the house, changing her husband's decanter and stirring giant stews to feed her son who failed to yield to bigness. It killed his father to see a son in his own spindly image; it killed him that he'd failed, among the many things he'd failed at, to better himself in the least. Little did he know that Big had a burgeoning, mean fat man concealed within his winnowed self; little did he know that Big intentionally kept his father down by burying his food in the backyard and mindfully taking after him.

The red of an exit sign lit Nancy's pen like a bordello. When he approached her, the red on her whiteness made her look like she'd been skinned.

He'd start by washing her with a bucket of water and a piece of old shirt. He'd feed her a plum and wipe her teacups clean. He'd wet her thin mane and wind it up like a tiny pastry on her neck. Then, he would take his clothes off. His buckle made a sound on the floorboards like he was doing something wrong. When Nancy was happiest with her plumpit, he'd lift a leg over her back. He'd watch with shame as his genitals, so big now that the rest of him was small, dangled in the red exit light, sore-looking. He'd rest those very same genitals—soft, mind you—against her back. Even the soupy weight of his testicles made her spine crack, just once, just twice. He'd start sweating then, the excess stuff he'd dispensed with long ago still pouring out of him.

He bent his knees by hundredths of degrees. First his testicles became ovals, then pancakes. He could feel the sharp point of each individual Nancy hair being driven into his inner thighs until the hairs buckled and became an indistinguishable pelt of softness. He felt the point of a vertebra dovetail with the crease of his buttocks. Nancy's back made teething noises as he descended, clacking and chomping.

His pelvis firmly on her back, he'd begin to lift his feet, starting with his toes. With all toes lifted, he'd raise his heels, first the left heel, then the right. When he was resting on the balls of his feet, always perched on the balls, her spine would cave in. He would howl in pain as a loose jowl of testicle was vised in the swaybacked collapsing of her vertebrae. He'd stand abruptly, pulling the skin loose. He'd watched as four drops of blood landed on her back, bristling outward into starshapes as the hair soaked him in.

He'd run home the way he'd come, remembering to fetch his cardigan. Always, stray dogs had pissed on it. Always, the failing bush was a little bit closer to dead.

After two years, ten years, Big wasn't one for counting years, Sal decided she wanted a Seven.

I do prefer the odder numbers, she'd say, hint hint, wiping the grapey chickeny stains off the faces of Three and One with a carboned oven mitt.

Every night with the lizards down she'd wait in the bed for Big to climb inside her and make a seven. After a few months of his purported trying, however, Sal started to accuse him.

What the hell do I know you're doing up there? she asked. Big reddened. In truth he was reading what the lizards had written, in truth he was napping. Sal demanded he show her his business on a handkerchief; she wanted proof of the ghost he'd produced. And because he was too small a man for discord, he'd balance on the balls of his feet in that darkened, slumping womb, he'd whittle away at his genitals until the walls were smeary, the words unreadable. He'd wipe them clean with a paper towel and thrust it out for her to see.

He had never bettered himself in the past no matter how many women he'd been inside, and assumed his bettering fluids to be worthless. After a few months of whittling and still, nothing, Sal closed the gates on Big. He pretended to scrabble at her iron thighs, because, as her husband, he knew this sort of pestering was his duty.

After three months of exile, Big found he'd begun to want Sal. Never much of one for the sexual act proper, Big missed the solitude of fucking her. There was nowhere to escape the sounds of the lizards digging. They were diggers, all six of them, and the yard looked like a frozen brown ocean, peaked and choppy. When he asked them what they were digging for, they kicked him in the shins. Most afternoons, he pressed his head against the white noise machine. He tried to imagine milk, a world of milk, when his headaches got the worst of him, because milk was the quietest thing he could think of.

He spoke of it to his friends at the rodeo. He'd gotten too wispy to ride Biscuit Killer and etc. He worked in the tack room, chipping old grass out of mouth bits.

Sal won't give it up, he said.

L. Ray chewed his thumb.

Just like a wife, said Fellows. Blown wide open by bettering herself, thinks she can wither back just by being scarce.

I don't know that's it, exactly, Big said.

Gotta take it by force, if its not coming to you easy, Fellows said. He had never kept a wife longer than a year. They always ran off with harder men than he.

Force was not Big's forte, but quiet was. That night, Sal halfwakened as he tried to enter her, toes first.

What! she asked.

Nothing, said Big.

Sal fell back asleep and Big slithered northward. It was tighter quarters than usual inside Sal's uterus, and he worried that he was gaining weight. He pinched and poked and checked his belt buckle. He knocked against something squishy and heard a mousy squeak. It was dark and he struck a match against the pocky walls.

Goddamned, said Big.

The embryo was orange and see-through. It had eyes like a shrimp, two black beads stuck to the outside of its head. Its hands were like patties, the rest of it like a legume, that's what Big thought, it looks like a legume, though he'd never in his life seen a legume. The Legume wasn't much for talking, but it would squeak—not unhappily—when Big rubbed what he presumed was a nose.

Every night now, Big made love to Sal without her knowing it. He was careful not to whittle himself in front of The Legume; this seemed improper. Every morning he'd ask Sal How're you feeling? and Sal would simply shrug and take a family-sized breakfast waffle from the freezer, tossing it THUNK on the counter like a roof tile. She was distant, Sal was, she didn't even bother to wipe down the lizards when they got syrupy.

He was sure she didn't know about his nightly amours. He was sure she didn't know about The Legume. He found that the solitude he could achieve in the company of The Legume was superior to any solitude he'd ever experienced alone. He talked to The Legume about his life, hoping this littlest of lizards might take it upon himself to write the Story of Big on the blank wall nearest to his patty hands.

For posterity, he'd say, clapping The Legume on his shoulder-looking part, but The Legume remained uninspired.

He didn't tell the boys in the tack room about The Legume, but they seemed to know something, whispering and then shushing when he came into earshot. They smiled in that sorry way that said ENJOY LIFE WHILE YOU CAN, COWBOY. Sometimes he'd squeeze into Nancy's pen, sit on the floor and let her eat tobacco out of his palm. He'd tell her that he was going to be a father, and she would whinny and try to toss him onto her back with her nose. She would bite at his pants and his shirt. Big never came around her pen at night anymore.

It started with bacon scraps, as almost all failures do. Big'd nibble the fat curls that one lizard, a sketchy little dishwater blond of sixish, left on her breakfast plate. From bacon scraps he moved to bread crusts. From bread crusts to old noodles. From old noodles to nuts. It wasn't because he was hungry or bored or forgetful that he forsook his bean eating, it was the fact that he was going to be a Daddy, at least that's what he told himself as his waist snuck over his belt buckle and his bones filled in. Soon it was hard to make love to Sal without her waking up, he was so all-there. Most nights, now, he'd just put his head against her flabby middle and talk into it, echoing his story through Sal's layers of bobble to the watery ears of The Legume.

I know you can hear me, Big would say. And then there was the time I rode Randy Bottom almost to the moon...

What? Sal would say, shifting.

Nothing, said Big.

When he got to the part about Nancy, he found himself crying against Sal's stomach. Wet little mouthy cries. Your fat old daddy is a failure, he told The Legume. The one thing in my life I've ever wanted. I just wanted to ride her. I wanted to be the one man who'd never hurt the world's most hurtable thing.

Sal grew restless and itchy as he cried against her and rolled onto her stomach. Frustrated, he got out of bed. He donned a cardigan (it almost fit) and wandered down to the horse stables. He tried to feed Nancy a rosehip, but she turned away, flicking her fishing line tail. He took his clothes off and whittled himself against the wall of her pen where nothing was written.

* * *

He started riding again, Biscuit Killer and Tom. Biscuit Killer would kick up and send Big as far as the first row of bleachers, where nobody sat. He had bruises from landing where the women never were. He was too big for the sky now, and no horse was strong enough to send him there. Sal sat in the topmost row and pretended not to know him as he dusted off his pants.

He was dying to make love to his wife but she refused him. I want you, Sal, he said, but what he really wanted was to see what The Legume had made of him.

So he decided to get her drunk.

He waited until the night of the rodeo Christmas party, because Sal was a sucker for eggnog. She drank half a punchbowl and disappeared for two hours. Fellows found Big looking at the magazines, waiting for Sal. Better take that wife of yours to bed, he said. Sal was sprawled on a cowhide rug, her panties missing.

Big brought Sal home and put her into bed. He found her panties in her coat pocket as he undressed her. When he was certain she was unconscious, he pried her legs open and squeezed inside.

Big felt like a mouse being swallowed by a python, but Sal was a mother six times over and she gave. He made kicking motions with his legs and wrestled his way up, up, into the solitary middle of his wife.

Big was so happy to see The Legume, glimmering orange through the tiny peephole to Sal's womb. He lit up a smile so big it trapped him in the birth canal.

Hey little buddy, Big said, pulling himself through. How you been?

The Legume didn't respond. He didn't seem to recognize Big.

It's me, Big said. It's your goddamned Daddy.

The Legume let out a burp.

What're you been up to? he asked, feeling his way along the scarred-up wall. He pushed his way past The Legume to see what he had written.

Big blinked and blinked. It was hard to see in that dark, slumping room.

What is this shit? he asked The Legume.

The Legume did not so much as peep.

He pinched The Legume's nose, he pinched his feeding tube until his black eyes popped and his belly bloated. He pinched his patty hands until they bled.

Stupid fucking lizard, he said, leaving the way he'd come.

Big walked along the road toward Nancy's pen. His head was busy with writing.

YER LADY MAN SHOOTEN BLANKS, SAL. NOT LIKE YER VARY ERN LOHRINSE RAY.

OH. EL RAY. EL RAY. EL RAY. OH.

But this was not the most disturbing writing, no it was not.

Big could not entertain thoughts of that most disturbing writing. All he could think about, as he watched his belly swing over the road, was how that spine was going to sound when he sat on it. The very sound of that back breaking bringing a smile to his face, a smile that almost blotted out the sound of the other writings (WHAT NOTHING WHAT NOTHING WHAT NOTHING) that pattered around his fat head.

Heather Swain

What You Won't Read in Books

WHEN YOU DECIDE THAT YOU ARE READY TO HAVE A CHILD, YOU will read in books every glorious and gory detail of pregnancy. You will trace on colorful diagrams the intended path of the embryo that will lodge between your hipbones, reenacting the universe from black hole to big bang to self-sustaining planet circling your sun. First a blob, then a sea monkey, eventually a viable fetus. Impending hemorrhoids, constipation, episiotomies and engorged breasts. Squealing baby, red and wrinkled, angry at the world. All of this is labeled the miracle of childbirth and you will believe every word of it like a born-again Christian accepting the Gospel as truth.

You chart your cycle in red pen on the wall calendar. It coincides with the moon. Waxing and waning ovaries releasing a half-life every twenty-eighth day until one lazy Saturday in May the egg you have expelled collides with the squirming sperm army ejected from your panting husband. One of those brave swimmers unites its chromosomes with yours but you will not feel the ping deep inside your body that you have expected. Pregnancy is far too gradual a condition to be a suddenly monumental event. So you continue to do the things you normally would do, including slugging back margaritas at a smoky bar until two a.m., silently daring with your debaucherous behavior that little zygote into existence. It floats, free form, unconcerned with your intemperance as it searches for a wall in which to implant.

You will not even suspect it is there until two weeks later when your breasts feel like water balloons left on the tap too long. And you unaccountably want to take a nap every day at eleven then at four. And the faintest odors of garlic or a sweaty sock strike you as the most vile assault of rancid cheese. You count days on your calendar and realize that seventy-two hours ago you should have seen the first trace of bright red blood in your panties. Dutifully you pee on the pregnancy stick then stand over it, watching for a purple line to transverse the square box. When it does, you slide down to the floor and laugh, then cry, because you realize that already your child has a life you know nothing about.

A funny coincidence. Your agent calls later that same morning to say a woman's magazine wants a story from you in which one of your trademark female characters will be pregnant. Your books and stories are hailed as hip and downtown. You write about Girls (who used to be called women but have now embraced the diminutive just as homosexuals took back queer and African Americans reclaimed nigger.) The Girls in your stories are smart, successful, fashionable, thin, and voraciously sexual. They compare vibrators in snappy dialogue over stiff pink drinks in elegant glasses at trendy bars. They understand stock portfolios, contribute regularly to their IRAs and willingly submit to bikini waxes.

Your agent says that babies are hot now. Everyone wants one since *Newsweek* did an exposé on infertility after age thirty-five. You debate about telling your agent that you are pregnant but you've only known yourself for less than three hours. You haven't even called your husband at work yet because you like having this knowledge all to yourself. Basking in it makes you feel powerful. You say yes to the story, of course, and eagerly begin sketching the plot.

In books you read about the progression of your embryo. At four weeks it is tiny. Nearly microscopic. Even though it has no eyes or fingers or toes, just a blob of tissue and a bundle of nerves, (you know just how it feels), you want to take it out and play with it as if it were an itty bitty doll. Dress it up and show it off, nestled in the palm of your hand. "Look what I made!" you want to shout. Already you are a pushy, overbearing mother.

You love writing the story about the pregnant Girl. She has a cute belly popping out from between her jutting hipbones, but she still looks ravishing in her low rider jeans and tank tops. Later, she wears her husband's salmon-colored cashmere sweater that brings out the glowing pink tint to her skin. Her boobs, her weight, crying jags, cravings, and hemorrhoids are the crux of every joke in the story. The Girl's friends are supportive and interested in her pregnancy, but just a little bit jealous. They gather around during her long but hilarious labor. Then coo over her perfectly formed baby girl, named after the Girl-heroine's dead grandmother. Childbirth in your imagery world is one big belly-laughing folly.

Writing the story makes pregnancy feel more real to you. Otherwise, sometimes you forget that you are pregnant. Just for a minute while you are eating olives or reading a magazine or waiting for the F train, you feel like your old self again. Just you. Only you. But when you write, you remember there is someone lurking inside of you now. You decide it is a girl, carrying the eggs of another generation, making you a temporary Russian nesting doll, housing your child and your grandchildren all at once.

You know that you will be forever changed by this experience and you wonder who you will be after you have this child. Who was your mother before she had you? She is thrilled that you are (finally) having a baby. Her first grandchild. She has bought the baby's first gift, an antique pink milk glass plate and saucer. It waits at her house, delicately wrapped in tissue paper.

According to the books, your baby is having its first growth spurt. This explains why you feel sick and bloated and tired, and why you cry so easily now. You see squirrels and you cry. You can't find the tea bags and you cry. You cry and then you cry about crying. Some days you think it is convenient to have such an excuse for being an emotional wreck. Other days you feel like a blithering idiot.

The books say your embryo is now a quarter of an inch long. She could sit comfortably on your thumbnail. You could carry her between your toes like lint. Her heart is the size of a poppy seed and already beginning to beat. She has buds for arms and legs but still looks like a tiny tadpole swimming deep inside your belly. You can't locate her with your finger but she has become your new center of gravity. Although no one else notices, you feel your body changing. Your bottom blossoms lotus-like. The scar of your navel announcing the severed connection with your own mother pulls taut.

You carry your daughter heavy, hidden in the place where all your other secrets lie. She knows everything about you right down to your sacred DNA, but she will tell you nothing about herself. What color will her eyes be? Her hair? Will she be tall and lanky like your husband or short and compact like you? Will she have your temper and his sense of humor? Although she is inside of you, although you are giving her life, although without you she is literally nothing, already she is her own person and your life will be endless variations of letting her go. Motherhood sounds so hard.

At eight weeks, you visit your kooky OB-GYN for your first sonogram. She uses words like pee-hole instead of urethra and recommends heavy drinking during labor. She pats you on the knee and scratches dandruff out of her eyebrow then rolls a condom over the magic ultra sound wand. She swishes it around inside of you as if she were Glenda the Good Bitch in a lesbian porno flick called the Wizard of Jizz. You hold your husband's hand and watch intently the scratchy black and white screen positioned between your knees. You are eager to see your daughter.

Your doctor frowns and swashes the wand around more urgently. She makes a clicking sound with her tongue against her teeth and this irritates you greatly. You do not want to be a pansy and cry with a quivering voice, "Is everything okay?" So you wait, forgetting to breathe until she takes out her pen and points to the screen.

"See this black blob?" she asks. Your husband and you peer more closely and nod. "That is your uterus."

It seems so small and ordinary to you. You expected something large and bright, pulsating like a disco ball, your tiny embryo shaking her groove thang to your amniotic beat. Or at least something cozier. An English drawing room with a glowing fireplace and over-stuffed wingback chairs covered in flowered chintz where your wee girl sits embroidering her first nightie.

"See this bright dot?" the doctor asks. You try hard to see it but you don't really know what she is pointing at. "That's the embryo." You squint disbelieving because how can some dot, however bright, be your daughter? In the books, an eight-week embryo has form, substance, pizzazz. A kidney bean with great black eyes and a tail. This dot looks like nothing. A speck. A blip. Hardly something to pin all your hopes and desires on.

The doctor taps the screen and says, "It should be bigger by now."

At home in bed, you look at books but you do not read the thin chapters called "Pregnancy Loss" because that is a stupid title. As if some negligent mother has misplaced her pregnancy like an errant set of keys. As if she could look between couch cushions or inside her overcoat pockets and well, there it is! That darn embryo. Always getting lost.

Instead, you look at development charts. You study what your baby is supposed to look like now. She should be an inch long, the size of your thumb tip and perfectly formed with a head and dark spots for eyes and even the beginnings of soft eye lids. She should have elbows and wrists that waggle her tiny webbed hands while her feet paddle, frog-like below. Inside, her organs are sketched to be filled in over the next week—heart, lungs, spleen, kidney: love, breath, anger, waste. With her grape-seed lungs and miniscule finger buds she could play a tiny oboe as she somersaults inside of you. You put your hand down below your belly button and you concentrate quietly, but you can't feel her, no matter how hard you try. So you tell her silently that you love her and hope that she will stay with you, even if she is a little bit small right now.

For several days you wait and the world seems particularly bleak. You even cry yourself to sleep a few times. You tell yourself this is silly. That everything might be fine. That you are getting worked up over nothing and wasting valuable energy. The doctor told you to come back in one week. She would look again. Maybe the embryo was turned a funny direction and couldn't be seen clearly on the screen. Perhaps your girl is shy or a very private person. Who are you to be peeking into her immaculate sanctuary, anyway? So, you try to remain cheery. You put on your best Polly Anna face and tell anyone who asks that you feel GREAT!

Secretly you wonder if your baby is dying. If she is releasing some chemical into you that makes you feel her small death without really knowing it. This seems egregiously unfair. You should know if your daughter is alive inside of you or if you are carrying something dead. From the beginning, you have been amazed at how separate and independent your child is from you, but you are not from her. You want your daughter to tell you everything. If she is in distress you want to console her. Take her pain for your own. Yet you won't let your own mother do the same for you. You avoid her calls, claiming that you are busy or too tired. In truth you are hiding. Not from your mother, but from the impending sorrow that you could never disguise if your mother were to hear your voice.

One morning, you bask in the warm bed beside your husband, chasing the fuzzy memory of some pleasant dream, forgetting just then that you are worried about this pregnancy. Forgetting that today you are supposed to return to your OB-GYN for another sonogram to see if the embryo has grown. In those moments everything is fine and you are happy. But soon you have to pee, because now you always have to pee. You pull yourself from the bed and stumble sleepily to the bathroom, content, until sitting on the toilet, you see a bright red stain of blood in your panties and you whimper.

As soon as the office opens, you call your OB-GYN who says there is nothing she can do for you. That you are likely miscarrying and you have to let your body take care of itself. It might take several days, like a heavy period. You feel shunned and ashamed. How dare you bother this doctor with the death of something not yet a life? Crawl away, you think, into a hovel.

Your husband offers to stay home from work, but you say no. What's the use? He can't do anything for you, either. This is your body, your problem. Before he leaves, he buys you five different kinds of sanitary napkins (with wings and propellers, parachutes and jump seats, but no escape hatches; you are in this for the long haul). He brings you crossword puzzle books, potato chips, and funny movies. He calls you every hour.

You decide to prepare yourself so you read everything about miscarriage in your pregnancy books. They tell you to expect some heavy bleeding and cramping and passing of tissue, as if you have been gestating a box of Kleenex. They tell you to take it easy and use a heating pad. You nap often. Cry sometimes. Watch as much confessional TV as you can stomach. Occasionally the cramps take your breath away.

When your husband comes home you tell him that you want to get out of the house. Go out to dinner and take a walk. Get your mind off of what is happening in your body. He asks if you are sure you are up for it and you say yes because you know what to expect now. You have done your research. You have read in books that a miscarriage is nothing more than a severe period. You can handle that.

But, nothing will ever prepare you for that full moon night when gravity loosens the grip of the fetus dying in your body. And it plummets in a sickening slide from between your soft labia to land in a quivering mess, like a gelatinous comet trailing it's own life support system. You are on the street corner across from your house with your husband beside you when this happens. You gasp, and cry out for God repeatedly. Your husband has no idea what is happening or why you are squeezing his fingers until they are red then white. He gingerly helps you across the street as if you are suddenly old and infirm. You walk like an elderly woman with slow unsure steps and you feel ancient because at that moment there is more death in you than there is life.

Your husband brings you into the house where you walk hunch-backed to the toilet, gasping shrilly for breath between huge aching sobs. You shut the bathroom door then slowly lower your jeans with your eyes half-closed because you do not want to see what has come loose from your body. It feels gigantic and you are afraid of it.

You sit on the toilet, weeping, and carefully pull out the sanitary napkin. You hold it up with both hands as if it were an altar that you are offering to an angry God. And you keen, a sound so desperate and sad that it even surprises you. You feel bewildered. The books said that you would bleed, but this is not blood. This is life rejected. This dead thing would have been your child and it is huge. The books said it was an inch. The tip of your thumb. The pictures make it seem as if the baby floats happily around inside of you like an alien astronaut (with its outsized noggin and paddle arms) attached to you by a long thin cord. But no. That's not it at all. All kinds of extrane-ous material held everything in place and gave your daughter what she needed. Now, all of it has fallen out of your body to lie in a bloody heap in front of you.

Nowhere in that mess do you see the body of your daughter because she is packed inside a yellow orb. A spaceship built for one. Time traveling through a wormhole between you legs. Part of you wants to touch the quivering glob in your hands. Break it open with your fingernail like a soft egg and expose her to the world. You want to see her, just once. Hold her miniscule hand and look into her eyes. But it seems profane to disturb her cocoon so you do not touch it.

You want to create some sort of shroud from gauzy fabric and carve a box from fragrant wood in order to bury what you've lost. But when your husband knocks on the door and pleads to know if you are okay, you panic and quickly wrap up the remains in wads of toilet paper to spare him the sight of your failure. He enters and gently takes the bundle from you. In his confusion he places it in an oversized trash bag as he gathers everything else from the floor around you (ruined panties, tissues, unused pads) as if all of it has been contaminated.

This part kills you. You did not mean to dispose of her so easily. Where is she now? Deep space of the garbage can. How could you have thrown her away like that? Like she was nothing but leftovers. As if you never loved her tadpole self. But you were too horrified to tell him to stop. That *that* was your daughter.

Your husband brings you water and fresh panties and anything you want. But you sit on the toilet for a while longer because you are bleeding torrents now. All that potential down the drain. This thought makes you bark a weird strangled laugh and you know that something must truly be wrong with you if your stupid inappropriate sense of humor is already back.

When you go to your wacky OB-GYN for a check-up, she names your disorder "Blighted Ovum". You think this sounds like a Grrl Riot band from Seattle so you say, "I have their first album, *Spontaneous*

Abortion." The doctor glances uneasily at your husband who sits rigidly in the chair beside you. He shrugs helplessly. You fill up the awkward silence with that weird strangled laugh of yours.

The OB-GYN tells you that you are passing this pregnancy beautifully. She says that you can start trying to get pregnant again in three months. You say no way. This was it. You are already 33 and that is close to 35 so your ovaries are probably as dried and shriveled as currants. What you really think, but don't dare say, is that you could never stand this loss again.

The doctor pats you on the knee and tells you that what has happened to you, happens to a lot of women and it is perfectly normal. You want a certificate proving that you are perfectly normal because so far you only feel fat and ugly and stupid. The Girls in your stories would never feel like that. They would be able to go water skiing on the day they had a miscarriage. All you can do is cry and sleep and bleed.

You cannot believe how much blood your body can lose without killing you. Ropy red nodules will fall out of your cunt. This will get old quickly. You wonder what will fall out next. A shoe? An old tire? Jimmy Hoffa? Nothing would surprise you. You smell meaty, musky and strange dogs sniff your crotch suspiciously. You wash and wash the blood away. Watch it circle pink into the drain. You can't imagine what it is like not to bleed anymore. And you are afraid of when the blood dries up because then it is all over and you will have to move on.

You feel fat and wonder why every other woman looks better than you do. You remind yourself that not every other woman has just been pregnant for ten weeks and then lost a baby. This is part of your new plan to be kind to yourself. To accept yourself as you are. But this is too hard so you decide to blame society instead.

You become angry at how unfair it is to expect women to work and be successful and have babies but never have an ounce of cellulite on their thighs. You vow to join Andrea Dworkin and her soul sisters in the Womyn's Movement. They have been right all along!

You will throw out your hot pants and Tootsie Plohound heels. Trade them in for overalls and Birkenstocks. Embrace words like healing and closure. Buy crystals and listen to Hearts of Space on NPR.

But you do not find comfort in those things. They make you feel syrupy, as if you have eaten too much candy. You wish you had a fashionable vice like shooting smack or drinking lighter fluid. This won't work either because you've never smoked an entire cigarette without nearly coughing up your spleen and one glass of wine gives you a headache.

Still, you desperately need to purge your culpability, so you delete the computer files with the beginnings of your newest novel about the Girls. Then you empty the cyber trash to make sure the Girls are good and gone. This thrills you. You look for more files to delete, reasoning that you have brought this whole thing on yourself. Losing a baby is karmic retribution for creating the Girls with their perfect lives no woman could possibly emulate. Blaming yourself is comforting.

Your husband can do nothing right, anymore. Although he tries. Very hard. He tries to be understanding and comforting but he isn't. He asks you numerous times a day how you are. He hugs you and kisses you with more frequency. Holds your hand on the street and while sitting on the couch. He compliments your appearance and your cooking and tells you that he is so lucky to have you. After a week of this, you answer each inquiry into your well-being with, "Feeling better every day" or "More and more like myself" or finally the biggest lie of all in which you claim to be "Fine" because really by now, you should be.

Just in case you haven't sounded convincing, you ask your husband how he is doing. If he is getting any support in all his effort to be supportive of you. Who he is talking to about his feelings. You ask these things not because you really want to know. You don't. What you want to know is how he can be so fucking cheery all the time.

Why he hasn't missed any days of work when you haven't been able to write a word. Why he refuses to call what you lost a baby, instead always referring to it as a fetus. What you really want to do is kick him in the shins and pummel him with your angry fists because he is not as sad as you are. And, if he were as sad as you then you would want to beat him around the head, screaming, "You have no right to be this sad! I'm the one who lost her. I'm one who held her in my hands. Not you!"

Since you cannot do any of those things, you pick fights with him. First you pick small ones over who cleaned the toilet last or how much is the appropriate amount to tip the slutty waitress at a diner. When that is not enough, you go for the throat. You want to push him as far as you can. How long will he be nice to you? As you lay in bed beside him, sulking after accusing him of not loving you enough or never having loved you in the first place (or some variation on this theme) he finally loses his infinite patience and snaps, "When are you going to get over this!"

That's enough. That's all you need to heave a martyred sigh, rip the covers off your body and scream, "I lost a baby and you want me just to forget about it! You never did love me! You are probably glad I lost it so now you can leave me!" Then you explode into convulsing hysteria.

You feel shattered and alone and the deep and urgent need to be very far away from him because there is nothing that could convince you that he does not truly (and rightfully) hate your guts. You think, of course, I will lose him. I had a baby inside of me. I imagined its future. I loved it dearly. And it should have lived, but it died. For no reason that anyone knows. It just died. That's not supposed to happen, but it did. So of course, it's possible that your husband might not love you anymore, either.

There are times in life when you know what it feels like to be a crazy person. A person who is out of control. A person who is blathering and in danger of hurting herself. When reality slides away and what's inside your mind is your entire universe and you don't realize that you have ended up downstairs, crouching on the floor, your face frozen in the mask of a silent scream. You don't realize it until that little part of you that stays attached to reality (and at that moment it feels like the merest sliver of a string) holds on, pulls taut, wakes you up just enough to find yourself clawing at the carpet. You hear your words, "I miss my baby so much, I want my baby back," like some creepy Doo-Wop song. Knowing what you are saying breaks your heart all over again because you remember just how much you had wanted that pregnancy and how much you had lost when your husband threw away those bloody gobs of tissue wrapped delicately in toilet paper.

On the floor you sob and mutter. You say out loud to no one but the chair legs, how alone you feel. How nobody knows how you have tried to get over it but you can't. And for the first time in your life, you truly do not know what to do. You could cry yourself to sleep on the floor, but that's not what you want. You could leave but you have no place to go. You could return to bed where your ungrateful husband no doubt sleeps happily now that you have gone.

Before you are able to execute any plan, your husband creeps down the stairs. Like a squirrel caught inside, you scurry across the floor in the dark. You want to hide. You consider closets. Consider fleeing out the front door but you don't want to make any noise. So you do what any lunatic would do and you shuffle off into a corner as if you will become invisible in a smaller space. The truth is that you want him to find you, but you don't want it to be too easy.

He turns on a light but he doesn't see you. This goes on for several seconds and for a moment you fear that you really have disappeared. So you say, "What do you want?" with as much venom as you can muster just to prove that you still exist. He comes to you with outstretched arms. He says he wants to hug you. To hold you. You dutifully refuse and curl into a ball and say no, that you are going to stay right there. He pulls you up anyway and wraps you in his long arms. He kisses the top of your head and rubs your back as you stand rigidly, huffing against his chest because you are damned if you are going to cry or carry on in front of him any more. But he keeps repeating his gentle mantra, "Let me hold you. I love you. I want to hug you. I'm so sorry."

Through clenched teeth and fists, you tell him that you are FINE. You say that you shouldn't have gotten so upset. That you will be all right and you don't need him just then. You apologize for being hysterical. You say that he is right. None of this is such a big deal. You should be over it by now. It was just a baby. Not even a real baby. A fetus. People lose them all the time. It's nothing. You can handle it. And you are sorry to be such a burden.

You hear yourself say it all and you cringe with every word until your stomach squeezes and you think that you might vomit. Who is this woman who would apologize for grief? Who is this woman who would blame herself for something beyond her control? Other women do that. Women from the 1950s who were unfulfilled and hid behind the identity of their husbands. Mrs. Bud Simmons from 15 Nutmeg Lane in a shirtwaist dress and Betty Crocker apron would do that. Not you.

But at that moment apologizing and accepting every ounce of blame is the only solution you can see. Because if this man is angry with you for being sad and losing the child of your union then you have to make things right. You must not burden him with your sadness so he will love you enough again to allow you back into his bed where you so desperately want to be. So you blather on, hating yourself and hoping that he will stop you.

Finally he hugs you so tightly that you lose your breath and he says "Shhhh," until you quiet down. You relax against his chest and cry quietly, wondering when you were reduced to this sniveling stereotype of a woman. The kind you promised never to write about.

Eventually the bleeding tapers off and slowly you begin to feel like you again. Sometimes you completely forget that you were pregnant. Sometimes the whole experience seems like someone else's. Someone less fortunate than you and you feel sorry for her. Other times it hits you, like a sucker punch in the gut and you are sad for days. Somehow all of this is comforting because as long as you have the strangulating grief, then you have a piece of the baby that you lost.

Your story about the pregnant Girl is published. You hate every word of it. The only thing you like is the picture of you that your husband snapped on the day you submitted the story. You love it because it is the only photo of you when you were pregnant with your first child. That little lost soul.

Your agent calls to congratulate you on the story. She asks how you are and for some reason (the anonymity of the phone, the easy timbre of her voice, the ache of holding it all in for too long) you confide everything to her. She tells you that she lost her first one, too. You listen to each other breathe and you feel grateful for this covenant.

She finally says, "Of course, you will use this, right? When you are ready. Give one of the Girls a miscarriage."

But you know the Girls are dead and gone now. Emptied in their virtual trash like your daughter. You will never resurrect them.

"It's important," she says. "All of these women go through it but nobody talks about it. How are we supposed to know what it's like?"

You are quiet because you have no answer for her. How *were* you supposed to know? Who was supposed to teach you? Your mother? Your best friends? Your doctor?

"So you'll write about it, right?" she asks.

You hesitate. You want to appear to consider her suggestion, but already you know the answer. Let someone else expose herself. Grapple with her grief. Gestate it until she can smooth it black and white across the page, a story with a beginning, middle and an end. You will not write about it, though, because this is something that you never want to read in books. The story of your daughter will remain interred. Wrapped in the gauzy fabric of your sadness. Enclosed in the intricate carvings of your womb. This, the final and proper burial that she never received.

John McNally

Creature Features

IN APRIL OF 1971, MY PARENTS SAT ME DOWN AT THE DINING ROOM table and delivered the horrifying news: I would no longer be the only child in the family.

I said nothing. Rain pounded our windows, and our lights blinked off and on. When lightning zapped a nearby tree, I jumped a good inch off my chair. It was the first serious thunderstorm of the year.

Mom did all the talking. According to her, she was already four months along. Dad, who normally did all the talking, pulled a napkin free of its holder and dabbed at the sheen of sweat across his upper lip. He looked from one corner of the ceiling to the other, as if anticipating a leak to start any second. He was a roofer; a leak was something he could fix.

"So?" my mother asked. "What do you think, Timmy?"

"Huh!" I said, nodding. I was eight years old. The only things I cared about were monsters. Movie monsters, to be precise. I wouldn't talk to anyone unless they had something to say about monsters. If the word *monster* didn't come up within the first few seconds of a conversation, I quit listening. Monsters was the only acceptable topic—the only topic, in fact, worthy of my undivided attention. When my father brought home a schnauzer from the pound, I named him Dr. Jekyll. When he brought home a parrot in a cage, I named him Quasimodo. Whenever Mrs. V., our neighbor, knocked on our door, I'd open it slowly and, in a thick Eastern European accent, say, "I bid you welcome." Weekends, when my father took me to the dusty Twin Drive-In flea market, I spent hours flipping through boxes of musty monster magazines with titles like *Castle of Frankenstein*, *Mad Monsters*, and *Fantastic Monsters of the Films*. I searched for the magazines that cost a nickel, since those were the only ones I could afford.

My mother wasn't talking about monsters, so I felt no obligation to listen to what she was saying.

"I have to admit," she said, "you're taking the news awfully well."

I nodded. I smiled. I imagined biting her neck, turning into a bat, and flying out our kitchen window.

We lived in a two-bedroom apartment in Chicago. Most nights I fell asleep on the couch with the TV still on. Freight trains chugged behind our building all day long, and the Stevenson Expressway hovered above our third-floor window. My parents complained about the noise, but I didn't notice. It was like living in a valley except that there were no valleys in Chicago. There were only overpasses and underpasses. We lived under an overpass. I could climb up to the expressway and motion for the semi drivers to honk their horns, or I could stand by the railroad tracks that ran below and yell for the conductor to throw chalk. Why train conductors carried chalk with them I didn't know, but occasionally a huge chunk would come sailing toward me, and I would then spend my afternoon drawing peace signs on every Dumpster in my neighborhood. What more could I ask for?

The highlight of my week, however, was Saturday night at ten-thirty when "Creature Features" aired on channel nine. "Creature

Features" was like any other station's late-night movie, except that it starred a monster. Since our tiny black-and-white TV had pretty bad reception, I would start fiddling with the antennas a full half-hour beforehand, twisting them back and forth, then toward me and away. In desperation, I sometimes wrapped a sheet of aluminum foil around them. Eventually the snowy images cleared and recognizable objects came into focus. With my parents sound asleep, I turned out the lights, settled into the couch, and, keeping the volume low, waited for "Creature Features" to begin.

In truth, "Creature Features" wasn't much of a show. There was no host; there weren't any contests. Except for the opening sequence—a series of short clips featuring all of my favorite monsters, including Dracula, whose hand slithered out of a coffin, and the Wolf Man, who loped angrily through a layer of waist-high fog—there wasn't anything more to "Creature Features" than the monster movie itself. But a movie with a monster in it was enough for me.

The monsters reminded me of certain groups of kids at school. There would always be the popular ones—the Frankensteins, the Wolf Men, the Draculas of the playground—and then, off in the corner, the less popular ones—your Creatures from the Black Lagoon, your Mummies, your Invisible Men. I loved all the monsters, but my hope was always to spend time with the popular ones, and so my heart sunk, if only momentarily, whenever the Mummy came on, much as it sunk each time Raymond Gertz, with his sagging pants and bad breath, joined me on the blacktop to see why I hadn't come over to his house lately. I liked Raymond—he was okay—but he wasn't Dracula.

I usually fell asleep right around the time the monster started running amuck. By morning, the TV would be turned off, my father'd be smoking a cigarette at the dining room table, and my mom would be in the kitchen making pancakes and bacon. The apartment was laid out in such a way that I could see from one room to the next without having to budge. There was Mom, there was Dad, and here I was on the couch: the complete family unit.

On this particular Saturday night, while my father prepared himself for bed (preparations that included, among other things, plucking long hairs that had appeared suddenly from the cave of a nostril) my mother plopped down next to me on the couch. She ruffled my hair and pulled me close to her. I had been trying to read a monster magazine in preparation for "Creature Features," but I couldn't concentrate with all of Mom's squeezing and touching.

"When the baby arrives," she said, "you two are going to have to share a room. You realize that, don't you?"

"What baby?" I asked.

Mom sighed. "*You* know what baby," she said. "We talked about it the other day. Remember?"

I shrugged. I folded open my magazine, creased it down the middle, and held it out for my mother to look at. "Iron-on monsters!" I said, pointing to the advertisement.

My mother wouldn't even glance down. "You don't need iron-on monsters," she said.

I read the description aloud, as if I hadn't heard her. "*Any two monsters, one dollar.*"

"You don't need iron-on monsters," she repeated.

I shut the magazine. I got up and put a leash on Dr. Jekyll. "Come on, boy," I said. "Let's go for a walk."

Dr. Jekyll sniffed the same spot outside but wouldn't do anything. "Do something," I begged. "*Please.*" I was the only one who ever defended Dr. Jekyll. Whenever he messed in the house, I blamed it on his alter-ego: Mr. Hyde.

The last time Dr. Jekyll made a mess, Mom and I stood outside the sad circle of pee on the rug and stared down at it. "That wasn't Dr. Jekyll," I said. "Mr. Hyde did that."

Mom shook her head. "Dr. Jekyll. Mr. Hyde. It doesn't make a difference to me. I'm going to ring his little neck the next time he messes inside."

I gave the leash a gentle tug now and said, "Why won't you do anything?"

Mrs. V., who was retired and lived across the hall from us, wobbled over with her cane. She was blind, but she always knew where I was. According to her, I talked too much. "I can hear you through my walls," she'd told me once. "You never stop talking."

Today, Mrs. V. said, "How's that dog of yours?"

"He's okay," I said. "He won't pee, though."

"How's your mom?" she asked.

"Mom?" I said. "She pees all the time."

Mrs. V. pursed her lips. She didn't like me, but I didn't like her, either, so it didn't really bother me that she didn't like me. She said, "I hear you're going to have a baby brother or a baby sister soon."

"Really?" I said. "I haven't heard that."

Mrs. V. stared in my general direction for a good fifteen seconds before turning and caning her way back toward the apartment building. I finally gave up on Dr. Jekyll and led him back upstairs. I didn't want to miss the opening to "Creature Features." Mom and Dad were already asleep; their light was out, and the door was shut. I gave Dr. Jekyll a corn chip.

Tonight's movie was one of my favorites, *The Wolf Man*. It was the story of Larry Talbot who, after years away from home, returns to Europe and falls in love with a girl, only to be bitten by a werewolf and then, once he turns into a werewolf himself, is beaten to death by his father.

One thing I loved about monster movies was how different everything in them was from my life. I lived in an apartment building with my mom and dad; Larry Talbot lived in a castle with his father. When the lights went out, my parents lit a few squatty candles; the Talbots owned fancy candelabras. When my neighbors were angry, they swore at each other and made threats before slamming their doors shut; in monster movies, when people were angry, everyone gathered in the town square, and then they hunted down whatever they were mad at, using guns, dogs, and torches. *The Wolf*

Man had all of this and more—spooked horses in the fog; fortune-telling gypsies; walking canes with silver wolf-head handles.

If you watched enough monster movies, you started noticing how one movie interlocked with another. Lon Chaney, Jr.'s father was Lon Chaney, who played Quasimodo in *The Hunchback of Notre Dame*. Lon Chaney, Jr. played Larry Talbot, who turns into the Wolf Man. Claude Rains, who played Lon Chaney, Jr.'s father in *The Wolf Man*, also played the Invisible Man. Bela Lugosi, who played Bela the Gypsy in *The Wolf Man*, was the original Dracula. From where I stood, the monster community looked like one big happy family.

When Larry Talbot's father started talking about the legend of the werewolf being nothing more than a myth about the nature of good and evil in every man's soul, I pulled the blanket up to my chin. Dr. Jekyll hopped onto the couch with me, curling up and pressing himself against my belly, and together we watched mere men turn into wolves. "Look," I said, nudging Dr. Jekyll when Larry Talbot changed into the Wolf Man. "That's one of your relatives," I said. "What do you think about that?"

I opened my eyes. I sat up and looked around. "What was *that?*" I asked, blinking. A loud thud, in the vicinity of my head had woken me.

"I got these at a garage sale yesterday," Dad said. "Left them in my trunk overnight. Almost forgot about them." He pointed with his cigarette to a stack of four medical encyclopedias that smelled like they'd been fished out of Lake Michigan. Mold dotted their spines. "Fifty cents," he said. "Not bad."

I blinked some more, trying to focus. "Thanks," I said. I was afraid to ask—I didn't want to hurt his feelings—but I decided to ask anyway. "What are they *for?*"

"In case you wanted to, you know, read about what your mother's going through. It's all there under 'p.' Or maybe it's under 'b.' I'm not sure. I didn't look."

"'P,'" I said.

"Or 'b,'" he added. "You know. For *birth*."

"Where's Mom?" I asked. "What's for breakfast?"

"I took your mother out this morning. A treat." When he saw that my feelings were hurt, he added, "We didn't want to wake you." He turned away from the intensity of my glaring. He said, "I dropped her off at Mary Rudolph's."

The Rudolphs lived around the corner. I was in love with Eileen Rudolph, who was two years older than me and epileptic. She liked monsters, too.

After Dad left, I searched the apartment for a pair of gloves so I could open one of the books without actually having to touch it, but all I found were big, puffy winter gloves. I put them on, anyway. Turning pages with such huge gloves proved nearly impossible. Instead of finding the entry for *pregnancy*, I ended up at *psoriasis*. "A common immune-mediated chronic skin disease," it said, "that comes in different forms and varying levels of severity." On a glossy page next to the definition was a color photo of a woman's face with red patchy spots all over it.

"Ugh!" I said and shut the book.

Later, bored, I picked up one of my monster magazines and examined, at great length, the face of Lon Chaney as Quasimodo in *The Hunchback of Notre Dame*. One eye was white and kind of bulged out. His cheeks were abnormally puffy. Dirty, crooked teeth erupted from his down-turned mouth. Quasimodo, I concluded, probably had psoriasis, but by the look of things, psoriasis was the least of his problems.

I held the photo up to the bird cage and said to the parrot inside, "Look. This is who you're named after. What do you think?"

When my mother came home from the grocery store, she wrinkled her nose at the encyclopedias and said, "P. U.! What garbage can did you find those in?"

"Dad bought them for fifty cents," I said. "Not bad," I added.

Mom rested her twined fingers over her belly. "Is there anything about pregnancy in there?" she asked, smiling.

I shrugged. I opened the book to the photo of the woman with psoriasis. "You don't have *this*, do you?"

She shook her head.

I shut the book and pulled a monster magazine from my back pocket. I showed her some of the other things I could order from the back pages, but it didn't matter what I showed her—"Monster Notebook Binders," "Punch-out Monster Masks," or the "Frankenstein Target Game"—she always came to the same conclusion: I didn't need it.

"Okie doke," I said. I put the leash on Dr. Jekyll. "Come on, boy. Let's go outside."

Eileen Randolph was the only girl I knew who faithfully watched "Creature Features." When I biked over to her house Sunday night to ask her what she thought about *The Wolf Man*, she raised her hands up like paws, bared her teeth, and growled at me.

"So you liked it?" I asked.

She growled again, exposing her Wolf Man-like underbite, and nodded.

"Me, too," I said.

When she finally transformed back into herself, she looked like she was going to cry. "It was so sad at the end, though," she said.

"I guess," I said. "But he *was* a monster, you know. You can't let monsters run loose."

"Maybe not," Eileen said. And then she did the very thing I'd hoped she wouldn't do: she stared intensely into my eyes. Whenever she did this, I had to look away. I didn't want to tell her that I was in love with her, but I was. She wore her hair really long, like Susan Dey in *The Partridge Family*, and she wore necklaces strung with candy. Sometimes when I was talking to her, she'd lift the string of candy up to her mouth and take a bite. It killed me every time.

"When's your Mom due?" she asked.

"Due?" I said. "Due how?"

"When's she having her baby?"

"What baby?" I asked.

Eileen punched my arm. She was strong for a girl, and whenever she punched me, I ended up with a dark bruise the next day. "*You* know what baby," she said.

"If I knew," I said, "I'd tell you, but I don't, so I can't."

"When are we going to kiss?" she asked. Kissing was Eileen's new favorite subject. Before that, it had been God. Before that, frogs. She'd been putting a lot of pressure on me lately to kiss her, but so far I had managed to wiggle out of it. She whispered into my ear, "I'm epileptic. I could die any minute, so we should kiss."

Whenever Eileen started mixing kissing and dying together, I clammed up. Some days I would start picking at a scab on my knee or elbow, or I'd simply change the subject and talk about monsters she might not have heard of, like Nosferatu or Mothra, but today I decided to take action. I straddled my bike and started pedaling as fast as I could.

"Where are you going?" Eileen yelled after me.

"Away from you!" I yelled back without turning around.

Weeks went by before I finally broke down and opened the encyclopedia to the part about pregnancy. The first section began with three see-through pages. What you saw, with all three pages together, was an illustration of a pregnant woman wearing a blue maternity blouse and white pants. She looked like a grown-up and pregnant Jane from the *Dick and Jane* books at school, but when I peeled back the first see-through page, Jane was totally naked.

"Wow!" I said. Her belly was gigantic, and her belly button was poking way out. I wanted to keep looking but didn't want to get caught staring at a naked pregnant woman, even one in an encyclopedia. So I quickly turned to the final see-through page, which showed the inside of her belly, where a sleepy, drunk-looking baby floated around.

My heart continued to thump hard. I wiped the sweat from my palms onto my thighs. A few pages later I found a black-and-white photo that looked like a scene from the scariest monster movie ever: a small but slimy melon was popping out of the top of someone's bushy, split-open head. I brought the book close to my eyes, then held it away, hoping everything would come into focus. When I still couldn't make any sense out of it, I read the caption: "A newborn baby passing through the mother's vaginal canal." I screamed and threw the book.

Mom rushed into the living room. "What happened? Did Dr. Jekyll bite you?" At the mention of his name, Dr. Jekyll's tail started thumping.

"No! I'm fine." I tried catching my breath.

"If you're fine, why did you scream?"

"I didn't scream," I said.

She narrowed her eyes. "You're an odd one. Do you know that?" Then she looked beyond me, out the window behind my head. "Look at the moon, Timmy," she said, pointing. "It's so huge."

The moon, like an old movie, was always in black-and-white. I cleared my throat. "Even a man who is pure in heart and says his prayers by night may become a wolf when the wolfbane blooms and the autumn moon is bright." This was what everyone had told Larry Talbot in *The Wolf Man* before he turned into a wolf himself.

Mom stared at me for so long, I worried that a pentagram—the mark of the werewolf—had appeared on my forehead, but then she leaned toward me and kissed my cheek. "Nighty night," she said.

"Night," I replied.

The following Saturday, my father took me to the drive-in's flea market. The sellers, who parked their vehicles next to cast-iron poles that held the heavy speakers, displayed goods on either fold-out card tables or blankets spread over the gravel. My father liked to get there early to haggle before the noon crowd showed up. Noon crowds, according to my father, were the worst. "They're not shoppers," he said. "They're browsers. All they do is get in your way."

Week after week, I was stunned by the junk that people had the nerve to put out to sell: dolls missing heads, tools fuzzy with rust, an Etch-a-Sketch without knobs.

"If you see that Dr. Spock book," my father said today, "let me know. Your mother loved that book when she was pregnant with you, but I don't know what happened to it. I might have thrown it out."

I'd had no idea that Mom was a *Star Trek* fan. I was the only one who ever turned it on to watch. "*Mr.* Spock," I said for clarification.

"*Mr.* Spock. *Dr.* Spock. Whatever. Just don't spend more than a nickel on it."

Later, while digging through a deep box, I found a sci-fi maga-zine with Leonard Nimoy on the cover. I held it up and showed it to my dad.

"Look!" I said. "Mr. Spock!"

Dad nodded; he wasn't impressed.

"You don't want it?" I asked.

"Why would I want it?"

"For Mom," I said.

Dad shook his head, and I tossed it back into the box.

When we got home and I saw Mom, I raised my hand and gave her the *Star Trek* greeting. "Live long and prosper," I said.

Mom smiled. "What a sweet thing to say," she said. "I hope you live long and prosper, too, honey."

The bigger my mother grew, the less desire I had to crack open the medical encyclopedia and find out what was going to happen next. The less I knew, the better. The photo of the kid with the slimy head popping out of his mother had made me want to believe that nothing like that was going to happen to anyone—*ever*. But there were worse thoughts. I tried pushing them out of my brain, but the scariest of them—that *I* had once been that slimy-headed kid—kept returning. And once I started thinking about myself as the slimy-headed kid in the photo, a thousand more questions followed: How was it possible that I had once been *inside my mother?* How had I managed to breathe while squeezing myself out? Why couldn't I remember any of it?

It was all too disturbing to think about, and every time a new question popped into my head, I'd start walking for blocks and blocks, zombie-like, wondering how everything had gone so wrong so fast. I had always been a good boy, the sort of boy that women in grocery stores commented upon, and at a very young age, three or four, I knew how to feign shyness, how to duck my head at compliments, how to look at my shoes, how to twist my feet ever so slightly inward and tap the tips together, a kind of Morse Code that women—mothers, especially—intuited as gestures of a modest boy. "Oh, *look* at him," they would say, and I would clutch the bottom hem of my mother's blouse and, wide-eyed, give it an almost imperceptible tug, further cementing public opinion that I was such a *cute little boy*.

But those days were gone.

When Jerry Stroka showed me the final card of his *Partridge Family* trading card collection—the much-coveted "Road to Albuquerque"—I ripped it in half and gave it back to him. I expected Jerry to punch me, but he didn't. He broke into tears, his face as raw and open as a sliced tomato, and he took off running.

When Joey Rizzo showed me his can of Silly String, I took it from him, shook the can for a good half-minute, the way my father shook cans of spray paint, and then I sprayed Joey's face. When I was done, Joey looked like someone had thrown a huge plate of foam spaghetti at his head.

"I'm blind!" he yelled, clawing at his face. "I can't see!"

What I did, I did without emotion. I felt no malice toward these boys; I felt no jealousy or rage. The sad truth was, I felt nothing—nothing at all. Something inside me was happening. I was becoming a different boy, and there was nothing I could do about it.

*   *   *

"Timothy O'Reilly," Mom said before I could shut the door. "Guess who just called me."

I looked down at my mother's belly and then back up at her. I shrugged. Mrs. V. was smoking a cigarette at our dining room table. She said, "I better skedaddle," but she couldn't resist smiling, thrilled at the prospect of my getting punished. For Mrs. V., who was blind, each day must have been like a monster movie turned inside-out in that *everyone* was the Invisible Man. She smashed out her cigarette and then walked toward the door, hitting me with her cane. If Eileen wasn't busy giving me bruises, Mrs. V. picked up the slack. Tomorrow I would have a new one, purple and puffy, on my shin.

With Mrs. V. gone, Mom said, "Do you have any idea why Joey Rizzo's mother might call me?"

I walked the rest of the way inside and shut the door. I took off my coat. I hung it on our wobbly coat rack. I understood now how Dad felt when he came home from a long day at work only to find himself interrogated about one thing or another the second he opened the door. In all fairness to Mom, she didn't interrogate Dad very often, and she always had a good reason when she did. Even so, my heart went out to my father.

"What's gotten into you lately?" Mom asked. "You used to be such a good little boy. I'm not even sure I recognize you anymore. Do you have anything to say for yourself?" She waited for an answer. "*Nothing?*" she asked.

I growled, just enough to let her know that I was in no mood, before heading for my bedroom and shutting the door between us.

When summer came to an end, so did my trips to the flea market.

"It's the same old stuff, week after week," Dad said.

"What about garage sales?"

"Wrong time of year."

"Are there any good flea markets in Michigan?" I asked.

My father gave me one of his are-you-out-of-your-gourd looks.

"You got a wad of bills burning a hole in your pocket or what?"

Instead of driving me around to look for old monster magazines, my father went out by himself, returning later with things for my mother, like Italian beef sandwiches, which she craved all the time now, or boxes of cookies he bought at the factory outlet store, where he was putting on a new roof. The cookies were cheaper because they were damaged, but Mom claimed that she preferred crumbs, anyway. I kept wanting to ask Dad, *What about me? What about the things I want?* but I knew I'd sound like a big baby.

"Since when do you like crumbs?" I asked Mom after Dad left the room.

"Shhhh," Mom said. "You'll hurt his feelings."

One night during "Creature Features," our telephone rang. I was watching *The Creature Walks Among Us*, in which a team of doctors decide that the Creature from the Black Lagoon (a.k.a. Gill Man) would be happier if he could walk around like the rest of us, so they try fixing up his looks by cutting, sewing, burning, and scraping him. I sat on the edge of the couch, leaning toward the TV. I was appalled at all the different kinds of torture the doctors were putting the Creature through, but I was kind of enjoying it, too. When the phone rang, I nearly wet my pants.

My father bolted from the bedroom, yelling, "What's that noise?"

I pointed to the phone.

Dad stared at it, as if it were a smoking meteorite, before looking at the clock on the wall and then picking up. "Yeah? . . . Yeah? . . . *What?* . . . We'll be right over." Dad hung up. "That was Bill Rudolph. Eileen's having seizures. They're taking her to the hospital, and he wants us to watch the kids." I stood to get ready, but Dad motioned for me to stay put. "Just watch your movie," he said.

"But it's *Eileen*," I said.

"We'll call you if there's a problem," Dad said. "Otherwise, we'll see you in the morning."

It took my parents no time to get ready. Mom slipped back on the clothes she had worn earlier that day, while Dad put on a thick coat, winter gloves, and a knit cap. When he left the apartment, though, he was still wearing his pajama bottoms.

I got up and fiddled with the TV antennas. Despite all the advancements in modern medicine, Gill Man was still having a difficult time adapting to life among humans. At the sight of all the injustices Gill Man suffered, my upper lip started to tremble, and my vision got blurry. Poor guy, I thought. Poor fella. I knew exactly how he felt. I *was* Gill Man.

When my parents returned to our apartment early the next morning, I figured Eileen must have been okay. Mom walked over to the couch, but I kept my eyes shut and forced my teeth to chatter.

"Look how cold he is," Mom said.

"He's fine," Dad said.

Mom rested her palm on my forehead. "He's *warm*. Maybe he's got the flu."

"Just throw a bunch of blankets over him," Dad said. "I'm going to bed."

Mom piled several blankets over my trembling body. "There there," she said, and kissed my head.

By the time school started up in the fall, word had spread about what I'd done to Jerry Stroka and Joey Rizzo, and my old friends kept a safe distance from me, fearful that I might grab hold of someone's exposed underwear and rip the elastic band free, or that I might remove my left-handed scissors from a pocket and quickly cut a patch of hair from an innocent kid's head. Overnight, I had become a boy capable of anything.

Meanwhile, my mother's stomach grew to ungainly proportions. When she walked, she tilted from side to side. She sometimes stopped whatever she was doing to let out a long sigh. *"Whew,"* she'd say and then take a deep breath before carrying on. She spoke more often to the kid inside her than to me. "You must be sleeping on my kidney, kiddo," she'd say. Or, "Your *brother* didn't even kick this much."

One afternoon, while my mother napped on the couch, I tiptoed up to her and had a few words with her belly.

"The bedroom's all mine," I said. "Find your own damned place to live." I stared at my mother's stomach, hoping my words were penetrating. I leaned closer and said, "I like monsters. If you don't like monsters, don't even talk to me, okay?" I waited a few seconds before adding, "Are we clear on things?"

Mom opened her eyes. It reminded me of a scene from *Dracula*: You think Dracula's asleep in his coffin, but then he opens his eyes and your heart clenches like a fist. "Who are you talking to?" she asked.

"Quasimodo," I said. I reached over and stuck my finger inside the bird cage, but he bit me, thinking my finger was a cracker.

"Oh," Mom said. "Do you think you could whisper then?"

Okay, I mouthed. I zipped my mouth shut. I put the leash on Dr. Jekyll. "Shhh," I whispered. "Don't bark."

The baby was due on September 8, 1971. I wasn't sure how they knew the exact date, but they did.

One day in late August, while Mom sat at the dining room table writing down possible names for the baby, I suggested naming it Boris after Boris Karloff, who played the Frankenstein monster, if it was a boy; or Elsa after Elsa Lanchester, who played the monster's disappointed bride, if it was a girl.

"I'm not naming the baby after a *monster*, for Pete's sake," Mom said. The pencil slipped from her hand and fell to the floor. When she leaned sideways to pick it up, she looked like she was going to fall over. Her stomach was that big. I reached down, picked up the pencil, and handed it back to her.

"Those aren't *monsters*," I clarified. "They're the names of actors who *played* monsters."

"Boris," Mom said and snorted. "What kind of name *is* that, anyway?"

The due date—September the eighth—came and went. So did September the ninth. On Saturday the eleventh, I biked over to Eileen's to ask her if she was going to watch *Frankenstein* on "Creature Features" later that night. Neither of us had ever seen the original *Frankenstein*. We'd seen *Bride of Frankenstein, Son of Frankenstein, The Ghost of Frankenstein, Frankenstein Meets the Wolf Man, House of Frankenstein,* and our favorite, *Abbott and Costello Meet Frankenstein.* How was it possible we'd seen all of these but not the most famous monster movie of all time?

We were sitting on a pile of logs behind the tool shed in her back yard. Her mother had made us a pitcher of Tang, and we each had a tall glass.

"I hear he drowns a cute little girl," Eileen said.

"Who?" I said. "Frankenstein's monster?"

"Who else."

"I can't wait," I said.

Eileen set her glass of Tang on the ground. She took my glass and set it next to hers. And then Eileen did the one thing I kept hoping she would never do: she leaned in and kissed me. Her lips actually touched my lips. I expected it to be worse than it was. Surprisingly, it wasn't too bad. She was chewing a wad of Bazooka Joe, and since I chewed Bazooka Joe all the time, her mouth tasted a lot like my own mouth, only better—better because it *wasn't* my mouth.

"Do you know how to French kiss?" she asked.

"Do *what?*" I said.

Instead of answering, she showed me. It was shortly after this that I might have blacked out. I didn't actually black out, but I lost all track of time, the way Larry Talbot, after he turns into the Wolf Man and kills innocent villagers, wakes up the next morning confused, only to discover paw prints on the carpet and then dirt on his feet, leaving him with one logical conclusion: He *is* the Wolf Man!

When Eileen slipped her hand up under my T-shirt, touching my bare skin, I told her I needed to go.

"Why? Don't you like this?"

"It's okay," I said. "But I don't want to miss *Frankenstein.*"

"You'd rather watch *Frankenstein* than kiss me?" she asked.

It was a crazy question; I almost didn't answer. I gave her one of my father's are-you-out-of-your-gourd looks. A whine crept into my voice when I said, "But it's *Frank-en-stein.*"

"I see," Eileen said. She stood up and brushed herself off. I could tell by the bounce in her step as she walked toward her house that she was mad.

"Now, don't be like that," I said. My words were eerily familiar, but it was only after Eileen had stopped abruptly, the way my mother would have stopped, that I realized the words I spoke belonged to my father. It was something he said at least once a week.

"Like what?" Eileen said. When she turned around, I saw that she was crying. "Like *this?* I could die tomorrow. I *could,*" she insisted, "and what do you care?" She waited for me to answer, but I didn't know what to say. I felt weak, like I'd been punched. It was starting to drizzle. I wanted to go home. But then Eileen delivered the final blow. "I don't even *like* monsters," she said.

"You *what?*" I said. Eileen was already opening her screen door to go inside. "You lied!" I yelled once the door shut. For good measure, I added, "How could you not like monsters? What's wrong with you?" The porch light flipped off, leaving me in the dark. "Eileen?" I called out, but no one answered. I looked closely for her shadow against the shut curtains, but when I didn't see anything that looked like her, I got on my bike and headed for home.

The rain came down in heavy sheets, and the roads were especially slick. I was so wet by the time I reached the apartment, my pants and shirt clung to my skin. Every time I peeled my shirt away from me, it slowly suctioned itself back to my flesh. My shirt was like a living thing, the way the Blob was a living thing: it wasn't human and it wasn't animal, but it was going to eat me alive if I wasn't careful. Even after I changed my clothes, rain continued to roll from my hair and down my face.

A note was taped over the TV screen. I was afraid it was there to let me know the TV was broken, but it was a note about Mom.

> WENT TO HOSPITAL.
> NEW BABY ON THE WAY.
> COULDN'T WAIT FOR YOU.
> DAD

I looked down at Dr. Jekyll. "Did you know about this?" I asked. He cocked his head, then wagged his tail. For Dr. Jekyll, every question was the same: *Do you want a treat?* I gave him a Cheez-It.

Rain hammered our windows, and I could hear a steady plop somewhere inside the apartment. I marched from room to room until I found the problem: rain was dripping from the kitchen ceiling. I set a sauce pan down to catch the drip.

Quasimodo squawked, and I said, "Easy, boy, it's only water," but then I saw that rain was dripping into his cage. When I picked up the cage to move it, Quasimodo squawked again. "You're welcome," I said.

By the time I turned on the TV and settled onto the couch, "Creature Features" was already starting. I covered my entire self with blankets, except for my eyes and the top of my head. At last, I was going to see the greatest monster movie of all time—*Frankenstein!* What a lot of people didn't realize was that Frankenstein wasn't the name of the monster. Frankenstein was the last name of the scientist who created him. It had crossed my mind that if I ever created a monster, people might start calling it O'Reilly. The very name O'Reilly would cause women to scream and men to gather their weapons.

Quasimodo squawked some more—an angry squawk this time. The rain had followed him, still dripping into his cage. "I'm going to miss the *movie*," I whined. I threw off my blankets and quickly moved the bird cage again.

As Dr. Frankenstein and his hunchbacked assistant, Fritz, started digging up the freshly buried corpse, rain poured in from new places in our ceiling. During the first commercial break, I found more pans and cups to place strategically around the apartment. If Dad was here, he would have known what to do.

"Dr. Jekyll," I said. "Do you know how to swim?"

His tail wagged. *Yes*, he was saying. *I'd love a treat.*

My lips still felt like they were touching Eileen's lips. It was like being kissed by the Invisible Man. Even the smell of Bazooka Joe lingered. What if she was telling the truth? What if she *was* going to die any day now? I was almost too upset to concentrate on the movie, but I watched it anyway, lying across the couch with Dr. Jekyll curled up next to me. I decided that I would memorize everything in the movie so that I could tell Eileen about it tomorrow: the way Dr. Frankenstein's laboratory was in a watchtower, the way Fritz climbed down a long rope from the top of the tower, the way the monster was strapped to a table, still dead. And then there was the laboratory itself with all its flywheels, chains, and glass bubbles. I would buy Eileen a box of chocolate. I would give her some of my favorite monster magazines. I knew she was lying, of course; her knowledge of monsters was too great for her *not* to like them.

It was storming in *Frankenstein*, a storm as bad as the one outside. At the height of the storm, Dr. Frankenstein cranked a flywheel, and the table upon which the monster lay rose to the very top of the watchtower. My hands were sweating. Rain hit the top of my head, one thick plunk after another. Electricity struck the bolts sticking out of the monster's neck and then Dr. Frankenstein lowered the monster back to ground level.

The telephone rang, and I clutched my chest. This was the most famous part of the most famous monster movie of all time, and I wasn't going to miss it for anything. The phone rang two more times before it stopped.

I had to squint through the rain to see the lightening on TV. Dr. Jekyll whined and looked up at me, and Quasimodo squawked. There was a knock at our door. "Go away!" I yelled, but then came another knock. I groaned and stood. I looked out the peephole. It was Mrs. V.

"What?" I yelled through the door.

"Your father is trying to call you!" she yelled back.

"So?"

"Your mother had a baby girl!"

"That's great!" I said. "Is that all?"

"What are you doing in there? Why won't you open the door?"

"None of your business," I said.

"You're an evil little boy," she said. "Did you know that?"

"I'm not a boy," I said. "I'm a monster."

At this, Mrs. V. backed slowly away from the door. She looked like a movie being run in reverse. My heart was pounding. *My mother had a baby*, I thought. *I've got a sister now.*

I pulled my eye from the peephole. "Wow," I said. "A sister." When I reached the couch, I watched the monster raise his hand all by himself.

"Look," Dr. Frankenstein said. "It's moving. It's alive."

"Look!" I said to Dr. Jekyll. "It's moving."

"It's alive!" Dr. Frankenstein bellowed. "It's alive! It's moving!"

Dr. Frankenstein looked so happy. I imagined my mother and the new slimy baby. I imagined my father towering over them, smiling like Dr. Frankenstein. I walked to the window and opened it wide. I was already soaking wet, and Dr. Jekyll was crawling under the couch for shelter. I poked my head out the window and yelled, "It's alive! It's alive!" Sheets of rain smacked my face.

Dr. Frankenstein continued to yell: "It's alive! In the name of God, now I know what it feels like to *be* God!"

"It's alive!" I yelled again. I was shivering, but I didn't mind. I was happy. I was happy for Mom; I was happy for Dad; I was happy that I had a plan to win back Eileen. I was even happy for the slimy baby I hadn't yet met.

Mrs. Willis, who lived below us, opened her window and looked out to see who was making all the noise. Mr. Sleezak, who lived next door, opened his window, too, and poked his head outside. A family running through the rain to their car paused to peer up at me. Behind me the TV sizzled and popped a few times, and then something inside it exploded. A glass tube, I suspected. From under the couch, Dr. Jekyll barked.

"In the name of God!" I shouted.

Tomorrow, I would knock on Eileen's door, and when she answered, I would take her in my arms. I would whisper into her ear that she wasn't going to die. Not anytime soon, at least. And not before we'd kissed some more.

"What's *wrong* with that kid?" Mr. Sleezak asked Mrs. Willis.

"I don't know," Mrs. Willis said, "but I always suspected he wasn't right in the head."

I held my hands out into the rain, as if to catch a falling baby, and yelled, "It's *alive*! It's *alive*!"

Laurie Lindop

Sunday Morning

KELLY STUDIED THE SPERM BANK CATALOG THAT SARAH HAD brought home yesterday. Donor 142 was of Scandinavian-English background with light brown hair, a complexion that was listed as "fair but tans well." Donor 245 was Korean with rosy coloring and type O+ blood. "I think a woman must compile these lists," Kelly said. "What man describes himself as *rosy*?"

"Hmm?" Sarah lowered the Sunday newspaper and looked across the table at her.

"Black guys seem the most popular," Kelly said. "They all have only 'limited inventory available,' except this one. Oh, but he's 5 foot 6. I wonder why they even bothered to collect from him."

"How about French-Scottish with gray curly hair?" Sarah was French-Scottish with graying curly hair.

"Nope. Only one Scottish and he's part Indian. Doesn't say which kind of Indian. That's an interesting combo, though, either way." Kelly shut the catalog. On the cover was a photo of sperm wriggling against a dark background, little comets of glowing whiteness against a night sky. Back when she was a teenager and trying hard to convince herself she wasn't a lesbian, she'd gone on the pill, but then couldn't stop worrying about the errant 2% in the pill's 98% success rate and so she insisted her boyfriend wear a condom. She'd be damned if she was going to have his sperm sneaking their way up her fallopian tubes to screw up her life.

"Sperm is now my friend," she declared.

"What?"

"It's a strange concept to wrap my brain around after all these years."

A while ago, when Sarah had starting showing signs of going into pre-monopause, they had agreed that Kelly would get pregnant by the time Sarah turned forty-eight, and yesterday had been Sarah's forty-eighth birthday. Over their celebratory dinner last night, Sarah had shown Kelly the catalog that she'd picked up at the sperm bank. *I bet not many women my age come through their doors*, she'd said, describing how the receptionist had given her a doubtful look. *I told her I had a partner who's a hot younger babe with ovaries ripe as little grapes.*

You did not, Kelly had laughed while trying to grasp all that it meant. It shouldn't have come as a surprise—they had made this plan, after all, and over the course of their seven year relationship, they had periodically debated whether or not to take the leap at various points. In the past, there had always been good reasons to wait. There were good reasons now. On the other hand, Kelly knew that they couldn't put it off forever—if she got pregnant today, Sarah would be in her sixties by the time their kid graduated high school.

Kelly gazed across the kitchen table at Sarah as she read the newspaper. Her lover was ten pounds too thin and her bathrobe was open just enough to reveal the hard bones of her chest, the jutting clavicle; she had keen dark blue eyes and a face that was all planes and hollows; her skin was so pale it appeared almost translucent and Kelly could see the squiggly vein running alongside her temple. When asked, Sarah would say that as a professor she was demanding, a harsh but fair grader. Every semester she acquired a small group of acolytes. Dr. Prescott's Girl Groupies, Kelly called them, and at the end of the year she and Sarah always hosted a Groupie dinner party. At this year's party, Kelly had grilled salmon and served it with her signature mustard-dill sauce and Asian coleslaw; when the dishes were cleared, Sarah had brought out her fiddle. Kelly's job was to urge everyone to get up and square dance. Sometimes she secretly felt that the girls would think it stodgy if she wasn't there. Oblivious, Sarah had done the calling while her bow glided quickly across the strings. Before long, the Groupies were happily weaving in unison around the back yard. More than once at these parties, a Groupie who had drunk too much wine confided to Kelly that she was absolutely in love with Dr. Prescott. In love with Kelly as well. In love with *all of this*, indicating their tall and narrow Victorian house, the pretty backyard, the girls dancing arm-in-arm.

Getting up from the breakfast table, Kelly now went to the sliding glass doors and looked out at the rectangular space they had excavated to put in a bluestone patio. She had done ninety percent of the work—tearing up the grass and leveling off most of the soil in preparation for the stone dust that was going to be delivered this morning. It had to be spread in a perfectly even layer in order for the stones to lie flat on top of it. She pictured plastic toys scattered around the finished space, maybe a swing set beside the birch they'd planted in honor of her mother who had recently passed away. The clock ticked down the hallway and she thought of her sister's house, the constant hubbub, the crying and crumbs, the sticky fingerprints on the refrigerator, the strong sweet smell of baby lotion, and always a hint of dirty diapers. But she and Sarah weren't going to have a whole gaggle of kids, just one, an adorable tomboy—*their* little girl— who would zigzag amongst the square-dancing Groupies and spin around in circles on the patio so that her hair flew out.

"We better go out and level off the rest before the stone dust comes," she said to Sarah who was smiling slightly at something in the paper. "Can you hurry up and get dressed?"

"I was going to make some eggs."

"Make them later. The dump truck could be here any minute and I need help."

Sarah folded up the newspaper, went over and put it in the recycling bin, then opened the basement door.

"What are you doing?" Kelly asked.

"I need to do a load of laundry first. I have a meeting at eleven—"

Kelly irritably pulled open the sliding doors and went outside into the unseasonable spring heat. Sarah's bad back made her virtually useless anyhow. Grabbing a shovel, Kelly dug into the soil that sloped down the rise of their yard. As she heaved up a load, she thought about how her boss had hinted that he might be leaving his position as head registrar. If he did, she would definitely get a shot at replacing him. How could she then go out on maternity leave? She wondered if Sarah had bothered to consider this before charging off to the sperm bank yesterday.

"All right, what do you want me to do?" Sarah came out dressed in her work jeans and a t-shirt with the university logo on it.

"I've got it." Kelly heaved up another shovel full.

"Let me help."

"You'll hurt your back." Or else complain that your joints are stiff.

"I could pack it down." Sarah went over to the uneven lower corner and began stomping on it in her docksiders.

"Now you're in my way."

Sarah stopped and studied her for a moment. "What's the matter?"

You turned forty-eight and that trumps everything else that might be going on in my life? Kelly wanted to ask. Although in truth, her boss had been hinting he would quit for more than a year and still hadn't done anything concrete. There would always be reasons to wait. "Nothing's the matter," Kelly finally said. "And, really, I can do this on my own."

Sarah gave her an uncertain nod and then came over, touched her lightly on the cheek. "Sweet girl," she said and then went back towards the house.

Kelly closed her eyes. They had moved to this neighborhood specifically because it had a good school system with a number of gay and lesbian families. The second floor sewing room would make an ideal nursery. When the child got older, Sarah would give up her large attic office and they'd turn it into a bedroom. More than once, Kelly had gone up there and envisioned Pooh Bear stenciled on the white wall, a dollhouse that she'd build herself standing where Sarah's file cabinet was now. All of a sudden, she felt tears well up. Her mom wouldn't be around for the biggest event in her life. She wouldn't be here to offer tips on reducing her swollen ankles or to reassure her that everyone felt like crap in the last trimester. As she rubbed her eyes, Kelly reminded herself that she couldn't be sure how her mom would have reacted to the news. Perhaps she would have immediately set to work needlepointing a Christmas stocking for their baby the way she'd done for all of her sister's kids. But what if she hadn't? There still wasn't a stocking for Sarah while her mother had knit one for Wendy's husband before they were even engaged. Sarah refused to take it personally: *We only see her a couple of times a year, Kelly, and she's at your sister's every single week. If we lived out there and saw her all the time, then I'd feel bad.*

Kelly wasn't nearly so forgiving. When she'd found out that her mother had decided to move into Wendy's house after her last round of chemo, her first thought was, *no surprise you picked them.* It wasn't rational—she couldn't expect her mother to move all the way across the country to be with her and Sarah; at the same time, she knew that her mother would always prefer Wendy's traditional all-American family.

Kelly scooped up more soil and tossed it behind her. Her mother had been living at Wendy's for a couple of weeks when she had flown out to Los Angeles to see her mother for what turned out to be the last time. Her sister had met her at the airport and warned her to be prepared. Kelly had tried, but was still surprised by the loss she felt at finding her mom without her lush, carefully coiffed hair. A dark fluff had started to grow in its place and her eyebrows were penciled in as mountain peaks. That evening, Kelly had offered to help her mother take her bath. While they waited for the tub to fill, her mother had sat on the closed toilet in her robe and Kelly dipped a washcloth in Noxzema to wipe away the eyebrows, momentarily smearing brown across her brow before quickly swabbing it off. Without those mountain peaks, her mother took on a startled look so that Kelly had suddenly and clearly imagined how she must've wondered many times since her diagnosis, *Why me? Why does it have to be me?* Not that her mother had ever mentioned such worries to her. Maybe to Wendy, but not to her.

Kelly remembered how her mom had said, "It's good to have my girls together." Her mother had reached out a hand and Kelly had held it gently, so birdlike with its small brittle bones. "I love you," her mother had said in her hoarse, wheezy voice. "And I worry about you. You know, honey, it's not too late to find someone."

"What are you talking about? I have Sarah."

"But don't you want to settle down and have a family?"

Kelly had dropped her mother's hand, gone over to the tub, and turned off the water. "I want Sarah and Sarah wants me, period."

"Yes," her mother had sighed and put her hands on the toilet's sides trying to stand.

Kelly had hurried over and grabbed her mother under the arms. She'd kicked plastic toys out of the way as they slowly shuffled to the tub and then held her mother around the waist while loosening her robe's belt. As it fell away, Kelly's heart had caught—how thin her mom had become, the skin hanging from her ribs and drooping from her stomach. There was a fearsome bruise on her arm from the IV.

"Oh, Mom," she'd whispered, pressing a finger to her lips then lightly touching the purplish splotch.

"It's all right."

"You're brave," Kelly had held her around the waist as her mom gingerly lifted a leg over the tub's side.

"It's not as if I've got a choice, honey."

When she was seated, Kelly had taken a plastic Minnie Mouse

cup and scooped up water, letting it spill over her mother's freckled back and bony shoulders. Then she dunked in the bar of soap as her mother reached for a large inflatable Snoopy bath toy. She clasped it to her front as Kelly soaped the hard bones of her back, the loose skin moving in patterns under her touch.

"Let me get the front, Mom."

But her mother had shaken her head, still clasping the Snoopy toy to her breasts. Kelly had dipped the plastic cup in the water and poured a stream over her mother's upper chest hoping it would seep under the toy and down. It was hardly satisfactory but she wasn't going to force the issue.

After she got her mother in her nightgown and tucked her in bed, she'd gone down to the kitchen where her sister sat drinking a cup of tea.

"I had no idea Mom was so modest," Kelly had said, making herself a cup as well.

"Mom? She's not modest."

"She lets you wash all of her? Her back and front?"

"Of course. Why?"

Perhaps her mother had simply felt like hugging something at that moment. To think anything else hurt too much.

Now Kelly stopped shoveling for a moment and gazed at the birch tree, wondering if she should have told her mother that she and Sarah planned to have a child one day. Their very own love. Their little muffin. It would've been just one more thing for her mother to worry about. Kelly shook her head and resumed working.

A short while later, she heard a truck pulling into their circular driveway. She went around to the front of the house where the big truck idled with its rusty front grill rising nearly as high as her head. The driver pushed open his door and swung down from his seat. He came towards her with a bowlegged walk. He was sunburnt, with a reddish crew cut and wrap-around sunglasses. *Five foot eleven*, Kelly guessed, *of Irish descent and a freckled complexion*. She noticed the cigarette stuck behind one ear and added, *heavy smoker*. It struck her that the sperm bank catalog hadn't mentioned any such details, not smoking, not drug use, not alcoholism.

"Hi. You ordered stone dust?"

"Could you dump it down there?" she pointed. "Right in the center?"

"You bet." He went back to his truck, put it in gear, and drove out their driveway to turn around in the street. The warning signal beeped as he starting going in reverse. Kelly moved out of the way as he approached the grassy incline that led down into their backyard. As the truck rumbled past her, she noticed the bumpersticker affixed to the side of his faded blue cab: *My wife said it was the gun or her. I sure will miss her.*

"Asshole," Kelly said softly and then followed the muddy tracks he'd left in their grass down to the space that she had excavated. The truck's flat bed rose up on its hydraulic lifts and before she could stop the driver, the rear gate swung open, allowing a load of blue-gray stone dust to slide onto the uneven corner that Sarah had attempted to tramp down. Kelly watched the flat bed clank back into place and smelled the exhaust as the driver put it in gear and roared back up the incline, adding two more muddy tracks.

Kelly took her shovel and began heaving up stone dust, moving it away from the unprepared section. The kitchen door slid open and Sarah came out.

"Do you know how much fucking extra work he just made for me?" Kelly demanded. "I told him the center and this is where he left it."

"Why don't we just hire someone to do it?"

Kelly shook her head. She liked the feel of working with her hands and having something to show for it afterwards.

"Well, at least let me help, then."

"This stuff's heavy."

"I'll be careful." Sarah went to the shed and took out the other shovel. Coming back, she scooped up a wimpy load and tossed it aside.

As they worked quietly, Kelly considered how some jerk like this morning's truck driver might have donated semen, which meant she could end up having his wife-hating, gun-loving sperm swimming around inside her. "You know that BTK guy?" she suddenly asked. "The murderer?"

"Oh, yeah," Sarah nodded. "What was it they dubbed him? Bind-Torture-Kill?"

"That's right. Did you know he had a family? Three kids and a wife who all said they had no clue." In the newspaper photos she'd seen of him, he'd appeared balding, fat-faced, ordinary. Surely there must have been indicators, though. Such extreme sickness would have to ooze into his family life, wouldn't it? Perhaps there was something off about the way he tied up the kitchen garbage bag, pulling the plastic ties into an excessively forceful knot, or his habitual lingering over the bolts of thick rope at the hardware store. Something.

Kelly paused in her shoveling. "What if our kid does something weird one day," she asked Sarah. "Won't we wonder if it was because Mr. Korean Rosy Cheeks was secretly a psychopath like BTK?"

Sarah dusted off her hands and leaned on her shovel. "Kids do weird stuff all the time, Kelly. I ate a lizard. It doesn't mean anything."

"You did? My God, why?"

"I don't know. I was four years old or so, and my brother dared me. I thought it was dead and I ate its foot. It wriggled on my tongue and I started screaming and swallowed it."

"See, that's exactly it, if our kid eats a lizard, I can try telling myself that it's all right, but in the back of my head, I'll be worrying about who, exactly, donated sperm. Genes *do* matter. Look at all those studies of twins separated at birth who end up being exactly like each other. I need to know more than that our kid's dad is a Scandinavian who tans well or a truck driver with red hair."

"They give you full dossiers about the donor. That catalog I brought home is just a starting point."

Kelly considered this and then said, "But wouldn't it be better to see him face to face? Then we could look in his eyes and study his hands and see the way he cuts his meat."

"You want to see him cut his meat?"

"I don't care how big of a dossier they give me on someone, it won't tell me who he is deep in his soul."

Sarah gazed at her intently. "Are you reconsidering?"

Kelly gave a tiny shrug.

Sarah dropped her shovel, came behind, and wrapped her arms around her. "I thought we both wanted a baby."

"We do. I think."

"You *think?*"

Kelly pulled loose from her. "*I'm* the one who's going to have to get shot up with semen from some guy who jacked off in a paper cup." She fell silent, staring down at the turned-over ground. "I want it to be equally yours. I want *our* child to be *our* child and not someone else's."

"But it will be ours," Sarah said.

Kelly felt how if it was Sarah's genes melding with her own to make a baby, the trepidation would be gone and in its place a humming, intimate excitement. Instead, there was this sense of others intruding where they had no right to go.

"It will be *ours,*" Sarah repeated with conviction. "Our sweet little baby with perfect tiny little hands and the cutest little feet who smells like milk and talcum powder."

Kelly smiled slightly.

"Our little baby falling asleep in her green snuggly suit with teddybears on it."

Kelly imagined coming home late from the office and going upstairs to find Sarah reading a good night story. The baby's room would be dimly lit and a music box softly playing. Leaning over the crib rail, she would rub circles across their baby's back while Sarah's voice rose and fell in a sing-song, and their baby's breathing grew more rhythmic with sleep. She did want this. Her own little family. She would simply not allow herself to think about the stranger's role in it all. But even as Kelly decided this, she knew there would be moments when, despite herself, she'd conjure him up. Their kid would eat a lizard or pretend a stick was a machine gun or get drunk at a high school party and the sperm donor would be there, a ghostly presence hovering around them. To try to get rid of him would be like trying to convice the brain that a limb has indeed been lost—a hard snap of the fingers against empty air could still send a jolt, no matter the truth and no matter how much one might will it otherwise. At such times, she must never let on to Sarah or their child what she was thinking, because that would only make the ghost more substantial. Kelly gazed over at Sarah as she scooped up a small amount of stone dust. She had been in love long enough to know that not all things needed to be shared, not all thoughts spoken aloud.

Molly Jong-Fast

Letters From a Young Fetus

May 8th 2005

Dearest soon to be mother darling,

It is your first mother's day and though you are not technically a mother yet, I know you will be brilliant at it. Ten years in the magazine business will have prepared you well for mothering. After all as a magazine editor you get to spend a lot of time with art-directors and writers. Needless to say there are a lot of similarities between writers and babies; for one thing, both of us are cute, and for another, both love mashed bananas and mushy peas, yum.

For your first (in a sense) mother's day I congratulate you on the many things you are doing well: taking prenatal vitamins, eating lots of vegetables and pound cake, and giving up diet coke. I am a little disappointed with your choice in fathers for me, but you and I and my good friend Raoul Felder will sit down and talk about that after I come into this world via c-section (please, I just can't have a mashed head. I think someone as into botox as you are can understand the importance of having a non-mashed-up face.)

Love,

Your fetus

June 5th 2005

Dearest soon-to-be-mommy,

I'm sorry I've been a bit remiss in writing. I've been really busy. I had the hiccups like seven times yesterday, and then I guess you had some Mexican food. Was that Mexican food? It seemed like you ate a monster burrito. Or was that some kind of hero sandwich from hell? Whatever it was, cut it out—I mean it. I'm so gassy and weird I don't know if I'm coming or going.

Love,

Just call me fe-tus

July 9th 2005

Yo moms,

Again I've been busy. I guess the growing is very tiring, which is ironic. Okay, maybe that's not what I mean, but the point is, enough with the Mexican food. I'm not going to say it again but salsa isn't really the food group you clearly think it is.

As for this dad thing, I must confess I had my trepidation (see my letter from May 8th), but I am pleased with the progress he is making. I was impressed when he went with you to order the David Netto furniture. I mean, $1390 for a crib is pretty excited about having a baby. And the way he sprang for the changing table ($1,395) and the dresser ($1,425)—why, that is one excited and generous daddy. We'll keep him for now.

As for your choice of apartments, I am sad to say I do not share the same enthusiasm. For one thing, I am vaguely embarrassed by your choice of a new-money condo, yeck. Also I am slightly horrified by your living all the way over by the Hudson River, grosser still. Also, let me say one last thing. The 1960's were not a time famous for their architecture (with some exceptions, like van der Rohe, obviously), and I have to wonder what kind of message you are sending me by bringing me into this world in a building that looks like the hideous stepchild of an eastern bloc communist-era bomb shelter and the modern pink granite mosque on ninety-sixth street.

A few more thoughts before I leave you—pound cake is not a meal, power bars don't make you powerful, and Tasti-Delite (even peanut butter flavored) has no nutritional value.

Love,

FEE

August 19th 2005

Yo chica,

I am so over prenatal yoga. It's just not that comfortable for me, and I know the only reason you go there is so you can hang out with Molly Shannon, which personally I think is pretty pathetic, being that Tina Fey could whip her ass any day of the week (you may be asleep while daddy watches Saturday Night Live but I am not).

Otherwise keep up the good womb-ing.

Talk next month, and please I beg of you, stay off the Mexican.

Hot diggety fee-tuss

September 4th 2005

Moms,

Sorry about the events of September 2nd and 3rd. I think you remember and don't need me to spell it out for you, but okay, basically I tried to make a break for it at 28 weeks. Did I mention I'm sorry? Maybe it was all that high priced baby furniture that freaked me out or maybe it was all the pre-natal massages, pre-natal yoga, the maternity Dianne Von Furstenberg dresses, etc. It's a lot of pressure for someone who's only 28 weeks old. How can I possibly be worth the thousands of dollars you've already spent on me? Is it possible that I have already peaked? I just can't imagine how I can't disappoint you.

I'm sorry to be so depressed. Maybe I'm on my way to a lifetime of Prozac and Woody Allen movies, but I have to ask this, How could I possibly achieve more in my life than you and dad have? You are the editor of a magazine. Dad runs a billion dollar hedge fund. What magazines could I edit that would be bigger than yours? Could I run a two billion dollar hedge fund? It just seems to me from where I swim that the only place to go is down, and that's a little worrying.

Just thinking out loud,

Your fetus

P.S. Just curious: what's my name?

October 5th 2005

And so we find ourselves at 32 weeks, I, a strapping six-pound fetus with eyes and ears and nose, and you a somewhat, well, I hate to say it, mom, but you've been porking up the last month. I know, I know I was the one who said to lay off the yoga a bit, but (and I think I mentioned this a while back) pound cake really isn't a food group.

Also, I hate to find fault with things but I hate your president. As a fetus I think I have the right to speak against him. After all, he's always speaking for me. For one thing, he's got a tiny head, like a pin-head. Why would anyone want a president with such a tiny head? And another thing: I may have complaints about your interior decoration, but that doesn't mean that I am alive. Sure I'm cool, sure I have better taste than you ever will, but quite frankly, until I have a circulatory system of my own, I find myself not to be a person. Am I crazy? Perhaps? Is this really just a manifestation of my own self-loathing and depression?

xxx fetus

November 6th 2005

And it's count-down time, babe!

I have to be honest, I'm not really looking forward to being born. Maybe I'm nuts but it just doesn't seem that great out there. First of all, I hate Asian fusion food. I don't dislike Asian food, and I don't dislike fusion, per se, but I just can't get with Asian fusion, and while we're on the topic of things I hate—I hate cilantro, the fake old phones from the pottery barn, rap music ring tones, the sounds that America Online makes, the clothing from Banana Republic, and of course lattes. I just don't understand how coffee can cost five bucks.

Tea doesn't cost five bucks! But seriously, people, I really want to get back to what I was talking about in September. I feel a bit cowed by the world I am coming into. Also I just feel like the expectations of me are far far too high.

Yes, mom, I heard you talking to the head of development at the Dalton school the other night and I have some news for you. I might not be a good test taker. I might not do well on the ERBs. I might not do well on the puzzles section. Yes, it's very possible that I won't do well on puzzles. That could sink me, no matter how much money you give to Dalton. And even if I get into Dalton, that doesn't mean that I'll get into Yale. And even if I get into Yale, which I think is pretty unlikely, what if don't get into Yale Law School? What if I only get into Harvard Law School, which is significantly less selective, and then I don't get a job at Davis Polk? What if I end up at Kramer Levin with the other losers from Harvard? And what if I don't make partner? Then what? Then do I go in-house somewhere to toil with guys from New Jersey who never slept in cribs that cost $1,300?

I know, I know, even as a lawyer I'll never be able to afford a rambling nine on Park Avenue. So what are my other options?

Father will say hedge funds. Grandpa will say something like construction, but he doesn't know that Dalton has made me too good for manual labor, or any kind of work that makes anything except art, letters, etc. which is excusable but really just for women.

Of course grandma will jump on this, as much as she can jump on anything from her seat at the bridge table at the Palm Beach country club. Grandmother will say that I should be an artist and produce art that no one will ever see; toil away in some industrial space in Brooklyn ripping things and breaking things and trying desperately to figure out what hasn't been done, because everything in art has been done a million times by people much more talented, and then, what then? In the end art often comes down to mailing lists and family money anyway. So are we really rich enough for me to become a painter anyway? Maybe you'll buy some paintings. Would you, mom?

Anyway, as you can see, I am very worried about this whole birth thing.

Love,

Doctor fetus esq.

December 6th 2005

Mom,

This is the last time I will write to you because I have a feeling I am going to be born tomorrow. I don't know why I feel that way. Maybe it's the scheduled c-section that makes me think that. Anyway, a few last thoughts before I come into this world. I know this might sound patronizing but it's not meant to be. I get a disconcerting feeling from the $750.00 stroller, from the $1,300 crib, from the baby nurse that you've already employed for the next three months, that perhaps you think this whole thing is going to be a bit like getting a King Charles cavalier spaniel.

Well baby, I ain't no spaniel, and perhaps that is the understatement of the year. For example, you can return a spaniel (yes, I know about that "incident" last year with the breeder in Connecticut) but you can't return a baby (or at least I hope you can't return a baby).

So as I leave you I remind you that you can't return a baby.

Love, fee-tus

P.S. See you soon.

Fred Leebron

Baby Girl

THE BABY WAS BORN ON A TUESDAY NIGHT AT THE END OF JULY, its mouth rimmed with a tarry green-black crust that had a sweet, pungent odor. "Now what do I do?" said the obstetrician.

"Bring her on up to Mom." The nurse stretched out her arms to receive the baby. "Cute little fella," she said. She lay the baby on the mother's chest.

Are you a boy or a girl, the mother wondered. "Hello," she said.

The baby's chest rose and fell in a rattle of inhalations. Its back left a soft green crud on the mother's breast. The nurse reached across and tapped the baby.

"Come on, baby," she said. "Breathe for your mother."

"Hi, honey," the father said. An hour before he'd taken a long look as the baby's head had begun to crown, and he'd seen the too-rich tangle of dark hair and announced she was a girl. He confirmed this as the nurse tapped the baby's chest again. He could not help but feel a little disappointed. He had wanted to name the baby after his father's father, because he did not respect his father and his father knew this, and he wanted to show his father that he loved him. He had imagined his father's teary voice on the other end of the line after he said, "It's a boy. We're naming him Jacob."

"We're going to have to take the baby," the nurse said. She pulled the baby back to her.

The father looked at the mother to see what he should do.

"Go with her," the mother said.

"I'll be right back," the father said.

"She's a little dusky," the nurse said.

He followed the nurse from the delivery room, the baby breathing a gravelly pant. They crossed an open area, to his left a bank of monitors suspended from the ceiling, men and women in scrubs standing under it, like passengers checking flight departure times.

"I could use a little help here," the nurse called.

She carried the baby into a dark room, the father close behind her.

"Could you get the light switch," she said.

In the dark the glass walls were opaque and tubes hung out of machinery. He felt frantically for a switch. When he flicked it on she lay the baby on a cold metal table. The baby rasped and wriggled. "Come on, baby," the nurse said. She tapped the baby's chest. The baby choked and coughed. She had narrow little legs and a proud yellow chest. Her face appeared blue. "Come on, baby," the nurse coaxed, reaching to her right for a forked tube, which she bit at and stuck one end of in the baby's mouth. Out a third end was a clear plastic bag. The nurse sucked, and greenish black matter began to fill the bag.

"Meconium," someone said.

A few people in scrubs had wandered in. The father knew what meconium was—in the opening of his life that was the onset of parenthood he'd heard any number of birth stories from new parents—Caesarean, vacuum, forceps—meconium wasn't a problem. During a trauma in labor, a moment he thought he could now clearly pinpoint, the baby had inhaled part of her first bowel movement. He drifted back as the medical people filled in the remaining space between him and the baby. The clear bag bloated with the meconium.

"You go on back to your wife," a man with a beard said. "We'll bring her to you."

A balloon-shaped bag hovered over the baby's mouth and the nurse drew the tube out as someone with a braceleted wrist hand-pumped air into the baby. Her chest rose and fell.

"You go on," the bearded medical person said to the father. "She'll be fine."

"He can come back in a few minutes to cut the cord," the nurse working on the baby said over her shoulder. The father looked at her. "If you want."

"Sure," he said.

She turned back to reinsert the tube into the baby's mouth.

In the cramped delivery room his wife was examining her placenta, while the obstetrician, with the assistance of another woman, stitched the episiotomy. The placenta sat in a beige plastic tub on a metal cart. Through its red bulb he could see pockets of the green-black tar.

"How is he?" the mother said.

"She's a girl," the father said.

"A girl?" the mother said. "I thought someone called her fella."

"They're working on her," he said. "She aspirated meconium." He gave an involuntary smile at the plucking of the words.

"That's what Ann and Jon's baby had," the mother said. "It took ten minutes."

"They said they'd bring her back," the father said.

"That hurts," the mother told the two women stitching her.

"Really?" the newly arrived woman said.

"Yes," the mother said.

"Where I was last," the obstetrician said, pointing at the mother's vagina, "we used to do a loop there."

The bearded man in scrubs came in and looked at the two obstetricians working, then at the wife, then at the husband.

"Your baby," he said. "They'll bring her back to you on her way to intensive care." He started to leave. "You still want to cut the cord?"

"Intensive care?" the mother said.

"Just for a little while. A couple hours, maybe a day. She should be fine."

The father squeezed the mother's hand and accompanied the man with the beard back to the glass room. The little girl lay on a white bath blanket with a tube running out her mouth, her round face yellow and her eyes open but inert. The father was given a pair of scissors and he cut the cord. The baby was screaming but she didn't seem to have any voice. He reached through the people in scrubs and touched her chest. The nurse smiled back to him. "We'll bring her in to Mom in a second."

In the delivery room his wife lay dazed and unattended on stained sheets, the placenta in its tub on the floor.

"They're bringing her back," the father said.

"I'm hungry," the mother said, her left hand still hooked to an IV. She studied the IV and he bent to look at the placenta. "You want to make the phone calls?"

He shrugged. It seemed a little soon, but he knew it would please her. "What should I say?" he said. She told him. "I'll be right back," he said.

He hurried out to the waiting area. In the new wing, uninhabited for another month, a pay phone had been planted into a wall of unpainted sheetrock. As agreed, he called her mother first, then her father, then his parents. He heard his voice say that the doctors said everything would be fine, that the baby was having difficulty breathing, that it was just meconium. The grandparents expressed elation. Plane tickets were already being bought. He saw fragments of his face in the mirrored metal of the wall unit. He nodded at himself as he listened to the sugary voices. An inexplicable hatred for all the grandparents came to him and settled in him. "Way to go, tiger," his father said.

Twenty minutes had passed. His wife still lay in bed. "Did they bring her by?" he asked.

"Not yet. Were the phone calls all right?"

"I'll go check on the baby," he said.

Out the other door, through the way station filled with medical staff halfheartedly eyeing the monitors, he found the glassed-in triage room empty. He turned to interrupt one of the staff. She looked at him indifferently.

"The baby who was in there." He pointed at the lit windows.

She shrugged. "There's a clerk out by the waiting area who can help you."

He exited yet another door and followed a bright hallway to where he recalled the intensive care nursery being, from the expectant parents' tour the month before. He stood in a narrow antechamber as a new group of medical personnel maneuvered around a warming bed that he surmised held his child. A woman saw him and touched the crossed heavy arms of a large man with a silver beard and a yellow gauze gown.

"The father's here," she said, loud enough for the father to hear.

The man looked up and smiled at the father. "Come on in," he said. "Put on a gown."

The father pulled a disposable yellow gown from a wall dispenser and thrust it on. A sign said to wash his hands for one whole minute, and he made himself do this as well. He stepped into the nursery and stood by the doctor in the matching gown.

"You have a very sick baby," the doctor said.

The father nodded. Through the tangle of tubes and arms he caught sight of her. Machinery gonged and beeped above her, and her mouth was pried open by a blue respirator tube. Her arms lay loose at her sides and her eyes were glazed under heavy lids. A white tube sprang from her umbilicus. She had IV's attached to a hand and a foot. From her forehead a toy-sized syringe projected. A diaper lay open under her bottom, making way for a catheter that fed a tiny plastic bag.

"At this point, we're just trying to stabilize her," the doctor said. "Why don't you come back in an hour or so with your wife. I'm sure she'd like to see the baby."

"What happened?" the father said.

The doctor recrossed his arms and leaned against a sink. "She inhaled too much meconium and it's settled so deeply in her lungs she can't process oxygen and we can't suction it out. It's a situation that will have to resolve itself."

"What are you saying?" the father said.

The doctor sighed and scowled and smiled. "We'll have to wait and see," he said. "Like I said, you have a very sick baby."

The father looked past the medical people at his little girl. He was reluctant to leave her to them, but he had to tell his wife. What would he tell her? He glanced sideways at the doctor in his yellow gown, the thick arms folded on the shelf of his belly. A woman in blue demanded, "What's her pH," and glared at a guy in green scrubs while he fumbled for an answer. The baby quivered under a bright yellow light aimed at her belly. The father wished he could close the diaper for her. He counted five people around the baby, plus the doctor. He wondered if the baby was warm enough. Labor had lasted nineteen hours and he was cold and knew he should be hungry, but he had no appetite. He followed the hallway back toward his wife's room, half expecting to find her gone.

She sat in bed, eating meatloaf from a styrofoam plate. She looked up at him; she was making herself eat. The sheet under her was a dark circle of blood.

"She's in the ICN," he tried to say evenly. "The doctor said we have a very sick baby."

She put her hand to her mouth and made herself swallow the food in it. She shut her eyes, nodded, and opened them. She pointed to a red carton of juice on her tray.

"I saved this for you," she said. "Is she going to die?"

"I don't know," he said.

"Did you ask?"

"He said we have a very sick baby." He took up the carton and forced it open, took a sip of the juice.

"I need to pee," she said.

He came around the other side of the bed, to where the IV hung from a metal pole. She held on to him and he pulled the pole along on its wheeled stand as they made the difficult walk across the room to the bathroom. She sat gingerly on the seat and looked up at him. Small blood vessels had popped under her eyes from the pressure of pushing the baby out.

"I can't," she said.

"Try," he said.

She remained on the toilet

"Should I close the door?" he said. She shook her head. The faintest line of water sounded from the bowl beneath her. Her face flushed. He touched her hand, careful not to disturb the IV. After the sound ceased she wiped herself and he helped her from the seat. There was blood in the bowl and blood on the back of her gown and blood dripped in drops onto the bathroom floor.

"I'd like to put on some underwear," she said.

He nodded and went to the packed bag with the teddy bear and the new nightgown that opened down the front so that she could breastfeed, and he found a pair of fresh underwear while she leaned against the bathroom doorframe.

She looked at the small, white underwear. "I guess not," she said.

He helped her back to the bed and she leaned carefully against it and eased herself onto the dark stain of blood that marked where she should sit.

"Could you get me a cup of ice?"

He'd been getting cups of ice all day. In the waiting area, a pregnant woman sat on a wooden chair waiting to be admitted. She clutched a string of beads—a rosary, he guessed—and muttered words, her eyes shut. The ice machine was clogged with ice that had partially melted and then refrozen again, and he took a metal fork and poked at its mouth and gouged and slashed until the ice fell free. He held a cup to it, pressed the button, and ice overflowed onto the floor. The hallway was empty. He took the full cup and stepped over the tricky cubes of ice back down the hall.

She was not in the delivery room. A wheelchair which had sat waiting in a corner was gone. He hurried out the corridor to the ICN. As he approached he could see the back of her in the chair wheeled up close to the warming bed. Her cotton gown fell slightly open at the back, her pale skin cold in the bright light of the nursery. The yellow gauze of the required gown was looped around her neck. The nurse who'd brought her down stood waiting to take her back. He came right up beside his wife, not bothering with the gown or a hand wash, and the nurse retreated. His wife moved her left hand, the one with the IV still in it, up and across her chest until it rested on his hand as it curled around the top of the wheelchair. The baby lay just out of reach on the warming bed with her diaper thrown open, her eyes nearly shut, her face puffed and swollen, and stale pinpricks of blood flecked on her skin where the tubes and lines had been inserted. Someone from x-ray was due to take a picture of her lungs and the second blood gases were expected in ten minutes.

"You should get some rest," the doctor said to the mother.

"Yes," the mother said. She bent her head and looked at her lap, at the crusty nearly transparent hospital gown under the sterilized gauze of the ICN gown, then looked up at the baby again. White adhesive strips were taped tightly around her mouth to keep the respirator tube in place. "Could she die?" the mother said.

"What?" the doctor said. The father thought he could sense the various men and women around the bed pause in their ministrations, listening with a defensive professional instinct.

"I said, 'Could she die?'" the mother said.

The doctor readjusted himself against the sink, his folded arms resting in a fresh position on his belly. "Yes," he said.

They made the phone call to her mother at one-thirty her time. The husband made it because the wife was afraid she wouldn't be able to say what needed to be said. She was now free of her IV and she sat in the wheelchair by him in the starkly lit unpainted new wing while he punched in all the numbers and the phone rang twice and then the tired voice came on the line. He carefully explained to her mother all that he knew and when she interrupted to ask if the baby could die, he gave the same simple one-word answer the doctor had given and she let out a sharp intake of breath as if she'd been struck and her voice for the next few seconds was only a whimper. He waited a moment and then told her why they needed her help and what perhaps she could do for them and through the phone line he could feel her nodding yes, yes. She would make phone calls to her colleagues in the pharmaceutical industry, wake people, to find out possible prognoses and treatments. She referred to the baby as "our baby" and he was nervous. She took notes, posed pointed questions, and hung up without remembering to ask to speak to her daughter.

"She'll call around," he said to his wife.

They took the elevator to the fifth floor, where from their Lamaze classes they knew was an alcove of vending machines situated outside a short cafeteria. A janitor stood at the other end, working a mop and bucket, carefully ignoring them. They bought shrinkwrapped food—a burrito for him that he had to microwave, a ham and cheese sandwich for her—and took it to a large empty waiting room that serviced the geriatrics unit. They sat side by side against a long wall and ate. There was a television which the husband wanted to turn on to get some noise in the room. There was a pile of magazines and an empty flower pot.

"We should get back," she said. She stood up and threw away the remainder of her sandwich. He helped her from the room, holding her elbow gently. The elevator was waiting for them.

Outside the ICN they washed and gowned themselves, only to be told by a nurse that it was change of shift and they'd have to come back after midnight. They could barely see the baby on her warming bed, her head resting to one side, the wide white adhesive tape obscuring most of her face.

His wife now had a bed on the maternity ward, across the hall from labor and delivery. It was a three-bed room, the beds planted at crazy angles to one another to accommodate the dividing curtains. He set up his wife with a sitz bath in the narrow bathroom. Through the curtains he could hear a nurse scolding one of the new mothers. "You have to change him," she said. "It's your responsibility." The walls of the bathroom were green and when the door opened and his wife came out from her sitz bath and maneuvered herself into bed, her section of the room was washed with a greenish light. He tucked her in and asked if she wanted her teddy bear. She shook her head no.

He was not allowed to stay in any of the parents' rooms because they had all been previously booked, and he was not allowed to stay in his wife's room. He found a small waiting room across from the nurses' station and covered himself with a lap blanket from his wife's bag. The room was airless and dark and cold, and he did not think he could sleep.

He woke to the feeling of someone covering him with the blanket.

"Is that you?" he said. "What time is it?"

"A quarter to four."

He made himself get up into the cold room. He walked out into the hallway with her. There were still skins of little puddles where he'd dropped the ice. As they hurried along the corridor to the ICN he asked her if she'd heard anything. "Nothing," she said.

Their baby's side of the nursery was well-lit. In an enclosed room off to the right a woman in blue scrubs bent over a spiral notebook with a four-color pen. She looked up, nodded at the parents, and scrawled on a ruled line. They washed their hands for one minute and pulled on the sterile yellow gowns. He put his arm around her shoulder and they walked out to the baby. They stood by the side of the bed. Her belly was puffed up and her chest fluttered in regular wingbeats as the respirator fed her air. A dark ring of crusted blood had formed around the white tube at her umbilicus. Her cheeks pursed against the white adhesive tape and dried perspiration left a film around her eyes and on her forehead. At two of the IV insertions, one at the foot and one on the hand, little bulbs of orange light had been attached in an almost ornamental fashion.

"You can touch her," someone said behind them. "And talk to her, too. She'll recognize your voices."

It was the doctor, leaning against his sink.

The mother reached out and stroked an unmarred length of the baby's arm. When she was finished, the father felt along the soft skin, patches flaking with a layer of birth fluid.

"You're the only ones who touch her and won't hurt her," the doctor said. "Whenever one of us touches her," he smiled apologetically, "it's to start an IV or suction the breathing tube."

The mother bent down to the baby. "Hi, sweetie," she said.

"How is she doing," the father said.

"The pictures were not good." The doctor looked at both of them as the mother turned from the baby. "But she's shown great resiliency. Her heart is normal. She's urinating, which means her kidneys are in order." He pointed at the respirator settings. "You can see for yourself she needs a hundred percent oxygen, eighty breaths a minute. She's not processing it that well. We'll have to wait and see."

"She's not stable?" the mother said.

"She's critical," the doctor said.

"How many cases of this do you see a year?" the father said.

The doctor shrugged. "Three. Maybe four."

"What happens next?" the mother said.

"We'll have to see."

The father touched his daughter's arm, gently scraped away some of the flaking. An alarm gonged. The father was horrified. The woman in blue scrubs came out from her office and shut the sound off, looked around at the father and the mother and the doctor. "I don't think you should touch the baby," she said.

"They can touch the baby," the doctor said.

She pulled up a high, cushioned chair on wheels and sat next to the bed with her notebook.

"Where were we?" the doctor said.

The father was torn between wanting to be with the baby as closely as he could, to let her know he was there, and wanting to listen to the doctor. The mother lay a pinky in the baby's hand and the baby squeezed it, her face grimacing around the white tape. Another alarm beeped. The woman rose from her chair, sighed, and clicked it off.

"Do you have any family here?" the doctor said to the parents.

"No," the mother said. "They're all on the east coast."

"They'll be coming out," the father added quickly.

"Good," the doctor said. He started to leave, then tapped the white index card on the side of the warming bed that said BABY GIRL KEENAN. "Let us know when you name her," he said.

When he was gone the woman in scrubs looked up from her book. "I didn't mean to be rude," she said. "It's just better for the baby if she rests as quietly as possible." She got up and retreated to the little office behind the glass windows.

They stood by the baby. In the mother's bag in her room was a list of a half dozen boys' and girls' names, but they had virtually agreed on which two it would be—Jacob, for the boy, Emery for the girl, after the mother's grandfather. The girl lay there in sleep with her knees at a slightly jaunty angle, as if perhaps she could push herself up and run off. The father didn't want to name her just yet. To name her would be to somehow condemn her. He felt superstitious, just as he'd been about calling the grandparents. He felt it was better to wait until everything was in the state it ought to be. He could feel the pressure of his wife beside him, wanting to name her, wanting to welcome her into the world, wanting to say you are one of us and you have a name. He didn't want a particular name attached to this moment in her life, fixing her in it. He wanted to wait. He needed to wait. Didn't he have any faith in her? He touched her wrist. "We name you Emery Keenan Brooks," he said.

In the late morning they had a long meeting with a second doctor assigned to the ICN. He was younger than the first, in his late thirties or early forties, with thin black hair and hornrimmed glasses, and he assured the mother and the father that the situation was not so bleak. "She's not on pavulon, for one thing," he pointed out. "And we haven't had to hook her up to dopamine yet. Beyond that, there's always the lung bypass machine. Am I going too fast?"

The father and mother shook their heads. The doctor had already sketched a diagram showing how the lungs refused to process oxygen and how the baby had reverted to a type of breathing that she'd been doing in the womb—persistent fetal circulation. Very rare, and in the first four days of life, "very difficult," the doctor said. And the father had spent a half hour on the phone with a doctor at his mother-in-law's pharmaceutical firm, a man who had been woken up at two in the morning and sounded as if he lived for that kind of phone call and had spent the next nine hours reading up on the baby's illness and consulting colleagues in and out of the firm. "The doctor on your case," the pharmaceutical doctor had said, "is a top guy." Now the father would have to ask about this new doctor.

A woman popped her head into the doorway. "When you're done with these two," she said with a Caribbean accent, pointing at the mother and father, "I need to talk to them. I'll be in my office. See you guys soon."

"The social worker," the doctor explained. He continued with a discussion of the lung bypass machine, that this particular hospital didn't have one and the baby would have to be transported across town to the university hospital. "ECMO," the doctor called it. "It's like a spaceship. It's the latest thing." He waved his hand. "Anyway, it has its risks. We don't need to talk about it quite yet."

The father rose from his chair. He liked being in the room listening to the doctor, listening to all the possibilities that existed, how *possible* they all seemed. He liked the closed, sealed feeling of the office with its certificates and family pictures. He liked the doctor. The mother got up, still moving with fatigue and pain. They thanked the doctor and crossed the hall to the social worker's office. It was smaller and no framed diplomas hung on the wall.

"How you guys doing?" the social worker said. She gestured them into hard plastic chairs.

"Fine," the mother said.

"I have a few things I want to go over with you." She reached across the desk and handed both the parents her business card. She told them about pumping breast milk and bringing it into the ICN to store for when the baby was ready to eat. She told them about the rules for booking the parents' rooms, how they were only for parents of babies awaiting discharge, so they could become accustomed to nighttime changing and feeding. It was best to sleep at home until that time, the social worker said. "Although you're welcome at any time to visit her," she said. "She's a cute baby." She fetched them sealed bottles of sterile water to empty and store the breast milk in, and she called and reserved an electric breast pump for them and doublechecked to make sure their insurance covered the cost. "Is there anything else I can do for you?" she said.

"I don't think so," the father said.

"I'm here Monday through Friday, eight-thirty to five." She stood up and shook both their hands. "You just come in if you want to talk." She pointed at her card that the father held in his palm. "I have voice mail, too."

"Great," the mother said.

On the wall outside the social worker's office was a large corkboard filled with pictures of ICN parents departing with their babies, with birth dates and birth weights and discharge dates written in ink below each photo. The parents paused to study it, looking for a baby like their baby, but all of the babies had been preemies.

Back on the maternity ward the mother climbed tiredly into her bed, her face pale. It was almost noon. Curtains around the beds were all drawn, and they could hear the cooing and gurgling sounds of mothers with their babies.

"Hey there!" a man's voice announced. "Can I come in?"

"What is it?" the father said.

A white-haired man in a red volunteer's blazer parted the curtain. "I'm here to help you fill out the necessaries on your child's birth certificate."

The father's stomach cinched and he looked stricken.

"What is it?" the mother said.

"Nothing," he said.

"What's the child's name?" the volunteer said, his pen poised over a clipboard.

The mother looked at the father and when it was clear to her that he didn't want to say it, she asked, "Do we have to do this now?"

"I only come around once a day," the volunteer said.

"Emery Keenan Brooks," the father said.

"Could you spell it?" the volunteer said.

The father spelled it.

"That's it." The volunteer looked at his clipboard. "I have everything else. The certificate will be available for you to pick up at the records office downtown in three weeks. But you have to pick it up. It won't come to you. And it costs ten bucks."

"Right," the father said.

The volunteer headed on to the next mother.

"You ought to get some sleep," the father said.

The mother lay against the hospital mattress, its slightly scooped angle.

"I'm checking out today," she said. "They wanted to keep me another day but I told them no."

"Good," the father said.

Tears ran from the corners of her eyes down the sides of her face. She shut her eyes and her face trembled.

"I guess I'm really tired," she said.

He climbed in beside her. Her back was to him and he reached around and held her and she shook. She was very quiet. He could feel the curtains of their third of the room close around them. He wanted to whisper that it was going to be all right. He said, "We're going to be all right." His wife continued crying in that silent way. Every few moments he'd pull himself up and see the tears streaming down the exposed side of her face. They'd known each other seven years, they'd been married three years. His father had almost died, had lain in a strange hospital in a strange city for three months after a complicated open heart surgery. The baby herself had had trouble very early, in the fourth or fifth week of pregnancy, and a doctor had announced that they were going to lose her then. There'd been pre-term labor in early June that confined the wife to bedrest for a month. Past the middle of her labor, late yesterday afternoon, the mother had requested something for pain and the anesthesiologist had injected so much epidural anesthesia into her spine that she was numb from the neck down and her blood pressure had dropped to seventy-two over forty and the baby's heartbeat had decelerated so precipitously it appeared almost to have stopped. Doctors and nurses had burst into the delivery room, a rush and swirl of activity that the husband had been both sucked into and pushed out from, as he felt his wife's life and the baby's life and even his own life pulled from him, and they'd injected the wife with Adrenalin, and attached a fetal heart monitor to the baby's scalp. Five minutes later they declared that everything was fine, and that she could proceed with a vaginal delivery. And now here they were. Soon the wife would finish crying and the husband would rise from the bed and hug her and go out the door and down the corridor to the elevator, which he'd take to the lobby, where outside he'd catch a taxi almost precisely 24 hours from when the taxi had dropped them off at the hospital. At home he would arrange for a rental car; perhaps a phone call or two would trap him; though he would try not to answer but, of course, he would *have* to answer. He'd pick up the rental car downtown, pick up the electric breast pump, and return to the hospital for his wife. They'd spend that night at home, and every night at home, curled up in bed by the telephone, spent from the days of back-and-forthing to the hospital and pumping milk and sterilizing equipment every three hours and waking in the middle of the night to pump some more and sterilize and call the hospital, until one

night the phone would ring, or perhaps they'd even be there at the
hospital, and an ultimate shift would occur that would change
their lives forever. One day their baby would breathe air again.
Though lying in bed with his wife now, waiting for this sequence
to unravel, he knew they were already changed. He held his wife
tightly, as she cried herself out, and he was astonished at how
much they could hold between them, and how hard it could be to
name.

Steve Almond

Shotgun Wedding

CARRIE HAD NEVER SEEN DR. JOEL OLEFEEDER BEFORE, BUT HE was the only one available under her medical plan—the old HMO clusterfuck—so here she was. She sat in his waiting room, reading a *Time* from three years ago. Racism was out of control. Civil war was savaging the Balkans. Hollywood was auto-cannibalizing. *Time* made it all seem delightful.

Dr. Olefeeder's nurse, Delores, had attended the same high school as Carrie. She too had been one of the fat girls who stood by, year after year, and watched the others dance. Now they pretended they didn't know each other.

"You can go on back to room seven, Miss Stoops," Delores said. She wore a wedding ring but was still a tubbo.

Carrie, through a glum devotion to celery in its many enticing forms (stalk, juice, pudding) had entered the land of the slim five years ago. She was sure this was why she always felt a little cold— lack of adipose. She shivered as she undressed and slipped into her hospital gown. Delores came in to take her temperature and check her blood pressure. She wanted to say something to Delores, something like: *I'm sorry you're still so fat. Being skinny isn't really so much better in the end. No, I'm not just saying that.*

But Delores wouldn't even look at her.

She left finally and Carrie passed the time browsing medical supplies. Tongue depressors. Disposable thermometers. A jar of K-Y Jelly the size of a newborn. She plucked a pair of latex gloves from a box on the counter and touched at her face absently. The gloves were coated in a chalky film—reptilian. Was this what it would feel like to be a snake handler? But snakes weren't really chalky, were they?

Behind her, Doctor Olefeeder cleared his throat.

"Sorry," Carrie said. She pulled off the gloves. "Just testing for quality."

The doctor smiled quizzically. He was a large man with a swirl of hair that sat on the crown of his head like a danish. His ears were red and damp, as if they had just been defrosted. "What can we do for you today, Miss Stoops?"

"I'm having some pain in my abdomen," Carrie said.

"The abdomen!" Olefeeder said brightly. "Yes!" He gestured for her to lie down on the exam table and raised her gown and set his hands, both his hands, on her belly. Carrie braced for the inevitable prodding. But Olefeeder's touch was surprisingly light. His fingers danced over her skin and he closed his eyes and let his head loll from side to side. He looked like a blind piano player.

"Could it be my appendix?" Carrie said. "I was worried, you know, because if you wait too long—" She made a small explosion noise.

Olefeeder's great body tensed. His fingers fell still. Then he began, again, a delicate glissando of touches from her belly button to the sensitive flesh at the top of her thigh.

Carrie didn't know what to do. Olefeeder wasn't hurting her, exactly. This was more in the nature of a caress. It felt . . . nice. Carrie had always suspected that blind men would be good in bed. She began to envision a scene in which she was assigned the task of leading Ray Charles to his private room, which included a jacuzzi, a heart-shaped jacuzzi. This was after a concert or something. Ray was in a thin silk robe and he asked her, in that gentle husky voice of his, would she help him find the top step and shed his robe right there and set his hand on her arm, his gentle, gentle, hand. And just at this moment—as Carrie gazed at his physique, the old braided muscles and smooth dangling sex, as she prepared to shed her gown and join Ray in this exciting new world of aqua-erotic tactile exploration—just at this moment, Olefeeder removed his hands and lowered her gown.

Carrie let out a little moan of disappointment, which she then tried to camouflage, absurdly, by pretending to sneeze.

"When was the last time you had sexual intercourse?" Olefeeder asked.

"*Intercourse?* I'm not sure I understand. Is there something wrong?"

"Not at all!" Olefeeder smiled broadly. His teeth were the color of newsprint.

Carrie winced her little wince of mortification. "A month ago," she said. "Six weeks, maybe." An image of Brian's torso flashed above her, narrow and thickly sprigged with black hairs; his lips peeled back to reveal pale gums. This was his *I'm coming* face. The expression always reminded Carrie of the novel *Jaws*, in which a woman describes her lover as looking like a shark. The association struck her as somewhat pathetic.

"What sort of birth control did you use?" Olefeeder said.

"My fiancé uses condoms, the kind with spermicide." Carrie had gone off the pill last year, after Brian moved to Milwaukee. The idea—as she had presented it to him—was to minimize side effects. But she had done this mainly to punish him for leaving. His response had been mordant whimsy. ("I suppose this means an end to the days of wine and douches?") That was Brian all over: good-humored to the point of exhaustion.

"Well," Olefeeder said. "My diagnosis is: you're pregnant."

"*Pregnant?*"

"Pregnant!" Olefeeder said the word as if he had just hit a bingo.

"No. I'm sorry. That's impossible. I haven't seen Brian in more than a month. I got my period after he left."

"I wouldn't know anything about that," Olefeeder said cheerfully.

Carrie shook her head again. "I don't mean to question your expertise, or whatnot. But, I mean, what are you basing this on?"

"I see your point." Olefeeder nodded vigorously. He turned to the drawer behind him and removed a needle and a small vial.

"You're not considering taking my blood."

"That's really the only way to know for sure."

"Wait a second. I don't think we're communicating." Carrie had now begun speaking extremely slowly. "I came in here with a sharp pain in my stomach, on the right side of my abdomen. Somehow, that's led you to conclude that I'm pregnant. But as I've explained, that's just not possible."

Olefeeder tapped the chart with his pen. He looked a little wounded. "Very well then," he said softly. "You may put your clothes on."

On her way out of the office, Carrie spotted Delores leaning over the copier. It was now obvious why she looked so slag-bellied—she was pregnant.

"The whole thing was just totally crazy," Carrie said. She was on the phone with her friend Maggie.

"What was crazy?"

"This doctor. You'll never guess what he told me. Are you ready for this: he thinks I'm pregnant."

"That's so *weird*," Maggie said. "I thought there was something different about you. Like this glow."

"I'm not pregnant, Mag."

"I thought you said—"

"I said he *thought* I was pregnant. He thought that. But I'm not. It's been, like, two months since I had sex."

"I thought Brian visited last month."

"Early last month. And I'm sure I got my period after he left. I remember, because it was that same weekend we went to Scottsdale."

"When did we go to Scottsdale?" Carrie could hear the *bolt-bolt-bolt* of Mag's sewing machine. She was a set designer who seemed to do most of her work while on the phone. Once, in a last-minute whirl to prepare for La Traviata, Mag had sewed the phone cord into one of her scrims.

"This guy isn't even a gynecologist. He's just one of those, whatever they're called, general doctors."

"Did he give you a test?"

"He didn't even do an exam. That's what I'm telling you."

"Are you going to get one?" Maggie said. "If my doctor thought I was packing fetus, I'd get a test."

"That's absurd," Carrie said. "I don't have a single symptom."

"Are you going to tell Brian?"

"Why should I tell him? There's nothing *to* tell him. That some quack believes I'm knocked up based on my having a stomach ache. This is exactly what I'm talking about. Just because he's a doctor and a man you immediately believe him. When I'm the one, it's my body, and goddamn Brian, he probably wouldn't even—"

"Why are you screaming?" Maggie said. She had stopped sewing.

Carrie took a breath and something in her throat caught.

"Are you okay?"

"PMS," she said quietly. "Goddamn PMSing."

All the next day, Carrie was hounded by babies. Precious little airbrushed babies gazed down from billboards. Real-life babies with faces like plum tomatoes wailed next to her at traffic lights. Babies on the TV at work sat in the middle of radial tires, burbling in a manner meant to suggest all-weather traction. At the bank, she got in line behind a woman who was dressed in a snappy pantsuit. Incongruously, she had a baby flung over her shoulder. The infant, dressed in a canary onesie, slept peacefully. And then, right in front of Carrie, the child opened its mouth and released a gout of cloudy liquid, most of which landed on his mother's sleeve.

"Oh! Diego!" The woman set the kid in his stroller and examined her sleeve. "Wouldn't you know it? The one time I leave the diaper bag in the car!" The woman gestured at the baby, then, as if by some previous arrangement, at Carrie. "I'll just be a minute!" A rancid odor rose from the boy's pale scalp. His eyelids were threaded with tiny pink veins. Diego? There was nothing to suggest even a trace of Latin blood. His mother—she was now, for some reason, haranguing the branch manager—looked Jewish.

Brian was half-Jewish. "The lower half," he liked to joke. He had an endearing way with his insecurity, but there was something deeply clannish in his mindset. It seemed to Carrie that she was always being kept just beyond range by his ambitions. He could be terrifically persuasive and passionate, even charming when the occasion demanded. But the word that lept to mind when Carrie thought about him was *overdetermined*. His marriage proposal had sounded like an arbitration ruling.

Diego's mother (*Mrs. Diego?*) now returned and lifted her child from the stroller. "Thank you so much," she told Carrie. "You're a gem. Something must have disagreed with his little tummy. Is that right? Did something disagree with your little tummy?"

The child, Diego, spat up again.

Carrie's boss Neil was pacing. This was fine. Neil paced a lot. He was an edgy man. He *needed* to pace. The problem was that he was pacing in Carrie's office.

"Haven't we talked about this?" Carrie said.

"Talked about what?"

Carrie walked to her desk and picked up the brass nameplate. "It's really better that you don't come into my office unless I'm here, Neil. Unless you're invited."

"Yeah—"

"See, when you come into my office and I'm not here I get worried that you might be checking through my drawers, trying to find my Big Pink Work Vibrator with the special Rotating Clitoral Cuff."

"I don't know anything about that," Neil said.

Carrie made it a point to mention sex toys, because she knew this would put Neil on the defensive. This was where you wanted a boss like Neil, whose loneliness bled into his duties and made him tenacious in unreliable ways. He had confessed to Carrie, during last year's Christmas party, that he feared he would never find a woman who could love the real him. This seemed a reasonable concern. And yet, it infuriated Carrie that he had singled her out for this declaration, as if they now shared the burden.

"I just wanted to know if you'd looked over the memo," Neil said.

"The memo?"

"The new maternity leave policy memo."

"As a matter of fact I haven't."

"Did you check your e-mail? It's been in your e-mail since Friday."

Carrie sat down at her desk and picked up her framed photo of Brian dressed as an elf and considered hurling it at Neil's head. "Why are you bringing this up now?"

"You're the one who brought it up," Neil said. "*You* brought it up. Last year. Remember? You said any civilized office should have a policy. That was the language you used, if I recall. I thought this would make you happy, Carrie."

Neil was pivoting into his self-pity offensive.

"I'll take a look at it," Carrie said. She began inspecting her mail.

Neil cleared his throat. "While I'm here," he said, "could we discuss the new account?"

"The consulting group?"

"No. The moisturizer."

"The moisturizer."

"Babyface."

"Babyface?"

"Right."

Carrie's stomach ache was gone, but it had been replaced by waves of nausea, one of which now rose saltily into her mouth.

"What?" Neil frowned and his chin pitted up. "You don't like the name?"

"The name's fine."

"Is something wrong? You look green, sort of."

"I'm fine, Neil. Just give me a minute."

Carrie spent half an hour bent over the toilet bowl, waiting to throw up. Was this a flu? Something acquired from little Diego? But she didn't feel achy. Or hot. The only symptom was this queasiness, along with a certain amorphous heaviness in her limbs. On the way home, she stopped off at Eckerd's and bought a home pregnancy test.

The nausea kept her from eating much at work. But now, at home, having gnawed through a plate of rice cakes and carrot sticks, she began fantasizing about a Philly cheesesteak. In high school, she had gorged herself on cheesesteaks. She and her boyfriend Tony Ducati would cut seventh period and head over to the Black Spot. The place was full of longshoreman, burly guys who smelled of Old Spice and low tide. There were no tables. Everyone stood at the counter, shoulder to shoulder.

You always hoped Vic was working (as opposed to Constantine) because he used three steaks per order, peeling the paper-thin filets from an overhead freezer and flipping them across the grill like playing cards. The steaks took only a minute to brown. Vic would parse off a spatula's worth of onions and peppers from the heap at the center of the grill and slather them across the steaks. Next came the cheese, three squares of white cheddar laid, always, corner-to-corner atop the onions, like yield signs. The cheese began to melt almost immediately, to bubble and curl, and Vic delivered four or five quick strokes with the edge of the spatula, then layered the jumble onto a long roll from the Portuguese bakery next door. Carrie could still taste those rolls, gummy with juices from the seared meat and the sharp cheddar and the sweet caramelized onions.

Those sandwiches had been her first idea of physical passion, the drip and warp of love, its redolent flagrancy. She could taste the cheesesteaks on Tony Ducati, on herself, on their joined breath as they bounced on the blue sofa in the basement of the apartment house where his mom ran a laundry service.

Her own mother despised the very idea of a Philly cheesesteak. And she always knew when Carrie had indulged herself, always, no matter how many capfuls of Scope her daughter gurgled. She could scent a cheesesteak at 20 paces.

Grease—and all that grease implied—was now the enemy. Carrie had to remind herself. There was such a thing as self-control. She marched to the kitchen and popped a V-8. The drink tasted like chilled blood.

Carrie switched on her laptop and checked her e-mail. She read over Neil's maternity leave memo, which was dreary and predictable until the last paragraph, which read: "In conclusion, I would like to cite Miss Carrie Stoops, senior account executive, for initially suggesting and vigorously advocating this policy."

The memo was cc'ed to the entire division.

The next seventeen messages were from colleagues. The subject line of the first read: *Knocked Up???*

So now she would have to race over to Neil's pathetic little duplex and drive a stake through his heart. And then, of course, there would be an inquest, and they'd dust the stake for fingerprints, meaning Carrie would have to wear gloves and, perhaps, a blond wig. And where was she supposed to get a stake from, anyway? Who sold stakes anymore?

But even if she killed Neil, the questions would continue: Were she and Brian finally going to tie the knot? Had she given any thought to a midwife? And now Carrie remembered the pregnancy test, which sat on the kitchen table in its plastic bag with the receipt still inside. No. Perhaps she should kill Neil first. Murder then pregnancy test? Pregnancy test then murder? Where was Miss Manners when you really needed her?

Carrie pulled a manila folder from her briefcase. Inside was the proposed photo for the Babyface Moisturizer ad: a toothless infant seated against a blue velvet background, pouring a bottle of Babyface onto its head. The child looked ecstatic. Carrie had never seen a happier child. She suspected it had been given drugs.

On a yellow pad, she doodled possible slogans:

You're never too young to fight wrinkles!

Recommended by four out of five infants!

How come my head feels like a porn star's?

Help! My mother is taking 70 percent of my gross earnings!

In years to come, when I have grown ugly and desperate and lonely, I will gaze at this photo and want to kill myself!

It was now time for Carrie to have some wine.

When she woke, the apartment was dark. That was the problem with wine—it put her out. Brian used to complain, early on, when he was famished for her body all the time, though later he came to see this, the strategic glass of wine, as a useful ally in the management of what came to be described as her *moods*. But before that, no, she wasn't allowed to drink on visiting days, which was what Brian called their overnights.

Carrie was still in her work clothes. This was no way to feel: wrinkled and gross, with a head full of mud. She needed a shower and stripped off her clothes and let the hot water jazz her boobs and soaped herself down below with the gentle, all-natural soap that never stung. Quietly, happily, she leaned against the tile. She imagined Tony Ducati begging her to open her legs, a little wider, just a little wider. His eyes were closed and his shiny brow was quivering.

That's how happy Tony Ducati was. For the sake of posterity, Carrie had granted him long sideburns and cleaned up his skin a little.

"Just a little wider," he murmured.

But there was a strange and familiar ring to this phrase. And suddenly Carrie realized why: during her nap, she had dreamed of giving birth. She lay on some kind of padded rack in her office. Brian stood to one side in a labcoat. He was explaining something: the child was stuck. They were going to have to call in a specialist. A specialist in stuck babies. Dr. Olefeeder bustled in, damp and joyful. He bent to examine the situation and pulled on a pair of latex gloves, the cuffs of which snapped against his wrists. Then he set to work, twisting the baby round and round, like a cork. There was a loud and embarrassing pop as the child finally broke free. "A girl," Brian said. "A little baby girl." He handed her to Carrie. But what was this? Her daughter was covered in some kind of thick white emollient, almost like . . . exactly like . . . Babyface.

Carrie shut the water off. This was just the kind of crap she had come to expect from her subconscious. A truly disappointing subconscious. Ham-handed and prosaic. *This is your brain. This is your brain on advertising.*

She and Brian had discussed having kids. They had. But not for quite some time. Carrie recalled one conversation that took place a few months after they got together. They had both called in sick. She'd been a little frightened to make love during the day, with all the sun that poured across Brian's mattress. But the experience had been breathtaking. Her own body, his body, the happy desperation of their hands.

"Maybe we should have used protection," Brian said.

"I thought you were going to put something on."

"I was, before you scissor clamped me."

Carrie giggled. "Liar."

"I've got bruises!"

She was close to her period, pretty close, and anyway she liked this guy, really liked him. She straddled him and ran her fingers through the hair on his chest and yanked the pale skin beneath. "You're in big trouble if you knock me up."

"Why?"

Carrie slumped back onto his belly and considered this question. "I guess it might be kind of cool to have a kid."

"As long as it gets your eyes." Brian fluttered his lashes. "Seriously, we could make a beautiful kid."

Carrie felt swimmingly alive. She reached behind her and massaged his crotch. "I hope it gets your cock."

"I hope it gets your tits." Brian reached up and cupped her.

"We could sell it to the circus."

"And use the money to move to France."

"No, Italy."

"Mmmmm, I'm hungry."

There were other discussions. But these had been grim and cautious, more in the spirit of negotiations. The idea of children had been subsumed into the larger looming ideas of cohabitation and marriage. These, in turn, had been weighed against issues like career advancement and logistics. Brian didn't avoid these matters. He was too clever for that. Instead, he slowly bled them of passion.

Now he was in Milwaukee, heading his own agency. ("This is something for us," he'd told her. "For our future.")

Carrie sat in her dark apartment and gritted her teeth. Her tits were sore. She wanted a Philly cheesesteak.

The phone rang eleven times before Brian answered.

"Hey," she said.

"What time is it? For Chrissake, it's 2 A.M."

"Funny. It's only midnight here."

"Have you been drinking?"

"Yeah," Carrie said. "I just drank an ass pocket full of whisky. I'm an alcoholic now, Brian. You're engaged to an alcoholic."

"Should I guess as to the purpose of this call?"

"Aren't you going to tell me you have a presentation tomorrow? I just love it when you talk about your *big, hard* presentations. It makes me *hot*."

Brian whistled in a manner intended to suggest his bottomless patience. "I take it then, that Ms. Grumpy has arrived." This is what he called her period.

"As a matter of fact, no, she hasn't." Carrie glanced around the room, at her elegant pointless furnishings. "I'm pregnant."

There was a clunk—Brian propping himself up in bed. "You said pregnant?"

"That was the word, yes."

Brian's breathing took on an accelerated rhythm.

"Is there a delay on this line?" Carrie said.

"Okay okay okay. Enough with the smartass. You've got my attention. Talk to me, Carrie. Details."

"I went to see my doctor yesterday. He said he thought I might be pregnant."

"Your gynecologist?"

"No. Just a general doctor."

"And he gave you a test?"

Carrie paused. "No."

"How did he know you were pregnant?"

"He said I have the symptoms."

"So what is this, speculation?"

"I took a test," Carrie said quietly. This was, in the technical sense, a lie. But what she needed was for Brian to stop questioning her and really, she needed this quite badly.

"One of those *home* tests? Why didn't the doctor give you a test?"

Carrie squeezed the phone. She could see Brian and his ridiculous, sharky orgasm face. His breath rattled around inside the receiver, tense and rhapsodic.

"There's nothing to get panicky about," he said finally. "Those home tests, you know ... what do they cost, twelve bucks? The first thing to do is go see your gynecologist and get a real test. If this is for real, if you're really pregnant, this is something, you know, we'll deal with this. It isn't the end of the world."

Carrie felt her anger boiling off. Instead, she was growing sad and there was an immensity to her sadness, a weight she could feel on her chest. Brian continued talking, making plans. He was good at plans. "You'll make an appointment and get a test. That's first off. Until then, you are not to worry. Do you hear me, sweetie? Neither of us, until we're sure there's something to worry about. Worrying doesn't solve anything. Can you do that? Call me right when you know. On the cell. We'll work this thing out, baby. If it comes to that."

In the olden days, this would have been the end of the line. No more wiggle room. Just a daddy with a shotgun (or a broadsword or a nice big rock) and a few witnesses and the couple themselves, the sweaty groom and the pink bride, stepping awkwardly onto the long, gray carpet of compromise.

Brian was prattling on about flights, airlines, contingencies, managing the problem. This was how he saw things—no occasion for joy, no happy accident—and Carrie felt her heart crack, a big crack right down the side. And the weight pressing down on her, which she saw now was the weight of her own knowledge, and the beginning of her life without Brian, the familiar comforts and miseries.

The receiver, balanced on Carrie's clavicle, slipped free. The tiny male voice grew fainter and fainter, until it was just a scratch in the dark air. Carrie returned the receiver to its cradle and unplugged the phone.

It was just after midnight. She went to the kitchen and got the pregnancy test and went into the bathroom and followed the instructions and sipped a glass of wine as she waited. In the Yellow Pages, she found a listing for a sub shop and dialed it on her cell.

"Big Mike's," said the voice on the other end.

"You're open!"

"All night, lady."

She could hear the sizzle of the grill in the background and a warm shuffling of voices. "Do you make cheesesteaks?"

"How many you want?"

"Just one." Carrie glanced at the pregnancy test. "Do you deliver?"

"Not after midnight."

"But it's just past twelve. Could you bend the rules?"

"Sorry."

"Would it be possible, could I talk to the owner? Is Big Mike there?"

"You're talking to him."

"What if I told you this was an emergency, Big Mike? A potential emergency craving situation."

"I don't know nothing about that."

"Please," Carrie said. "I really need this."

Big Mike sighed.

Carrie could tell from the timbre of this sigh, a deep suffering vibrato, that he was relenting. This was Big Mike's secret: he was a softy. A big, gruff softy in an apron. She heard him yell something and slam his spatula. "Now listen, my delivery boy, he was on his way out the door. I promised him a decent tip if he does this last run. You understand?"

"Absolutely," Carrie said.

"They got child labor laws in this state."

Carrie felt as supple and tingly as a teenager. Where was Tony Ducati these days? Laid out upon some worn blue sofa? In a bedroom of exorbitant mistakes? She glanced again at the pregnancy test, the invisible ring beginning to form. Or not form. How sweet it would be, in either case, to sip again from the grail of the dangerous and possible. To do just the wrong thing in the right spirit. Carrie glided through her apartment, snapping off lights. Then she dumped her wine in the sink, curled up on the couch, and waited in the dark for the kid to show up.

Yiyun Li

Prison

YILAN'S DAUGHTER DIED AT SIXTEEN AND A HALF ON A RAINY SATURDAY in May, six months after she had got her driver's license. She had been driving to a nearby town for a debate when she lost control. The car traveled over the median and ran into a semi. The local newspapers put her school picture side by side with the pictures from the site of the accident, the totaled black Nissan and the badly dented semi, the driver standing nearby and examining the damage to his truck, his back to the camera. The article talked about Jade's success as an immigrants' daughter—the same old story of hard work and triumph—how she had come to America four years earlier knowing no English, and had since then excelled in school and become the captain of the school debate team. It also quoted Jade's best friend, saying that Jade dreamed of going to Harvard, which was a dream shared by Yilan and her husband, Luo; and that she loved Emily Dickinson, which was news to Yilan. She wished she had known everything about Jade so she could fill the remaining years of her life with memories of her only daughter. At forty-seven, Yilan could not help but think that the important and meaningful part of her life was over; she was now closer to the end than the start, and within a blink of the eyes, death would ferry her to the other side of the world.

The year following Jade's accident, however, stretched itself into a long tunnel, thin-aired and never-ending. Yilan watched Luo age in grief and knew she did the same in his eyes. He had been a doctor in China for twenty years; they had hoped he would pass the board exam to become an American doctor, but, too old to learn to speak good English, he now worked in a cardiology lab as a research assistant and conducted open-heart surgery on dogs twice a week. Still, they had thought that the sacrifice of both their careers—Yilan had been an editor of an herbal medicine journal—was worthwhile if Jade could get a better education.

The decision to immigrate turned out to be the most fatal mistake they had made. At night Yilan and Luo held hands in bed and wept. The fact that they were in love still, despite twenty years of marriage, the death of their only child, and a future with little to look forward to, was almost unbearable in itself; sometimes Yilan wondered how it would feel if they could mourn in incommunicable solitude.

It was during the daytime, when Luo was at work, that Yilan had such thoughts, which she felt ashamed of when he came home. It was time to do something before she was torn in half into a nighttime self and a crazier, daytime self, and before the latter one took over. After a few weeks of consideration, she brought up, at dinner, the idea of adopting a baby girl from China. They would get a daughter for sure, for nobody would be willing to give up a son.

Luo was silent for a long moment before he said, "Why?"

"All these stories about American parents wanting their adopted girls to learn Chinese and understand Chinese culture—we could do at least as much," Yilan said, her voice falsely positive.

Luo did not reply and his chopsticks remained still over his rice bowl. Perhaps they were only strangers living in the illusion of love; perhaps this crazy idea would be the gravedigger of their marriage. "Other people's unwanted child won't replace her," Luo said finally.

Even though his voice was gentle, Yilan could not help but feel a slap that made her blush. How could she expect that a girl not of their blood—a small bandage on a deep, bleeding wound—would make a difference? "Such nonsense I was talking," she said.

But a few days later, when they retreated to bed early, as they had done since Jade's death, Luo asked her in the darkness if she still wanted a child.

"Adopt a baby?" Yilan asked.

"No, our own child," Luo said.

They had not made love since Jade's death. Even if pregnancy was possible at her age, Yilan did not believe that her body was capable of nurturing another life. A man could make a child as long as he wanted, perhaps, but the best years of a woman passed quickly. Yilan imagined what would become of her if her husband left her for a younger, more fertile woman. It almost seemed alluring to Yilan: she could go back to China and find some solace in her solitude; Luo, as loving a father as he was, would have a child of his blood. "I'm too old. Why don't I make room for a younger wife so you can have another child?" Yilan said, trying hard to remain still and not to turn her back to him. She would not mind getting letters and pictures from him from time to time; she would send presents—jade bracelets and gold pendants—to the child so she would grow up with an extra share of love. The more Yilan thought about it, the more it seemed a solution to their sad marriage.

Luo grabbed her hand, his fingernails hurting her palm. "Are you crazy to talk like this?" he said. "How can you be so irresponsible?"

It was a proposal of love, and Yilan was disappointed that he did not understand it. Still, his fury moved her. She withdrew her hand from his grasp to pat his arm. "Ignore my nonsense," she said.

"Silly woman," Luo said. He explained his plan. They could find a young woman to be a surrogate mother for their fertilized egg, he said. Considering potential legal problems that might arise in America, the best way was to go back to China for the procedure. Not that the practice was legal in China, he explained—in fact, it had been banned since 2001—but they knew the country well enough to know that its laws were breakable, with money and connections. His classmates in medical school would come in handy. His income, forty thousand dollars a year, would be insufficient for carrying out the plan in America, but they were rich for the standard in China. Besides, if they brought the baby back to America, there would be less worry about the surrogate mother later wanting to be part of the baby's life, as had happened to an American couple.

Yilan listened. Luo had been a surgeon in an emergency medical center in China, and it did not surprise her that he could find the best solution for any problem in a short time, but the fact that he had done his research and then presented it in such a quiet yet hopeful way made her heartbeat quicken. Could a new baby rejuvenate their hearts? What if they became old before the child grew up, and who would look after her when they were too frail to do so? An adopted child would be a mere passerby in their life—Yilan could easily imagine caring for such a child for as long as they were allowed and sending her back to the world when they were no longer capable—but a child of their own was different. "It must be difficult," Yilan said hesitantly. "To find someone if it's illegal."

Luo replied that it was not a worry as long as they had enough money to pay for such a service. They had little savings, and Yilan knew that he was thinking of the small amount of money they had got from Jade's life insurance. He suggested that they try Yilan's aunt, who lived in a remote mountain area in a southern province, and he talked about a medical school classmate, who lived in the provincial capital and would have the connections to help them. He said that they did not have much time to waste; he did not say menopause but Yilan knew that he was thinking about it, as she was. Indeed it was their last chance.

Yilan found it hard to argue against the plan because she had never really disagreed with Luo in their marriage. Besides, what was wrong with a man wanting a child of his own? She should consider herself lucky that Luo, with a practical mind and a methodical approach to every problem in life, was willing to take such a risk out of his love and respect for her as a wife.

Yilan was surprised, when she arrived at her aunt's house in a small mountain town, by the number of women her aunt had arranged for her to consider. She had asked her aunt to find two or three healthy and trustworthy young women from nearby villages for her to choose from, but twenty thousand yuan was too big a sum for her aunt to make any decision, so what she did, instead, was to go to a few matchmakers and collect a pile of pictures of women, their names, age, height and weight written on the back. Some pictures were even marked with big, unmistakable characters about their virginity, which made Yilan wonder how much these women, or her aunt and the matchmakers, understood the situation. Even she herself doubted now that she saw all these faces, staring at her, from which she had to pick one as a hostess for her child. What was she to look for in these women?

"No virgins, of course, or first-time mothers," Luo said when she called collect and told him of the complications that they had not expected. He was waiting for his flight, two months later than Yilan's, to the provincial capital where, with the help of his classmate, Yilan would have already finished her hormone therapy for the ovulation. It would have been great if he could have accompanied her to pick out the surrogate mother, and for the treatment before the in vitro fertilization, but he had only a few weeks of vacation to spare, and he decided that he would wait till the last minute to travel to China in case the procedure failed and he needed to spend extra time for another trial.

"You mean we want to pick someone who has already had a child?" Yilan said.

"If we have options, yes. A second-time pregnancy will be better for the child," he said.

Luo had arranged to rent an apartment in the provincial capital for a year where Yilan and the surrogate would spend the whole pregnancy together. It was his idea, as they had to be certain that the baby they got in the end was theirs—he could easily imagine them being cheated: an unreported miscarriage and then a scheme to substitute another baby, for instance, or a swapping of a baby girl for a baby boy. It surprised Yilan that Luo had so little trust in other people, but she did not say anything. After all, it was hard for her to imagine leaving her child to a stranger for the pregnancy and coming back only for the harvest; she wanted to be with her child, to see her grow and feel her kick and welcome her to the world.

Yilan had expected a young widow perhaps, or a childless divorcee, someone who owned little to her name but a body ready for rent. A mother would make the situation more complicated. "We can't separate a mother from her child for a year," she said finally.

"Perhaps it's not up to us to worry about it if someone is willing," Luo said. "We're buying a service."

Yilan shuddered at the cold truth. She looked out of the telephone booth—the four telephone booths in the main street, in the shape of fat mushrooms and colored bright orange, were the only objects of modern technology and art in this mountain town, and to protect them from vandalism as well as probing curiosities, the booths were circled by a metal fence and one had to pay the watchperson a fee to enter one of the booths. The watchperson on duty, a middle-aged man, was dozing off in his chair, his chin buried deeply in his chest. A cigarette peddler across the street sat by his cart with his eyes turned to the sky, daydreaming. A teenager strolled by and kicked a napping dog, and it stirred and disappeared among a row of low houses, behind which, in the far background, was the blue and green mountain.

"Are you still there?"

"I'm wondering," Yilan took a deep breath and said. "Why don't we move back to China?" Perhaps that was what they needed, the unhurried life of a dormant town, where big tragedies and small losses could all be part of a timeless dream.

Luo was silent for a moment and said, "It's like a game of chess. You can't undo a move. Besides, we want our child to have the best life possible."

Their child, she thought. Was it reason enough to make another child motherless for a year?

"Yilan, please," Luo said in a pleading tone. "I can't afford losing you."

Shocked by the weakness in his tone, Yilan apologized and promised that she would follow his instructions and choose the best possible woman. It saddened her that Luo insisted in holding onto her as if they had started to share some vital organs during the twenty years of marriage. She wondered if this was a sign of old age, of losing hope and courage for changes. She herself could easily picture vanishing from their shared life, but then perhaps it was a sign of aging on her part, a desire for loneliness that would eventually make death a relief.

The next day, when Yilan brought up her worries about depriving a child of its mother, Yilan's aunt laughed at her absurdity. "Twenty thousand yuan for only one year!" her aunt said. "Believe me, the family that gets picked must have done a thousand good deeds in their last life to deserve such good fortune."

Yilan had no choice but to adopt her aunt's belief that she and Luo were not only renting a woman's womb, but what was more, they were granting her and her family opportunities that they otherwise would not have dreamed of. Yilan picked five women from the pile, the first pot of dumplings as her aunt called it, to interview, all of them mothers of young children, according to the matchmakers. Yilan and her aunt rented a room at the only teahouse in town, and the five women arrived in their best clothes, their hands scrubbed clean, free of the odor of the pigsty or the chicken coop, their faces over-powdered to cover the skin chapped from laboring in the field.

Despite her sympathy for these women, Yilan could not help but compare them to one another and find imperfections in each one. The first one brought the household register card that said she was

twenty-five, but she already had sagging breasts under the thin layers of the shirt and the undershirt. It did not surprise Yilan that the
village women did not wear bras, luxuries that they did not believe
in and could not afford, but she had to avert her eyes when she saw
the long and heavy breasts pulled downward by their own weight.
She imagined the woman's son—two and half, old enough to be
away from his mama for a year, the woman guaranteed Yilan—dangling from his mother's breasts in a sling and uncovering her breasts
whenever he felt like it. It made Yilan uncomfortable to imagine her
own child sharing something with the greedy boy.

The next woman was robust, almost mannish. The following
woman looked slow and unresponsive when Yilan's aunt asked her
questions about her family. The fourth woman was tidy and rather
good-looking, but when she talked, Yilan noticed the slyness in the
woman's eyes. The fifth woman was on the verge of tears when she
begged Yilan to choose her. She listed reasons for her urgent need of
money—husband paralyzed from an accident in a nearby mine, aging
parents and in-laws, two children growing fast and needing more food
than she could put in their mouths, a mud-and-straw house ready to
collapse in the rainy season. Yilan thought about all the worries that
would distract the woman from nourishing the baby. Yilan was
ashamed of her selfishness, but then she did not want her child to be
exposed so early to the unhappiness of the world. Not yet.

At the end of the morning, Yilan decided to look at more women
instead of choosing one from the first batch. Even though Luo had
explained to her that the baby would be entirely their own—they
were the providers for her genes and the surrogate mother would only
function as a biological incubator—Yilan worried that the baby would
take up some unwanted traits from a less-than-perfect pregnancy.

When Yilan and her aunt exited the teahouse, a woman sitting
on the curb by the road stood up and came to them. "Auntie, are you
the one looking for someone to bear your child?" she said to Yilan.

Yilan blushed. Indeed the young woman looked not much older
than Jade. Her slim body in a light-green blouse reminded Yilan of a

watercress; her face was not beautiful in any striking way but there was not slightest mistake in how the eyes and nose and mouth were positioned in the face—the woman was beautiful in a way not to provoke but to soothe. "We're looking for someone who has had a child before," Yilan said apologetically.

"I have a child," the woman said. From a small cloth bag she wore around her neck with an elastic band, she brought out a birth certificate and a household register card. The birth certificate was her son's, four years old now, and she pointed out her name on the register card that matched the mother's name in the birth certificate.

Yilan studied the papers. Fusang was the woman's name, and she was twenty-two according to the register card, married to a man twenty years older. Yilan looked up at Fusang. Unlike the other married women who wore their hair short or in a bun, Fusang's hair was plaited into one long braid, still in the style of a maiden.

"Young girl, nobody's recommended you to us," Yilan's aunt said.

"That's because I didn't have the money to pay the matchmakers," Fusang said. "I had to follow them here."

"Why do you want to do it?" Yilan said, and then realized that the answer was obvious. "Where's your son?" she asked.

"Gone," Fusang said.

Yilan shuddered at the answer, but Fusang seemed to have only stated a fact. Her eyes did not leave Yilan's face while they were talking.

"What do you mean 'gone'?" Yilan's aunt asked.

"It means he's no longer living with me."

"Where is he? Is he dead?" Yilan's aunt said.

For a moment Fusang looked lost, as if confused by the relevance of the question. "I don't know," she said finally. "I hope he's not dead."

Yilan felt her aunt pull her sleeve, a warning about the young woman's credibility or her mental state. "Does your husband know you're coming to see us?" Yilan said.

Fusang smiled as if she was waiting for the question to come, and the fact that Yilan asked it only proved her judgment right. "My husband—he doesn't know his own age."

Yilan and her aunt exchanged a look. Despite the disapproval in her aunt's eyes, Yilan asked Fusang to come and see them again the next day. By then she would have an answer, Yilan explained. Fusang seemed unconvinced. "Why can't you tell me now? I don't want to walk all the way here tomorrow again."

"Which village are you from?" Yilan's aunt asked.

Fusang said the village name and said it took her two and half hours to walk to town. Yilan took out a ten-yuan bill and said, "You can take the bus tomorrow."

"But why do you need to think about it?"

Unable to look at Fusang's eyes, Yilan turned to her aunt for help. "Because we need to find out if you're lying," Yilan's aunt said.

"But I'm not. Go ask people," Fusang said and put the money carefully in the bag dangling from her neck.

Fusang had been sold to her in-laws at the price of two thousand yuan. Their only son was a dimwit whom nobody would want to marry, and they had to buy a young girl from a passing trader, one of those moving from province to province and making money by selling stolen children and abducted young women. Luckily for the old couple, Fusang was docile and did not resist at all when they made her the dimwit's wife. When asked where she had come from or about her life before, however, her only answer was that she had forgotten. The in-laws, for fear she would run away and they would lose their investment, kept her a prisoner for a year, but the girl never showed any sign of restlessness. The second year of the marriage, she gave birth to a son who, to the ecstasy of the grandparents, was not a dimwit. They started to treat her more like a daughter-in-law, granting her some freedom. One day, when the boy was two, Fusang took him to play outside the village. She came home reporting he was missing, and the villagers' search turned up nothing. How could a mother lose a son? her enraged in-laws asked her. If not for her dimwit husband, who had enough sense to protect Fusang from his parents' stick and fists, she would have been beaten to death. In the two years following the boy's disappearance, both in-laws had died and now Fusang lived with her husband on the small patch of rice field his parents left them.

This was the story of Fusang that Yilan's aunt had found out for her. "Not a reliable person, if you ask me," her aunt said.

"Why? I don't see anything wrong."

"She lost her own son and did not shed a drop of tear," Yilan's aunt said. After a pause, she sighed. "Of course, you may need someone like that," she said. "It's your money, so I shouldn't be putting my finger in your business."

Yilan found it hard to explain to her aunt why she liked Fusang. She was different from the other village women, their eyes dull compared to Fusang's. Young and mindlessly strong, Fusang seemed untouched by her tragic life, which would make it easier for her to part with the baby—after all, it was not only a service Yilan was purchasing but also a part of Fusang's life that she was going to take with her.

The next day, when Fusang came again, Yilan asked her to sign the paper, a simple one-paragraph contract about an illegal act. Fusang looked at the contract and asked Yilan to read it to her. Yilan explained to Fusang that she would stay with Yilan through the pregnancy and all living and medical expenses would be covered by Yilan; there was not any form of advance but the final payment that Fusang would get right before Yilan and the baby left for America. "Do you understand the contract?" Yilan asked when she finished reading it.

Fusang nodded. Yilan showed Fusang her name, and she put her index finger in the red ink paste and then pressed it down below her name.

"Have you had any schooling?" Yilan asked

"I went to elementary school for three years," Fusang said.

"What happened after the third grade?"

Fusang thought about the question. "I wasn't in the third grade," she said with a smile as if she was happy to surprise Yilan. "I repeated the first grade three times."

Luo arrived two days before the appointment for the in-vitro fertilization. When he saw Yilan waiting at the railway station, he came close and hugged her, a gesture too western that made a lot of people stop and snicker. Yilan pushed him gently away. He looked jet-lagged but excited, and suddenly she worried that Fusang might not arrive for the implantation of the embryo. It had been two months since they had talked, and Yilan wondered if the young woman would change her mind, or simply forget the contract. The nagging worry kept Yilan awake at night, but she found it hard to talk to Luo about it. He did not know Fusang's story; he approved of her only because she was young and healthy and her body had been primed for pregnancy and childbirth.

Fusang showed up with a small battered suitcase and a ready smile as if she was coming for a long-awaited vacation. When Yilan introduced her to Luo, she joked with him and asked if it would be hard for him to be away from his wife for a year, and what he would do. It was an awkward joke, to which Luo could only respond with a tolerating smile. He acted deferential but aloof toward Fusang, the right way for a good husband to be, and soon Fusang was frightened into a quieter, more alert person by his unsmiling presence.

The procedure went well, and after two weeks of anxious waiting, the pregnancy was confirmed. Fusang seemed as happy as Yilan and Luo.

"Keep an eye on her," Luo said in English to Yilan when they walked to the railway station for his departing train.

Yilan turned to look at Fusang, who was trailing two steps behind like a small child. Luo had insisted that Fusang come with them. "Of course," Yilan replied in English. "I won't let our child be starved. I'll make sure Fusang gets enough nutrition and sleep."

"Beyond that, don't let her out of your sight," Luo said.

"Why?"

"She has our child in her," Luo said.

Yilan looked at Fusang again, who waved back with a smile. "It's not like she'll run away," Yilan said. "She needs the money."

"You trust people so easily," Luo said. "Don't you understand that we can't make even a tiny mistake?"

Shocked by Luo's stern tone, Yilan thought of pointing out that she could not possibly imprison Fusang for the whole pregnancy, but they did not need an argument as a farewell. She agreed to be careful.

"Be very vigilant, all right?" Luo said.

Yilan looked at him strangely.

"It's our child I'm worrying about," Luo said as if explaining himself. And after a moment, he added with a bitter smile, "of course for a loser like me, there's nothing else to live for but a child."

Yilan thought about the patients he had once saved, most of them victims of traffic accidents, as he had served for the emergency center that belonged to the traffic department—they used to make him happy but since when had he lost faith in saving other people's lives? "We can still think of coming back to China," Yilan said tentatively. "You were a good surgeon."

"It doesn't mean anything to me now," Luo said and waved his hand as if to drive away the gloom that was falling between them. "All I want now is a child and that we give her a good life."

The first few days after Luo left, Yilan and Fusang seemed at a loss to what to do with each other's company. Yilan made small talk but not too often—they were still at the stage where she had to measure every word coming out of her mouth. And the only meaningful thing, besides waiting, was to make the apartment more comfortable for the waiting. A shabbily furnished two-bedroom apartment in a gray, undistinguishable building among many similar buildings in a residential area, it reminded Yilan of their first home in America, with furniture bought at the local goodwill store and a few pieces hauled in from the apartment dumpster. Jade, twelve and half then, had been the one to make the home their own, decorating the walls with her paintings framed in cheap frames bought at the dollar store; Jade had always been good at drawing and painting, which baffled Yilan, as neither she nor Luo had any artistic cell.

Yilan had brought with her a few books of paintings that Jade had loved, and now, when the stay in the apartment was confirmed, she took them out from her luggage and put them on a rickety bookcase in the living room. "I brought these for you," Yilan said to Fusang, who was standing by the living room door, watching Yilan work. Clueless like a newborn duckling, Fusang had taken on the habit of following Yilan around until Yilan told her that she could go back to her own bedroom and rest. "In your spare time," Yilan said and then paused at her poor choice of words. "When you feel OK, spend some time looking at these paintings."

Fusang came closer and wiped her hands on the back of her pants. She then picked up the book on the top, paintings by Jade's favorite artist, Modigliani. Fusang flipped the pages and placed a hand over her mouth to hide a giggle. "These people, they look funny," she said when she realized Yilan was watching her.

Yilan looked at the paintings that she had tried hard to like because of Jade's love for them. "They are paintings by a famous artist," Yilan said. "You don't have to understand them but you should look at them so the baby will get a good fetal education."

"Fetal education?"

"A baby needs more than just nutrients for her body. She needs stimuli for her brain, too."

Fusang seemed more confused. Yilan thought about Fusang's illiterate mind. Would it be an obstacle between the baby and the intelligence of the outside world? Yilan did not know the answer, but it did not prevent her from playing classical music and reading poems from the Tang Dynasty to Fusang and the baby. Sometimes Yilan looked at the paintings with Fusang, who was always compliant, but Yilan could see that Fusang's mind was elsewhere. What did a young woman like Fusang think about? Jade used to write journals that she had not thought of hiding from Yilan so Yilan at least got to know the things Jade had written down. Fusang, however, seemed to have no way of expressing herself. She talked less and less when the increasing hormones made her sicker. She spent several hours a day lying in bed and then rushing to the bathroom with horrible gagging sounds. Yilan tried to remember her own pregnancy; Jade had been a good baby from the beginning, and Yilan had not experienced much sickness at all. She wondered how much it had to do with a mother's reception, or rejection, of the growing existence within her body. She knew it was unfair of her to think so, but Fusang's reaction seemed unusually intense. Yilan could not help but think that Fusang chose to suffer from the pregnancy. Would the baby feel the alienation, too?

Such thoughts nagged Yilan. No matter how carefully she prepared the meals, with little salt or oil or spice, Fusang would rush to the bathroom. Yilan tasted the dishes—Tofu and fish and mushroom and green-leafed vegetables—they tasted perfectly bland; she did not see why Fusang would not eat.

"You have to force her," Luo said over the phone. "You're too soft-handed."

"How do you force a grownup to eat when she doesn't want to?" Yilan said in a low, frustrated voice. She had told Fusang to take a nap in her bedroom when she picked up Luo's phone call, but now she hoped that Fusang would hear the conversation and understand their displeasure.

"There should be a clause somewhere in the contract. You could tell her that we will not pay her the full sum if she doesn't cooperate."

"You know the contract doesn't protect anyone on either side at all," Yilan said.

"She doesn't know. You can frighten her a little," Luo said.

"Wouldn't a frightened mother send some toxic signals to our baby?" Yilan said and then regretted about her sarcastic tone. "Sorry," she said. "I don't mean to be so cross with you."

Luo was quiet for a moment. "Think of a way to improve," he said. "I know it's hard for you but it's harder for me to stay here, doing nothing."

Yilan imagined her husband spending his days at the lab and nights thinking about their baby. She should be more patient with him, she thought. It was not like she herself was pregnant and had a right to throw a tantrum at a helpless husband.

That evening, when Fusang returned to the table with a hand on her mouth, Yilan said, "You need to try harder, Fusang."

Fusang nodded, her eyes swollen and teary.

"You're a grownup so you have to know the baby needs you to eat."

Fusang glanced at Yilan timidly. "Do you think I can eat some really spicy food?" Fusang said.

Yilan sighed. Spice would give the baby too much internal *fire*, and the baby would be prone to rashes, bad temper and other problems. Yilan wondered how she could make Fusang understand her responsibility to have a good and balanced diet. "Did you also crave spicy food last time you were pregnant?" Yilan asked.

"Last time? For three months I only ate fried soybeans. People in the village all said I would give birth to a little farting machine," Fusang said and giggled despite herself.

Yilan watched Fusang's eyes coming alive with that quick laugh. It was what had made Yilan choose Fusang the first time they met. Yilan realized she had not seen the same liveliness in the young woman since she had moved to the provincial capital. "So," Yilan softened her voice and said, "Did you end up having a baby like that?"

"No. Funny thing was that his dad really worried. Isn't he a real dimwit, with a brain full of lard?" Fusang said, her voice filled with tenderness.

It was the first time Fusang had talked about her previous life, full of mysteries and tragedies that Yilan had once wanted to know but now made unimportant by the baby's existence. Yilan thought that Fusang would just remain a bearer of her child, a biological incubator, but now that Fusang mentioned her husband with such ease as if they were only continuing an earlier conversation, Yilan could not hide her curiosity. "How is your husband? Who's taking care of him?"

"Nobody, but don't worry. I asked the neighbors to keep an eye on him. They won't let him starve."

"That's very nice of them," Yilan said.

"Of course," Fusang said. "They're all thinking about my twenty thousand yuan."

Yilan thought of telling Fusang not to underestimate people's kindness, that money was only a small part of a bigger world. She would have said so had Fusang been her own daughter, but Fusang had lived in a world darker than Yilan could imagine, where a girl could be stolen from her family and sold, a son could disappear into other people's worlds. "Are you going back to your husband?" Yilan asked.

Fusang studied Yilan for a moment and said, "I'll be honest with you, Auntie, if you don't tell this to others. Of course I'm not going back to him."

"Where will you go then?"

"There is always some place to go," Fusang said.

"It would be hard for a young girl like you," Yilan said.

"But I'll have the twenty thousand yuan you pay me, right?" Fusang said. "Besides, what do I fear? The worst would be to be sold again to another man as a wife, but who could be worse than a dimwit?"

Yilan thought about the husband who had enough feeling and intelligence to save Fusang's life from his parents. She could easily end up with someone with much more to be feared, and twenty thousand yuan, barely enough to cover two years of rent for an apartment such as the one they lived in, was far from granting her anything. Yet Fusang seemed so sure of herself, and so happy in knowing that she had some control of her future, that Yilan had no heart to point out the illusion. She thought about her Chinese friends in America, a few divorced ones who, even though much older than Fusang, could still be a good choice for her. But would it be a wise thing to make that happen, when in reality the best thing, as her husband had said, was to conclude the deal after the baby's birth and never have anything to do with Fusang again?

They became closer after the conversation. Fusang seemed more settled in the apartment and in her own body, and she no longer followed Yilan around like a frightened child. Despite her husband's phone calls reminding her about nourishing both the baby's body and her brain, Yilan stopped filling every moment of Fusang's life with tasks. They found more comfort in each other's absence. In fact, Yilan enjoyed reading and listening to music and daydreaming alone now, and a few times, in the middle of a long meditation, Yilan heard a small voice from Fusang's bedroom, singing folksongs in a dialect that Yilan did not understand. Fusang's singing voice, low and husky, was much older than her age, and the slow and almost tuneless songs she sang reminded Yilan of an ancient poem that kept coming to her since Jade's death: a lone horse of the Huns running astray at the edge of the desert, its hooves disturbing the old snow and its eyes reflecting the last hopeful light of the sun setting between tall, yellow grasses.

Twice a day, Yilan accompanied Fusang to a nearby park for an hour-long walk. Yilan told strangers who talked to them that Fusang was her niece. Nobody doubted them, Fusang's hand grasping Yilan's arm in a childlike way. Yilan did not let Fusang go with her to the marketplace for groceries—there were many things that Yilan wanted to protect Fusang and the baby from: air and noise pollution from the street always crowded with cars and tractors, unfriendly elbows in front of the vendors' stands, the foul language of the vendors argu-ing with the customers when the bargaining did not work out.

Fusang's body seemed to have changed rapidly within a short time. By the tenth week of the pregnancy, the doctor prescribed an ultrasound, and half an hour later, Yilan and Fusang were both cry-ing and laughing at the news of a pair of twins snuggling in Fusang's womb, their small hearts big on the screen, pumping with a power-ful beat.

Yilan and Fusang left the hospital arm in arm, and on the taxi ride home, Yilan changed her mind and asked the driver to send them to the restaurant that had the best spicy dishes in town. She ordered more than they could consume, but Fusang only had a few bites of the spicy dishes. "We don't want the twins to get too hot," she said.

"It may not hurt to let them experience every taste before they are born," Yilan said.

Fusang smiled. Still, she would only touch the blander dishes. "I've always wondered what it'd be like to have twins," she said. "To think we'll have two babies that will look just the same."

Yilan hesitated at Fusang's use of 'we' and then explained that the twins came from the implantation of multiple embryos and that they would not be identical. They might not be the same gender, either.

"Let's hope for a boy and a girl then," Fusang said.

Yilan gazed at Fusang. "At my age, I wouldn't want to bargain."

"Auntie, maybe you hate people asking, but why do you want a baby now?"

Yilan looked at Fusang's face that glowed a soft peach color. The news of the twins seemed to have transformed Fusang into an even more beautiful woman. This was what Yilan was going to miss, a pregnant daughter sitting across the table from her, sharing with her the joy of a new life.

"Are you angry, Auntie? I shouldn't have asked."

"I had a daughter and she died," Yilan said. "She was five years younger than you."

Fusang looked down at her own hands on the table and said after a moment, "It's better now. You'll have more children."

Yilan felt the stinging of the tears that she tried to hold back. "It's not the same," she said. Luo had been right—nobody would be able to replace Jade. For a moment, she wondered why they would want to take the pains to get more children, whose presence could be as easily taken away as Jade's; they themselves could easily disappear from the twins' lives and leave them among the orphans of the world. Weren't they the people in the folklores who drank poisonous fluid to stop a moment of thirst? But it was already late to regret.

"You should stop thinking about your daughter," Fusang said. "It's not hard at all if you try."

Yilan shook her head and tried hard not to cry in front of the young girl.

"Really, Auntie," Fusang said. "You'll be surprised how easy it is to forget someone. I never think about my son."

"But how can you forget him? He came from your own body," Yilan said.

"It was hard at first, but I just thought of it this way: whoever took him will give him a better life than his own parents. Then it didn't hurt to think of him, and once it didn't hurt, you forgot to think about him from time to time, and then you just forgot," Fusang said.

Yilan looked at the young woman, her eyes in the shape of new moons, filled with innocent smile as if she was not talking about the cruelest truth in life. A fragile and illiterate young woman as she was, she seemed to have gained more wisdom about life than Yilan and Luo. Yilan studied Fusang: young, beautiful, pregnant with Luo's children—who could be a better choice to replace herself as a wife than Fusang? Such a thought, once formed, became strong. "Have you ever thought of going to America?" Yilan said.

"No."

"Do you want to?"

"No," Fusang said. "My tongue is straight and I can't speak English."

"English is not hard to learn," Yilan said. "Take me as an example." Take Jade.

"Are you matchmaking for me, Auntie? If possible, I want someone younger this time," Fusang said, laughing at her own joke.

Yilan could not help but feeling disappointed. Indeed Luo was too old for Fusang—her father's age already. It did not feel right, to marry someone your daughter's age to your husband, Yilan thought. "Where are your parents?" she asked Fusang. "Do you want to go back to them after this?"

"My mother died when I was two. I've never known her."

"What about your father? Do you remember him?"

"He leased me to a beggar couple for ten years so I could support myself by begging with them. They were like my own parents and had raised me since I was eight. They promised to return me to my father when I was eighteen with the money I made as my dowry so he could marry me off, but then they died and I was brought to my husband's village and before I knew it, aha, I was sold."

"Who sold you? Why didn't you report it to the police?"

"The man said he could find me a job so I went with him. The next thing I knew I was locked in a bedroom with a dimwit. And when they finally let me free, my son was already born," Fusang said, shaking her head as if intrigued by a story that did not belong to her. "What's the good of reporting then? They would never find the man."

Yilan looked at Fusang's calm face, amazed at how the young woman was strong enough to live through such pain and was still able to laugh at it, and meanwhile was compliant and never questioned the justice of the world.

Yilan and Fusang left the restaurant and decided to take a long stroll home. They were the reason for each other's existence in this city, and they had no place to rush to. Fusang's hand was on Yilan's arm, but it was no longer a hand clinging for guidance, their connection something between friendship and kinship. When they walked past a department store, they went in and Yilan bought a few maternity outfits for Fusang, cotton dresses in soft colors of pink and yellow and blue, with huge butterfly knots on the back. Fusang blushed when the female salesperson complimented her on her cuteness in the dresses. Yilan found it hard not to broadcast the news of the twins. An older woman passing by congratulated Yilan for her good fortune as a grandmother, and neither Yilan nor Fusang corrected her.

When they exited the store, Yilan pointed out a fruit vendor to Fusang. It was the season for new bayberries, and they walked across the street to buy a basket. As they were leaving, a small hand grasped Yilan's pants. "Spare a penny, Granny," a boy dressed in rags said, his upturned face smeared with dirt.

Yilan put the change into the straw basket the boy was carrying, in which were a few scattered coins and paper notes. The boy let go of Yilan's pants and then grabbed Fusang's sleeve. "Spare a penny, Auntie."

Fusang looked at the boy for a moment and squatted down. "Be careful," Yilan said but Fusang paid no attention. She put a hand on the boy's forehead and he jerked back, but Fusang dragged him closer and said in a harsh tone, "Let me see your head."

The boy, frightened, did not move. Fusang stroked his hair back and gazed at his forehead for a moment. "What's your name?" she said, shaking the boy by his shoulder. "How old are you? Where are your parents? Where is your home?"

Before the boy could answer, a middle-aged man ran towards them from the street corner. "Hey," he said in a dialect not of the province. "What are you doing to my son?"

"But he's not your son," Fusang said. "He's mine."

The boy recoiled from Fusang, his eyes filled with trepidation. The man pulled the boy away from Fusang and said to Yilan, "Is she your daughter? Can't you see she's scaring my child? Don't think we beggars do not deserve respect and you can shit on our faces."

Yilan looked at the man, his yellow crooked teeth and big sinewy hands bearing the threatening of a lawless wanderer. He could easily hurt the twins with a mean punch to Fusang's belly. Yilan held Fusang back and said in a placating tone, "My niece lost a son so please understand that she might make a mistake."

"But I'm not mistaken," Fusang said. "My son has a scar here on his forehead, like a new moon, and he has that too."

Already a group of people had gathered for the free street show. Someone laughed at Fusang's words and said, "Five out of ten boys have a scar somewhere on their heads, haven't they?"

"Hear that?" the man said to Fusang. "How can you prove he's your son?"

"Can you prove he's your son?" Fusang said. "Do you have his birth paper?"

"Beggars don't bother to bring useless things with them," the man said. He picked up the boy and put him on his shoulders. "Brothers and sisters, if you have a penny to spare for me and my boy, please do so. Or we'll leave now so this crazy woman won't bother us."

Fusang grabbed the man's arm but with a small push he sent Fusang stumbling back for a few steps before she sat down on the ground. Yilan's heart quickened.

"If you dare leave now, you will not have a good death," Fusang said and started to cry. Neither her curse nor her tears stopped the man. The circle scattered to let him and the boy pass, and besides a few idlers who stayed to watch Fusang cry, the others left for their own businesses.

Yilan imagined the twins in Fusang's womb, shaken by anger and sadness that they did not understand. Yilan did not know how to comfort Fusang; nor could she believe in Fusang's claim of the boy's identity. After a moment, Yilan said, "Are you all right?"

Fusang put a hand on her belly and supported herself with another hand to stand up. "Don't worry, Auntie," she said. "The babies are OK."

"You could've hurt them," Yilan said. Her words sounded cold, and right away she regretted it.

Fusang quieted down and said nothing. Yilan called a taxi, and on the ride home, they let silence grow and distance them into strangers. When they got back to the apartment, Yilan told Fusang to take a rest and not to dwell on the incident; Fusang did not reply but followed Yilan to her bedroom. "You don't believe me, Auntie," Fusang said, standing at the door. "But he's my son. How can a mother make a mistake?"

Yilan shook her head and sat down on her bed. A moon-shaped scar could happen to many boys and it proved nothing. "You told me that wherever your son was, he was having his own life," Yilan said finally. "So don't think about him now."

"I thought he would have a much better life," Fusang said. "I thought people who wanted to buy a boy from a trader would treat him as their own son. I didn't know he would be sold to a beggar."

Yilan had heard of stories of people buying or renting children from poor villages and taking them into the cities to beg. The owners made big money from the small children, whom they starved and sometimes hurt intentionally so the children, with their hungry eyes and wounded bodies on display, would look sadder and more worthy of charity. She tried to recall the boy's eyes, whether they bore unfathomable pain and sadness unfit for a child his age, but all she could remember was the man's big hand on his small arm when he was taken away from Fusang.

"Had I known this, I wouldn't have let the trader take him away. I thought any parents would be better than his dimwit father and me," Fusang said.

"Did you give your son away to a trader?" Yilan asked.

"We couldn't give the boy a good life," Fusang said. "Besides, his grandparents deserved it because of what they had done to me."

Yilan was shocked by the venom in Fusang's word, the first time Yilan detected the young woman's emotion about her past. "How could you make such a mistake?" Yilan said finally. "You're the birth mother of your son and no one could replace you."

"But if someone could give him a better life—" Fusang said. "Just like you'll take away the twins and I won't say a thing because you'll give them more than I can."

"The twins are our children," Yilan said and stood up abruptly. She was stunned by Fusang's illogic. "You can't keep them. We have a contract," Yilan said.

"If they're in my belly, won't they be my children too?" Fusang said. "But don't worry, Auntie. I won't keep them. All I'm saying is sometimes mothers do give away their children."

"Then stop thinking of getting him back," Yilan said and then regretted her frustration. "And perhaps he's not your son at all," she added in a softened voice. "Your son may be living a happy life elsewhere."

Fusang shook her head in confusion. "Why is it that no one wants to believe me?" she said. "He is my son."

"But you have no way to prove it," Yilan said.

Fusang thought for a long moment. "Yes, there is a way," she said and suddenly became happy. "Auntie, can you give me half of my money now? I'll go find the man and offer ten thousand yuan to buy the boy back from him. He won't sell the boy if he's his son, but if he only bought the boy from a trader, he'll surely sell the boy to me, and that will prove that he is my son."

Yilan did not know how to reply. Ten thousand yuan was a big sum and Fusang might be able to buy the boy from the beggar, if indeed he was only the owner of the boy instead of the father, but that did not make the boy Fusang's son. Or did it matter whether he came from her blood or not? She believed him to be her son, and he might as well become her son, but what did Fusang have, except for the rest of the money she would earn from the pregnancy, to bring the child up? Fusang was still a child herself, acting out of wrong reasoning; she herself needed a mother to pass on generations of wisdom to her.

"Auntie, please?" Fusang said, her pleading eyes looking into Yilan's. "I can send him to his father for now if you don't like him around."

"But you're planning to leave your husband," Yilan said. "Plus, he can't possibly take care of a small child."

"I'll find someone to take care of him in the village. I'll stay with my husband if you think I shouldn't leave him," Fusang said. "Please, Auntie, if we don't hurry, the man may run away with my son."

What would Fusang do with a small child? Yilan thought. She found it hard to imagine Fusang's life without her own presence, but what would Luo say if she told him about the situation and suggested they find a way to help Fusang and her son to America? Luo would probably say there was no clause about an advance or any other form of payment beyond the twenty-thousand yuan. How could she persuade him to see that sometimes people without any connection of blood would also make a family—and Fusang, wasn't she their kin now, nurturing their twins with her blood?

"Auntie?" Fusang said tentatively and Yilan realized that she had been gazing at the young woman for a long time.

"Fusang," Yilan said. "Why don't we sit down for a moment? We need to talk."

But Fusang, mistaking Yilan's words as a rejection, stepped back with disappointment. "You can say no but remember, your children are here with me. I'll run away and sell your children if I like. I can starve them even if you find a way to keep me here," Fusang said, and, before Yilan could stop her, she ran into kitchen and climbed onto the dinner table. Yilan followed Fusang into the kitchen and looked at Fusang, her small figure all of a sudden a looming danger. "I can jump and jump and jump and make them fall out of my body now," Fusang said. "I don't care if I don't earn your money. I have a husband to go back to. I will have more children if I like, but you won't ever see the twins if you say no to me now."

Yilan looked at Fusang, whose face was no longer glowing with a gentle beauty but anger and hatred. This was the price they paid for being mothers, Yilan thought, that the love of one's own child made anyone else in the world a potential enemy. Even as she was trying to find reconciling words to convince Fusang that she would do whatever she requested, Yilan knew that the world of trust and love they had built together was crushed, and they would remain prisoners of each other for as long as they stayed under the same roof.

Whitney Gaskell

Trying Again

I WALKED ALONG THE JUNIOR HIGH SCHOOL TRACK, STEPPING BRISKLY and pumping my arms to burn more calories. The exercise was making me feel virtuous, and almost made up for the double hot fudge sundae I'd had the night before. And the chocolate croissant I'd had for breakfast. And the pre-walk snack of a Hershey's bar dipped in peanut butter, even though I considered that to be a much needed carbohydrate-slash-protein boost.

I was near the end of my second trimester, and my itchy pregnant belly was stretching the extra-large men's t-shirt out as far as it could go without bursting the seams. *If I get much bigger, I'm going to have to go around swathed in a sheet, toga-style,* I thought. Actually, the idea had some appeal to it—at least a toga wouldn't dig into my skin like the waistband on my maternity shorts, which had seemed so voluminous when I first bought them.

An older woman in her late sixties started to pass me by. A few months earlier being passed on the track by anyone, much less a senior citizen, would have gotten my competitive juices flowing and spurred me into running just that much faster. Now I was happy to be waddling along at my own pace, and so I just smiled pleasantly at her.

The woman noticed my hugely swollen stomach, and did a double take.

"Do you have twins in there?" she asked me.

I gave her the stink-eye, although since I was wearing sunglasses, it likely lacked the effect I was hoping for. Why does anyone ever think that's an appropriate question for a pregnant woman? No one likes to have her expanding girth pointed out, and when you add a potent dose of pregnancy hormones into the mix, you're just asking for tears. Or homicidal rage. Or both.

"No, just the one," I said brightly.

"Are you sure?" she asked.

Sigh. She was asking for it, she really was. But it was a beautiful summer day—the first in a long while that wasn't already scorching hot by eight in the morning—and I decided she just wasn't worth getting my blood pressure up over.

"Pretty sure," I said. I patted my round stomach. "He's just a big boy."

"Is he your first?" the woman asked.

This seemingly innocuous question never failed to shake me. And it was one that everyone felt the right to ask, from the cashier at Target to the lab tech at my obstetrician's office.

And the answer was no. There had been another baby, a beautiful little boy with a cloud of downy hair, a pink rosebud of a mouth, round hands, long feet and eyes that would never open. He had arrived into the world without ever taking a breath, and he never had the chance to gurgle with laughter, or suckle at my breast, or gaze with wonderment at all the newness that surrounded him. Losing him had shattered me.

There is no polite way to introduce a dead child into the conversation, I've learned. I've tried, I have. I've stumbled out an awkward explanation of the baby I "lost," as though I just happened to misplace him somewhere, like a neglected pair of earrings. It's not just that people blanche and look away, muttering their apologies, while looking for an escape route (there's something unnatural about a mother who survives her child that no one is comfortable with) . . . but that I still couldn't mention my sweet boy without tears stinging my eyes and the words choking in my throat, without the horror washing over me anew.

And so it was not for her sake, but my own, when I shook my head slightly and said, "This is my first," while offering a silent apology up to my first son.

"Well, don't worry about the delivery," the woman said, settling into what I'd quickly learned was a favorite pastime of busybodies everywhere—doling out unsolicited advice to pregnant women. "No matter how big the baby is, they always manage to get out somehow."

"Actually, it really doesn't matter what size he is," I said, smiling ruefully. "I'm having a c-section."

The woman looked sharply at me, her eyes snapping with unmistakable judgment.

"Why, are you too chicken to go through labor?" she asked.

I blinked, and came to an abrupt halt. Was a suburban matron really calling me *chicken*? What the hell was *that*? I was just out for a walk, getting the exercise *What To Expect When You're Expecting* has insisted was the necessary, and out of nowhere I was being attacked for my birth choice.

Not that I even had a choice. The first pregnancy had ended with an emergency surgery, when they'd wheeled me into a room so cold and white it felt like a set for a Stanley Kubrick film, before putting me completely under with a general anesthesia. The doctors didn't want me to see them lift the tiny still body from my womb, I suppose, although my husband and mother did watch from a few feet away. Later, my mother and sister would bathe and dress our son in a tiny blue romper, while I lay in post-op, puking up cranberry juice the nurses were pushing on me and begging for my morphine drip, with my pale husband at my side. We were united in our shock at how what had begun with my triumphantly waving the positive home pregnancy test over my head had ended so terribly wrong.

Fast forward six months, and I was lying on the doctor's exam table, wearing only a flimsy paper gown while my obstetrician had a sonogram wand stuck up my crotch.

"Let's see," Dr. Vella said, twisting the wand around as she gazed at a television connected to the sonogram machine. She pointed to the blurry image on the screen. "That's your uterus. And there! Do you see that?"

My husband nodded, and squeezed my hand. I craned my neck up, trying to make out what they were both looking at.

"What? Is everything okay?" I asked, panic prickling at me.

"Everything looks perfect. That dot right there . . . that's your baby's heartbeat," the doctor said, beaming down at me.

I stared hard at the screen, and finally saw what looked like a grain of rice, pulsating on the screen. I inhaled sharply, and tears sprang into my eyes. *Your baby.* My baby.

Please, I thought. *Please let me keep this one. Please.*

"You're going to be classified as high-risk this time around, which basically means that we'll be watching you like a hawk," Dr. Vella said. She pulled the wand out of me, and snapped off her rubber gloves. "The results from the blood tests your perinatologist ran came back. Did he go over them with you?"

"Yes," I said, struggling to sit up. I smoothed the wrinkled paper gown over my lap. "He said that I have a genetic condition that puts me at a higher risk for forming blood clots, and that they can . . .." I swallowed. "Put the baby at risk."

The doctor nodded. "He's recommended that you take an injectable anticoagulant every day during your pregnancy. When we're through, I'll have a nurse come in to show you how to inject yourself."

"*Inject* myself?" I repeated. I stared at her, horrified. "You mean, with a needle?"

"Just a small one," she said soothingly. "It's the same size needle that diabetics use."

"Those aren't so bad," my husband said. "I'll help you."

I shook my head. "No. No way. No needles. I'm afraid of needles. Isn't there a pill or something I can take instead?"

"The medication has to be administered subcutaneously. I'll give you some needles to practice with on an orange at home," Dr Vella said. She smiled and rested a hand on my shoulder. "It won't be so bad, once you get used to it."

Yeah, right. As if I'd ever get used to starting off my days by being stabbed with a needle.

"And it's not too early to start thinking about the delivery," Dr. Vella continued. "Unfortunately, because of the blood clotting issues, you're not a candidate for attempting a vaginal birth. You have to stop taking the anticoagulant two days before delivery, or else you'd be at a risk for bleeding, so your delivery has to be scheduled. And patients who've had caesareans can't be induced, since there's a chance of uterine rupture. So, we're looking at a repeat c-section." She closed my chart. "It's the only option we really have."

"That's fine," I said without hesitation. "I don't care if you have to pull this baby out of my armpit, as long as he or she makes it here safely."

But not everyone shared this view. I'd already had words on the subject with a particularly strident member of my online pregnancy board.

"Women who have c-sections are denied their right to experience labor. You're not doing your son any favors by having a repeat c-section," she'd informed me.

"Yes, actually, I am," I replied. "It's the only way he can be safely delivered. I'm considered too high risk to attempt a vaginal birth."

"Your doctor's only telling you that because she's worried about her own liability. I would never trust a doctor to deliver my baby. That's why I'm having a home water birth with only my husband and midwife present," she'd said smugly.

When I'd told my husband about the conversation, he'd rolled his eyes.

"Some random stranger on an Internet message board knows more about your medical condition than your doctor? Please," he said.

"But she acted as though she was a stronger woman . . . and a . . . a better . . . *mother* for having a natural childbirth," I said.

My husband hugged me from the side, which was the only way he could pull me close now. It looked like I'd swallowed a beach ball.

"You're already a wonderful mother," he whispered in my ear. "And it's none of her fucking business."

And yet . . . and yet. There was the lingering guilt that gave my grief an even sharper edge. What kind of a mother was I, really, when I couldn't even keep my first son safe?

Now, as the sun rose higher, and the heat began to shimmer over the spongy red track, my enthusiasm for taking a walk faded into the fatigue that seemed to always cling to me these days. I looked squarely at this woman who didn't know anything about me, and yet felt perfectly comfortable sneering at my birth plans. She'd also come to a stop and was gazing back at me, looking curious.

"Are you all right?" she asked. Was I imagining it, or did she seem a bit hopeful that I was not, in fact, all right? She was probably hoping that my water had broken, so she could be the one to call for an ambulance.

"I don't know what she'd have done if I hadn't been there," I could just hear her telling her friends, as she cast herself in the role of heroine. "Poor thing, she was so frightened of giving birth, she was planning on having an elective c-section. Can you *imagine*? So I just held her hand, and told her to take deep breaths, and that she didn't have anything to be afraid of. Not one thing."

Anger welled up inside of me. Nothing to be afraid of, of course, other than the constant dread that I'd wake up once again to feel my child having gone still inside of me. That I'd have to see the horror on the face of the ultrasound technician as she said softly, "I'm sorry, but there's no heartbeat." That I'd yet again leave the Labor and Deliver wing of the hospital with only a stack of Polaroid photos and the ashes of my son contained in a heartbreakingly small urn.

"No. I am not. Afraid. Of labor," I said, so furiously I was practically spitting the words out of my mouth.

And it was only at that moment that she realized she had crossed a line. Either that or she was genuinely frightened by how pissed off I must have looked.

"Oh, I was just kidding . . . just kidding," she trilled, and then she turned and hurried off in the opposite direction.

I stared at her departing back, and for a moment considered going after her, grabbing her by the wrist, and telling her about all of it—my dead son, the battle I was going through with my treacherous body, the mottled map of purple and yellow bruises the injections left on my tender stomach, the constant and consuming fear that this child would also be taken from me—whether or not she wanted to hear it, so that next time she'd think twice about picking on an unsuspecting pregnant woman.

But since I couldn't have waddled fast enough to catch up with her, even if I wanted to, I had to let her and her prejudices go. And so I turned, and started for home, my son nestled safely inside me, rocking gently in the darkness.

Lewis Robinson

Cuxabexis, Cuxabexis

ON THE FERRY, ELEANOR RECLINES IN A PLASTIC SEAT BOLTED TO the linoleum floor with her feet resting on a suitcase. Bill sits next to her, by the window, legs crossed, silver glasses crammed against his face—scanning the *Courier-Gazette*. She has never been on a boat before, but then again, she has never before been pregnant, either— she is six-weeks in—so she's not sure which is contributing most to her mood. She is irritated with Bill. Doesn't he know he should be feeding her? He should know she needs meat. The issue is rarely quantity of food, or variety—it's access. And she imagines there won't be anything to eat on the island, which will be Bill's fault.

"Meat," she says.

"Yes?"

"That's what I need."

He doesn't raise his eyes from the paper. "This boat doesn't have a snack bar."

"But I saw vending machines," she says. He looks up at her and smiles, and this angers her at first, but his smile lingers and his glasses are so round—his nostrils are flared in a ridiculous manner—that despite her efforts, she can't be annoyed. "Sit tight," he says. He folds the paper and sets it on the floor. "I'll check the Coke machine for hamburgers." He steps over her legs, and as he walks from the passenger cabin—his shoes snapping on the linoleum—she watches his ass, his dress shirt tucked neatly into his wool slacks.

Then, the thought descends: this is not how it's always been. She is different than she once was. How simple an idea that is! Just a few years ago, her life had been stacked in three neat piles. For money, she waited tables—at a place called Enrique's on the Upper West Side. Seven shifts a week: three lunches, four dinners. Bring the people their food. Ask polite questions about what is needed. Grit teeth. Balance drinks on a tray. Run credit card through machine; smack machine and run card again. After work, there was action sometimes. She had various sleep-over friends, men who didn't bother her otherwise—one she knew from college, one she worked with at the restaurant, one she'd met at the library. Then there had been her schoolwork—never a problem. The prize was entrance to medical school, Columbia.

But things have slipped. Eleanor loves her brain, but she has started to saturate. In medical school, she has learned that everything can and will go wrong with a body, and that too many of the drugs she is studying—of various synthetic origins—cause hives, breathing difficulty, and dizziness. There is so much to learn. (Surgery has been better: she likes to cut, and the muscle-flexing culture of surgeons amuses her.) After she stopped seeing her sleep-over friends, she met Bill.

Bill is from Maine. Bill is from Cuxabexis Island—though he lives in Boston now. And he is off looking for meat, for her. It's March and the clouds are low and the water is hazel, the color of Bill's eyes. It's snowing. Looking at the water gives Eleanor the feeling she gets at the end of a long shift on her surgical rotation, a weakness in her abdomen and legs—fatigued from remembering, and from the actual labor of cutting, or watching the doctors cut. The water looks very solid and thick, and she finds it hard to imagine all that's below her; she fears falling and sinking, hypothermic shock, being swept by the tide onto the shore of a barren reef, ice in her hair, matted with seaweed. She's not afraid of sharks or lobsters or jellyfish, but the whole dark world underneath—the droopy, slow-moving spiny fish, the eels, the currents and sinkholes—these things make her want to hurry back home, ride a heated subway car to the movies, where she can be absolutely sure what will happen.

Bill had suggested the trip; he has nostalgic feelings about the place, about his childhood. He tells her it's where he feels most alive.

The snow is falling heavy on the ocean, dissolving into it, swirling on the front deck of the ferry. For a minute, Eleanor can hardly believe what she's seeing—the huge iron boat, painted blue, named for a governor; the gray water—a mile deep?—the big flakes of snow. She can't see anything in the distance.

Her enthusiasm for Manhattan goes up and down, but she's been feeling especially steeled for battle, feeling there is no other place she could live. She's in her third year of medical school, and while she spends most of her days exhausted and depressed, the occasional aortic anastomosis—cross and connect, like radiator hoses—amazes her; the resilience of the body calms her. She does not worship procedures in the same way some of her fellow students do, but a week earlier, when she first saw an open chest cavity, she forgot herself—and Bill—and thought only about her child, growing inside her. She saw a glimpse of the ribs, which have a plastic sheen, and she saw the turmoil inside this patient's body—a fatty heart, dark lungs—and she dreamed about the perfection of her child. Her most recent guess: he (she has decided the baby is male) will be a trombone player in his middle school band, and he'll be an actor, preferring musicals, and he'll eat cereal by the bowlful. She sees blond hair and skinny legs. It made her so wistful and worried, she nearly left the operating room.

And this as well: he will live a long life; he will watch Eleanor grow old and die, and he will have his own family, and perhaps a woodshop in his garage, and he will be fascinated by other things, by the habits of turtles, perhaps, or the geology of Antarctica.

Bill returns with a miniature bag of pretzels which he drops in her lap. "We'll find something when we arrive, sweetie," he says. Then he's back to reading the paper.

(At first, Bill's laconic manner made her nervous; she liked the muscles in his legs, and his dark eyes, but she wondered if he was smart enough. She realizes now that he is.)

They've been living apart because of Bill's job. He writes about food, and it's the *Globe* that gives him work. He's made a name for himself. He is unconventional and fickle. He gets a lot of hate mail. He fixates on one thing—the mushiness of the cauliflower marranca, for example—then drums his point to death. Eleanor finds his articles hilarious. She tries to visit him as much possible, which ends up being very rarely, but when she does they go out to dinner on the *Globe* and he writes about it. When Bill visits Eleanor in New York, she treats him to stories of pig vivisection, which is what she's been doing lately as part of her training. It's not what she expected: she had never seen a pig before, either. She was thinking slick and pink and round but these pigs have grayish-black hair and are skinny— they look almost like cats.

When they're not together they talk on the phone at night. There's been a lot to talk about lately. She's easily discouraged. Who has a baby during medical school, and who in his right mind marries a pregnant medical student living four hours away? Bill is an optimist. He says they can do it all. She asked him, marriage? He said, sure. Was that a proposal? They were on the phone and she told him, come on, let's do this correctly. If we're doing this over the phone, you should at least be kneeling.

"I'll wait until I see you," he said.

Bill sees things at face value. He has the enviable ability to recognize—in the most straight-forward of ways—how much he loves her. She's supposed to be the literal-minded one, the scientist, the pragmatist, but Bill, he's a stickler for the truth. He has beliefs. She admires his intelligence, his memory, his ability to synthesize squirrelly ideas. His thoughts come choreographed, tightly outlined. Bill will teach the child how to tie a slip hitch, fold clothes, speak grammatically.

The ferry's route winds through a tight passage, and she's amazed there's enough depth to keep it from running aground. They're going much slower now, and they steam past a fluorescent green navigational marker—Bill calls it a can. There is an austere bird with a hooked beak nested on top, staring at the ferry through the snow.

"Eagle?" she asks.

"Osprey," he says.

"Are you sure?"

"Positive," he says. "They're everywhere up here. It's the Cuxabexis mascot."

"No chance it's an eagle? It looks like one."

"It does," he says. "But it's an osprey."

This is Bill at his best. She doesn't like it when he backs down. When they visit each other, they wrestle—they spar in bed, or on the living room floor—and he has learned not to let her win. In high school, his Cuxabexis basketball team traveled the state. He was the point guard and his dad was the coach. Bill uses some of his father's old expressions. Persistence pays. That's one. Another: Life is not fair. His father was a geometry teacher, too, and would bring a tape measure to the first practice every season, showing his team that the diameter of the basket is exactly twice the diameter of the ball. Bill tells this story with great pride; his father died a year ago, of a heart attack.

His father also insisted that bank shots, correctly calculated, are more accurate and much more satisfying than non-bank shots. Bill is a bank-shot man.

The ferry slip on Cuxabexis is made of long grey wooden planks nearly as tall as the boat itself. The nearby wharves are covered with tangles of frayed green nylon rope, rubber boots, and tubs of fish.

The harbor is silent. The thick spruce forest comes right down to the shore, with gnarled trees growing on the rocks.

They stay with Bill's aunt, Fran—the sister of his dead father. She looks about sixty with long hair and a steady chin. She has Bill's pretty eyes. She walks them to their room on the second floor, and she smiles at the poster bed with its pink pillows and red blankets. The remainder of the room is empty except for a plain wooden dresser topped by a bowl of heart-shaped soaps. The view is the neighbor's house, plastic stapled over the windows, aglow with green light.

"You two are a handsome couple," she says, and suddenly, Eleanor is struck by Fran's beauty. She looks like an old film star. "We'd love to see you have some babies, Billy."

"In time," Eleanor says.

"Soon," says Bill—but Eleanor pinches his arm. She's not ready to talk about the baby with anyone.

"Well, it would make me happy," says Fran, giving them a smile. She is wearing a maroon cotton dress. Her stare is unfocused but kind. "This island has always been a good place for growing a family. I've raised ten children here. Maybe you should move back, Billy." She winks.

"We're just here for two nights," Eleanor says.

"That'll be long enough," says Fran.

Bill sits on the poster bed. "Big game tomorrow night—how's George playing?"

"He's on top of it," she says. "We're undefeated."

But meat is the issue most pressing to Eleanor. "Are there restaurants here?" she asks.

"You can eat with me, dear," says Fran. "We'll start at seven."

Then she leaves, and Eleanor closes and locks the door after her. She moves toward Bill on the bed. She unzips her jeans.

"Hi," says Bill. He lies on his back and she pins him. He puts his right hand on her left breast, over her shirt. She leans down and bites his neck, and he pulls her underwear down enough to get his fingers on her. He starts very slowly.

She tumbles over on her side, keeping a knee raised. She unbuttons the top three buttons of his shirt and reaches in to put a hand on his warm chest. She kisses him again and his face is concentrating.

When she comes, her legs close on his hand. She keeps it that way, her own hand gripping the back of his neck.

Bill had slept with six women before Eleanor, and she knows all of their names. They are no match for Eleanor. The first time she had sex with Bill—he was a senior in college and she had a research job at Mass General—was awful. He had her on her back, he didn't look her in the eyes, and he pumped like an piston drill. She didn't know quite how to take it; she thought, at first, he was being ironic, but then she realized he needed some guidance.

"That's quite something," she had said. He lived in a basement apartment, with windows near the ceiling.

"Really?" he said. He had a colorless imagination back then; he thought she was complimenting him.

You're an automaton, she thought.

She got him to slow down, relax, and she felt less lonely. Bill became her earnest student. They were at a Ukranian restaurant in Watertown when she told him she loved him—the first time she had said such a thing—and when they woke up the next morning together, Eleanor's brain was unusually quiet.

Fran's kitchen has a low ceiling and none of the hokey charm Eleanor expected—there's a TV next to the microwave, and empty boxes of sugar cereal stacked by the trash.

"Going to the pep rally?" asks Fran. She has changed out of her dress and is wearing purple sweatpants and a purple t-shirt. When she sets the bowls of soup on the table, her round biceps show under her loose skin.

"Definitely," says Bill.

"Everyone's going to love seeing you, Billy," she says. "George wants to play you sometime."

"Your grandson?" Eleanor asks.

"My son," says Fran.

"Oh," says Eleanor. "Excuse me." Bill has told her little about Fran—she was a relative he'd always liked, but he'd never spent much time with her as a kid.

"He's fourteen," she says. "A full six-four."

"Great news," says Bill.

"So, when's the wedding?" Fran asks. She blows on a spoonful of soup, then puts it in her mouth.

Bill says, "Well, we haven't—"

"Why not?" Fran asks. Her look is earnest; she seems genuinely concerned.

"We'll tell you when we're ready, Fran, I promise," says Bill.

"Okay, Billy," says Fran, smiling. Eleanor has just started her soup but Fran ladles her more.

Eating the soup has calmed Eleanor. She reaches under the table and feels for Bill's crotch. He swells in her hand. "I'm pregnant," says Eleanor.

Bill looks as though he swallowed wrong.

"That's wonderful! I could almost tell," says Fran, reaching across the table and squeezing Eleanor's arm.

"You're the first person we've told," says Eleanor.

"Your father would be so happy," says Fran.

"Yes," says Bill, and his face is flushed—he's happy. Eleanor knows exactly what he's thinking: My wacky girlfriend, so unpredictable.

Fran takes Bill's empty bowl to the stove and fills it. "You know, the rabbits that went into this soup—they're amazing," she says. "One of them gets born on a Monday, and by the middle of the following week, he's a granddaddy."

"That sounds kind of impossible," says Bill.

"I'm not sure on the math," says Fran. "Believe me, though, these bunnies are out of their minds."

The soup is delicate, plenty of bay leaves and marjoram, and the cubes of meat are lean but not dry.

"Have you ever seen rabbits do it?" Fran asks. "It's damn exciting. Not in a perverted way, either. It's just that they're efficient. Strenuous. It's really very inspiring."

Eleanor wonders if Bill is used to conversations like this with his family. "When do you watch them?" she asks. Bill is turning his soup spoon in the bowl, still flushed and smiling.

"Up at Gus Reed's farm. I walk up there sometimes. We'll go tomorrow. They have these little tiny penises—"

Bill laughs. "So what do you think of Cuxabexis, sweetie?"

"Great soup here," says Eleanor. Everything feels exciting: the trombone player in her uterus, Bill's family, being on an island where rabbits are fucking.

"You two do the dishes," says Fran. "I'll get my coat and we'll leave in ten minutes." Before going upstairs, she looks at Eleanor and smiles, puts her hand lightly on Eleanor's cheek and says, "You're very lovely."

The pigs she's been operating on in school: they make her sad. All of the students wear gowns, gloves and masks, but nothing is sterile, probably because they aren't concerned about fulminant sepsis in patients who will be euthanized at the end of the hour. She tells Bill that the worst thing about it is that she uses Nembutal, which works as an anesthetic but not a paralytic. That means when Eleanor grazes a nerve with her scalpel, the pig's muscles twitch. She's cutting him up, the little guy, and he's moving all around.

"But the pig is basically dead, right?" asks Bill.

"I guess so," she says. "He won't ever wake up." She gives him the Nembutal, intubates and hooks him up to a ventilator, then takes out a lung, or cross-connects blood vessels, whatever she's told.

"It's a pig, though, sweetie," says Bill. "Just a pig. Think about how much you're learning."

"You should see them," she says. "They're just so small and skinny, and they're on their sides, asleep. Dreaming of the old days."

"The old days?" asks Bill. "What?"

"You know, back with their mom, running around outside."

"Pigs don't remember like that. They don't dream."

"I bet they do."

The snow has stopped and the clouds are lifting, billowing together, dark bluish-grey on the horizon, clearing patches of night sky. The road has already been plowed. The sidewalk, too, has been cleared; it's set above the road, in the side of the hill by the harbor, and Bill and Eleanor and Fran walk along it under pine boughs. Fran is dressed entirely in purple: purple boots, purple sweatpants, purple down coat and purple bandana around her head. There are no boats in the harbor, but the clean, sturdy wharves are well lit by high-set street lamps, giving the path where they walk an orange hue. The wind is picking up, but Eleanor feels warm. In front of every house they pass, there is a neatly stacked pile of green-wire lobster traps, and symmetrical bouquets of fluorescent lobster buoys, tied together for safe keeping. All the vehicles they see are trucks, all of them high-gloss reds and blues and dark greens.

"See the flags?" Fran asks. Every wharf has a flag pole—shorter than usual, bare wood bleached by the sun—and each one flies an American flag and two others.

"The blue one's Maine," Bill says to Eleanor. "The brown spot in the middle's a moose."

"We got our flag—it's that white one—before Maine was even a state," Fran says, proudly. "French pirates. They stockpiled firs here." Eleanor nods—she sees the pirate in Fran, and she's envious.

In town, they turn off the main street and walk up a steep hill past a cemetery full of enormous, ornate tombstones and mausoleums. The wind is warm.

The further they get from the harbor, the warmer it gets, and by the time they reach the high school, Eleanor's face is flushed and her feet are sweating. It feels like a different season. There are birds overhead—ospreys?—that are making their high-pitched calls, circling near the wide, thatch nests they've built in the top tiers of the spruce trees. Eleanor hears water running beneath the ice on the creek by the road.

Fran pounds three times on the side door. When it opens, a young girl peers out. She looks at Eleanor and Bill, her brow wrinkled. "Hey, Fran," says the girl.

"This is Billy," Fran says to the girl. "You're too young, dearie, to know who he is. He's a legend."

The gym is small, but the bleachers are packed—it must be the entire town, and many are dressed like Fran, in purple. They murmur. When the three of them get to the center of the bleachers, the crowd parts and they climb to the back row. A man in overalls in the third row winks at Fran, then smiles. Everyone is staring at Bill. The back row makes room, and Bill and Eleanor sit on either side of Fran.

Eleanor has never seen anything like this. It feels like church. "Why is this pep rally closed to outsiders?"

"We've had people from the other islands come over, try to get our game plan," Fran says. Then she takes Eleanor's hand and says, "I'm so glad you're here."

The cheerleaders arrive first, and they are magnificent stock—tumblers, cartwheelers, smiling hard. They bounce on powerful legs, spring into pyramid formation.

"Go Ospreys!" they scream, all strong shoulders and flat chests. Eleanor has always resented cheerleaders, but she loves these ones. They're doing their job, red-cheeked and loud.

Then, blasting from a side door, the team. CUXABEXIS on their chests, purple letters on brilliant white uniforms. They are all tall with lithe, pale muscles and crew cuts. They slam the ball against the hardwood in their sprint to the basket, and then—flash!—they're up by the rim and ever so gently laying the ball in the basket. The cheerleaders are feeding on it, jumping by the sidelines. Everyone's on their feet now, and the fight song kicks in:

> *Cuxabexis, Cuxabexis*
> *From the spruce trees on high!*
> *Cuxabexis, Cuxabexis*
> *'Til the day that we die!*

"That's George, there, number twenty-four," shouts Fran, and Eleanor sees the resemblance. He has bright eyes and a high forehead—another pirate. As he waits in line to do his layup, he jogs in place. He has hairless, strong legs. When he gets the ball, his movements are hesitant, but he leaps up to the basket and slams the ball down.

"Wow," says Bill.

"His daddy can jump, too," she says, winking at Eleanor.

A middle-aged man with slicked-back grey hair, dressed in a tie and tweed jacket with blue jeans and farm boots, walks from the bleachers to the microphone at center court. He taps on it and it whines. The crowd silences. "Ladies and gentlemen, we have a special guest tonight. Many of you remember the '89 tournament, when our Ospreys torched Ilsesboro for ninety-nine points to win States. The point guard on that team, the son of Bill Haskel, Sr., scored thirty-one to lead the team. He's come all the way from Boston today, and I hear he's got a happy lady with him, who's soon to be bringing us Bill the Third. Let's have one more *Cux, Cux* for Billy Thrill Haskel."

Later, in the poster bed, Eleanor's on top of Bill. He's inside her. "Billy Thrill," she says. She is no longer mad the secret is out; after all, she is the one who told Fran, and Fran is a pirate. Bill is slow in his fucking. In the end she relaxes all her weight on him.

"Will you marry me?" he asks.

"What?"

"I'm asking in person," he says.

He gets out of bed and kneels on the wood floor, naked, wincing at first from the pressure it puts on his bad knee.

"Billy Thrill," says Eleanor. "Yes."

After, they lie on their backs and Bill pulls the blankets up. She listens to their breathing for a while, then she says, "Let's get up early and walk around the island," but Bill is already sleeping.

There is a knocking at the door. It's barely light. Eleanor looks at the digital bedside clock which reads 6:55.

"Hello?" she mumbles.

"Hey, it's George," says a voice behind the door. "Mom told me to get you guys up. She said you want to see the rabbits."

"Give us a few minutes, okay?" says Eleanor.

"No prob," he says.

Bill has slept through this exchange, but when Eleanor rubs his head and kisses his cheek his expression turns cross.

"Jesus," he says.

"Come on, time for a walk."

"Right," he says. "Go to it." He pulls the blankets over his head.

Eleanor gets up and spends a minute on her knees in the bathroom, gripping the sides of the toilet. She vomits. She brushes her teeth and puts a cold washcloth on the back of her neck. Eleanor sees that Bill has guilted himself out of bed and is putting on his pants. His hair is flat on his head and he yawns wide. His face is grey and his eyes are nearly shut and Eleanor tries to guess what he's thinking. She wonders if she should know, now that they're getting married.

For the walk, George is dressed in jeans and matching jean jacket. He wears huge untied purple sneakers and holds a bright orange basketball. Bill and Eleanor are on the sidewalk and George is in the road, walking in long strides, bouncing the ball, weaving it between his legs and behind his back. It's early but it's warm; there's a trickle of snowmelt between the road and the sidewalk. Fran is off running errands.

"I always keep a ball with me," says George, smiling. "For good luck, you know?"

He's a skinny giant who seems to take his life quite seriously. He's got the soft close-cropped hair of a baby starling, no whiskers at all, red cheeks. Eleanor can't imagine how his team wouldn't win the game; the island feels mysteriously pointed in that direction.

"George, you know what we're coming up on, around the corner," says Bill. George grins, staring down at his shoes. They're on a road with a long row of small white houses built close together under large bare oak trees, a post office and a coin-op laundromat. Then, a basketball court comes into view. The air smells salty, and with the sun shining through the trees, the shadows are sharp.

Bill points to the court. "You ready, hotshot?"

"I probably shouldn't," says George, still smiling. "I've got a game tonight." But he's taking off his jeans, and he's wearing his uniform underneath.

"I'll take it easy," says Bill. "Just a friendly game. My knee's gimpy, anyway." Eleanor knows they'll both kill for a win: George wants to beat the legend, and Bill wants to prove he's still young.

"Where's the farm?" asks Eleanor.

"Just up the hill," says George. "You can't miss it."

Bill strips down to his t-shirt and tightens his sneakers. When they step on the court, he lets George have the ball first. Bill crouches in his defensive stance, no smile. Billy Thrill.

"I'll be back," says Eleanor, but neither responds.

She climbs the hill. A breeze comes through the spruce trees. By the side of the road, fiddleheads poke through the bramble. In the clearing at the top of the hill sits a modest white farmhouse with a wide wet lawn spotted with melting snow. There's a large pen up near the house with a low, wire-mesh fence. An old man stoops in the pen with a bundle of hay in his arms. He has the ground nearly covered, sprinkling the hay here and there. When Eleanor gets close, she sees a huddle of white, black and brown rabbits by the side of the barn, at the edge of the pen. There are perhaps thirty of them. They're not moving much; their heads are down, and they're nestled up close to each other.

"Hello, dear," says the man, looking over at Eleanor. His hands are bloody and he wears a darkened smock.

"Are they cold?" she asks.

"Not sure," he says. "They usually do this before I clean them. They must know."

"Can I help?" she asks.

He looks at Eleanor hard. Then he smiles. "I don't really need the help, but you could do the knots. My fingers are bad." He sprinkles the last of the hay and then holds his hands out to her, palms up. He has blood up to his elbows. "I've got a bit of a shake," he says, and he does, but his hands are huge and strong-looking. He opens the gate for her.

"Saw you at the rally last night, dear," he says. "So glad to hear you're bringing Billy back home. Hope I'll be around to watch Billy Three play."

She nods.

"Billy's a good kid," he says.

He walks slowly to the bundle of rabbits and picks out a white one by the scruff of its neck. He hands it to Eleanor.

"First we've got to tie its back legs," he says. "They don't like it much, but I can pop the neck straight-away and then they don't feel anything."

"Okay," she says.

In the barn, a rope is hanging from a roughly hewn rafter, leading down to a stool. She takes the rabbit's hind feet and cinches them with a square knot. The rabbit kicks and kicks. Then, as swiftly as promised, the man puts a thumb into the back of its neck and with his other hand pulls its head back. Then he cuts into it with a quick jerk of his knife. Blood streams to the hay. He skins it with one pull. The muscles are encased in a bluish, shiny membrane. She puts her hands around the slick, hot carcass. She's amazed.

"Yup," says the man. "That's all there is to it."

She thanks the man and says goodbye, looking once more at the beautiful huddle of rabbits, thinking again about her baby—wondering if she's ready to take care of something so helpless. She walks down the hill, past George and Bill, blood sticky on her hands, feeling excited. She loves Bill, but she can't talk to him now, she needs some time alone on this island. She watches George glide past him, leaping up to the basket and with one hand cramming the ball in the hoop. A question from Bill about the rabbits, about the blood on her hands, would depress her. *You helped Gus Reed kill his rabbits?* He would only be curious, but there are so many things she can't explain to him. He helped, but the baby is hers. In seven months she will be as big as a phone booth. She will ride the subway to the hospital to give birth. I'll be there with you, Bill has said, I will.

Okay, Bill, okay.

This baby is hers. She already loves it so much she could eat it— this is something else which Bill wouldn't understand. *I don't mean that literally,* she'd have to say. She keeps walking, all the way to the far side of the island, on a road without houses, the thick spruce forest coming right down to the edge of the road. The warm wind gives her chills.

When she reaches the ocean—a house on a small plot with open views to the east—she sees waves slamming the nearby shore, loud and dramatic. Beyond this, though, are miles and miles of water, a surface as smooth and shiny as the hood of a car. This calms her, for now, which is what she'd always hoped an ocean could do.

Mummy Dust Tea

EPIFANIA FIGURED IT HAD HAPPENED EITHER THAT TIME IN RUBÉN'S electric blue Jetta or else that time in the graveyard grass by the mummies' cave. There were no tourists at night, so everyone went there to do it, outside the single underground corridor that was the mummies' tiny museum.

The doctor behind the gas station said it had been about two months, and Epifania remembered lying pressed in the customary candy skull-scattered field after *el Día de los Muertos*, the Day of the Dead, which was two months ago. It was also two months ago that Rubén finally got his sunroof fixed, so that she could again look up and see the stars of heaven instead of the cave.

Epifania and Gabriela skipped morning classes in favor of cigarettes and pineapple soda. The two were inseparable; Gaby went to the mummies with one of Rubén's brothers, each of whom ran his own branch of the family yarn store. Both Epifania and Gaby had the fairer skin and rounder cheeks of those who weren't gravediggers, those who drove Jettas instead of VW bugs. Epifania's hair was even lighter than Gaby's. It sprang in feather formation from her scalp and picked up the gold in her green eyes.

Epifania and Gaby inhaled, swallowed some soda, and then exhaled through glossy lips. "It must have been the *pinche* gearshift in that Jetta," Epifania told Gaby between smoke rings. "Of course now I'll have little baby Volkswagens."

"*Cállate,* Epifania," Gaby jabbed a nail file toward Epifania's nose. "I'm writing you down the name of the doctor I used. Everything was fine. You remember." Gaby pulled a leather memo pad from her purse and scribbled something with the matching pen, her fingers spread apart so her nails wouldn't smudge.

Epifania arrived back at school just as her mother pulled up. On the way home for *comida* she chatted about the morning's classes in practiced detail, taking her cues from borrowed notes. Today in psychology they had discussed how children act out reality in games with dolls, and later they learned two Good Morning songs.

Epifania was studying to teach kindergarten because she'd always liked kids. She went to the Normal school in the city with many of her friends from high school; she had lost touch with the ones who had gone to the nursing school or gotten married, though she still ran into them at the disco or at night by the mummies.

Like many of her cousins and friends, Epifania would graduate with a job teaching kindergarten in a hut. Her bus would stop where the pavement did, at the beginning and the end of a single dirt road that is a coffee-picker school district. The children that had not been taken along in the picking truck would spot their *maestra* as she passed, her tennis sneakers skimming the rubble, and would run barefoot to follow, papaya-sticky hands jingling the bangles on her wrists, pleading for a piggyback.

Squinting as the rear-view window mirror rosaries caught the hazy sunlight, Epifania wondered how on earth she could have gotten pregnant. Rubén said he always stopped in time, and she always said the protective spell that Lupe, the family housekeeper since Epifania's birth, had taught her. Maybe one time she got distracted and didn't say it, maybe that time in the grass when she turned her head to the side and saw the festival candy skull frosted with a girl's name. Yes, that was the time. Because right then Epifania imagined fleetingly, recklessly, that that name would be their baby's name. Only now she couldn't remember what it was.

At bedtime Epifania's mother came in to cross her and say *que duermas con los angelitos*, Epifania, may you sleep among the little angels. Mama, Epifania thought, you would have to cross me backwards enough times to undo seventeen years of bedtimes if you knew you'd just crossed my baby too. Both Epifania and her baby could not sleep among the little angels.

That night Epifania decided she did not like her own mother enough to be one herself. She wished the baby had never had a name, whatever it was, because that made it hers. Like the way the mummies in the museum were amusing until you knew who they were. Epifania thought of her housekeeper and nursemaid, Lupe, whose mother and grandmother were in that cave.

The price of renting a grave, like most prices, went up every year. The families of the deceased always had genuine intentions of paying the installments, unable to predict that one day they would have to admit that keeping the dead buried is not necessary to the survival of the living. When the rent was overdue, the body would be dug up and replaced. The cemetery management knew each family well enough to estimate how deep they should bother burying the body. At six feet a body would usually stay buried; some waited at two feet.

Their insides would dissolve, but the peculiar brew of dusts, winds, and rains in the region turned out to preserve the shriveled shells of skin. The resulting mummies were propped in glass cases along a single dim corridor in a shallow cave. For a token fee, visitors and tourists could pay their respects to the brown bodies, skin sunken and draped across wiry bones. They were finely detailed, yet still incomplete, like an artist's pencil study of a figure. Their heads drooped forward like heavy, wilted blooms. One man had a visible bullet hole; one woman, buried alive by mistake, had never unclenched her fists. The tattered lace of a baptism smock still clung to what was left of a baby, edging a tiny yawn where her stomach had been.

On the night when Rubén told her it was time, Epifania had decided that doing it by the mummies could not be a sin, because the mummies proved that there was no heaven.

The next day Epifania and Rubén walked through the town plaza, past the bandstand and soda fountain cloistered by sherbet-colored houses with iron balconies and indoor orchards. Rubén had narrow cheeks, long fingers, and pants with lots of pockets. For the moment he was doing all right, running one of the family yarn stores like each of his four brothers. Still, Rubén was not accustomed to planning ahead. He was thinking about becoming a priest, but he always forgot to close the Jetta's sunroof during the season of night rains.

Rubén pulled off his sweater and Epifania could feel the staticky prickle from his hair on her forehead. *"Claro,* our parents would disown us. But that's okay, we'd have to run away anyway to find a place to live where nobody knows us," Rubén said. He lit a cigarette. "I hope I will have a son."

"Rubén, *¿no es obvio?"* Epifania stopped walking and faced Rubén. "You promised I wouldn't get pregnant. Lupe promised I wouldn't get pregnant. Well, you lied. You both lied to me. So now I can't be pregnant anymore." She ground out her cigarette on a cobblestone. "I'm calling Gaby's doctor."

"Epifania, I didn't lie," Rubén said. "I just said what I said at the wrong time. That's not as bad a sin as killing the baby." He put his arm around Epifania's waist and smiled with his lips closed over his teeth. "Think of all the clothes you can knit for him, free, with yarn from my store."

Epifania shook his arm off. Tears had begun to hop down her face. "Oh. So we're taking your store when we run away?"

They turned a corner and faced the church and graveyard. Epifania's memory hurried like a tourist down the museum's single corridor. Even that little baptized baby had not gone to heaven. No *angelitos* slept with her.

Epifania made Rubén drive her straight home. In order for her baby not to be a sin, she would have to leave it to the mummies, not to the doctor.

Even if it meant talking to Lupe, with whom she was very angry at the moment. Epifania found Lupe ironing in the laundry room. Lupe grinned widely and motioned to offer the iron to Epifania. Ever since Epifania was a little girl she liked to press in sharp creases and then erase them away just as quickly. But this time Epifania looked the way she looked when she came to confess that the blood Lupe had warned her about had arrived. This time Lupe knew right away that Epifania was not in the mood for ironing.

"Great spell, Lupe," Epifania stared at her, arms crossed at her stomach.

"Oh, *mi hija*," Lupe rose from her stool, her bulky frame throwing a pear-shaped shadow that twisted on the clothesline as the sheets flapped. Although she fit under the clothesline without ducking, she was densely packed into her brown skin, and no one dared challenge her place in the milk line. Her eyes shone at Epifania like ripe berries in a dark thicket of wrinkles.

Lupe took a sleepwalker's step forward. Her heavy brown hands moved to cover her open mouth, then to shrug helplessly, and then to reach out to Epifania, palms bloodless.

"So. Got another one?" Epifania tried to stare hard enough to make Lupe's eyeballs hurt.

"Yes, *mi hija*. Find me in the kitchen when your parents have gone to sleep."

Lupe kissed Epifania and hurried out, berating herself for not sprinkling protective herbs among Epifania's sheets the last time she made up her bed.

"But, Epifania," Lupe said, pausing in the doorway, "it's going to taste terrible."

Epifania tiptoed into the kitchen when it was safe. Lupe was stirring a small pot on the stove where a gritty black liquid churned. Its stench threatened to snap the bands of moonlight that stretched through the window.

"Tea with dust from the mummy ground," Lupe said. "Doesn't kill, just dissolves."

Lupe poured the liquid into a mug, holding her breath as the steam passed under her nose. She passed the cup to Epifania.

"You have to drink every drop, *mi hija*," Lupe said. "Every drop. I'm sorry."

Epifania breathed all her air out through her nose the way Gaby had taught her to do before doing a tequila shot. She poured the tea down the back of her throat.

Every inch of Epifania's skin ripped down her throat with the tea. The taste seared hot stars through her body, turning it inside out. Lupe carried Epifania to her bed, making her swallow the drops that swung from the corners of her mouth.

When Epifania awoke she went to the bathroom and saw blood on her white lace underwear. Someplace inside her had caved in. The *angelitos* were gone, and Epifania felt something sucked out of her where her stomach had been.

Laura Catherine Brown

Leftover Gonal-F

ALL HER LIFE, SINCE SHE WAS VERY YOUNG, BEFORE SHE HAD EVEN learned how babies were made, Eleanor had known she didn't want them. They were brats, they ruined lives, messed up everything and ate you out of house and home.

She survived several baby booms with her resolve intact.

The first was a no-brainer. Within a year after high school graduation, Eleanor's three best friends had husbands and babies. Eleanor, away at college, felt betrayed, mortified. Didn't they see they had set their fates in stone: to live out their lives in the same small upstate town, dealing with the same small upstate people, getting old and peripheral? She didn't envy their weddings, their receptions at the local firehouse, or their husbands, whose idea of a compliment is to tell the wife she's fat and can't cook—but they want her fat so nobody else will.

Eleanor can't get used to walking through these glass doors on the second floor entrance of the medical building, with the starkly impersonal words etched in them: Center for Reproductive Technology. She feels like she has stepped into someone else's life as she signs her name on the list. Already twenty women ahead of her, how did they manage to arrive so early? She can't get used to waiting in this crowded room with its mauve carpet matching the upholstery, probably supposed to be calming. She can't take for granted the bathrooms stacked with pads and tampons, from overnights with wings and super-plus to panty-liners for everyday and juniors, covering every possible aspect of a woman's cycle. They give the impression of abundance. But in this world menstruation signifies failure.

She remembers when getting her period was a cause for relief. Oh, thank god, I'm not pregnant! Seems like a long time ago.

At forty, Eleanor works in the graphics department of a financial firm, laying out newsletters, brochures, annual reports. It's not sexy but it pays okay. The hours are decent. There is satisfaction, certainly, in knowing a craft, learning software, pleasing others; but the satisfaction is incomplete, lacking spiritual fulfillment, or a sense of meaning. On bad days, there is simply no reason at all to do anything and she surfs the web while her life passes her by. She's been there a long time now, almost a decade—funny how that happens.

In her spare time Eleanor paints. For many years she had painted with oils. Then, because they were less smelly and dried more quickly, with acrylics. She stopped stretching her own canvases too. She paints lurid colorful snakelike shapes and squiggles, amoeba swallowing smaller amoeba. Her favorite painters, the ones she studies and admires are Kahlo, Miró, and Gorky. A couple of evenings a week, she lugs her equipment to an open studio where models pose nude, to paint from life. She has had a couple of paintings in group shows. She doesn't care that she'll never be famous.

The second baby boom to bypass Eleanor happened right after college. She and her friends were all moving to New York City to find jobs, living six to an apartment, single and free. Some of her friends had been gay as undergraduates. They talked a good feminist game about equal pay for equal work, about refusing to settle for half-lives and how they wouldn't stand for asshole guys. They passed the joint around at night after work—they all had shitty, time-consuming jobs that insulted their intelligence and paid far too little—talking about what they were going to do with their lives. Paint. Write. Act. Sing. Invent. Sell. Make a killing. Smoking pot was required to keep the illusion going. They had one-night stands and crushes that didn't last. Their loyalty was to each other.

Until it wasn't. Within a year, Eleanor's friends paired off with guys, no longer one-night-stands. They moved in with boyfriends, spent time with new, boyfriend-linked circles of friends and got together as couples. Eleanor attended their weddings, these women she thought she knew. Most appallingly, as if they had been pro-grammed, her friends moved to the suburbs. No one had ever divulged a desire to live in the suburbs. Eleanor became estranged.

I can't believe you want to be so boring! she cried.

Who are you to judge, was the response. So what if we want to get married. So what if we want kids. Maybe you're the boring one.

Eleanor's doctor encourages her to have kids. Nobody who has children regrets it, he says. But people who don't have them do.

He has two children, now adults, and a few grandchildren. Eleanor doesn't argue. She doesn't say, nobody who has children regrets it *openly*. Except my mother. And my sister. And you obviously don't know anyone without children who loves their life. She resents his condescension. She appreciates that he's trying to encourage her. She has learned that if she argues it will only extend his talking. So she listens and nods, and accepts his prescription for folic acid.

Eleanor didn't get married until she was thirty. She fell in love with Jack, a man with light brown hair and light green eyes, a shy quick smile. He was different than the other guys she'd met. He wasn't macho. He didn't conduct monologues and then say, you really under*stand* me. He hated sports. He was thin and waif-like. He wore pointy black shoes and crisply ironed shirts. He reminded her of her father, though she had never known him except from photographs. He had abandoned the family when Eleanor and her younger sister Maxine, who calls herself Maxie, were still in diapers.

Jack seemed to float above the carpet at the party where they met. He was in a band. He played lead guitar. Yet he didn't make guitar sounds with his mouth or quote lines from songs he wrote. She liked that about him. They both had jobs to bankroll their vocations. A musician, he worked in computers. A painter, she worked in graphics. Neither was enamored of kids.

There's so much time to reflect when she's sitting in a room full of women at 6:30 in the morning waiting to have blood drawn. Twice a week or more she needs a sonogram to ensure that follicles are developing in her ovaries, plump ripe fruit of her loins.

She brings a biography of Georgia O'Keefe to read but can't concentrate, afraid she'll miss her name when they call it. On her buttocks she has drawn two circles in black permanent marker where Jack's supposed to administer the long syringe of the ovarian stimulation drug, Gonal-F. Quick and hard, he's supposed to push it in.

In the locker room at the gym the night before, she noticed a woman staring at her. Blushing, she remembered those round circles, the mark of infertility. She's disobeying orders because she needs to exercise. For sanity.

It's not me, it's him, she wants to say. But that's ridiculous.

Even though she was married by then, the "early-thirties" baby boom was easy to dismiss. Eleanor didn't envy her friends who married men with breeding agendas, who hounded and pressured them—reluctant wives—to bear children before they'd ever had their first solo shows, or written their books, or gotten that corner office, or even cultivated a sense of what they might achieve apart from motherhood.

Eleanor and Jack attended a party in Greenwich, Connecticut, for Suzanne's baby's first birthday. Suzanne had been Eleanor's college roommate and, later, her apartment mate. She used to eat psilocybin mushrooms and dance to the Grateful Dead and Talking Heads. She used to make intricate beaded earrings and bracelets. She had read constantly. She had written poetry. Now she said things like, I can't remember the last time I read a book, as if she was proud. She showed off her kitchen renovations. She talked baby talk.

The women at the party either had kids or wanted them. They talked about the quality of the babies' poop, about day care, potential pre-schools, and how once the siblings were born, the older ones regressed. The two year old was crawling alongside her little brother, as if she didn't know how to walk anymore. The mothers exchanged birth stories: vaginal vs. caesarian, drugs vs. natural, induced labor, episiotomy, perineal tears. The children tore around the house shrieking, faces smeared with chocolate cake.

Eleanor drank too much spiked punch and loudly proclaimed, I have no intention of having a baby. It's recreation, not procreation for me. The women seemed to feel sorry for her. I used to feel that way, they said, nodding to one another.

Jack was talking to a couple of the fathers, musicians he had once played a gig with at CBGB's Battle of the Bands.

I can't really gig anymore now that we have two, one of the fathers said, with less regret than Eleanor and Jack thought he ought to have. I sometimes dust my guitar off, another laughed. How could they give up something that meant so much? How could they all passively accept this fate to reproduce little versions of themselves? Where was the joy in that?

At least they had each other, she and Jack agreed. This kid thing was like a conspiracy.

Jack is summoned by a nurse and directed to the room where he's to produce sperm. Abashed, he's off to masturbate. Eleanor sits at a nurse's station, offering the milky inside of her arm for blood. Make a fist, the nurse instructs.

Doctor Waxman wears a permanent tan and speaks with an accent. Where is he from? Sweden? Israel? Germany? Impossible to know. A silver-framed photograph of a slim, lovely blond woman and two blond children in a garden sits on his desk—wife and kids? It faces out towards Eleanor and Jack during their consultation. They wait, novices, eager to please.

The doctor explains the results of the tests they've undergone. Morphology and motility, those are the words. He draws pictures of polyhedrons forming complex shapes indicating sperm functioning. Why is he doing that? His teeth are perfect. He was referred to her as: the best.

Testosterone won't do you any good, he says to Jack.

Jack is ashen. He hadn't bargained on it being about him, she can tell. Eleanor touches his arm softly and he grabs her hand.

She wants Dr. Waxman to notice them as a couple; unique among all the other couples he deals with. She wants to be his favorite. She always wants everyone to love her.

Dr. Waxman is efficient and businesslike. At your age, he addresses Eleanor and she shrinks back in her seat, we can't mess around with half-procedures like IUI and ZIFT. We go straight to IVF with ICSI. It's all acronyms, a language Eleanor doesn't yet understand.

In vitro fertilization with intracytoplasmic sperm injection. A breakthrough procedure, pioneered in Belgium. Injecting the sperm into the egg guarantees pre-embryos. Sperm quality doesn't matter anymore, Dr. Waxman says triumphantly. Jack seems to relax. Eleanor releases his hand.

Eleanor's mother has always been angry. For her, the sun does not illuminate, but casts shadows. Her mantra for years, the refrain of her life, is: I could have been a contender. Not very original and not a mantra Eleanor cares to inherit. If I said it once I said it a thousand times, you do not *have* to have children, her mother has said repeatedly. *I'm* certainly not going to tell you to have them.

Her sister, Maxie, had three children in five years, each with a different father, none of whom she lives with. She survived on Welfare until they kicked her off it with, as she calls it, Welfare Deform. Now she cleans houses for cash and she's returning to school because the state will pay for tuition.

Maxie calls Eleanor regularly, complaining about how noisy the kids are, how time-consuming, what a drag. The boy has a speech impediment. The youngest girl has ADD. The eldest was caught shoplifting a cat collar from Grand Union and has to do community service that Maxie has to drive her to. A fucking cat collar, Maxie tells Eleanor on the phone.

But Eleanor thinks it's touching and sad that her niece stole, not for herself, but for the cat, a gift.

She and Jack attend Eleanor's 20-year high school reunion. Jack wears a bright orange T-shirt and blue carpenter pants, purely by chance, the high school colors, which brings him popularity among these people he has never met before. Eleanor's women friends, the first round of baby-boomers, have several kids each. They don't have nannies or higher educations but jobs at Applebee's and Wal-Mart, where people aren't customers but guests, they break out laughing. They smoke cigarettes—especially at parties. Some of their kids are already graduating from high school. Yikes, says Eleanor. Does this mean we're old?

You don't have children? they ask, their pity palpable.

I'm into my life right now, Eleanor says, aware of how selfish that sounds, annoyed at their incomprehension that she could be without kids by choice. I have a cat, she offers. He's a big responsibility. And everyone laughs.

She goes outside to get stoned in the parking lot with a group of mothers, all of them reverting to their cliquish high school ways until one of them bursts into tears when she tries to explain how much— how terribly, painfully, unbearably—she loves her children. The others murmur agreement. Eleanor, too, feels overwhelmed in the presence of such mother love. A group hug ensues, something they would *never* have done in high school. When they go inside, stoned, the woman is still dabbing her eyes. But then, with the DJ playing The Ramones, it's easy for Eleanor to detach and judge the woman with her mascara smudged and lipstick smeared, as a maudlin drunk. Yes, that must be it, Eleanor decides.

But the memory lingers. The idea of that love disturbs the equanimity. Has she denied herself a world of emotional connection that she can barely fathom from her present perspective?

The final baby boom is underway. Friends Eleanor made in the working world, women with whom she has drinks after brutal days at the office, some married, some not, are getting pregnant. They don't drink anymore and seem pleased to be unavailable. They shop at Mimi's Maternity, discuss symptoms and ob/gyn visits.

Friends she paints with at the open studio are announcing their pregnancies, too. One of her fellow painters reveals that she has been trying for almost ten years. She cries when she says, it's finally happened, I'm four months pregnant and I'm so happy.

Is feminism as dead as the media declares it? The glorious world of opportunities available to women, the power, the freedom, the success and happiness, when will they manifest? Life is working a lot of hours, paying mortgage and maintenance, arguing about who spent what and where the money goes, struggling with fatigue while trying to paint in the evening. The bright future, if the present is any indication, will never come to pass. The future is now.

One acquaintance, then another, actually gives up working to allow their husbands to support them while they raise kids. How do they do that? Where's the income stream? Was the career thing a game they played while keeping this other option safely stored away?

Eleanor tries to paint her way out of this baby boom. She survived the others, she'll get through this one. She practices yoga. She stops proclaiming she'll never have kids. It's immature, maybe freakish. She used to live in a small universe of women who felt as she did, that children were not crucial to fulfillment as a woman and a human being, but now she finds lone stars here and there, oh, you don't have kids either, nice to meet you!

One evening at an Indian restaurant with their friends Charlotte and Ron, Jack orders a Kingfisher beer. Make it two, says Eleanor. Three, says Ron, an aspiring fiction writer with a full-time job in the financial industry.

I'm fine with water, Charlotte says. She's a secretary at the firm where Eleanor works. Ten years younger than Eleanor, she's taking a yoga teacher-training course and a fiction-writing workshop. You manage to balance your life so well without selling out, Charlotte has told Eleanor, infusing Eleanor with a sense of well being that her life is something someone might want to emulate. Unlike Eleanor, Charlotte gets a lot of pressure from her mother to bring a grandchild into the world. She acts like what I want doesn't matter at all, Charlotte has confided. Mothers, Eleanor, the elder, said.

No beer for you? Eleanor asks now, surprised. Charlotte can outdrink Eleanor any time.

Should we tell them? says Ron.

Charlotte's face lights up. Actually, I'm not drinking because I'm pregnant. Her smile is beatific.

We're so psyched! Ron says. It just happened. We weren't even trying.

Curry burns the inside of Eleanor's mouth. She lays her fork down, trying to smile. She swigs her Kingfisher. How are you going to write? she asks.

Aagh, Ron flaps his hand, dispensing with his creative dream as easily as breathing.

We'll manage, Charlotte smiles.

And Eleanor experiences a sudden, shocking pang of jealousy.

She can pinpoint the moment that closely. The subtly percolating underground spring of dissatisfaction explodes to the surface. The veils that have hidden the mystery fling open, revealing with utter clarity why a woman might want a child.

Charlotte, beaming, has a life with meaning.

I want a baby, Eleanor announces.

That's crazy, says Jack. We can't afford it.

Jack, too, had a lousy upbringing, a mother who lacked love and a cold, distant father.

You're just afraid, Eleanor says. We have a great relationship, why not bring a child into it?

Yeah, we have a great relationship, *why* bring a child into it?

They argue, an ongoing dispute picked up and left off like a marathon card game. Until she changed her mind, Eleanor thought the biological clock was a media-invented term designed to entrap women.

It's now or never, she says. I want the intimacy, the mess, the human relationship, the meaning.

You're obsessed! he says. You've been brainwashed. What's happening to you?

We don't have to become our parents, she tells Jack. It sounds cliché but it sinks into her heart, a heavy stone of truth.

She stops putting in her cervical cap. Sex is wonderful without birth control, so free and effortless, a plunge into pleasure. Jack admits, they should have done this years ago.

Every morning before peeing, she places a thermometer under her tongue. A higher temperature signifies ovulation. Clear discharge, too, signifies ovulation.

She tells Maxie, We're trying to have a baby.

I can't say I'm happy for you, Maxie says bleakly. She sits on Eleanor's sofa with her elbows on her knees. Her new boyfriend is taking care of the kids.

Wait a second, you're putting *that* in your mouth? Maxie says. That's an underarm thermometer! As a mother she knows these things.

Well, at least it's not rectal, says Eleanor, embarrassed.

It's a lot of bother if you ask me, says Maxie.

Eleanor watches babies in carriers on their father's chests at the farmers market, worn like living accessories. Babies are everywhere, in backpacks, in strollers, their expressions internal and satisfied, almost smug. She smiles at the toddlers clustered outside the nearby day care center, attended by their third-world nannies, the women who care for the children of the middle class in order to give a future to their own. She won't hire a nanny. She doesn't believe in it.

But she believes in the miraculous event of pregnancy, of birth, of growing children. She's joyful, anticipating joining her motherfriends, how they'll talk about their babies and day care and make play dates and stuff though she draws the line at poop. She imagines the relief of laying down her artistic aspirations like a sword and shield by the riverside. She worries about mercury in seafood.

She watches the older children who attend the Quaker school in her neighborhood. They're sure of themselves, brash, loud and beautiful. Dude, what's crackulatin? they call to each other. Peace out, they wave goodbye. Her kid will go there. They won't move to the suburbs.

She daydreams about leaving her job, how she won't miss it at all. Pregnant and bountiful, she'll paint and paint. When the baby is born, she'll wheel it to museums in a baby carriage and stand in people's way.

But a year of not trying not to get pregnant passes, and nothing. Everyone's having kids right and left, the easiest thing in the world, except for Eleanor and Jack.

Something's not right. She joins an organization called Resolve, serving the growing community of the infertile, and receives regular newsletters with articles entitled: *FSH Levels and What They Mean to You* and *The Donor Option*. A new vocabulary enters her lexicon: ovarian reserves, assisted hatching, cryopreservation, ovulation induction.

After their first visit with Dr. Waxman, she and Jack decide: they'll try the IVF with ICSI. Once. Their insurance won't pay for assisted reproductive technology—ART, the irony of the acronym not lost on Eleanor. It's all out of pocket except for the drugs. She's grateful that Oxford covers the drugs, which are costly.

Money is required upfront, a good portion of which will add up to twelve thousand dollars, their savings, which Jack begrudges. See? The kid's not even born yet and he's cleaning us out. I don't want to hear it, Eleanor says. Great parents they'll be, fighting like this already.

Still searching for options, Eleanor attends a fertility conference where Dr. Waxman's colleague, who specializes in male infertility, disagrees heartily with the "sperm quality doesn't matter" school. He talks about variocele, a condition of enlarged veins in the scrotum, the most common cause of infertility in men. He quotes statistics on the success of his surgical variocele repair, and the resulting improved sperm quality. At a symposium, he shows a film of himself performing microsurgery, slicing into the scrotum, removing the enlarged vein. When the lights come back up, the men are slumped in their seats, sickly green.

Dr. Waxman is also a keynote speaker. His topic: Newborns

Delivered After Intracytoplasmic Sperm Injection. The auditorium is over air-conditioned and freezing. Eleanor's teeth are chattering when she approaches him after his speech. Dr. Waxman, hi!

He doesn't recognize her. People clamor around him. He's famous in this world.

I'm your patient. Me and my husband, Jack?

I'm sorry, he says, I see so many patients. But yes, I think I do recognize you. How good to see you.

Once as a child walking across the school playground she had been hit in the head with a kickball. She was so embarrassed, the tears springing, the ridiculousness, that she kept walking, pretending nothing had happened, even as people ran over. Leave me alone, she told them. She had felt herself singled out by the universe for humiliation.

Will she ever be free of that feeling? Outside the auditorium, rows of booths offer services from IVF to egg donors to adoption to fertility drugs. They give the impression there's an epidemic. Eleanor snatches brochures, key chains, canvas bags, letter openers and pens, all decorated with logos from organizations and companies devoted to infertility.

The special guest speaker is a well-known playwright. She talks of her fifteen-year quest for a child as if she has undertaken an arduous journey for the sake of all women. She gave birth to a girl, three months premature. The baby's lungs were not yet fully developed and she spent several months in the infant ICU—but recently passed her first birthday. To think that I, a woman in her late 40s, and a single mom, live in a time and place where this is possible, she says over the applause.

She cracks jokes about infant ICU, the most prestigious, elite preschool ever. The audience of eager women laugh. But seriously, anyone who has gone through this knows it's hell. What did I do? I'm a playwright, she says. I wrote a play. And that play became a Broadway hit and won several awards. Which I couldn't have predicted! Ha ha ha.

Eleanor feels ill. She's going to explode. Jack refused to come so she's alone in a conference room where reality has skewed. She questions the playwright's sanity, her warped sense of perspective. Her story seems neurotic rather than courageous, revealing narcissism rather than determination.

Weeping, Eleanor takes the subway home. Why did she come to this conference? What did she expect? How has she landed here, in the world of the infertile?

Maybe you should have this variocele operation, she tells Jack.

I'm wearing boxers and I've given up hot baths. That's as far as I go, he says.

The cat meows testily for its dinner. Stupid animal that will never grow and develop. Stupid pseudo child.

At the clinic, Eleanor counts fifty women, most dressed for the office, hair highlighted and blow-dried, navy suits impeccable, talking on their cell phones. She remembers her first couple of jobs after college. Yuppie was the catchphrase then, describing young women who swarmed the streets in corporate suits and white sneakers, exactly what Eleanor did not want to be. The species seemed to vanish when the media lost interest.

But twenty years later they're here, leafing through magazines or filofaxes, retrieving messages on their Blackberries, issuing orders on their cell phones. There are the oddities, the lone Muslim woman in headscarf, the Hasidic Jewish woman in wig, the sweat-panted, stay-at-home mother hopeful, hair pulled back in a scrunchie. But most of the women seem to have jobs, like Eleanor.

She reads a flyer in the display, offering a women's drop-in support group. Attending would mean admitting she's one of these people. She overhears them exchanging stories, an informal support group in the waiting room. My third time, a woman says. I never knew I had endometriosis until I tried to get pregnant. My first was ectopic and I almost died. I had a high FSH and they're telling me to go for an egg donor. I went into hyperstimulation of the ovaries and I said to the doctor, why weren't you monitoring this? It's the injections that get me, I can't get used to them. The doctor told me my miscarriage was good because it means I can get pregnant. But a miscarriage isn't good. War stories.

The lump in her throat makes swallowing impossible. Why are we putting ourselves through this, she wants to stand up and shout. But in this world, she's only an initiate. A virgin.

Who are these determined couples—women really, for they're the ones who take the drugs and undergo the procedures—who will endure this process two, three, four times and more, who will switch clinics, carrying enormous volumes of medical records, who will insist on the transfer of multiple zygotes, take out second mortgages, work two jobs, go into credit-card debt, spend money, time and energy they barely have, and do anything, absolutely anything, to bear a genetic child of their own?

This isn't like cancer where you become accustomed to chemotherapy in a row of reclining chairs and weak thin people hanging on, just hanging on. She's not sick. She does not have to be here to live.

Yet here she is.

At the IVF orientation, mandatory for first timers, Eleanor takes note: Everyone else in the room is a couple. If she had insisted, would Jack have come? The middle of a weekday, he had to work. She has a job, too, but she got here. She feels sorry for herself. Each couple is given a folder containing instructions for their particular drug protocol. Eleanor gets her folder: Lupron, Gonal-F, hCG. Subcutaneous. Intramuscular. She pierces sponges with sample syringes.

Don't you worry, says a woman, you'll look like a pincushion by the end of all this. Eleanor's grateful for the interaction.

She will be taking Lupron for two weeks until Dr. Waxman is ready to start her cycle. In the world of infertility the cycle is the unit of measurement. Everything runs in cycles of approximately nine weeks.

Lupron is easy with its tiny needles and premixed fluid. Grab a roll of belly fat and dart the needle in. This will stop her cycle, turn her menopausal. She experiences no side effects that she can quantify. But her paintings become less colorful, more hard-edged, and she hates them. They look like the visuals on pharmaceutical ads. The color mauve creeps in.

Once she begins the follicle-stimulating drug, Gonal-F, she's not allowed to exercise, not even yoga. Ovaries are free floating, connected by flimsy ligaments to the uterus. You don't want to risk harming them, the nurse says. Eleanor has no choice but to believe her. She's ashamed of how little anatomy she knows.

The needle for the Gonal-F is six inches long. Glass ampules full of powder need to be mixed with saline solution. Jack pushes the needle in gingerly, afraid. Blood spurts from her right butt cheek. Pain spreads through her muscle. By the next morning a deep bruise has formed.

At work Eleanor confides in two freelancers, a single mom whose son seems to bring her nothing but joy, and a married woman with two kids. Eleanor tells them about the sonograms and the injections, the long syringes. Like heroin, say her confidants. Yeah, heroin in the butt, they laugh.

A nurse draws her blood in the morning. Another nurse calls her in the evening telling her the next day's dosage, depending on the hormone levels revealed in the blood test.

She sits at 7:00 A.M., waiting her turn for blood test and sonogram, her buttocks bruised from Gonal-F injections. She feels a bubbling deep in her lower abdomen, eggs rising like yeast muffins. She thinks of her high school friends whose children are already practically adults, and she's just starting. It's crazy.

It never works the first time, a woman in the next chair tells her. I'm on my third time. You have to do it at least twice. Don't even expect it to work.

Eleanor feels like a failure, as all these women must, these busy successful corporate types with their cell phones and beautiful suits, the stay-at-homes in designer sweat pants and yoga gear, the Hasidic Jewish women, the Muslims, all of them undergoing this tyranny of medicine because their bodies aren't producing what they're supposed to produce.

Sometimes there are toddlers at the clinic, born of IVF, with mothers returning in the hope of making siblings. The other women smile from their phones and magazines and Blackberries. The toddlers taunt and preen. They seem sadistic.

She sells a painting to friend of a friend who's opening a new design company in midtown. The painting is hung prominently in their reception area. There's a launch party for the company where Eleanor, standing in the corner with a glass of wine she can't finish, notices imbalance in the painting. The red is too dominant, too thick and heavy in the lower right corner. It looks as if it's spilling out. It's awful but she can't tell them that. She wants to take it down but that would be extreme. It's too late. Too late. Will that become her mantra?

In the morning before work, Eleanor hails cabs to the clinic. Initially she took the subway but they're unreliable at 6:30 A.M. If she gets to the clinic late, too many people will have signed in already and she'll be late for work, soliciting snide comments from her boss. The taxi drivers are morose. Nurses at the clinic are snotty and overworked. Jack is preoccupied by hair loss and his upcoming 50th birthday.

Things have been bad at work, competitive, destructive, dangerous. Eleanor has to team up with a new hire, Victoria. Victoria has two kids, a husband who cooks dinner, and a live-in nanny from

Turkey. But that's not enough. She wants power. Management is in an upheaval. People are going over other people's heads.

The former Eleanor would have quit. The present Eleanor can't. She needs the insurance to pay for her medication. What about when she has a child? It'll be even harder to leave because she'll need to pay for day care, college, braces, SAT prep classes. What if they fire her? She breaks out in a cold sweat imagining herself without an income, without insurance, beholden to Jack, complaining to Maxie.

Eleanor cries frequently, unable to practice yoga, which has offered sanity for years. She and Jack have forked over six thousand dollars already. It will end up costing—and this excludes the drugs—more than a car, a year of college, the down payment of a house in a depressed area, just to put it in perspective. She visits her friend, Lisa, the one she paints with at the open studio, bringing a gift for Lisa's daughter, born on Lisa's fourth IVF attempt. My insurance covered everything, Lisa says. I don't know how we could have done it otherwise.

Eleanor's envy rises from inside her like a hot flash.

When she gets home from work she takes out her paints but she feels empty and incapable. What to paint? Why bother? It'll be too heavy in one color or another, and end up hanging in an office lobby— if she's lucky and manages to sell it. The smallness appalls.

Maybe you're depressed, Jack says tentatively.

She hates that. If you don't like me or how I behave, you should just say it, she says.

You could try the support group, he says.

You could go to hell, she says.

Her eggs are developing. The sonograms prove it. Swollen orbs on a grainy, gray visual. Good, good, the nurse says, Dr. Waxman's very pleased.

Eleanor is proud, as if she has finally excelled at something. The clinic is the only place she feels normal anymore. Even if she's not one of them.

Jack has to attend a work-related dinner one evening. I'll give you the shot when I get home, he says.

But you won't be home until late. And it has to be given at 6:30.

They only say that so you don't forget to do it.

How do you know that? What do you know about it?

Really, he says, it's to give you a sense of control. Don't worry. I'll do it when I get home.

Don't patronize me, Eleanor snaps.

She calls the clinic. She wants to do it right. A nurse tells her it's very important to inject at the same time every day. For $25 Eleanor can hire a nurse to give her the shot. A lot of the women do it. One of the nurses lives in Eleanor's neighborhood.

At six, Eleanor walks to the nurse's apartment. Hi, I'm Eleanor. I'm Cindy, hi. No, I don't recognize you but there are a lot of people at the clinic.

Normally, my husband gives me the shot but he seems to think it doesn't matter what time it happens, Eleanor says.

You know, until there's an actual baby, some of the husbands just don't get it, says Cindy. It's not real to them. Maybe that's going on with your guy?

Eleanor panics. She's revealing too much of herself. She doesn't want to bitch about Jack to strangers. Paranoia tenses her limbs. Her neck is as stiff as a tree trunk.

Cindy mixes the medicine, preparing the shot. Eleanor takes in the apartment, small and immaculate. A tiny living room with a pretty braided rug, a rocking chair, a teddy bear. You have kids? she asks. Cindy smiles, a daughter.

It's too presumptuous to ask where the daughter is, Eleanor cracks her knuckles and tries to relax. Her body aches with the effort.

Cindy teaches Eleanor how to give the injection to herself. Quick and fast, don't hesitate. Just glance back at your rear end and boom. Shaking, Eleanor succeeds, sending the needle into her butt like a missile.

She strides home, empowered. She no longer needs Jack. You're off the hook, she says.

Why are you excluding me? He sulks. You say I don't support you but now you don't even want my help.

This isn't real to you, is it? she says.

What are you talking about?

She relents. He can do it if he's home by 6:30. There are two intramuscular injections now. Follicle stimulation and proges-terone—to create a more welcoming environment for an implanta-tion in her uterus. But no more subcutaneous ones. Not that they were ever a problem.

The night before the transfer, she has to take a new mixture, human chorionic gonadotropin, which triggers ovulation. Another long hypodermic syringe. Twelve hours later, at the clinic, they'll remove her eggs with an aspirator needle.

Jack comes with her. She's part of a couple like everyone else. But a nurse ushers her to a room, leaving him in the reception with the other husbands.

Eleanor has never had surgery, never been put under anesthe-sia. Her mouth is dry. She has fasted. In a hospital gown and slip-pers she sits with another woman. They exchange stories. The woman has a misshapen uterus because her mother took DES to prevent miscarrying. I don't blame her, the woman says. She wanted me to be born.

Eleanor is led to a gurney and wheeled into the operating room. The brightness of the lights astounds. She's afraid she will die as she tries to count backwards from 100. I'm still awake she says. It's okay, someone says.

She opens her eyes and Jack is there, looking sad and tired, with lines around his eyes and mouth. Thirteen eggs, the nurse tells her. Well. She might be forty but they got thirteen eggs out of her. She and Jack go home in a cab. Excitement has rubbed off on him.

Thirteen eggs, he says. I'm proud of you. She's allowed the luxury of lying in bed, reading. She sleeps. She feels pampered.

The clinic calls that evening. Take the progesterone shot. We'll let you know when we have fertilized eggs. Don't call us. We can't check up on cell division.

Names float around her mind. Ramona. Joan. Martin. She and Jack argue, a good kind of argument, about baby names.

Thirteen! She tells her friends at work. Go, girlfriend! They raise fists.

The clinic calls. They have viable fertilized eggs.

Eleanor panics. I don't want quintuplets! I'd rather have no baby than quintuplets!

Don't worry, says the embryologist. We're only transferring three zygotes. The others weren't viable. The transfer feels like nothing. A lab pipette with three invisible pre-embryos are carefully placed in her uterus. How can she be sure they're hers and Jack's? How can she be sure she's not the victim of an elaborate hoax? They hand her a printout with pictures of the blastocysts, fuzzy circles. Hello, sweethearts, Jack tells the printout.

Afterwards, there's nothing to do but wait. Two solid weeks of endless waiting. Eleanor cries several times a day. No call in the evening from a nurse. She hadn't realized how she had come to count on those phone calls. She snaps awake at 3 a.m., sweating, panting, the shreds of her dream slipping away. What if a baby brings no meaning or love to their lives? What if she's a horrible mother? What if it fails? What if she develops ovarian cancer from the drugs? Breast cancer? What if Jack dies?

No visits to the clinic in the morning. No exercise. The tears disappear at work when she has to function. But they lay in wait and spring forth as soon as she leaves.

Jack turns fifty. People used to think fifty was old. When the baby is twenty, Jack will be seventy. Eleanor will be sixty. Scary. But what about the famous eighty-year-old writer whose wife just had a baby? When his kid is twenty, he'll be a hundred.

Fifty's the new forty, his friends toast. Eleanor drinks juice, no alcohol. She's supposed to act like she's pregnant. I have a cold, she tells everyone. I'm on antibiotics. But how strange that there's this party, a milestone birthday for the man she loves, and she's barely participating. The center of her universe is inside her body. The rest is a dream.

Two weeks has never been so long. She ruffles the hairs of her paintbrushes but she can't bring herself to paint. She pets the cat and thinks about how neglected he'll be when there's a baby. If there's a baby. What if her baby grows up to be a murderer? What if she has to abort an embryo? She tries to meditate. She's going insane. She does a headstand even though she's not supposed to exercise. It's not really exercise. Headstands always calm her. Until she comes down and worries that she shouldn't have done it.

Desperate, she purchases a home pregnancy test at the drug store. Just what the nurses at the clinic told her not to do. But she must know.

The test is negative. Why did she do it?

She drags herself from home to work and back again. Victoria accuses her of carelessness. I can't believe you left the file like that when you knew it had to go to press. And you forgot to back up the latest version. And you left your applications open all weekend.

Two weeks pass, impossibly.

She waits in a different waiting room, an almost empty one, across the hall from the mob scene where she spent so much time. A chatty woman talks about beginning her fourth attempt. I'll get in on the next cycle, she says. She works at the clinic. They're the best here, the absolute best. My body's just not baby friendly. But I'll do this until I have one, so help me god.

When Eleanor sits across from the nurse squeezing a ball so the nurse can find a vein, she confesses. I took a home pregnancy test and it came out negative. She feels the tears coming.

If those tests were accurate wouldn't we tell everyone to take them instead of coming here? Why would we put you through this waiting?

Did I ruin my chances?

No, you just made it hard for yourself.

The DES woman and her husband are waiting for the elevator. Eleanor wonders about this husband, accompanying his wife, even to this final blood test. If only Jack were so devoted. Waiting was agony, wasn't it, they agree. Suddenly you have time again but then you can't sleep.

She's in the middle of a contentious meeting where egos are battling. Victoria insists the brochure for a risk-linked securities conference must be entirely redesigned because the marketing people want changes. Eleanor did the original design but what does she care? It's a two-color conference brochure. Her phone rings. Cindy on the other end says, since I know you, I thought I could be the one to call. I'm sorry. You're not pregnant.

Just like that.

Eleanor puts the phone down softly. Excuse me, she says to the others, I'll be right back. She slips out, down the corridor, past the cubicles and into the ladies' room where she barely manages to make it to a stall before she can start sobbing.

No baby, no savings, just a lot of costly leftover drugs, prenatal vitamins, baby names rattling around in her skull. At what point will the questions stop circling, stop trying to find blame? Was it the headstand? The stress at work? Jack's lack of support?

They sit in the living room, the cat between them. Jack plays his acoustic guitar quietly. We tried, honey. I'm sorry.

She doesn't want to blame Jack. We'll try again, she says. We'll pool money. If we refinance the mortgage, we have enough for one more time and . . .

But that's going into debt.

She imagines his lazy, badly shaped sperm as passive and resistant as he is. It's not debt; it's an investment. Why don't you get the variocele surgery? Insurance will pay for that.

Stop shouting.

You're not even upset, she says. You're relieved.

Not true. I got my hopes up. I'm sorry I wasn't into it like you were but I came around. I wanted it. Like you said, I was afraid.

They go for their final appointment with Dr. Waxman.

Why didn't it work? she asks. She doesn't mention the head-stand.

You had a 20% chance of a take-home baby. Obviously, it doesn't always work. You have a few choices. We can try the IVF with ICSI again. If you use a donor egg, your odds improve. Of course it's more expensive. Hands folded on his desk. Slim tan wife, two blond kids smiling in the photograph.

If you want to try again, you should schedule yourself on the earliest available cycle, as soon as possible, because of your age.

Eleanor concludes that Dr. Waxman never cared about them.

Why would he care? Jack says. It's a business.

She has to continue living, going to work, coming home, as if nothing has happened. But it's like someone died. She and Jack pick up the argument whenever they run out of distractions.

What about a sperm donor? Egg donor?

We said we'd do it once. No more.

We can adopt.

No, he says. Under no uncertain terms.

She can't do it alone. She can't carry all the enthusiasm.

You're ambivalent too, he says. You're just hiding yours behind mine.

She has to stop and think about that one. Not true, she says. But is it? Did she throw herself into the wanting only because she knew she was tethered by his lack of it?

Eleanor, honey, sweetie, I love you, he begs. You're the one I want to be with. And we were happy before this. You know we were.

But she can't remember back that far anymore.

She can't become a bitter, barren woman, caustically proclaiming, my husband was shooting blanks. Because of him we don't have kids. Either she is going to gather her resources and her strength and do it again. Or she is going to leave Jack and quickly find a man to have babies with, even if she doesn't like him. Or she is going to put an end to the wanting.

She menstruates. She practices yoga. She sleeps through the night. Her body belongs to her again. The crying jags dwindle. Her mood lifts. She no longer has to count the days in her cycle or give herself shots. Her hormones balance.

She inhabits her skin. She starts a new painting. One of her paintings gets in a group show. The difficulties at work revert to the background. Who cares if they fire her? She has no kids to support.

Eleanor meets an activist, a woman, at the opening of her group show. She has just returned from Africa where she was filming a documentary on AIDS in the Ivory Coast. They talk about children, how everyone's having them. The activist says, I'm child-free, honey. I don't need insta-meaning. I'd rather create my own. Anyone can have kids.

If only Eleanor had that myopic confidence. But she knows that not anyone can have kids.

At night, she sits on the sofa with the cat in her lap, no longer annoyed at him for not learning to talk, for being nothing but an animal. His soft body warms her. The vibration of his purr comforts. Will it ever be enough?

Until that dinner at the Indian restaurant, she thought she was happy. The urge to have a child came out of that happiness. It didn't arise because of a huge void in her life. It came from hope. She wanted to prove to her mother and to Maxie that children are not, as she had believed for years, a trap, a drain, an inconvenience. But rather a gift. That's why she wanted one.

In an empty cookie tin in the cabinet, she discovers unused syringes she doesn't know how to dispose of. She packs them up, along with the Gonal-F, the progesterone and the Lupron, and takes them to Lisa, her friend from the studio, who has a friend going through IVF with no insurance.

Lisa's baby is screaming when Eleanor arrives. She doesn't want to nap, Lisa says. I'm at my wits end. Her crying physically hurts me, you know? I think it's biological. I can't even complete a thought.

Eleanor hugs Lisa, noticing a slightly sour smell, not unpleasant.

It'll be okay, she says. But that endless crying jangles and jars. She's relieved to say goodbye.

Walking home from Lisa's, she notices the sun is shining. A breeze lifts her hair. She feels as if she could fly, utterly unencumbered. The feeling is so profound she's giddy. She leans against a building, breathing evenly

She gives notice at her job. They ask her to stay. They offer her reduced hours. She takes it. Free of the drugs, painting by herself, mixing colors, she finds a quiet fulfillment that she recognizes as familiar from a long time ago, from before she decided to have children.

The activist she met at the group show refers her for a part-time job teaching painting to teenagers after school, which brings Eleanor closer to kids than she has been in a long time. She's amazed at their loudness and their mess. How they splatter paint and laugh at nothing. They leave their backpacks and bags strewn around the room and load their canvasses with vivid, untamed imagery. They inspire.

She ponders her alleged ambivalence. She wanted to believe that she, too, is capable of the monumental love some women—not all—have for their children. So is it about loving and being loved?

She learns that the woman who used her leftover Gonal-F gave birth to a daughter. I didn't know whether it would make you feel sad. But I thought you'd want to know, Lisa tells her over the phone.

Eleanor waits for the sadness. Good for her. Someone got something.

Is it true, as her doctor said, that people who don't have children regret not having them? And people with children regret nothing? Surely, there are regrets either way? Just like the occasional bouts of sadness she experiences at being denied what might be an essential human relationship, that of mother and child, surely all parents have similar occasional longings to walk unfettered into a new and spacious existence where anything is possible.

Anything, that is, except that one thing.

Gina Zucker

Punishment

BUT FOR ONE THING, THE MAN AND HIS GIRLFRIEND WANTED THE same things. On the one thing, he tried to sway her. "Think of the lack of sleep," he said. "Think of the diapers. Do you really want anyone to need you that much?" His girlfriend laughed. "Don't exaggerate," she said, and her laughter flowed around him warm as milk. But as the years passed, she grew despondent. Sometimes she hit him. At other times she cried. It's funny how someone you love can transform over time and yet you're too close too see it. One day, as the man watched his girlfriend crawling around on the floor, he realized she had become someone utterly different from the person with whom he'd fallen in love. Everything about her had changed. Her body had shortened and rounded to an almost unrecognizable degree. She wore terry-cloth bodysuits. She garbled words and didn't bathe herself. She ate mashed peas. Most heartbreaking of all, she had managed, as if by some kind of magic depilatory device, to become completely bald.

After a particularly embarrassing dinner with friends during which his girlfriend had spit up on his shirt, the man confronted her.

"Look," he said, "Can't we discuss this like adults?" Instead of answering, she threw a bowl on the floor, spattering day-old peas. When he looked up, she grinned at him, toothless, ecstatic. It was too much. Scooping her into his arms, he ran from their building, through the darkened streets to the park. As he searched among the leafy paths for a place to leave her, he became aware of the small, if somewhat smelly, warmth of his girlfriend snuggled against his chest. He sobbed, fighting the urge to rub his nose on her scalp and kiss her with loud, wet smacks. As his tears fell on her head, she gazed up at him, wide-eyed. Pure, unadulterated trust stared him in the face. He gazed back. It was the beginning of a great love affair.

Arthur Bradford

Orderly: How I Spent that Year After High School

IT WAS AN IRRESPONSIBLE THING TO DO. I EVEN KNEW IT AT THE TIME, but still I went ahead. I was working as an orderly at The State Hospital, which wasn't really a hospital, but a mental institution and place for people with mild disabilities who couldn't function well in the outside world. Originally my job was to clean the residential areas, mop floors, disinfect bathrooms and so on. But they were short on staff and after a few months I began assist the professionals with the care of the residents. I would help lift someone from his wheel-chair to the bed, or walk with a resident to the cafeteria and help him choose his food. I enjoyed these tasks more than the cleaning.

One of the residents was a strikingly pretty woman named Elsa. I couldn't figure out why she was there. She seemed to be in control of herself most of the time, though she did walk with a limp. She had a shock of grey hair running from the top of her forehead and very intense, light colored eyes. Several times when I was in the cafeteria I noticed that she was looking at me. One time I led Joseph, the resident whom I was accompanying, over to her table and we sat down next to her. Joseph had a visual disability and would feel all of his food with his fingers before he ate it.

"I hope you wash his hands before he does that," said Elsa.

I said, "We always wash up before we eat, right Joe?"

"That's right," agreed Joseph, though now that I thought of it we had neglected to do so on that day. Elsa regarded his dirty fingers with disdain.

"My name is Arthur," I told her.

"I'm Elsa," she said.

I was going to extend my hand for her to shake, but I hadn't washed it and I figured she could tell. We ate the rest of the meal in silence.

Joseph told me that Elsa was "mental", that she would fly off the handle sometimes and she would have to be restrained.

"They give her drugs now," he said, "and she's more calm."

I had just finished high school that spring and while there I had only managed to have sex with one woman, and it only happened once. She was a substitute teacher who had supervised our algebra class for two weeks. I contacted her several times after our initial fling but she wouldn't return my calls. It turned out she had a husband. The other girls at the school were uninterested in me and I realized then that I had developed an attraction to older women. Elsa was perhaps thirty-five years old, and I found myself thinking about her quite a lot.

I suppose she could sense my attraction. One time when I was eating with Joseph she walked by and brushed her hand across my back. I was very startled by this. I followed her out of the cafeteria and she handed me a folded up paper towel and then turned away.

On the square of paper towel she had written, in crayon, "I am not crazy. Meet me. OK?"

By the time I had read it she was gone. I tried to figure out where she wanted to meet me and was frustrated at the vagueness of this request. But then, that afternoon, as I walked away from the main building toward the bus stop, I saw her sitting on the side steps smoking a cigarette. Most of the residents were not allowed to smoke. She had permission though.

I walked up to her. "I read your note," I said.

"Good," she said.

"What did it mean though?"

"I can't discuss that right now," she said, looking away.

"Okay," I said.

We talked a while longer about things unrelated to the note. She told me she was from Wisconsin. She fidgeted a lot. Abruptly, in the middle of a sentence, she stood up and limped back up the stairs and went inside.

Like I said before, I knew it was irresponsible to be flirting like that with a resident. But she didn't seem "mental" to me. She just seemed nervous. And she was older than me. At that point in my life I assumed that wisdom came with age.

A few days later I was working an overnight shift and she startled me. It was nearly four a.m. and I was on the covered walkway between the residential halls. She darted out from the shadows and took hold of my arm.

"This way," she said.

We went into the exercise center and there she removed my clothes and then she took off her pants. I wanted her to take off her shirt too, but she wouldn't. She lay me down and climbed on top and we had very quick, hurried sex on one of the firm vinyl covered mats. When it was over she grabbed her pants and shuffled off, leaving me there naked. I gathered up my clothes and finished my shift.

From that point on, whenever I had a night shift, we would meet up in the exercise room and have awkward, half-clothed sex. We rarely spoke and the when my shift was over I would walk home in the dim light of morning wondering if it wasn't a dream.

This pattern continued for perhaps two months and then she stopped meeting me. I tried to catch her eye in the cafeteria during the day but she wouldn't even look my way. I was sad and a little heartbroken, but took it in stride. I was beginning to notice a pattern in my relationships with older women, or so I thought.

Elsa and I hadn't spoken or made eye contact in over a month when she approached me in the hallway and shoved another folded up paper towel into my hand. This time she stayed where and waited for me to read it.

It said, "pregnancy test."

"You took one?" I asked her.

She shook her head. "I need you to buy one," she said. "Buy one for me."

"You're pregnant?"

"I need you to buy a test," she said, "from a drug store."

"Okay . . ." I said.

I fretted over this for hours until my workday was done. Then I went to the pharmacy and picked out the simplest looking test. I was mortified to be seen buying such an item. I looked over the directions and it explained that the woman had to pee onto a strip of paper. The paper would show one red line if she wasn't pregnant, and two if she was. What was it about pee that told you a woman was pregnant? I considered tampering with the test, peeing on the strip of paper myself so that the result would come out negative, but then I realized this wouldn't change things. I suppose I wasn't thinking rationally.

I returned to The Hospital and slipped the testing kit to Elsa. She thanked me and went on her way. I wanted to wait around for the result, but I there was no good excuse for me being there after the end of my shift. So I went home and didn't sleep at all.

The next day Elsa handed me the little plastic tube which held the all-powerful strip. I took it from her trying to gauge the results by the look on her face. I couldn't tell what was going on behind those skittish light colored eyes though. I realized then, as I looked at her for an answer, that she really was crazy. And then, a minute later, I stood alone in an empty closet gazing down at the strip of paper she had peed upon, and I saw the two red lines declaring she was pregnant with a child we had made together.

I was terrified. I ran out of the closet and searched the hallways for Elsa. That crazy woman! We were going to have a crazy child! A nutcase baby! She was gone though and people were staring at me running around like that. I left work early, without telling anyone, and I considered never going back.

I returned to the hospital a few nights later though, and I had a talk with Elsa. She sat on the cement steps looking up at me with her wide, shaky eyes, smoking one cigarette after another.

"I don't think you should smoke now," I told her.

"It calms my nerves," she said.

"It's bad for the baby."

"Babies don't smoke," she said, as if that somehow refuted the facts.

I asked her if she would consider having an abortion.

"No. Never," she said.

I felt a rush of blood to my head and had to sit down. I sat down next to Elsa and put my head between my knees. I know they say it is miracle, the act of creating life. I know they say it changes you forever, for the better, when you see your first child born into the world. But I felt only fear that night, fear and some kind of awful wrath unleashed upon me for the things I had done. I began to cry and between drags on her cigarette, Elsa rubbed my back with the heal of her hand. She hummed a song too, a strange song I'd never heard and it made no sense at all.

I wondered when the doctors would know about this. I wondered when I would get fired and if what I'd done was against the law. Over the next few weeks, as I watched Elsa walk around, I was sure I could see her belly growing. Other people must be noticing, I thought. I moped along thinking, when, finally, is the shit going to hit the fan?

I had a strange moment though, when I was back in the drugstore later that week. I walked by the shelf where I had picked up that little pregnancy test and I stared at all the different colored boxes thinking how each one was a box full of fate. Next to the boxes was a row of plastic bottles and some of them were labeled "pre-natal vitamins". I grabbed one of those, stuffed it in my pocket, and left.

I gave the bottle to Elsa and told her to take one a day, like the directions said.

"More pills…" she said to me.

It was during the night shift, a few days later, that I heard Elsa calling out my name. She wasn't yelling, she was just repeating my name steadily and it echoed down the hallway.

I ran to her room and saw that it was empty. She was in the bathroom down the hall. I tapped my fingers on the door.

"It's me," I said.

"Go away," she said.

I stood outside the door for two hours. Other staff members came and looked at me and one of the nurses called the police. I wasn't supposed to be in the women's wing at that hour. I wasn't supposed to be standing outside the bathroom door like that, blocking the way, and not listening to anything anyone said.

The police arrived and I stood my ground. They hauled me away and as they did Elsa came out of the bathroom, finally. She was pale and her eyes met mine and she nodded. The baby was gone.

They call it a miscarriage and it happens one time out of every five. That's what I read. Oh, maybe it happens more, maybe when the parents are like me and Elsa it happens every time. I never even saw Elsa after that. I was fired from my job at the State Hospital and in return for my silence on the matter my record stated only that I was terminated for personal differences, or something like that.

I'm a bit older now and I find myself wondering about the child that Elsa and I could have made. Children, I believe, can exceed the sum total of their parents. In their little genes lie some lessons learned from all of our past mistakes. We never could have raised that kid right, Elsa and I, but maybe she would still have grown up to be beautiful.

Angie Day

In the Darkness

"MARK, I CAN SEE PEOPLE RUNNING," AMY SAYS. HER FOREHEAD is pressed against the window of the office they share on the forty-second floor of a building in Manhattan. She is trying to angle a view of what is happening on the street below, but it is difficult when she is so far above it all.

Mark gets up from his desk and stands beside her. He looks down. "Oh my god. What's going on?" he says, his voice shrill.

One minute before, Amy had been talking on the phone with a chatty client in Dallas, who announced that his daughter had made the honors choir today. As he marveled at his daughter's perfect pitch, Amy wondered how different her life would have been if she hadn't moved to Manhattan ten years ago. Would she also have a child by now? Is it possible that she would have wanted one?

That's when the entire floor of her building went dark. Someone screamed.

"I'm sorry, I have to go," Amy said abruptly to the man, as she realized that something was very wrong.

"What, am I boring you?" he joked.

Amy hung up on him but did not lose her composure. She could feel her energy shift, a calmness kick in that was the exact opposite of what one might expect. That's when she looked outside and saw the suited men and women flooding out of their buildings and into the streets.

Now she is changing into the sneakers that she has kept under her desk just in case it happens again. She doesn't want to think about that day. It was years ago, but still the images flash through her brain. Right now she is thinking about the shoes. Two days after it happened, she'd returned to the downtown Manhattan loft she shared with Dean, then her boyfriend. As she walked through the deserted streets towards home, she'd seen hundreds of shoes littering the streets and sidewalks. Almost all of them were women's high heels that had been abandoned, she could only guess, because they were impractical for running away. For a year Amy wore nothing that she couldn't run in if necessary. By 2002, she was wearing flip flops again. By 2003, she would even wear high heels on occasion. But always she kept the sneakers under her desk, just in case she ever needed to escape.

Mark has only lived in Manhattan for a year, so he is panicking. "Holy shit, the whole city is dark," Mark says as he moves for the door. "Are you coming?" Amy knows what he is thinking, and it is simple, driven by fear: we are under attack. I have to get out of this building.

Amy's thoughts are more complex. "I'll be right behind you," she says as she slowly ties her second shoe, sure that he won't wait. She takes a moment to consider whether to evacuate. It has just occurred to her how brilliant it would be for someone to cut off all the lights in Manhattan, which would get people into the streets. But for what? She imagines that once everyone is outside, they might take this as their opportunity to gas everyone. She's not sure what gassing involves, or who "they" are, but she knows better than to underestimate. Her chest is tightening but she is not giving in to the panic. Instead she allows shock to take over and do its thing. She looks out her office door to see that the hallway is empty now. Despite her fears, she decides to evacuate with everyone else, admitting to herself that she is afraid to stay on the forty-second floor alone.

She places her cell phone, wallet, and water bottle in her purse, then quickly walks towards the emergency exit. She opens the heavy door to see that the stairwell is filled with people walking at different paces, some talking, a few crying. Together they slowly descend to the street, unsure of what awaits them.

Two weeks before, there had been a fight. It started with these words from Amy: "I know you don't feel ready, but . . ." It amazed her that she and Dean had been together for four years, and married for one of them, yet still she was embarrassed to bring up the topic. In North Carolina, where she grew up, all her friends from high school were on their second or third kid; yet here she was, thirty-two, so nervous about confronting her husband with a touchy subject that she was having a hard time eating the homemade ravioli that Dean had spent two hours preparing.

She took a long sip from her glass of wine, and spoke. "I know you don't feel ready but . . ."

"But what?" he said softly, already sensing where the conversation was going.

"I want to get a dog."

What followed was a familiar discussion that turned into a familiar fight. He told her that having a dog cooped up in a New York City apartment is cruel, and reminded her that boarding a dog takes a lot of money. "Our lives are complicated enough," he said. Amy countered that she would take care of the dog and cover the cost, and that Dean wouldn't even have to walk him. It surprised her to hear the tone of pleading in her voice, like a desperate child asking permission. Why was this dog so important to her?

Amy's mother had recently told her that this desire for a dog was proof that her maternal instinct was kicking in, and Amy knew that there was truth to that. But she also knew that the last thing she wanted right now was a baby. True, she and Dean have always agreed that they want children eventually; but so far, they have kept the idea comfortably in the abstract, because whenever they try to imagine a real living, breathing human being in their care, it becomes too overwhelming. It seems somehow irresponsible to bring up a kid in this city, or even this country, now that the world is so unsettled. She explained this to her mother once, who told her that the real problem was Manhattan. She urged Amy to move out of the city to someplace safer and less stressful so that she and Dean could move on with their lives, by which she meant reproduce. Amy finally stopped trying to explain how she felt. How can you make someone understand that every time you see the Brooklyn Bridge out of your apartment window, you imagine it blowing up; yet at the same time you are certain that you want to live near the Brooklyn Bridge for as long as it is able to survive?

At dinner, Amy continued to build her case. She talked to Dean about how an apartment is less cruel than a shelter, and that dogs are good for your health, good for anxiety. "I just think a dog loves in such an unselfish way, and that . . . I don't know. I just feel like I'm ready for a dog."

He sighed. "Amy, I never want to be the kind of husband who forbids you to do something, but if you want to do this, you're on your own."

"That really takes the fun out of the whole thing," she said, and it was true.

That night she spent two hours on petfinder.com, looking at the sorrowful pictures of the shelter dogs. There were Mindy and Mishka, two full-grown Golden Retrievers owned by a priest who had died suddenly. There was Boxie, who was found in a dumpster. There was Peanut, the one-eyed mutt. She wanted them all, but knew that she would never follow through, not because she was afraid of upsetting Dean, but because deep down she agreed with him.

Amy emerges from the stairwell of the building to find that it is a beautiful day outside, sunny, and warm. Her first instinct is to look up. The skies are almost as blue as the day in September that Amy doesn't want to think about. That day she'd been at home getting ready for work when the first tower fell, and evacuated minutes later after her apartment filled with so much acrid, gray dust that she had to hold a t-shirt over her nose and mouth to breathe. As she crossed the Manhattan bridge on foot—the Brooklyn Bridge was closed by then— there was a moment when everything went silent; the screams, the panicked shouts, all faded away at once. Instinctively, she stopped in her tracks and turned to see where everyone was looking. She was just in time to watch the second building fall, in her memory in silence and slow motion, with a backdrop of sky so clear that it seemed fake. Still, years later, the sight of a cloudless sky that shade of brilliant blue makes her heart clench, as it is clenching now. She blocks this thought from her mind and focuses on the situation at hand.

Just as she'd feared, the sidewalks are filled with people who have left her building, and the building across the street, and every building she can see up and down Broadway. They stand in huddles, attempting desperate calls on cell phones, taking part in anxious conversations. Again, she wonders what would happen if someone detonated a dirty bomb. They, the unnamed "they," could kill so many people right now. It would be ingenious.

Amy spots Mark, and decides that she will find out what he knows, then move on. "Is there any news?"

He shakes his head no just as someone shouts to the crowd, "Lights are going out all over the country." There is an audible gasp and one shriek.

"I'm just going to walk home down the West Side," she says, as calmly as she can. As she leaves the clusters of people in front of the building, trying and failing to call Dean on her cell phone, she feels sorry for those who aren't thinking quickly enough to move away, but she doesn't know how to help them. Most seem to be either staying put, which seems ludicrous, or heading down Broadway, through the gridlock, right towards Times Square, which is the last place she'd want to be. It is a symbol of America. A target.

Instead Amy is drawn to the city's edge, and the presumed safety of being near the water. She heads towards the West Side Highway so she can walk home along the Hudson River Park. Usually this riverside path is used by runners and cyclists, but today she knows it will be filled with people like her who are fighting the urge to swim away from the island. She'd heard that on that day in September, people had gotten into the water to swim, and although this was regarded as the actions of a few deluded crazies, she fully understood why they did it, and couldn't guarantee that she would not do the same today.

She is not at the water yet, but instead is crossing Eighth Avenue, then Ninth. The distance between them seems interminable. She wants to get to the water. She tries Dean again and again. There are no lines open. She wants to see Dean. The sidewalk is thick with people. She sees shoe stores that have brought sneakers out onto the street to sell to passersby in impractical footwear who didn't learn their lesson the first time around. She hears the radio screaming from parked cars with their windows down, blaring the news instead of music. There is no new information. She passes women crying as they try to hunt down their kids, and feels a deep sense of relief that she is not responsible for anyone's fate but her own. The lights are going out everywhere. The whole country could be in the dark soon. She has to reach Dean. She has to reach him. There are no lines. She tries again.

Two days after they fought about the dog, Dean and Amy went to brunch at a restaurant near Union Square that Dean said he'd wanted to try. After they ate, he told her that he wanted to pick up a few things at the farmer's market for dinner that night. They meandered through the tables topped with vegetables of every color, some she'd never heard of. There was something called an avocado squash, and burpless cucumbers. There were organic pies and elk steaks, jam and potted plants. And dogs.

There must have been about twenty of them, eyes sad and vacant, all wearing orange doggie vests that read *Adopt Me*. Instead of having owners at the ends of their leashes, they were being guided by kind-faced shelter volunteers who were parading the dogs through the crowd in hopes that someone would meet them, love them, and fill out an application to take them home. Amy knelt beside a cocker spaniel mix, so frightened that his hind legs were shaking.

"This is Marty," the volunteer explained, as Amy stroked his silky fur, wondering what sort of trauma he must have endured in his short little life. "He's house trained, but messes up sometimes. And he's not good around cats. He hates them," she said, smiling.

"Thanks," Amy said, as Dean came up to join her. "But we're not ready to adopt."

Just then a young woman plopped down beside Marty and pulled him into her lap, cooing, "How's the little puppy!" She was joined by an equally fresh-faced guy who scruffed Marty on the head as if he'd been his dog for years. Amy marveled at them the same way she marveled at people who were good with kids. How do you just know what to do?

Already forgotten by Marty, Amy stood up and grabbed Dean's hand, noticing that he looked sad. He had a tendency towards guilt, so she assumed he was feeling bad about their dog fight the other night. He wasn't. "Actually," he said, his deep eyes locking with hers, "I brought you here on purpose. I think maybe you're right," he said, now looking at his feet, at the traffic, at anything but her. "We can't hold off on a dog forever, right? I mean, people do harder things every day."

"Let's just look," Amy said, feeling both excited and nervous.

Over the next hour they met nine dogs. There was Petey, found wandering the streets in Brooklyn, who was known for his abundance of energy and bad chewing habits. There was Andy, the good-natured lab who was missing a leg. There was Mia the deaf dog. Mellow the lonely, cuddly dog. Miracle the abused dog. Alaska the sweet but anxious dog.

A part of Amy wanted to take every one of them home, quit her job, and just raise dogs. She imagined that she would be so happy then. But the other part of her kept finding something wrong with each of them. It wasn't that the dogs weren't good enough, but more that she wasn't good enough for them. She wasn't at home enough for a high energy dog. She wasn't experienced enough to give that one the training he needed. Their walls were too thin for a dog that barked. Their place was too small for a dog that size. And what would she do with a dog if the city was attacked again? How could she be expected to keep him safe when she might be miles away in midtown at work? She could feel her earlier excitement gradually transform to stress with each new dog, and wondered what was wrong with her. Everywhere she went she was surrounded by families who together seemed to be proof that parenting was natural and easy, the way of the world. Yet here she was, unable to take in an abandoned dog, afraid to commit, she thought, because she had learned that you can never promise to take care of anything. The world is too troublesome and unpredictable to ever promise something as important, as sacred, as that.

Exhausted, they took their vegetables and left, vowing to return next weekend to try again, both of them feeling relieved.

Amy is one of thousands walking along the river, and she is glad that no one is panicking. Instead, it is a calm progression towards home. Huge, overwhelming masses of people gather at bus stops and ferry stations, unable to use the subway, and it occurs to her that people must be stuck in the subways as well. She tries to imagine what she would do if she were in a subway that suddenly went black. She would probably have to evacuate through the tunnels. She thinks of the rats. This is no way to live.

Yet she wants to live. What the hell is going on? she wants to know. What is going to happen next? Again, her eyes search the vast, blue sky. There is nothing. She keeps her focus and tries not to give in to the panic, but it is coming. Suddenly everything seems futile. Right now the population of Manhattan is simply reshuffling itself. People who work downtown are working their way towards their apartments in midtown. People like her are moving in the opposite direction. How is this safe? Still, she wants to be home. Again she tries Dean. Again and again and again. There are no lines. She tries not to cry. And then her phone rings. "Dean? Are you OK?" she says, a touch of hysteria in her voice.

"You haven't heard?"

"No. Are you OK?"

"Baby, it's just a blackout."

He explains that there was a problem that started in Canada or somewhere, he's not sure, but that it's just a power outage. That's it. She is relieved but not yet convinced.

"Honestly, Amy, it's nothing."

"What happens when it gets dark?" she wants to know, thinking of a city this size engulfed in the blackness, with looters scurrying from building to building with the ease of roaches.

"I think we should still go home. It's not like anybody can work, anyway. We'll be fine. It'll be fun."

The weekend after Amy and Dean met Marty the dog, they didn't go back to Union Square to attempt adoption again like they'd said they would. They didn't even talk about it.

The blackout happened one week later.

The anxiety doesn't leave Amy right away. Instead, it gradually passes through her, until she feels completely serene, the flip side of shock. If this were her usual calm, she'd feel tired, maybe even a little lazy; but this feeling has an unmistakable high and clarity to it, as if she's just gone on a long run through the woods and feels drained, yet at one with her mind for the first time.

The path along the Hudson River is still packed with people, and the news of the blackout seems to have spread easily. Suddenly the mobs of people that had seemed so ominous before, like animals running from an unseen predator, have relaxed and taken on a certain beauty. It is like the perfect Sunday, where the whole of Manhattan is out on a stroll, collectively choosing not to watch television, not to talk on their cell phones, not to check in with work, but to simply enjoy the day. People who live nearby have re-emerged from their hot, unairconditioned apartments to soak in some sun in the park. She sees toddlers and their adoring parents frolicking on the lawn next to gay men tanning in miniscule swimsuits. There are groups of friends picnicking, feasting on expensive refrigerated foods that are sure to go bad soon. And now there are rollerbladers, joggers, weaving in and out of people like Amy who are still on their way home, simply passing through the park so that they, too, can begin their day off.

Amy stops at a small food cart with a line that is ten deep with other people like her who have been walking for an hour. They are out of water, so instead she gets ice cream. She doesn't understand why, but as she walks through this bustling scene, the ice cream melting just enough that she has to catch the drips on the side of the cone, her feet tired yet prepared to walk forever, her eyes well up with tears. It's been a common occurrence since that day in September. Sometimes it happens when she sees a low-flying plane, or when she's walking home from the movies in Battery Park, and passes people posing for pictures in front of the old site as if it were their own piece of history to claim, or when she walks by the Brooklyn Bridge and remembers the people she saw that day, who looked like powdered donuts, covered in the gray dust, doubled over and vomiting, or crying, or simply putting one foot in front of the other towards an undetermined final destination. But today it's different. It is the same level of emotion, but for the opposite reason. Before, these tears were because something had been taken away; but as she stares at this carefree Manhattan scene, like a summer snow day on an urban landscape, she is reminded of what was preserved.

When she gets home, Dean is sitting on the front steps of their building having a beer with their neighbors, whom they see almost every day but have never officially met. Their names turn out to be

Chris and Jessica, and they offer Amy a beer, which she accepts. Later they walk up the pitch black stairwell together, guided by a small flashlight, to the roof.

Amy wonders if Chris and Jessica remember that she had been on the roof with them on that day in September. As she got ready for work that morning, she watched on the news as first one plane, then another, flew into the tower. It didn't occur to her to call Dean about it, who was out of town on business. Instead, once dressed, she decided to have her coffee on the roof so she could see it for herself. Chris and Jessica had been up there, too, with their video camera, although she didn't know their names then. As they watched the smoking building, Amy told them what she'd heard on the news—that the towers had been hit by two small aircraft that had simply lost their way. Wasn't this the most absurd thing they'd ever seen? Chris told her she was wrong, then rewound the tape and played it frame by frame as the American Airlines logo struck. That was when she went downstairs to call Dean. When the first tower fell. When their apartment filled with the thick, gray air.

The day of the blackout isn't that day in September, but there are similarities. From the roof, she can look down below and see gridlock so bad that civilians are stepping in to direct cars through the unlit intersections. And, because the subways aren't running, the Brooklyn Bridge is as full of evacuating pedestrians as she's ever seen it, with people packed as densely as if they were leaving Yankee stadium, inching across the bridge in slow cooperation. She can just make out a group of kids who look like they're on a field trip, all wearing matching bright green t-shirts. Every time she looks up, they have moved another fifteen feet or so towards home.

That night, drinking beer with her neighbors, Amy takes in the most beautiful view she has ever seen. Building after building without lights. The sun fully setting on this city for the first time she'd ever known.

Soon they are joined by two more neighbors, who have brought up a bottle of wine and some cheese they feared would go bad. Together they talk like neighbors should, but rarely do anymore. They swap stories of their long journeys home today, walking for miles to get back from work or, in Jessica's case, hitching a ride on a stranger's motorcycle. They vow to get together sometime soon for a drink, and it is sincere. They talk and laugh until the city is engulfed in the blackness and together they navigate the depths of the stairwell.

Without electricity, their habits are impossible. Amy can't sneak onto her computer to check emails, and Dean can't watch TV. Amy finds herself wondering what it would have been like to live a hundred years before. She feels like she would have been smarter. She would have read more. She would have felt more. She would have noticed more. She would have wanted less.

They read by candlelight, the windows open and blowing in a much-needed breeze. Later he cooks her pasta on the gas stove and they play cards. She feels like someone she doesn't recognize, like someone at peace.

That night they surround the bed with candles and talk until they are tired, but they don't sleep. Instead they find each other in the darkness. There is that familiar moment when Dean is supposed to put on a condom, but their eyes lock and he doesn't. They know what they are doing. Or what they are trying to do. What they are OK with doing in this moment.

Two months later, Amy and Dean adopt a dog named Boots. He's a mangy black mutt with white paws, who is afraid of umbrellas and of large men, but other than that, he is perfect. She is not pregnant, and they are not trying. It is not that easy for them. But somewhere in their scars you can see their future, and there you will find that they are waiting for another day that they now know exists, a day when the world is so stripped of itself that—for the briefest of moments—life seems possible.

Charles Baxter

Saul and Patsy
are in Labor

THE MOONLIGHT ON THE SHEETS IS AS HEAVY AS DAMP COTTON, and Patsy, pregnant in her ninth month with a child who does not care to be born, sits up in bed to glare at whatever is still visible. The moonlight falls on the red oak bedroom floor, the carved polar bear on the bedside table, and her husband, Saul, under his electric blanket. Sleeping, Saul is always cold. His dreams, he has reported, are Arctic. Moonlit, he seems a bit blue. But soothes her, having him there: his quiet groans and his exhaling supply the rhythms of Patsy's waking nights.

She pulls back the covers, walks to the window, and sheds her nightgown.

Brown-haired, athletic, with a runner's body, she is ordinarily a slender woman, but now her breasts and belly are swollen, the skin stretched taut, her fingers and feet thickened with water. She finds herself tilting backward to balance herself against her new frontal weight. She feels like a human rain forest: hot, choked with life, reeking with reproduction.

Out in the yard the full-faced moon shines through two pine trees this side of the garage and on Saul's motorcycle parked in the driveway. Beyond the garage she sees a single deer passing silently through the field.

Patsy leans toward the desk in front of the window and permits the moon to gaze on her nakedness. She soaks up the moonlight, bathes in it. As she turns, she clasps her hands behind her head. She's had it with pregnancy; now she wants the labor, the full-blast finality of it. When she looks at the desk she sees the ampersand key on the upper row of the typewriter keyboard, the & above the 7. It's shaped like herself, distended and full: the big female *and*: &. The baby gives her a sleepy kick.

Hey, she says to the moonlight, *put me in labor. Pull this child into the world. Help me out of here.*

Three hours later, just before dawn, her water breaks.

The labor room: Between contractions and the blips of the fetal monitor, she is dimly aware of Saul. He's donned his green hospital scrubs. The wouldn't let him wear his Detroit Tigers baseball cap in here. He's holding her hand and his eyes are anxious with nervous energy. He thinks he's coaching her. But he keeps miscounting the breaths, and she has to correct him.

After two hours of this, she is moved into the huge circular incandescence of the delivery room. She feels as if she's about to expel her entire body outward in a floor flood. With her hair soaked with sweat and sticking the back of her neck, she can feel the universe sputtering out for an instant into two flattened dimensions. Everything she sees is suddenly painted on a wall. She screams. Then she swears and loosens her hand from Saul's—his touch maddens her—and swears again. The pain blossoms and blossoms, a huge multicolored floral sprouting of it. When the nurses smile, the smiles—full of professionalism and complacency from the other world—make her furious. The seconds split.

"Okay, here's the head. One last push, please."

Patsy backstrokes through the pain. Then the baby girl presents herself in a mess of blood and fleshy wrappings. After the cord is cut,

Patsy hears her daughter's cry and a thud to her right: Saul, on the floor, passed out, gone.

"Can someone see to the dad?" the obstetrician asks, rather calmly. "He's fainted." Then, as an afterthought, she says, "No offense, Patsy, but he looked like the fainting type."

After a moment, during which Patsy feels plumbed out and vacant, they give the baby an Apgar test. While they weigh her, a nurse squats down next to Saul and takes his pulse. "Yes, he's coming back," she says. "He'll be fine." His eyes open, and underneath the face mask he smiles sheepishly. The papery cotton over his mouth crinkles upward. It's typical of Saul, Patsy thinks, to have somebody make a fuss over him at the moment of his daughter's birth. He steals scenes.

"Is my husband okay?" she asks. She can't quite find him. Turning back to herself, she can see, blurred, in the salty recession of this birth, the paint of her toenails through her thin white cotton socks. Saul had painted those toenails when she had grown too wide to bend down and do the job herself.

"Here's the baby," the nurse says. The world has recovered itself and accordioned out into three dimensions again. The nurse's smile and her daughter's ancient sleepy expression sunspot near Patsy's heart, and the huge overhead delivery room light goes out, like a sigh.

Someone takes Patsy's hand. Who but Saul, unsteady but upright? Cold sweat drips down his forehead. He kisses Patsy through his face mask, a sterile kiss, and he informs her that they're parents now. Hi, Mom, he says. He apologizes for his cold sweat and sudden bout of unconsciousness. Patsy raises her hand and caresses Saul's face. Oh, don't worry, the nurse says, apparently referring to Saul's fainting fit. She pats him on the back, as if he were some sort of good dog.

They name their daughter Mary Esther Carlson-Bernstein. While making dinner, one of his improvised stir-fries, Saul says that he's been having second thoughts: Mary Esther is burdened with a lot of name, a lot of Christianity and Judaism mixed in there. Possibly another name would be better. Jayne, maybe, or Liz. Direct, futuristic American monosyllables. As he theorizes and chops carrots and broccoli before dropping the bamboo shoots and water chestnuts into the pan, Patsy can see that he's so tired that he's only half-awake. His socks don't match, his jeans are beltless, and his hair has gone back to its customary anarchy.

Last night, between feedings, Saul claimed that he didn't know if he could manage it, *it* being the long haul of fatherhood. But that was just Saul-talk. Right now, Mary Esther is sleeping upstairs. Fingering the pages of her magazine, Patsy leans back in the alcove, still in her bathrobe, watching her husband cook. She wonders what she did with the breast pump and when the diaper guy is going to deliver the new batch.

Standing there, Saul sniffs, adds a spot of peanut oil, stirs again, and after a minute he ladles out dinner onto Patsy's plate. Then with that habit he has of reading her thoughts and rewording them, he turns toward her and says, "You left the breast pump upstairs." And then: "Hey, you think I'm sleepwalking. But I'm not. I'm conscious."

They live in a rented house on a dirt road outside of Five Oaks, Michigan, and for the last few months Saul has glimpsed an albino deer, always at a distance, on the fringes of their property. After work or on weekends, he walks across the unfarmed fields up to the next property line, marked by rusting fence posts, or, past the fields, into the neighboring woods of silver maple and scrub oak, hoping to get a sight of the animal. It gives him the shivers. He thinks this is the most godforsaken locale in which he's ever found himself, certainly worse than Baltimore, and that he feels right at home in it, and so does that deer. It is no easy thing to be a Jew in the Midwest, Saul thinks, where all the trees and shrubs are miserly and soul-shriveled, and where fate beats on your heart like a baseball bat, but he has mastered it. He is suited for brush and lowland undergrowth and the antipicturesque. The fungal smell of wood rot in the culverts strengthens him, he believes.

Clouds, mud, wind. Joy and despair live side by side in Saul with very few emotions in between. Even his depressions are thick with lyrical intensity. In the spiritual mildew of the Midwest all winter he lives stranded in an ink drawing. He himself is the suggested figure in the lower righthand corner.

He makes his way back to the house, mud clutching fast to his books. He has a secret he has not told Patsy, though she probably knows it: he does not have any clue to being a parent. He does not love being one, though he loves his daughter with a newfound intensity close to hysteria. To him, fatherhood is one long unrewritable bourgeois script. Love, rage, and tenderness disable him in the chairs in which he sits, miming calm, holding Mary Esther. At night, when Patsy is fast asleep, Saul kneels on the landing and beats his fists on the stairs.

On the morning when Mary Esther was celebrating her birthday—she was four weeks old—they sat at the breakfast table with the sun in a rare appearance blazing in through the east window and reflecting off the butter knife. With one hand Patsy fed herself cornflakes. With the other hand she held Mary Esther, who was nursing. Patsy was also glancing down at the morning paper on the table and was talking to Saul about his upcoming birthday, what color shirt to get him. She chewed her cornflakes thoughtfully and only reacted when Mary Esther sucked too hard. A deep brown, she says. You'd look good in that. It'd show off your eyes.

Listening, Saul watched them both, rattled by domestic sensuality of their pairing, and his spirit shook with wild bruised jealous love. He felt pointless and redundant, an ambassador from the tiny principality of irony. His heart, that trapped bird, flapped in its cage. Behind Patsy in the kitchen spice rack displaced its orderly contents. A delivery truck rumbled by on Whitefeather Road. He felt specifically his shallow and approximate condition. In broad daylight, night enfolded him.

He went off to work feeling superfluous and ecstatic and horny, his body glowing with its confusions.

* * *

This semester Saul has been taken off teaching American history and has been assigned remedial English for learning-disabled students in the junior high. The school claims it cannot afford a specialist in this area, and because Saul has loudly been an advocate of the rights of the learning-disabled, and because, he suspects, the principal has it in for him, he has been assigned a group of seven kids in remedial writing, and they all meet in a converted storage room at the back of school at eight-thirty, following the second bell.

Five of them are pleasant and sweet-tempered and bewildered, but two of them hate the class and appear to hate Saul. They sit as far away from him as possible, close to the brooms, whispering to each other and smiling malevolently. Saul has tried everything with them—jokes, praise, discipline—and nothing has seemed to work.

He thinks of the two boys, Gordy Himmelman and Bob Pawlak, as the Child Cossacks. Gordy apparently has no parents. He lives with siblings and grandparents and perhaps he coalesced out of the mud of the earth. He wears tee-shirts spotted with blood and manure. His boots are scuffed from the objects he has kicked. On his face there are two rashes, one of acne, the other blankness. His eyes, on those occasions when they meet Saul's, are cold and lunar. If you were dying on the side of the road in a rainstorm, Gordy's eyes would pass over you and continue on to the next interesting sight.

He has so sense of humor. Bob Pawlak does. He brags about killing animals, and his laughter, describing how he has killed them, rises from chuckles to a sort of rhythmic squeal. His smile is the meanest one Saul has ever seen on an ex-child. It is also visible on the face of Bob Pawlak's father. About his boy, this father has said, "Yeah, he is sure a hell-raiser." He shook his dismayed parental head, smiling meanly at Saul in the school's front office, his eyes glittering with what Saul assumed was Jew-hatred.

Saul can hardly stand to look at Gordy and Bob. There are no windows in the room where he teaches them, and no fan, and after half an hour of everyone's mingled breathing, the air in the room is foul enough to kill a canary.

Yesterday Saul gave the kids pictures clipped from magazines. They were supposed to write a one-sentence story to accompany each picture. For these ninth-graders, the task is a challenge. Now, before school starts, his mind still on Patsy and Mary Esther, Saul begins to read yesterday's sentences. Gordy and Bob have as usual not written anything: Gordy tore his picture to bits, and Bob shredded and ate his.

> It is dangerous to dive into a pool of water without the nolige of the depth because if it is salow you could hit your head that might creat unconsheness and drownding.
>   Quite surprisingly the boys find among the presents rapings which are now discarded into trash a model air plan.

Two sentences, each one requiring ten minutes' work. Saul stares at them, feeling himself stumbling in the usual cognitive limp. The sentences are like glimpses into the shattered mind of God.

> Like the hourse a cow is an animal and the human race feasts on its meat and diary which form the bulky hornd animal.
>   The cold blooded crecher the bird will lay an egg and in a period of time a new bird will brake out of it as a storm of reproduction.

Saul looks up from his desk at the sputtering overhead lights and he grimy acoustic tile. It is in the storm of reproduction—mouths of babes, etc.—that he himself is currently being tossed.

He looks down at the floor again and spots a piece of paper with the words *you're a kick* close to the wastebasket. Finally, a nice compliment. He tosses it away.

The neighbors bring food down Whitefeather Road, indented with the patterned tire-tracked mud of spring, to Saul and Patsy's house. They've read Mary Esther's birth announcement in *The Five Oaks Gazette*, but they might know anyway. Small-city snooping keeps everyone informed. With the gray March overcast behind her,

Mrs. O'Neill, beaming fixedly with her brand of insane charity, offers them a plate of the cookies for which she has gained local notoriety. They look like molasses blasted in a kiln and crystallized into teeth-shattering candied rock. Anne McPhee gives Patsy a gallon of home-made potato salad preserved in pink translucent Tupperware. Laurie Welch brings molded green Jell-O. Mad Dog Bettermine hauls a case of discount no-name beer into the living room, roaring approval of the baby. In return, Saul gives Mad Dog a cigar, and together the two men retire to the back porch, lighting up and drinking, belching smoke. Back in town, Harold, Saul's barber, gives Saul a free terrible haircut. Charity is everywhere, specific and ungrudging. Saul can make no sense of it.

They all track mud into the nursery. Fond wishes are expressed. Dressed in her sleep suit, Mary Esther lies in the rickety crib that Saul himself assembled, following the confusing and contradictory instructions enclosed in the shipping box. Above the crib hangs a mobile of cardboard stars and planets. Mary Esther sleeps and cries while the mobile slowly turns in the small breezes caused by the visitors as they bend over the baby.

One night, when Mary Esther is eight weeks old and the smell of spring is pouring into the room from the purple lilacs in the drive-way, Patsy awakens and finds herself alone in bed. The clock says that it's three-thirty. Saul has to be up for work in three hours. From downstairs she hears very faintly the sound of groans and music. The groans aren't Saul's. She knows his groans. There are different. She puts on her bathrobe.

In the living room, sitting in his usual overstuffed chair and wearing his blue jeans and tee-shirt, Saul is watching a porn film on the VCR. His head is propped against his arm as if he were listening attentively to a lecture. He glances up at Patsy, flashes her a guilty wave with his left hand, then returns his gaze to the movie. On the TV screen, two people, a man and a woman are having showy sex in a curiously grim manner inside a stalled freight elevator, as if they were under orders.

"What's this, Saul?"

"Film I rented."

"Where'd you get it?"

"The store."

Moans have been dubbed onto the soundtrack. The man and the woman do not look at each other. For some reason, a green ceramic poodle sits in the opposite corner of the elevator. "Not very classy, Saul," she says.

"Well," Saul says, "they're just acting." He points at the screen. "She hasn't taken her shoes off. That's pretty strange. They're having sex in the elevator and her shoes are still on. I guess the boys in the audience don't like feet."

Patsy studies the TV screen. Unexpected sadness locates her and settles in, like a headache. She rests her eyes on the Matisse poster above Saul's chair: naked people dancing in a ring. In this room the human body is excessively represented, and for a moment Patsy has the feeling that everything in life is probably too much, there is just too much to face down.

"Come upstairs, Saul."

"In a minute, after this part."

"I don't like to look at them. I don't like you looking at them."

"It's hell, isn't it?"

She touches his shoulder. "This is sort of furtive."

"That's marriage-driven rhetoric you're using there, Patsy."

"Why are you doing this, Saul?"

"Well, I wanted a real movie and I got this instead. I was in the video place and I went past the musicals into the sad private room where the Xs were. There I was, me, full of curiosity."

"About what?"

"Well, we used to have fun. We used to get hot. So this . . . anyway, it's like nostalgia, you know? Nostalgia for something. It's sort of like going into a museum where the exhibits are happy, and you watch the happiness, and it isn't yours, so you watch more of it."

"This isn't like you, Saul. Doesn't it make you feel like shit or something?"

He sits in his chair, thinking. Then he says, "Yup, it does." He clicks off the TV set, rises, and puts his arms around Patsy, and they stand quietly there for what seems to Patsy a long time. Behind Saul on the living room bookshelf are volumes of history and literature—Saul's collections of Dashiell Hammett and Samuel Eliot Morison—and the Scrabble game on the top shelf. "Don't leave me alone back here," Patsy says. "Don't leave me alone, okay?"

"I love you, Patsy," he says. "You know that. Always have."

"That's not what I'm talking about."

"I know."

"You don't get everything now," she says. "You need to diversify."

They stand for a few moments longer, swaying slightly together.

Two nights later, Saul finished diapering Mary Esther and then walks into the upstairs hallway toward the bathroom. He brushes against Patsy, who is heading downstairs. Under the ceiling light her eyes are shadowed with fatigue. They do not speak, and for ten seconds, she is a stranger to him. He cannot remember why he married her, and he cannot remember his desire for her. He stands there, staring at the floor, angry and frightened, hoarding his injuries.

When Saul enters his classroom the next day, Gordy and Bob greet his arrival with rattle throat noises. On their foreheads they have written MAD IN THE USA, in pencil. "Mad" or "made," misspelled? Saul doesn't ask. Seated in their broken desks and only vaguely attentive, the other students fidget and smile politely, picking at their frayed clothes uniformly one or two sizes too small.

"Today," Saul says, "we're going to pretend that we're young again. We're going to think about what babies would say if they could talk."

He reaches into his jacket pocket for his seven duplicate photographs of Mary Esther, in which she leans against the back of the sofa, her stuffed gnome in her lap.

"This is my daughter," Saul says, passing the photographs out. "Mary Esther." The four girls in the classroom make peculiar cooing sounds. The boys react with nervous laughter, except for Gordy and Bob, who have suddenly turned to stone. "Babies want to say things, right? What would she say if she could talk? Write it out on a sheet of paper. Give her some words."

Saul knows he is testing the Cossacks. He is screwing up their heads with his parental love. At the back of he room, Gordy Himmelman studies the photograph. His face express nothing. All his feelings are bricked up; nothing escapes from him.

His is the zombie point of view.

Nevertheless, he now bends down over his desk, pencil in hand.

At the end of the hour, Saul collects the papers, and his students shuffle out into the hallway. Saul has noticed that poor readers do not lift their feet off the floor. You can hear them coming down the hallway from the slide and scrape and squeal of their shoes.

He searches from Gordy Himmelman's paper. Here it is, mad in America, several lines of scrawled writing.

> They thro me up in to the air. Peopl come in when I screem and thro me up in to the air. They stik my face up. They never catch me.

The next lines are heavily erased.

> her + try it out . You ink

Saul holds up the paper to read the illegible words, and now he sees the word *kick* again, next to the word *lidle*.

His head randomly swimming, Saul holds the photographs of

his daughter, the little kike thoughtfully misspelled by Gordy Himmelman, and brings the photos to his chest absentmindedly. From the hallway he hears the sound of lively laughter.

That night, Saul, fortified with Mad Dog's no-brand beer, reads the want ads, deeply interested. The want ads are full of trash and leavings, employment opportunities and the promise of new lives amid the advertised wreckage of the old. He reads the personals like a scholar, checking for verbal nuance. Sitting in his overstuffed chair, he scans the columns when his eye stops.

BEEHIVES FOR SALE—Must sell. Shells, frames, extractor. Also incl. smoke and protective hat tools and face covering. Good condition. Any offer considered. Eager to deal. $$$ potential. Call after 7 p.m. 890-7236.

Saul takes Mary Esther out of her pendulum chair and holds her as he walks around the house, thick with plans and vision. In the vision, he stands proudly—regally!—in front of Patsy, holding a jar of honey. Sunlight slithers through its glass and transforms the room itself into pure gold. Sweetness is everywhere. Honey will make all the desires right again between them. Gordy Himmelman, meanwhile, will have erased himself from the planet. He will have caused himself to disappear. Patsy accepts Saul's gift. She can't stop smiling at him. She tears off their clothes. She pours the honey over Saul.

Gazing at the newspapers and magazines piling up next to the TV set as he holds Mary Esther, Saul finds himself shaking with a kind of excitement. Irony, his constant companion, is asleep, or on vacation, and in the heady absence of irony Saul begins to imagine himself as a beekeeper.

He does not accuse Gordy of anti-Semitism, or of anything else. He ignores him, as he ignores Bob Pawlak. At the end of the school year they will go away and fall down into the earth and the dirt they came from and become one with the stones and the inanimate all-embracing horizon.

On a fine warm day in April, Saul drives out to the north side of town, where he buys the wooden frames and the other equipment from a laconic man named Gunderson. Gunderson wears overalls and boots. Using the flat of his hand, he rubs the top of his bald head with a farmer's gesture of suspicion as he examines Saul's white shirt, pressed pants, ten-day growth of beard, and brown leather shoes. "Don't wear black clothes around these fellas," Gunderson advises. "They hate black." Saul pays him in cash, and Gunderson counts the money after Saul has handed it over, wetting his thumb to turn the bills.

With Mad Dog's pickup, Saul brings it all back to Whitefeather Road. He stores his purchases behind the garage. He takes out books on beekeeping from the public library and studies their instructions with care. He takes notes in a yellow notebook and makes calculations about placement. The bees need direct sunlight, and water nearby. By long-distance telephone he buys a hive of bees, complete with a queen, from an apiary in South Carolina, using his credit card number. When the bee box arrives in the main post office, he receives an angry call from the assistant postal manager telling him to come down and pick up the damn humming thing.

As it turns out, the bees like Saul. He is calm and slow around them and talks to them when he removes them from the shipping box and introduces them into the shells and frames, following the instructions that he has learned by heart. The hives and frames sit unsteadily on the platform Saul has laid down on bricks near two fence posts on the edge of the property. But the structure is, he thinks, steady enough for bees. He gorges them with sugar syrup, sprinkling it over them, before letting them free, shaking them into the frames. Some of them settle on his gloved hand and are so drowsy that, when he pushes them off, they waterfall into the hive. When the queen and the other bees are enclosed, he replaces the frames inside the shell, being careful to put a feeder with sugar water nearby.

The books have warned him about the loud buzzing sound of angry bees, but for the first few days Saul never hears it. Something about Saul seems to keep the bees occupied and unirritated. He is stung twice, once on the wrist and once on the back of the neck, but the pain is pointed and directed and so focused that he can manage it. It's unfocused pain that he can't stand.

Out at the back of Saul's property, a quarter mile away from the house, the hive and bees won't bother anyone, Saul thinks. "Just don't bring them in here," Patsy tells him, glancing through one of his apiary books. "Not that they'd come. I just want them and me to have a little distance between us, is all." She smiles. "Bees, Saul." Honey? You're such a literalist."

And then one night, balancing his checkbook at his desk, with Mary Esther half asleep in the crook of his arm, Saul feels a moment of calm peacefulness, the rarest of his emotions. Under his desk lamp, with his daughter burping up on his Johns Hopkins sweatshirt, he sits forward, waiting. He turns around and sees Patsy, in worn jeans and a tee-shirt, watching him from the doorway. Her arms are folded, and her breasts are outlined perfectly beneath the cloth. She is holding on her face an expression of sly playfulness. He thinks she looks beautiful and tells her so.

She comes into the room, her bare feet whisking against the wood floor, and she puts her arms around him, pressing herself against him.

"Put Mary Esther into her crib," she whispers. She clicks off the desk lamp.

As they make love, Saul thinks of his bees. Those insects, he thinks, are a kind of solution.

Spring moves into summer, and the mud on Whitefeather Road dries into sculpted gravel. Just before school ends, Saul tells his students about the bees and the hives. Pride escapes from his face, radiating it. When he explains how honey is extracted from the frames, he glances at Gordy Himmelman and sees a look of dumb animal rage directed back at him. The boy looks as if he's taking a bath in lye. What's the big deal? Saul wonders before he turns away.

One night in early June, Patsy is headed upstairs, looking for the Snugli, which she thinks she forgot in Mary Esther's room, when she hears Saul's voice coming from behind the door. She stops on the landing, her hand on the banister. At first she thinks he might be singing to Mary Esther, but, no, Saul is not singing. He's sitting in there— well, he's probably sitting, Saul doesn't like to stand when he speaks—talking to his daughter, and Patsy hears him finishing a sentence: ". . . was never very happy."

Patsy moves closer to the door.

"Who explains?" Saul is saying, apparently to his daughter. "No one."

Saul goes on talking to Mary Esther, filling her in on his mother and several other mysterious phenomena. What does he think he's doing, discussing this stuff with an infant? "I should sing you a song," he announces, interrupting himself. "That's what parents do."

To get away from Saul's song, Patsy retreats to the window for a breath of air. Looking out, she sees someone standing on the front lawn, bathed in moonlight, staring in the direction of the house. He's thin and ugly and scruffy, and he looks a bit like a clod, but a dangerous clod.

"Saul," she says. Then more loudly, "Saul, there's someone out on the lawn."

He joins her at the window. "I can't see him," Saul says. "Oh, yeah, there." He shouts, "Hello? Can I help you?"

The boy turns around. "Sure, fuckwad. Yeah, you bet, shitbird." He gets on his bike and races away down the driveway and onto Whitefeather Road.

Saul does not move. His hands are planted on the windowsill. "It's Gordy Himmelman," he groans. "That little bastard has come on our property. I'm getting on the phone."

"Saul, why'd he come here? What did you do to him?" She holds her arms against her chest. "What does he have against us?"

"I was his teacher. And we're Jewish," Saul says. "And, uh, we're parents. He never had any. I showed those kids the baby pictures. Big mistake. Somebody must've found Gordy somewhere in a barrel of brine. He was not of woman born." He tries to smile. "I'm kidding, sort of."

"Do you think he'll be back?" she asks.

"Oh yes." Saul wipes his forehead. "They always come back, those kind. And I'll be ready."

It has been a spring and summer of violent weather, and Saul has been reading the Old Testament again, looking for clues. On Thursday, at four in the afternoon, Saul has finished mowing the front lawn and is sitting on the porch drinking the last bottle of Mad Dog's beer when he looks to the west and feels a sudden cooling of air, a shunting of atmospheres. Just above the horizon a mass of clouds begins boiling. Clouds that look like breasts and handtools —he can't help thinking the way he thinks—advance over him. The wind picks up.

"Patsy," he calls. "Hey Patsy."

Something calamitous is happening in the atmosphere. The pressure is dropping so fast that Saul can feel it in his elbows and knees.

"Patsy!" he shouts.

From upstairs he hears her calling back, "What, Saul?"

"Go to the basement," he says, "Close the upstairs window and take Mary Esther down there. Take a flashlight. We're going to get a huge storm."

Through the house Saul rushes, closing windows and switching off lights, and when he returns to the front door to close it, he sees out in the yard the tall emaciated apparition of Gordy Himmelman, standing fixedly like an emanation from the dirt and stone of the fields. He has returned. Toward Saul he aims his vacant stare. Saul, who cannot stop thinking even in moments of critical emergency, is struck into stillness by Gordy's presence, his authoritative malevolence standing there in the just mown grass. The volatile ambitious sky and the forlorn backwardness of the fields have together given rise to this human disaster, who, even as Saul watches, yells toward the house, "Hey, Mr. Bernstein. Guess what. Just guess what. Go take a look at your bees."

Feeling like a commando, Saul, who is fast when he has to be, catches Gordy who is pumping away on his broken a rusted bicycle. Saul tears Gordy off. He throws and kicks the junk Schwinn into the ditch. In the rain that has just started, Saul grabs Gordy by the shoulders and shakes him back and forth. He presses his thumbs hard enough to bruise. Gordy, violently stinking, smells of neglect and seepage, and Saul nearly gags. Saul cannot stop shaking him. He cannot stop shaking himself. With violent rapid horizontal jerking motions the boy's head is whipped.

Saul wants to see his eyes. But the eyes are empty as mirrors.

"Hey, stop it," Gordy says. "It hurts. You're hurting. You're hurting him."

"Hurt who?" Saul asks. Thunder rolls toward him. He sees himself reflected in Gordy Himmelman's eyes, a tiny figure backed by lightning. *Who, me?*

"Stop it, don't hurt him." Patsy's voice repeating Gordy's words, snakes into his ear, and he feels her hand on his arm, restraining him. She's here, out in the rain, less frightened of the rain than she is of Saul. The boy has started to sag, seeing the two of them there, his scarecrow arms raised to protect himself, assuming, probably, that he's about to be killed. There he squats, the child of attention deficit, at Saul's feet.

"Stay there," Saul mumbles. "Stay right there." Through the rain he begins walking, then running, toward his bees.

* * *

The storm, empty of content, tucks itself toward the east and is being replaced even now by one of those insincere Midwestern blue skies.

Mary Esther begins to cry and wail as Patsy jogs toward Saul. Gordy Himmelman follows along behind her.

When she is within a hundred feet of Saul's beehives, she sees that the frames have been knocked over, scattered, and kicked. Saul lies, face down, where they once stood. He is touching his tongue to the earth momentarily, where the honey is, for a brief taste. When he rises, he sees Patsy. "All the bees swarmed," he says. "They've left. They're gone."

She holds Mary Esther tightly and examines Saul's face. "How come they didn't attack him? Didn't they sting him?"

"Who knows?" Saul spreads his arms. "They just didn't."

Gordy Himmelman watches them from a hundred years away, and with his empty gaze he makes Patsy think of a albino deer Saul has insisted he has seen: half blind, wandering these fields day after day without direction.

"Look," Saul says, pointing at Mary Esther, who stopped crying when she saw her father. "Her shoe is untied." He wipes his face with his sleeve and shakes off the dirt from his jeans. Approaching Patsy, he gives off the smell of dirt and honey and sweat. In the midst of his distractedness, he ties Mary Esther's shoe.

His hair is soaked with rain. He glances at Patsy, who, with some difficulty, is keeping her mouth shut. She not only loves Saul but at this moment is in love with him, and she has to be careful not to say so just now. It's strange, she thinks, that she loves him, an odd trick of fate: He is fitful and emotional, a man whose sense of theater begins completely with himself. What she loves is the extravagance of feeling that focuses itself into the tiniest action of human attention, like the tying of this pink shoe. It's better to keep love a secret for a while than to talk about it all the time. It generates more energy that way. He finishes the knot. He kisses them both. Dirt is attached to his lips.

At a distance of a hundred yards, the boy, Gordy, watches all this, and from her vantage point Patsy cannot guess what that expression on his face may mean, those mortuary eyes. Face it: He's a loss. Whatever they have to give away, they can only give him a tiny portion, and it won't be enough, whatever it is. All the same, he will stick around, she's pretty sure of that. They will have to give him something, because now, like it or not, he's following them back, their faithful zombie, made, or mad, in America, and now he's theirs.

Well, maybe we're missionaries, Patsy thinks, as she stumbles and Saul holds her up. We're the missionaries they left behind when they took all the religion away. On the front porch of the house she can see the empty bottle of Saul's no-brand beer still standing on the lip of the ledge, and she can see the porch swing slowly rock back and forth, as if someone were sitting there, waiting for them.

About the Stories

Almond, Steve: Shotgun Wedding
Carrie rethinks her relationship with her fiancé when she learns she could be accidentally pregnant and he sees it only as a problem.

Baggott, Julianna: Girl Child X
The story of a woman from her own birth through the birth of her first child.

Baxter, Charles: Saul and Patsy are in Labor
An amusing look at the humor of labor.

Bender, Aimee: Marzipan
A ten-year-old girl's family is thrown into comic disarray when her father develops a hole in his abdomen and her mother becomes unexpectedly pregnant then gives birth to her own mother.

Bradford, Arthur: Orderly: How I Spent That Year After High School
A young mental hospital orderly deals with the consequences of having sex with a patient.

Brown, Laura Catherine: Leftover Gonal-F
After years of proclaiming she would never have a child, Eleanor suddenly feels compelled to get pregnant but must go through in-vitro fertilization without her husband's full support.

Day, Angie: In the Darkness
During the Manhattan blackout of 2002, Amy and her husband struggle to decide whether it's the right time to start a family.

Franklin, Emily: In the Herd of Elephants
Two women deepen their bonds of friendship in the last month of pregnancy.

Gaskell, Whitney: Trying Again
Following the stillbirth of her first child, a pregnant woman is ridiculed by a busybody for her choice to have a c-section.

Graver, Elizabeth: Mourning Door
While undergoing in-vitro fertilization, a woman constructs an infant from body parts she finds in her old home that's being renovated.

Harris, Lynn: Mummy Dust Tea
In Mexico City, Epifania chooses to end a pregnancy using her nanny's remedy of mummy dust tea.

Jong-Fast, Molly: Letters from a Young Fetus
A fetus writes letters to its mother about life in the womb and its fears of being born.

Julavits, Heidi: Little, Little Big Man
A very thin cowboy enters the womb of his wife to have conversations with his unborn child.

Langer, Adam: The Book of Names
A professor determines all the names that would be inappropriate for his child being carried by his former student.

Leebron, Fred: Baby Girl
A husband and wife go through the agony of learning their newborn has swallowed meconium during birth.

Li, Yiyun: Prison
Yilan returns to China to hire a surrogate mother after she and her husband lose their teenage daughter in a car accident.

Lindop, Laurie: Sunday Morning
Kelly and Sarah struggle to define their relationship as they study a sperm bank catalogue and plan for a child.

McNally, John: Creature Features
An eleven-year-old boy contemplates his mother's pregnancy while watching monster movies in Chicago.

Packer, Ann: Her First Born
Lise and Dean prepare for the birth of their child following the death of Lise's first baby from a former marriage.

Robinson, Lewis: Cuxabexis, Cuxabexis
Eleanor goes to Maine to visit her husband's family while newly pregnant.

Rubin, Emily: Ray and Sheila Have a Day
Ray and Sheila reprioritize their life when they discover their unborn child may have Down's syndrome.

Swain, Heather: What You Won't Read in Books
A writer struggles to deal with an unexpected miscarriage.

Zucker, Gina: Punishment
A woman morphs into an infant after her boyfriend tells her he does not want children.

About the Contributors

STEVE ALMOND is the author of two story collections, *My Life in Heavy Metal* (Grove 2002) and *The Evil B.B. Chow* (Algonquin 2005) and the nonfiction book *Candyfreak* (Algonquin 2004).

JULIANNA BAGGOTT is the author of *Girl Talk*, *The Miss America Family*, *The Madam* and, co-written with Steve Almond, *Which Brings Me to You*, as well as a book of poems, *This Country of Mothers*. She also has a series of novels for younger readers, *The Anybodies*, written under the pen name N.E. Bode. She teaches in the Creative Writing Program at Florida State University.

CHARLES BAXTER is the author of four novels, most recently, *Saul and Patsy* and *The Feast of Love*, both published by Vintage in paperback. He has also written four books of stories and two books of criticism, including *Burning Down the House*. He lives in Minneapolis and has one son.

AIMEE BENDER is the author of three books, most recently the short story collection *Willful Creatures*. Her short fiction has been published in *Granta*, *GQ*, *Tin House*, *Harper's*, *The Paris Review* and more, as well as widely anthologized. She teaches creative writing at USC, and lives in Los Angeles.

ARTHUR BRADFORD's first book, *Dogwalker* was published by Knopf in 2001 and is out in Vintage paperback now. He is the recipient of an O. Henry Award and his stories have appeared in *Esquire*, *McSweeney's*, *Zoetrope*, and *Bomb*. He is also the director of "How's Your News?", a documentary film series which features a team of news reporters with disabilities. It has appeared on HBO/Cinemax, PBS, and Channel Four England.

LAURA CATHERINE BROWN's first novel, *Quickening*, published by Random House in June 2000, was a Barnes & Noble Discover Great New Writers selection. The Ballantine Books paperback edition was published in February 2002. She received a Walter E. Dakin Fiction Fellowship for the 2001 Sewanee Writers' Conference. She has been awarded residencies at The Ragdale Foundation, Ucross Foundation, Vermont Studio Center, Norcroft Writing Retreat and Hambidge Center. She earns a living as a graphic designer, as well as teaching creative writing at Manhattanville College. She is currently working on her second novel.

ANGIE DAY is both a writer and a television producer. She is the author of the national bestseller *The Way to Somewhere* (Simon & Schuster, 2002), which was a finalist for the Best First Work of Fiction Award by the Texas Institute of Letters, and was the first book selected for the online book club network "Book Movement." She developed and was a supervising producer on the MTV series MADE, now in its fifth season. A native of Houston, Angie lives with her husband in New York City where she is finishing her second novel.

EMILY FRANKLIN is the author of *Liner Notes* and a fiction series, *The Principles of Love. Early Girls: A Novel in Stories* will be published in the fall of 2006 by William Morrow. Her nonfiction anthology of essays, *It's a Wonderful Lie: The Truth About Life in Your Twenties*, is slated for a January 2007 release from Warner Books. Her work has appeared in *The Mississippi Review* and *The Boston Globe*. Having spent her formative years half in London and half in Boston, Franklin studied at Oxford University, received her B.A. from Sarah Lawrence College, and her M.A. in Writing and Media Studies from Dartmouth College. She has been a part of the Boston Jewish Book Fair and on the staff of National Public Radio's 'Car Talk' show. She lives near Boston with her husband and three children.

WHITNEY GASKELL is the author of *Pushing 30, True Love (and Other Lies)* and *She, Myself & I*. She lives in Florida with her husband and son.

ELIZABETH GRAVER is the author of three novels: *Awake, The Honey Thief* and *Unravelling*, and a short story collection, *Have You Seen Me?*. Her stories and essays have been anthologized in *Best American Short Stories; Prize Stories: The O. Henry Awards; Best American Essays*; and *Pushcart Prize: Best of the Small Presses*. She teaches at Boston College and is the mother of two young daughters.

LYNN HARRIS is author of the comic novel *Miss Media* and its forthcoming sequel, *Death by Chick Lit*. A contributing writer for *Salon.com* and *Glamour*, she also writes frequently about gender, reproductive rights, and culture high and low for the *New York Times, Nerve.com*, and many more. Lynn is co-creator, with Chris Kalb, of the award-winning website *BreakupGirl.net*. She comments frequently in magazines such as *Us Weekly* on celebrity pregnancies and other matters that are really none of her business.

MOLLY JONG-FAST is the twenty-six-year-old author of the weirdly popular cult novels *Normal Girl* and *The Sex Doctors in the Basement* (both published by Villard). She has written for *The New York Times, The Times of London, Cosmo, Mademoiselle, Marie Claire, British Elle*, and many other newspapers and magazines. She has an MFA from Bennington College. She recently chronicled her wedding for *Modern Bride Magazine*. She lives in New York City with her husband, her child, their cocker spaniel Godzuki and Pete, the world's fattest cat. Her mother wrote *Fear of Flying*, her grandpa wrote *Spartacus*, and her great great grandfather was a herring merchant.

HEIDI JULAVITS is the author of two novels, *The Effect of Living Backwards* and *The Mineral Palace*, as well as *Hotel Andromeda*, a book collaboration with the artist Jenny Gage. She is a founding editor of *The Believer*.

ADAM LANGER was born in 1967 in Chicago. He attended Vassar College then returned to Chicago where he worked as an editor, nonfiction author, playwright, theater director, and very occasional film producer. He served as senior editor of *Book Magazine* in New York until that publication folded in 2003. He is the author of two novels, *Crossing California* (Riverhead Books, 2004) and *The Washington Story* (August, 2005). He now divides his time between Bloomington, Indiana and New York City.

FRED LEEBRON is a professor of English at Gettysburg College and Program Director of the MFA in Creative Writing at Queens University of Charlotte. His novels include *Out West*, *Six Figures*, and *In the Middle of All This*.

YIYUN LI grew up in Beijing and came to the U.S. in 1996. She started to publish in English in 2002 and her fiction and nonfiction have appeared in *The New Yorker*, *The Paris Review*, *Zoetrope: All-Story*, *Ploughshares*, *Glimmer Train*, *Gettysburg Review* and other magazines. Named by *Los Angeles Times* as one of the three writers to watch in 2005. Her first book, *A Thousand Years of Good Prayers*, was published in 2005 by Random House. She lives in Oakland, California with her husband and their two sons.

LAURIE LINDOP is the author of nine nonfiction books, most recently *The Starving Artist's Survival Guide* (Simon and Schuster, 2005). Her fiction has appeared in *Redbook*, *The Beloit Fiction Journal*, and elsewhere. She teaches writing at Boston College.

JOHN MCNALLY received his MFA in creative writing from the University of Iowa Writers' Workshop. He has edited several collections of short stories including *Bottom of the Ninth: 24 Great Short Stories about Baseball* and *Humor Me: An Anthology of Humor by Writers of Color* and is the author of *Troublemaker* and *The Book of Ralph : A Novel* which was published by Free Press in 2004.

ANN PACKER is the author of *The Dive From Clausen's Pier* and *Mendocino and Other Stories*. She lives near San Francisco with her children.

LEWIS ROBINSON is the author of *Officer Friendly and Other Stories*. A graduate of Middlebury College and the Iowa Writers' Workshop, Robinson received a Whiting Writers Award in 2003. He teaches in the Stonecoast MFA program and coaches basketball in Portland, Maine.

EMILY RUBIN has published her work in magazines and newspapers, including *New York Stories*, *Compass Rose* and *The Boston Globe*. She won the White Pines Fiction Contest for her short story "A Dusky Episode," and her short story "Days of Awe" was nominated for a Pushcart Prize. She is currently writing her first novel, which explores the intersection of interfaith marriage and motherhood. Much of Emily's writing inspiration comes from her two young sons, Sam and Jules.

HEATHER SWAIN came to literary attention through her short stories. In 1999, her story "Sushi" appeared in the anthology *Virgin Fiction 2* from Rob Weisbach Books as one of twenty winners in a national contest for new young writers. She is the author of two novels, *Eliot's Banana* and *Luscious Lemon* (Simon & Schuster/Downtown Press). Swain's short stories, personal essays, and nonfiction articles appear in *Other Voices*, *Potpourri*, *American Baby*, and *Salon.com* among other publications. She lives in Brooklyn with her husband and daughter.

GINA ZUCKER's fiction and nonfiction have appeared or are forthcoming in *Tin House*, *Salt Hill*, *failbetter*, *eyeshot*, *Elle*, *GQ*, *Glamour*, *Cosmopolitan*, *Redbook*, *Rolling Stone*, *TimeOut NY*, and elsewhere. She also writes for Lifetime Television, and teaches in the creative writing program at Pratt Institute, in Brooklyn, NY.

Permissions

"Shotgun Wedding" by Steve Almond, *New England Review*, 2003

"Saul and Patsy are in Labor" by Charles Baxter, *Believers*, Vintage, August 1998

"Marzipan" by Aimee Bender, *The Girl in the Flammable Skirt*, Bantam, August 1998

"In the Herd of the Elephants" by Emily Franklin, *LiteraryMama.com*, January 2005

"The Mourning Door" by Elizabeth Graver, *Ploughshares*, Summer 2002; *Best American Short Stories, 2001*; *Prize Stories 2001: The O. Henry Awards*; *Pushcart Prize XXVI: Best of the Small Presses 2002*

"Little, Little Big Man" by Heidi Julavits, *McSweeney's #7*, 2002

"Baby Girl" by Fred Leebron, *TRIQUARTERLY*, Number 93, Spring/Summer 1995

"Prison" by Yiyun Li, *Tin House*, (Forthcoming)

"Creature Features" by John McNally, *Virginia Quarterly Review*, 2005

"Cuxabexis, Cuxabexis" by Lewis Robinson, *Officer Friendly*, HarperCollins 2004

"Punishment" by Gina Zucker, *Failbetter.com*, fall 2002

2 - 9/07